Tidesong

Wendy Xu

Quill Tree Books
Imprints of HarperCollinsPublishers

HARPER
alley

Quill Tree Books and HarperAlley
are imprints of HarperCollins Publishers.

Tidesong
For information address HarperCollins Children's Books,
a division of HarperCollins Publishers,
195 Broadway, New York, NY 10007.
www.harpercollinschildrens.com

ISBN 978-0-06-295579-1 (paperback)
ISBN 978-0-06-295580-7 (hardcover)

The artist used an iPad with the Procreate art program
to create the illustrations for this book.
Typography by Cat San Juan and Andrea Vandergrift
21 22 23 24 25   EP   10 9 8 7 6 5 4 3 2 1
❖
First Edition

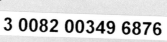

To my students at HCMS and HCHS:
It's okay to stumble in life, figure it out,
and do things your own way.
This one is for all of you.

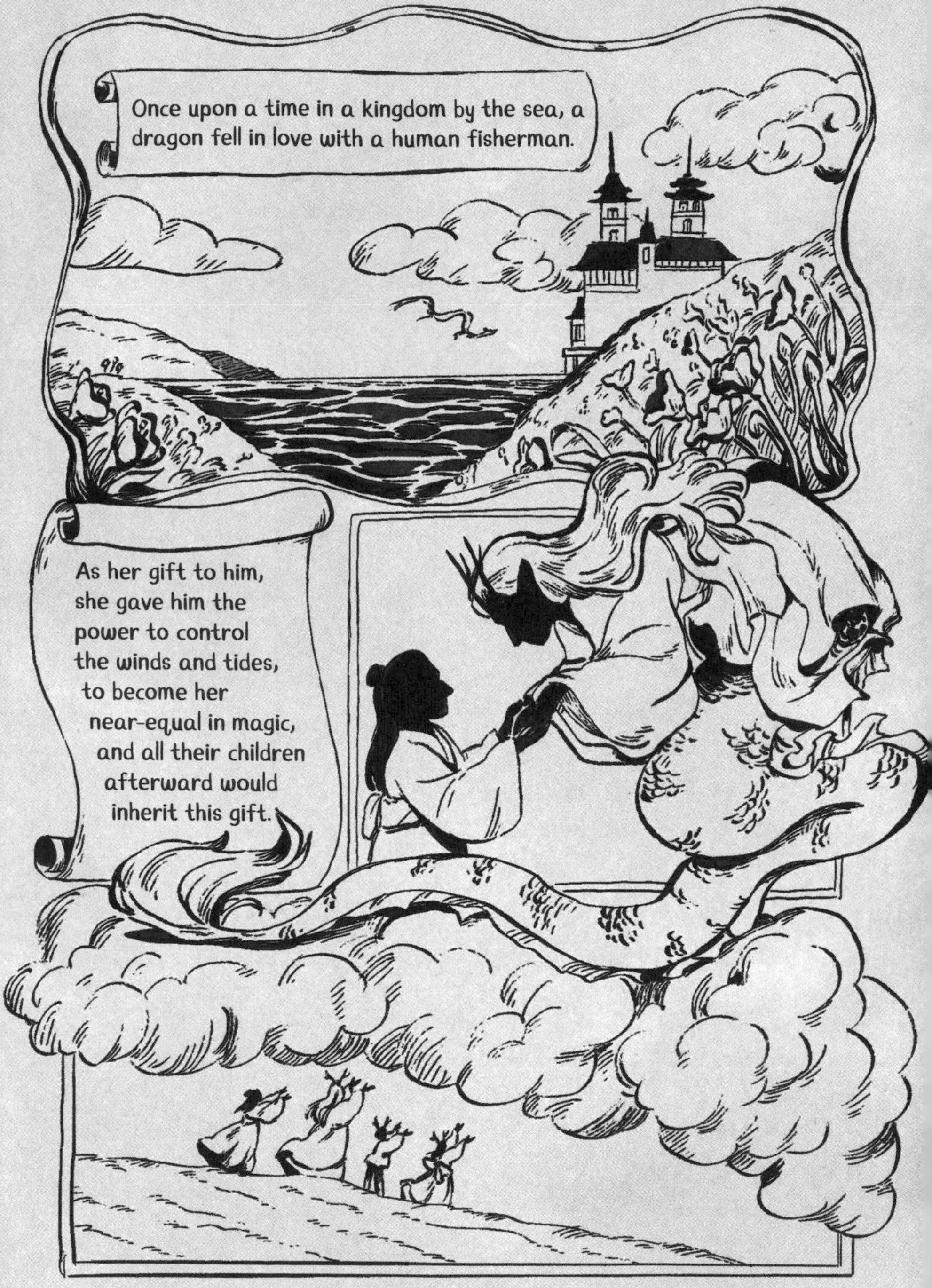
Once upon a time in a kingdom by the sea, a dragon fell in love with a human fisherman.
As her gift to him, she gave him the power to control the winds and tides, to become her near-equal in magic, and all their children afterward would inherit this gift.

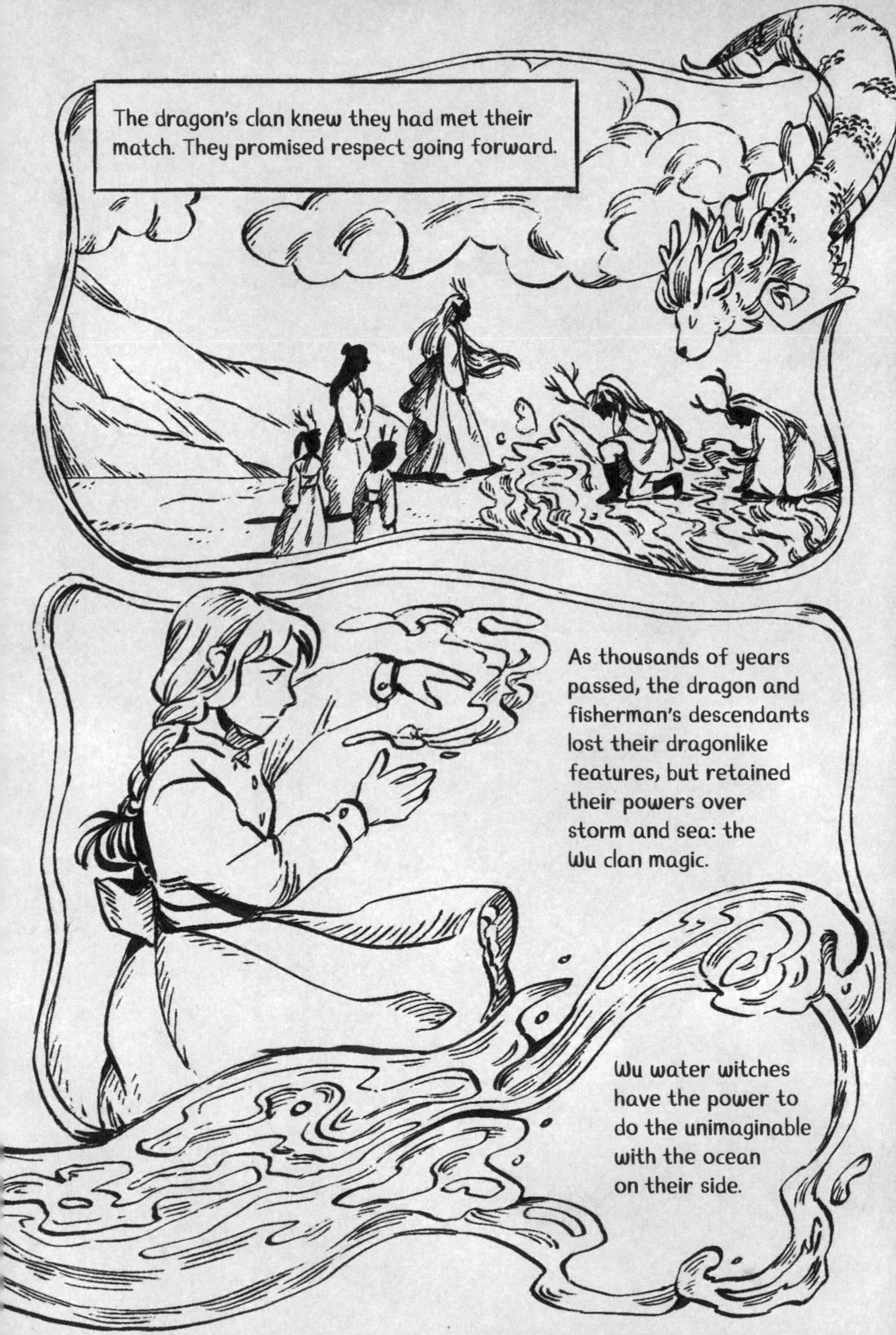
The dragon's clan knew they had met their match. They promised respect going forward.
As thousands of years passed, the dragon and fisherman's descendants lost their dragonlike features, but retained their powers over storm and sea: the Wu clan magic.
Wu water witches have the power to do the unimaginable with the ocean on their side.

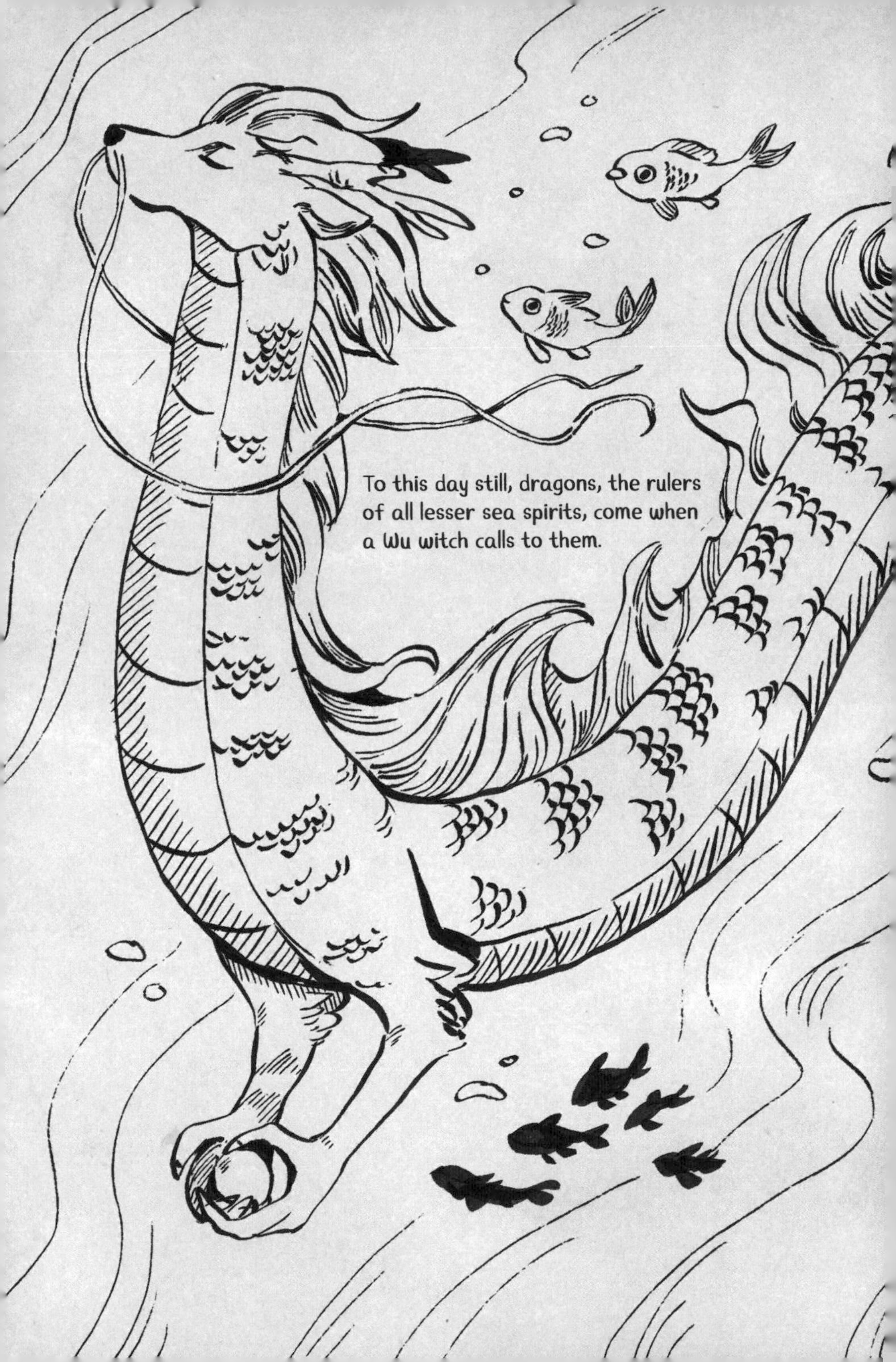
To this day still, dragons, the rulers of all lesser sea spirits, come when a Wu witch calls to them.

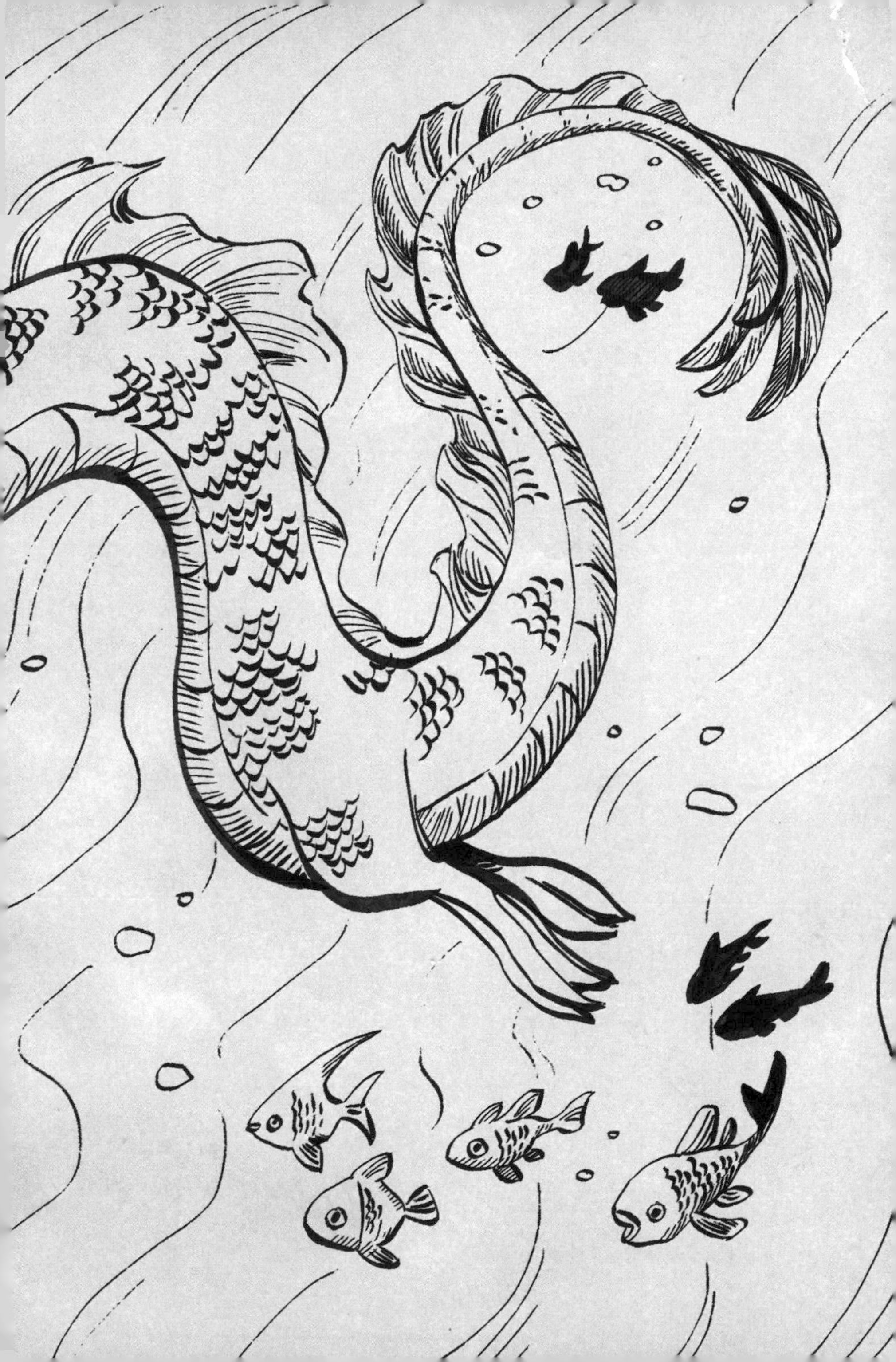

Chapter 1

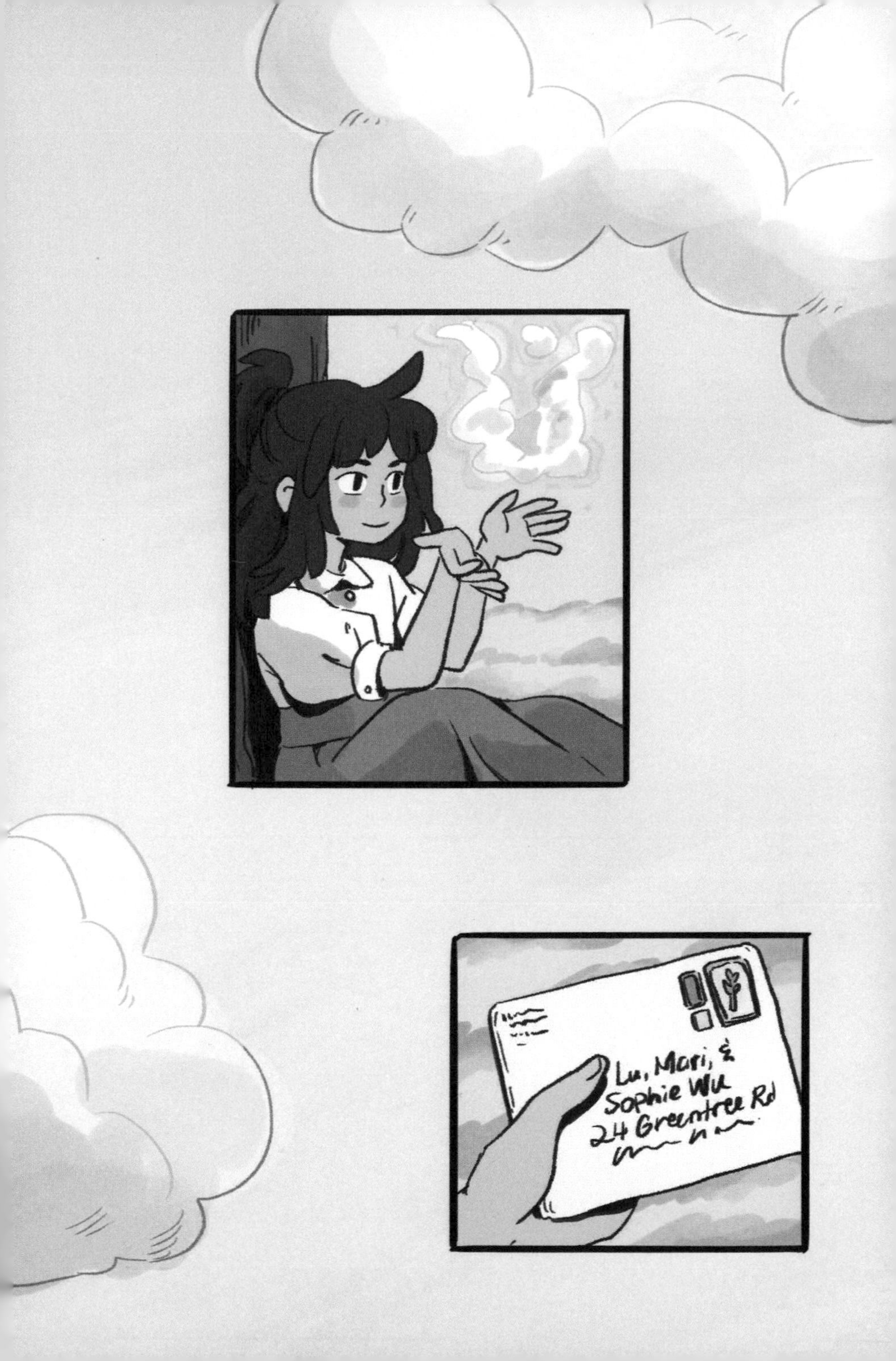
Lu, Mari, &
Sophie Wu
24 Greentree Rd

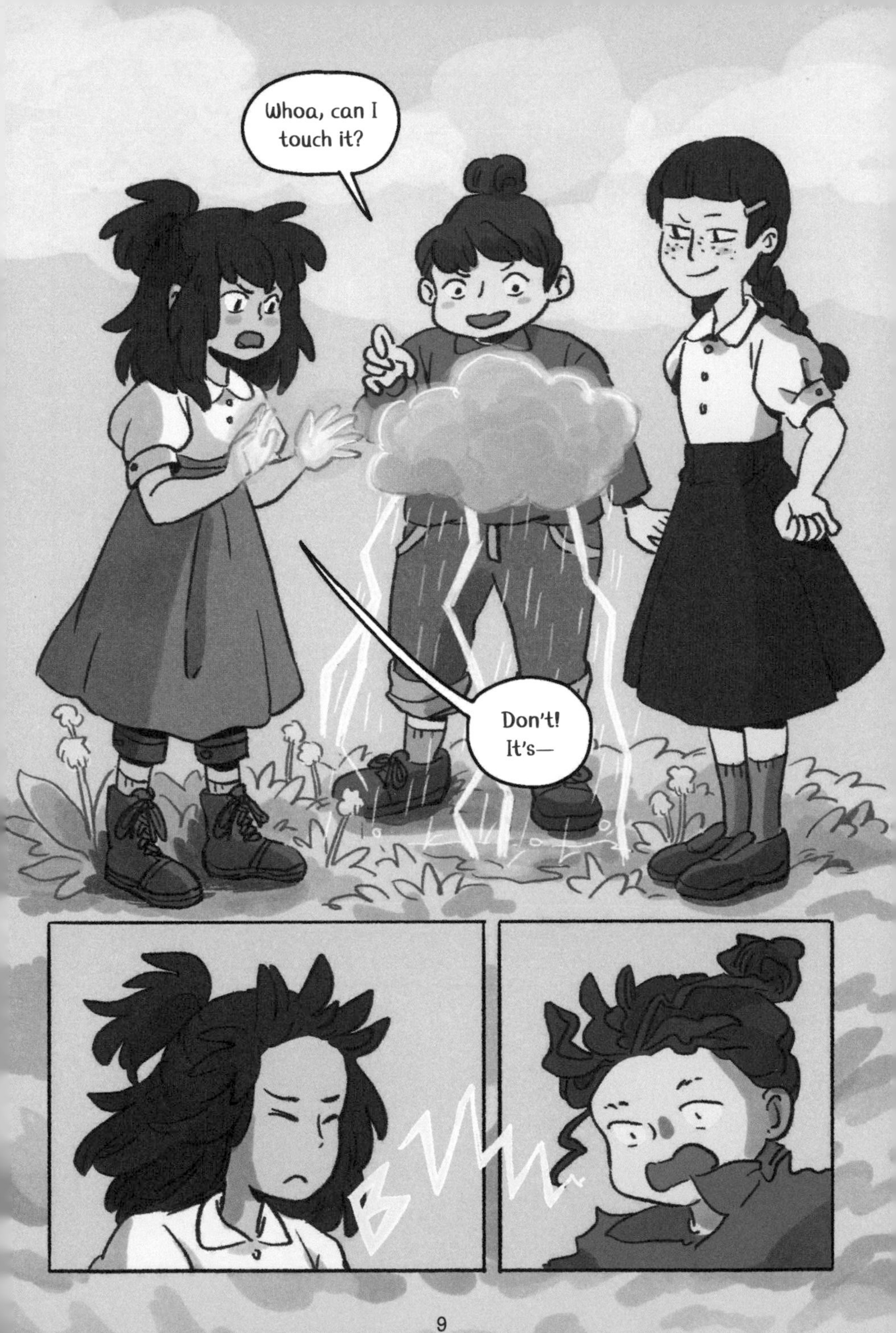
Whoa, can I touch it?
Don't! It's—
BW

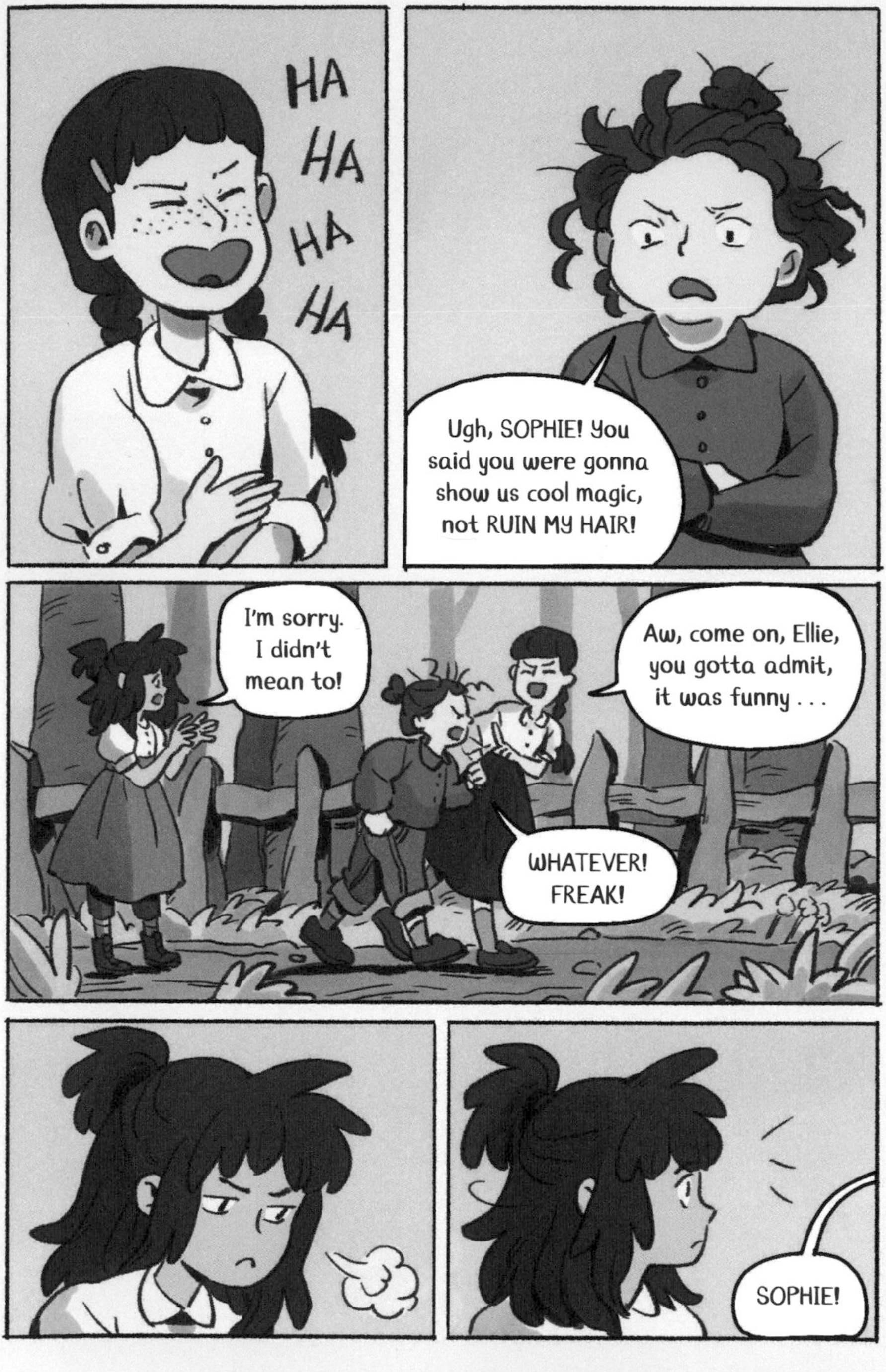
HA
HA
HA
HA
Ugh, SOPHIE! You said you were gonna show us cool magic, not RUIN MY HAIR!
I'm sorry. I didn't mean to!
Aw, come on, Ellie, you gotta admit, it was funny . . .
WHATEVER! FREAK!
SOPHIE!

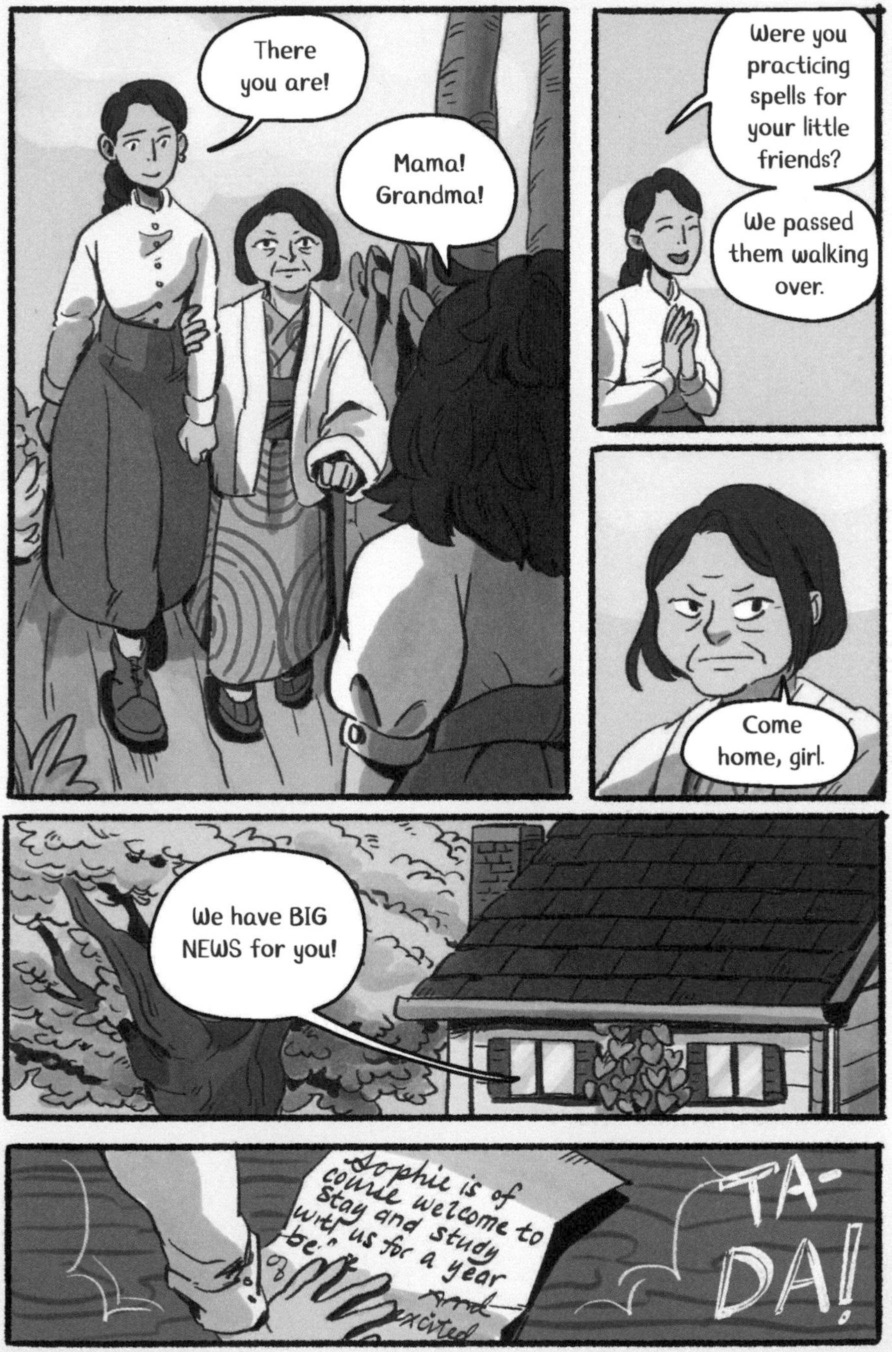
There you are!
Mama! Grandma!
Were you practicing spells for your little friends?
We passed them walking over.
Come home, girl.
We have BIG NEWS for you!
Sophie is of course welcome to stay and study with us for a year
TA-DA!

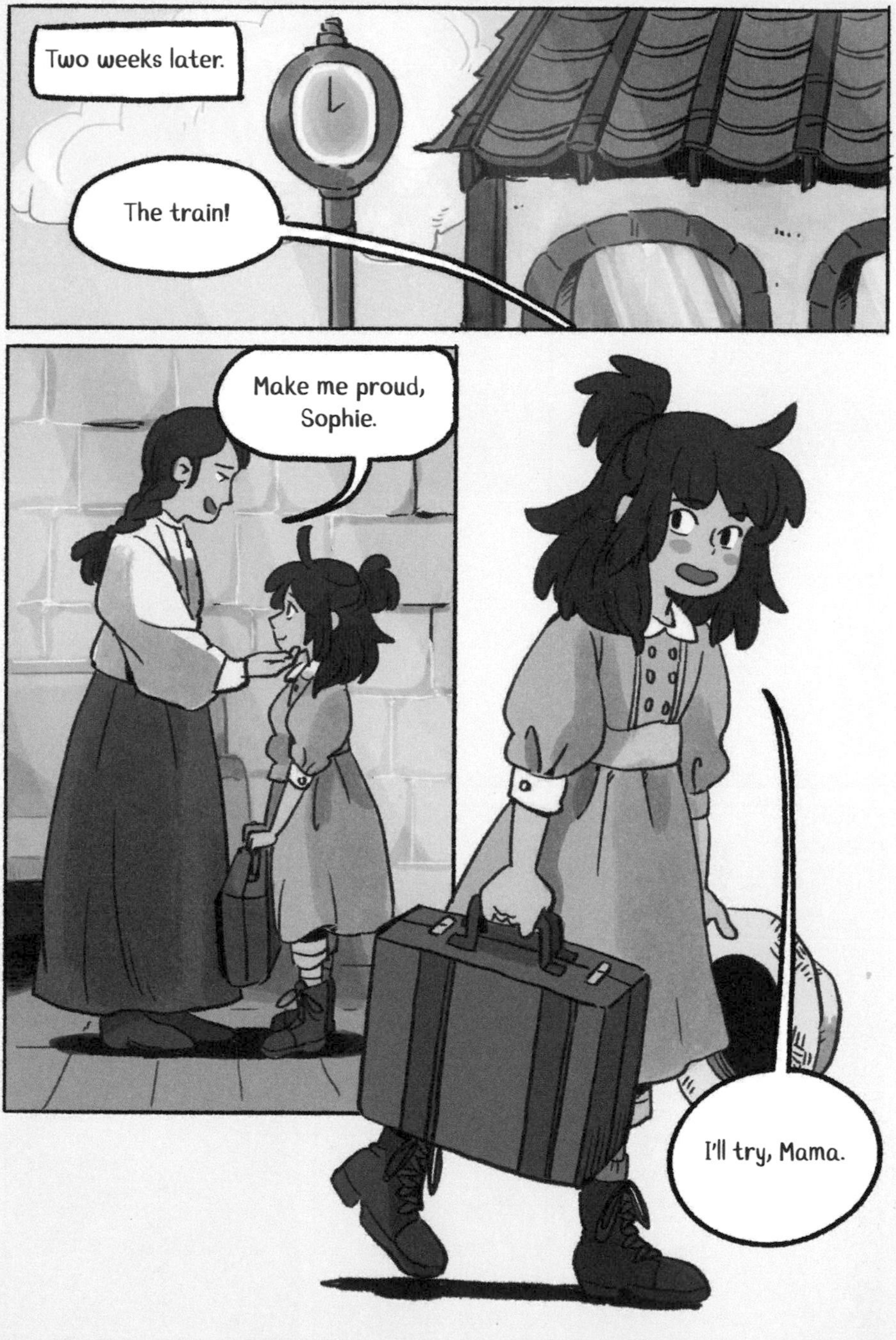
Two weeks later.
The train!
Make me proud, Sophie.
I'll try, Mama.

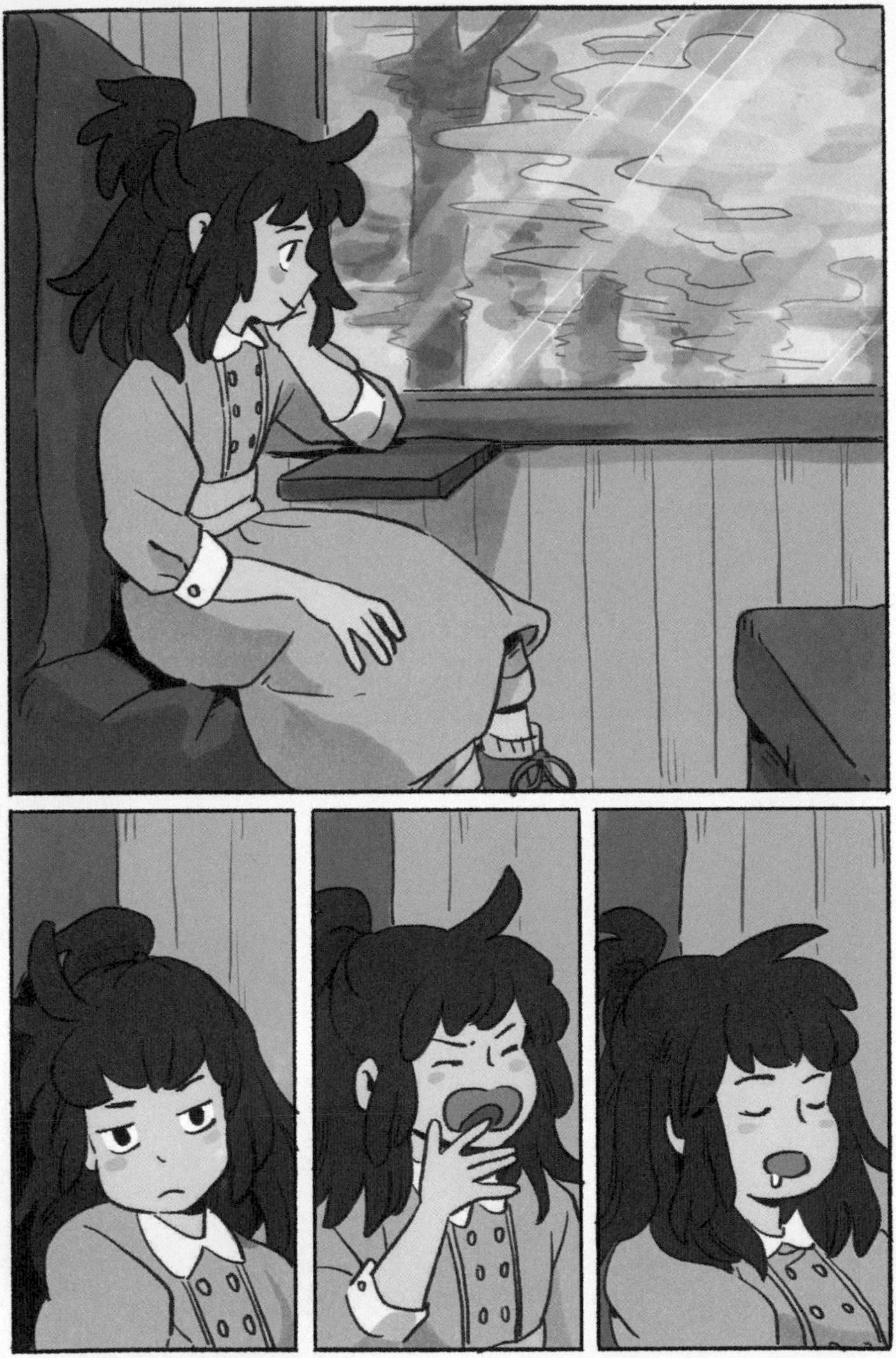

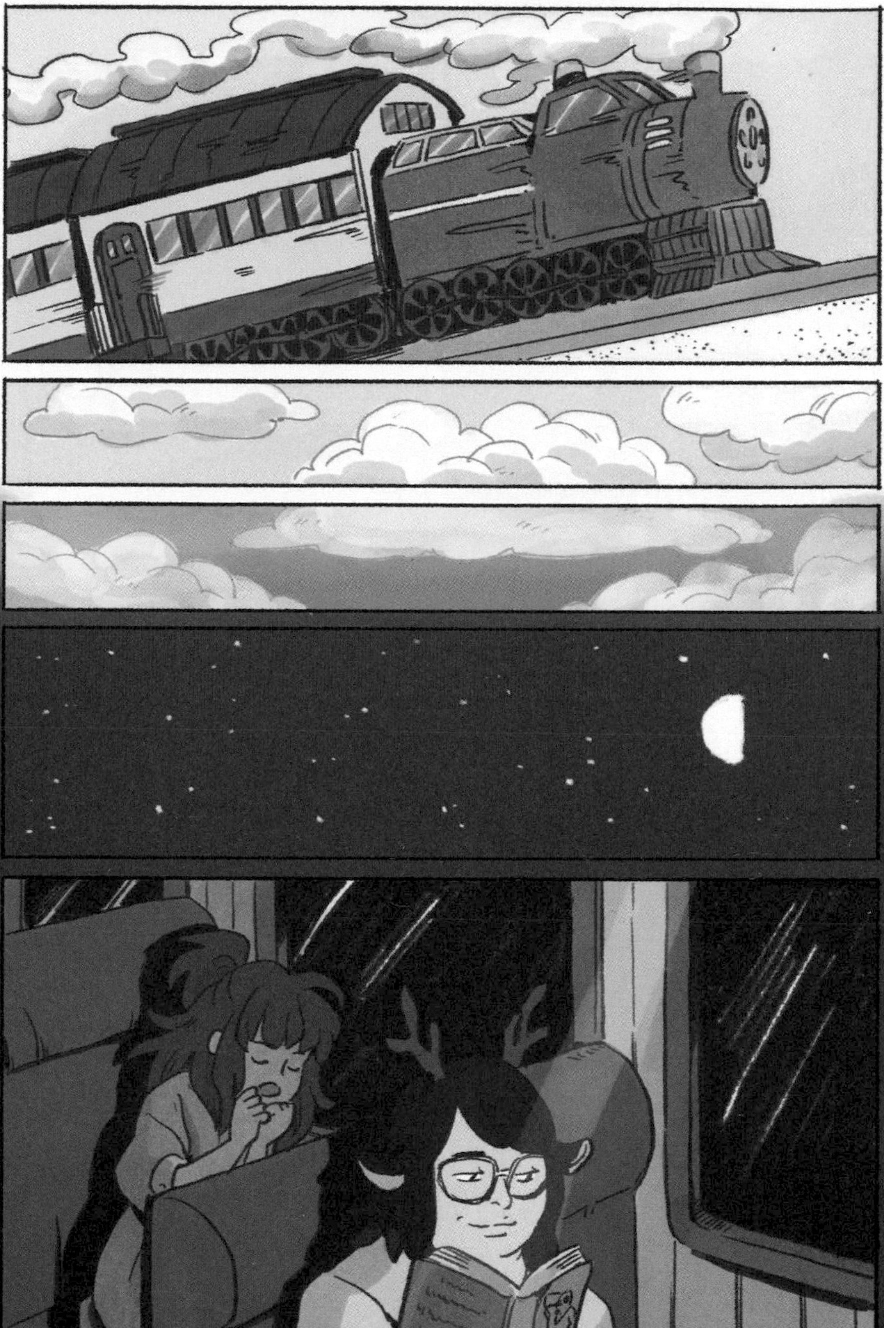

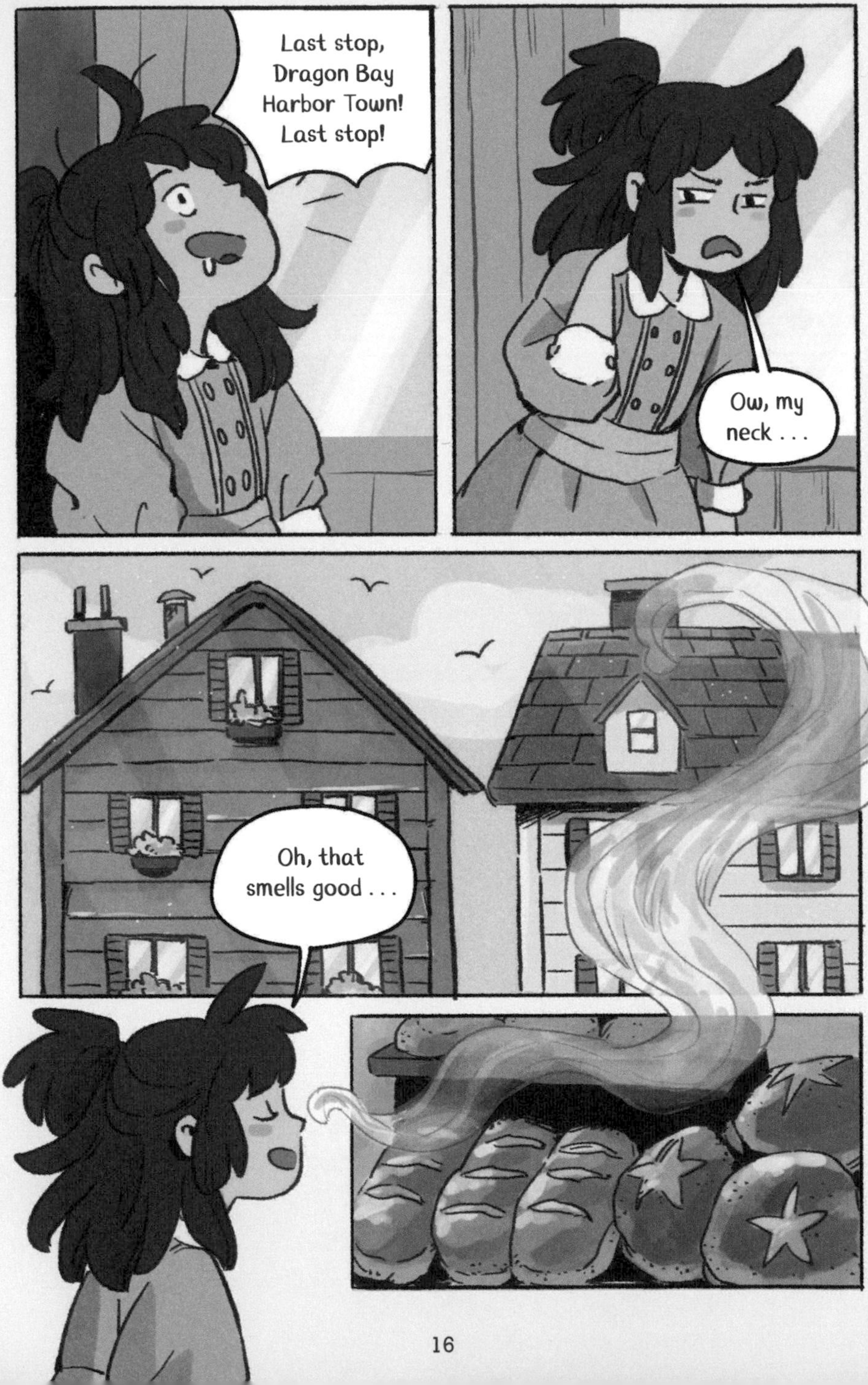
Last stop, Dragon Bay Harbor Town! Last stop!
Ow, my neck . . .
Oh, that smells good . . .

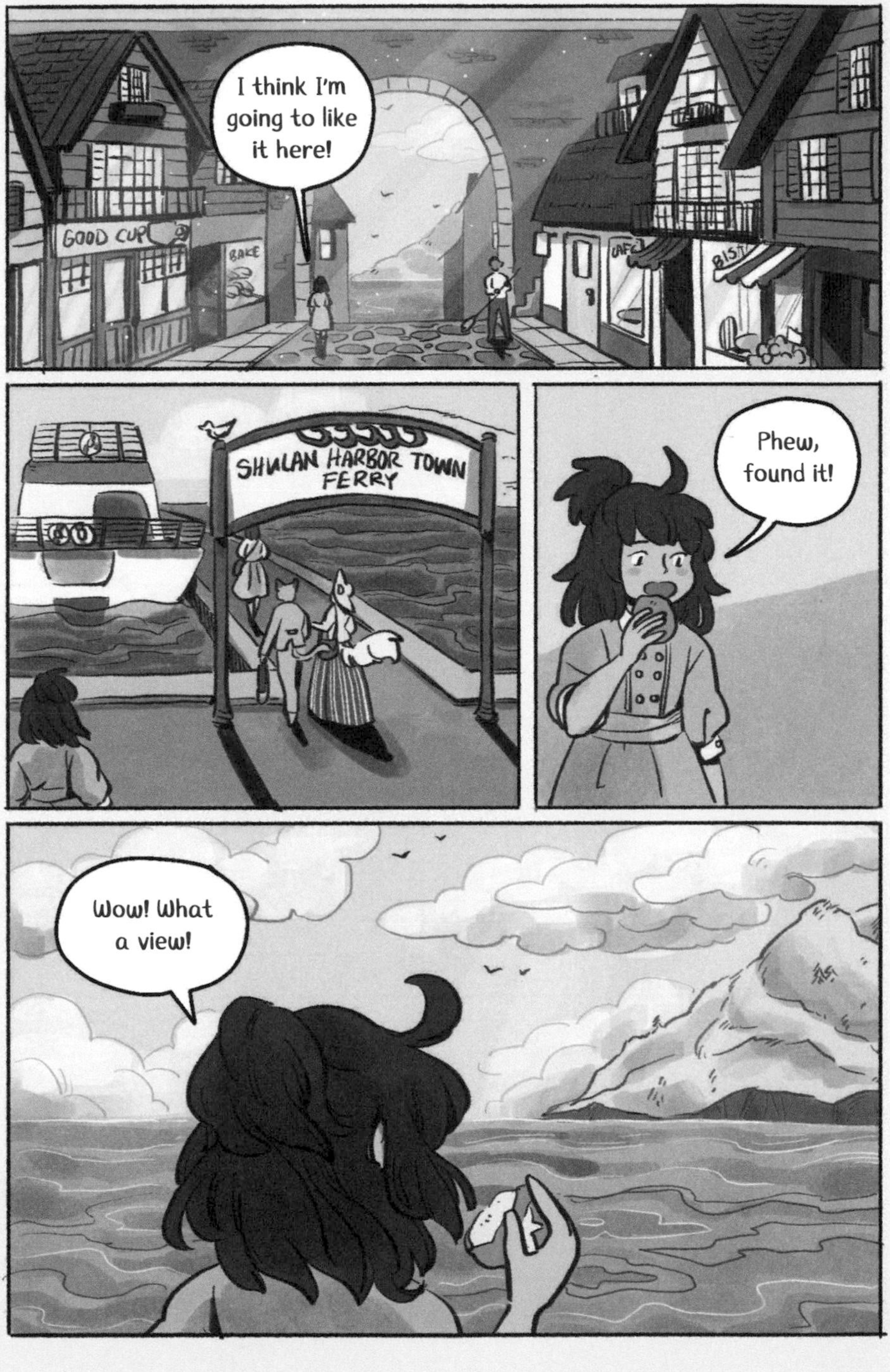
I think I'm going to like it here!
GOOD CUP
BAKE
SHULAN HARBOR TOWN FERRY
Phew, found it!
Wow! What a view!

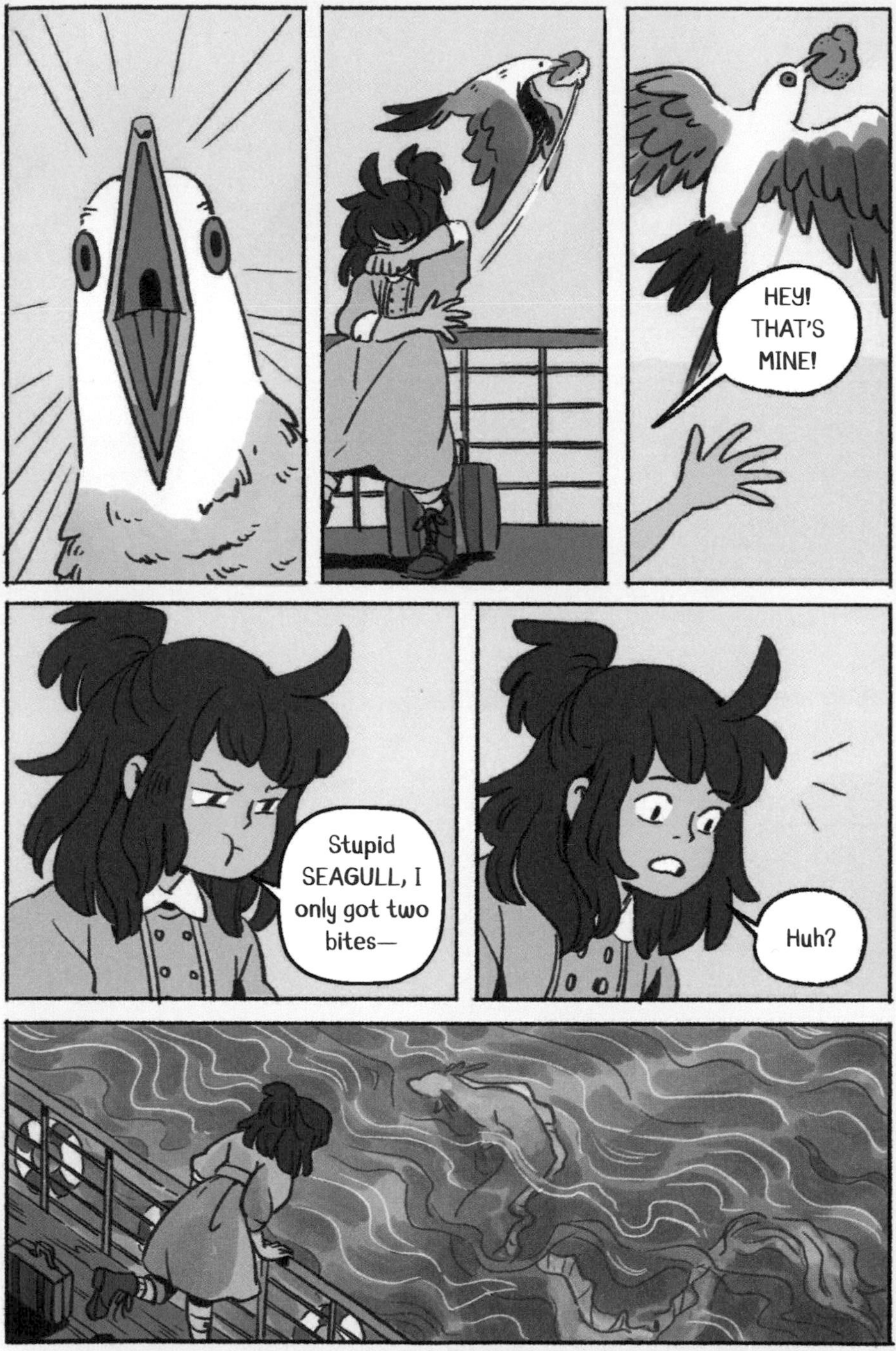
HEY! THAT'S MINE!
Stupid SEAGULL, I only got two bites—
Huh?

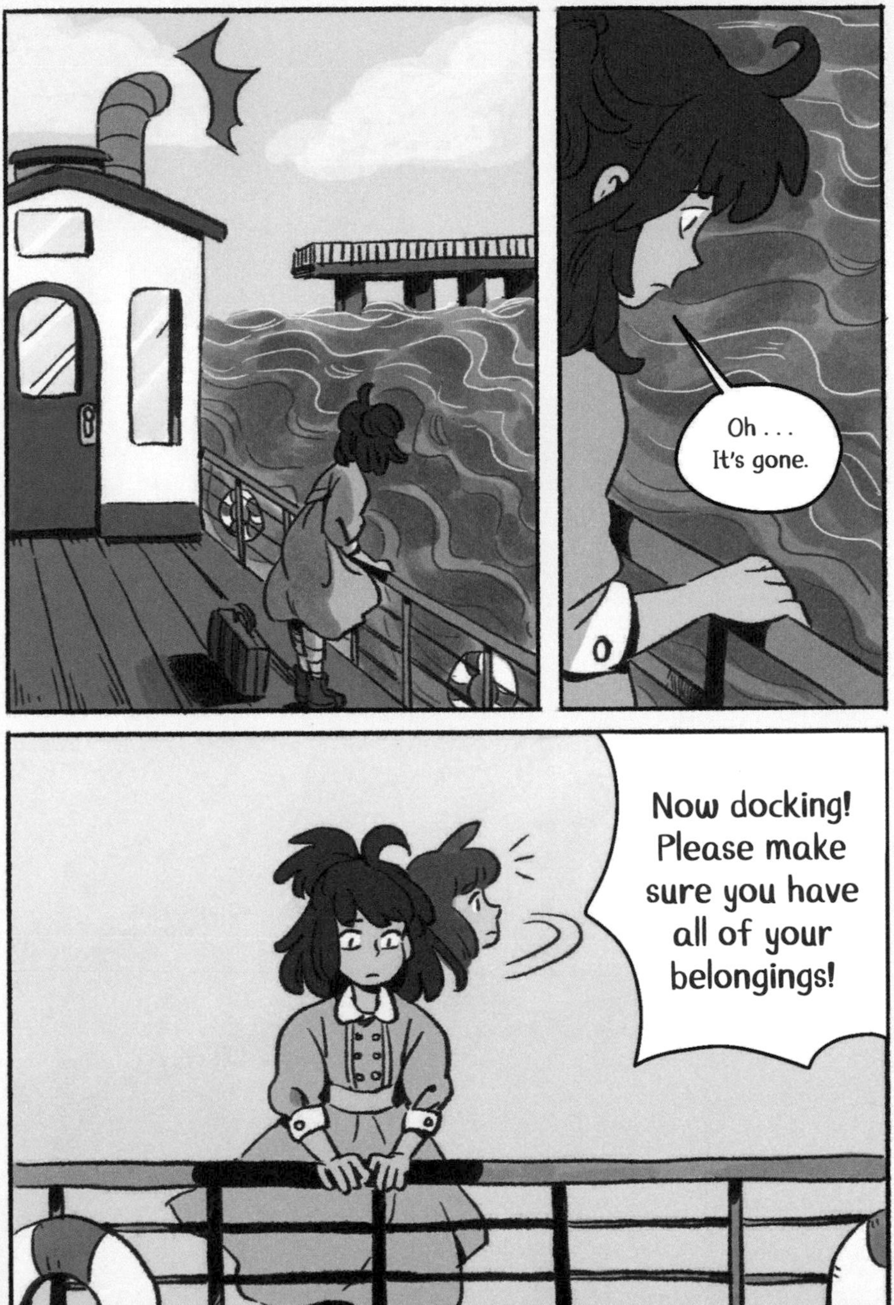
Oh . . .
It's gone.
Now docking! Please make sure you have all of your belongings!

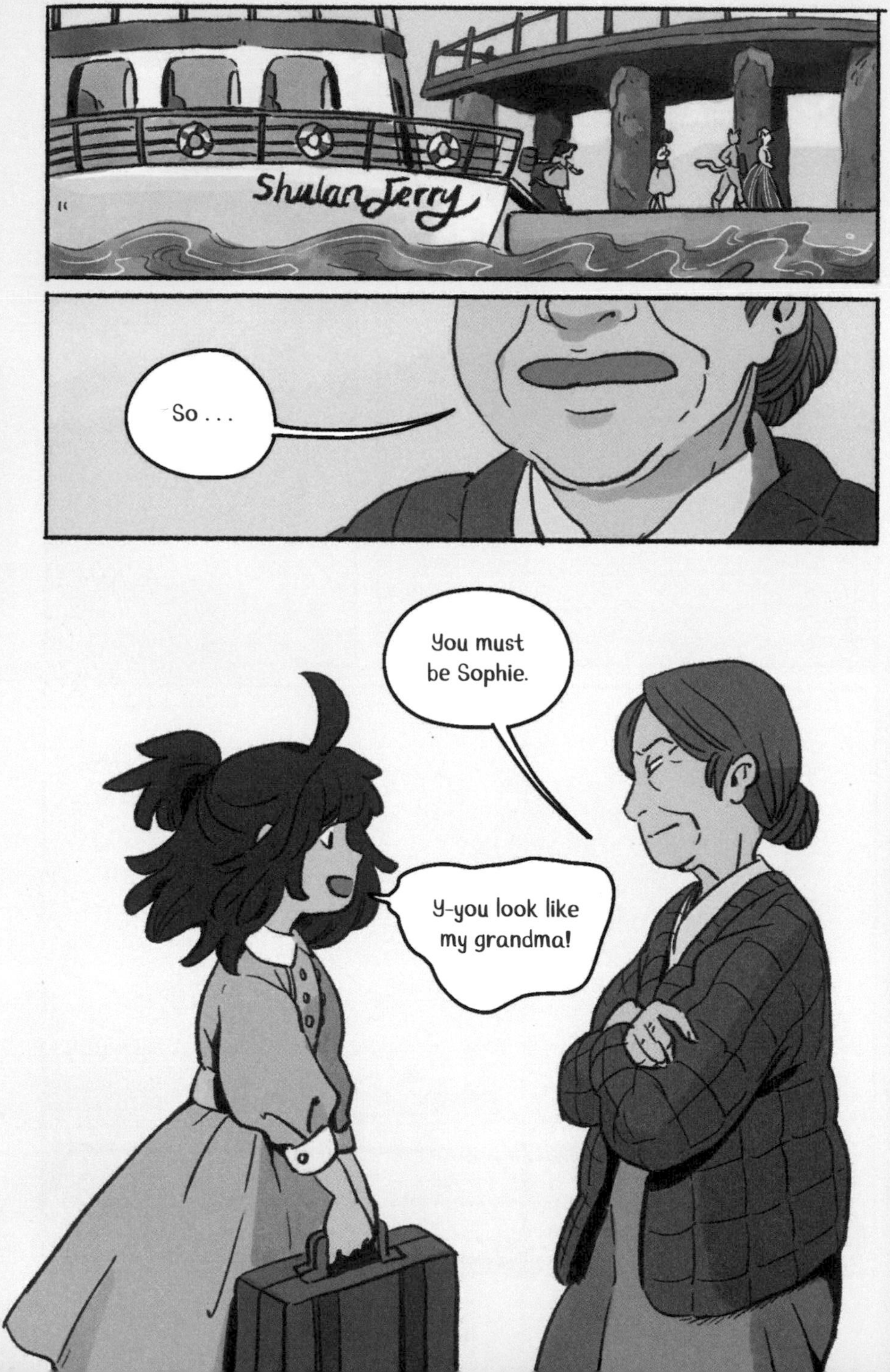
Shulan Ferry
So . . .
You must be Sophie.
Y-you look like my grandma!

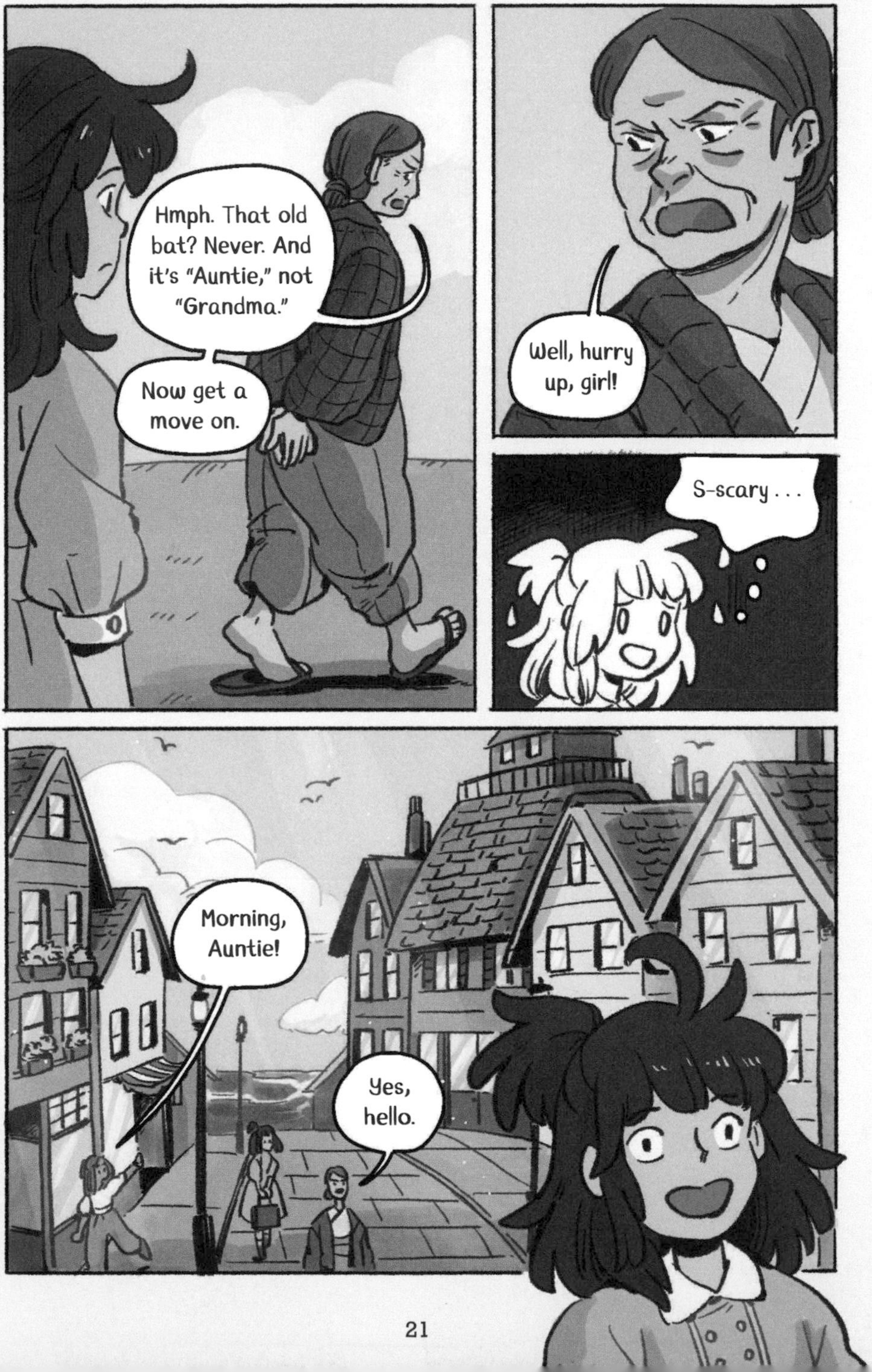
Hmph. That old bat? Never. And it's "Auntie," not "Grandma."
Now get a move on.
Well, hurry up, girl!
S-scary . . .
Morning, Auntie!
Yes, hello.

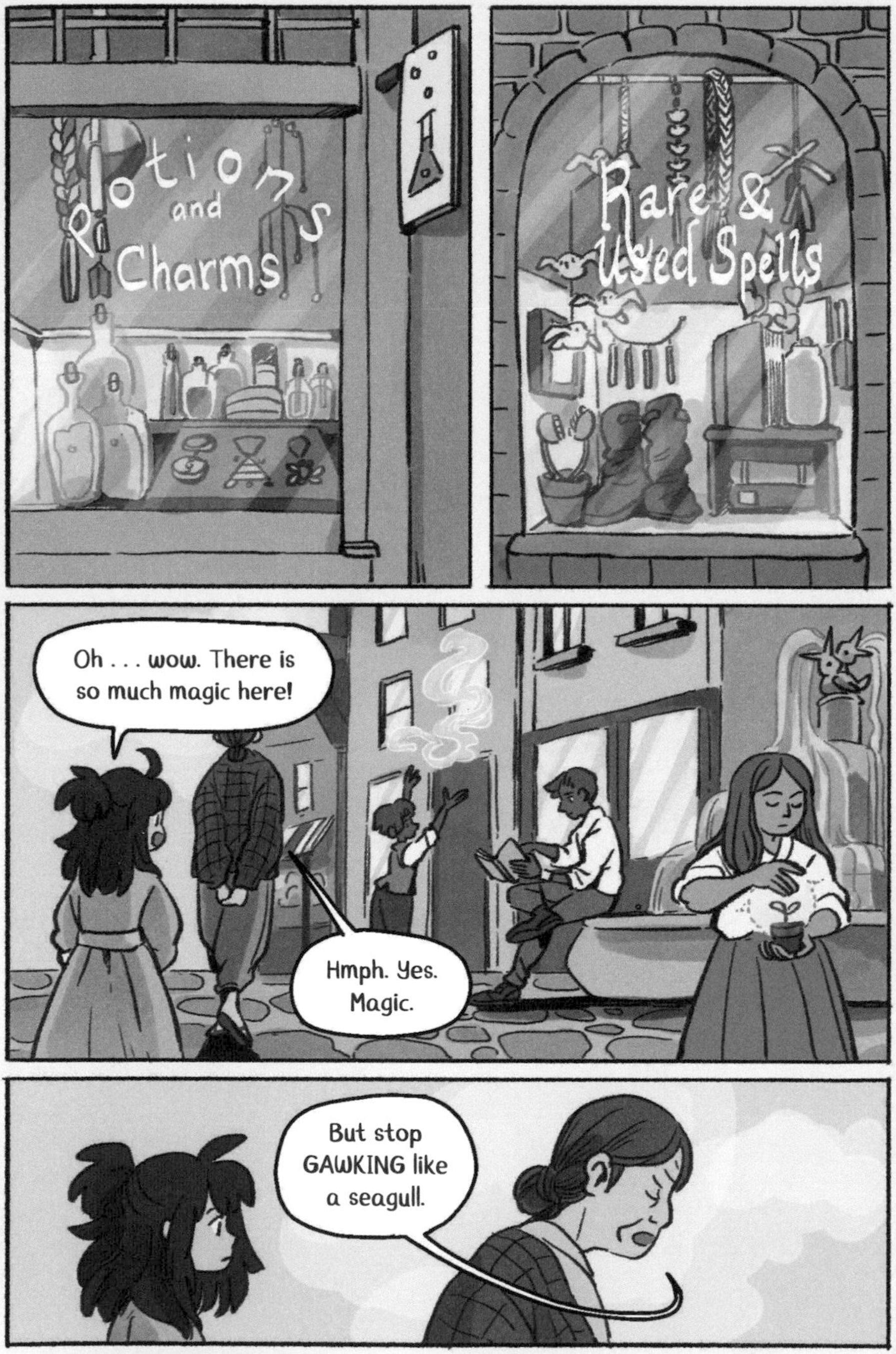
Potions and Charms
Rare & Used Spells
Oh . . . wow. There is so much magic here!
Hmph. Yes. Magic.
But stop GAWKING like a seagull.

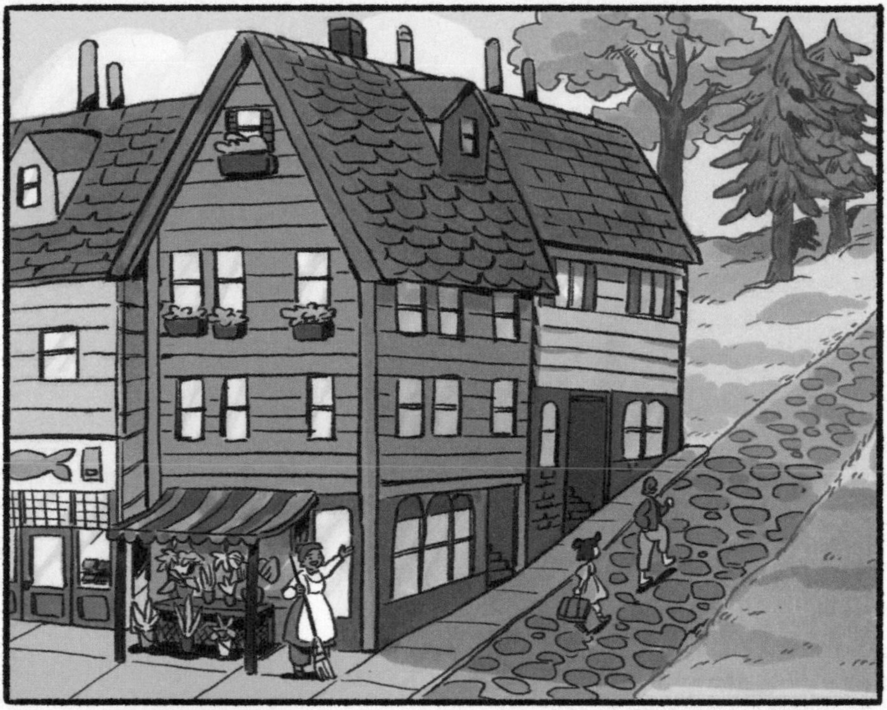

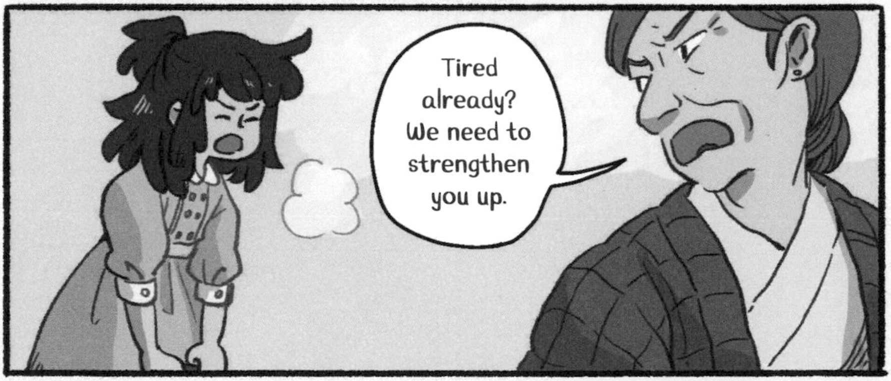
Tired already? We need to strengthen you up.

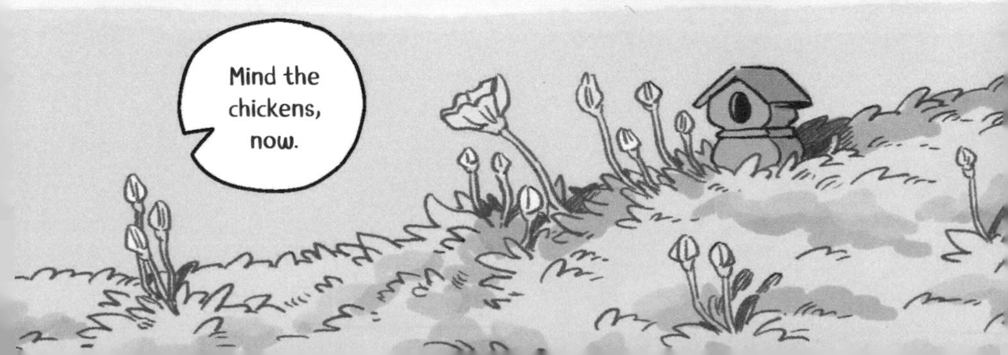
Mind the chickens, now.

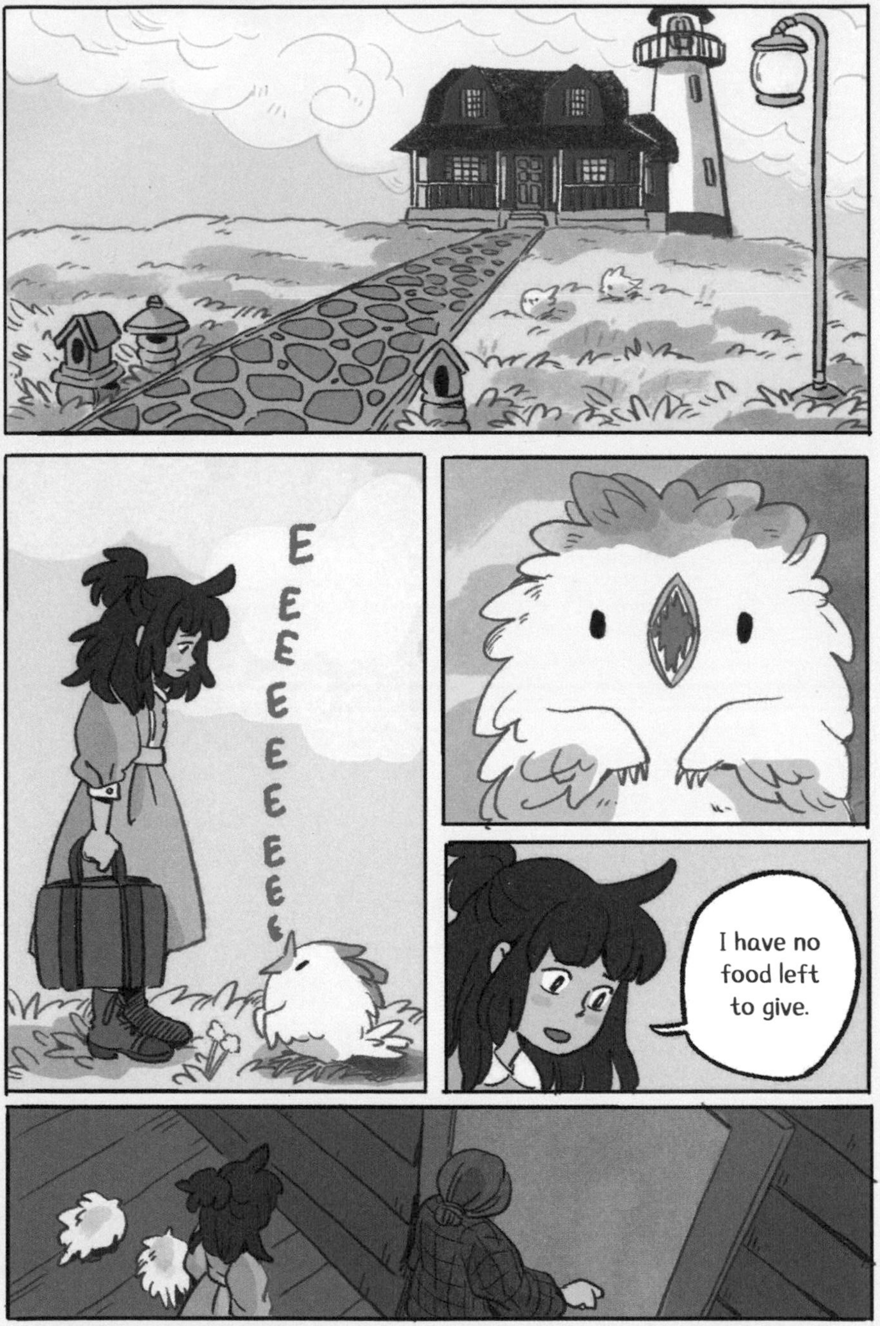
EEEEEEEEE
I have no food left to give.

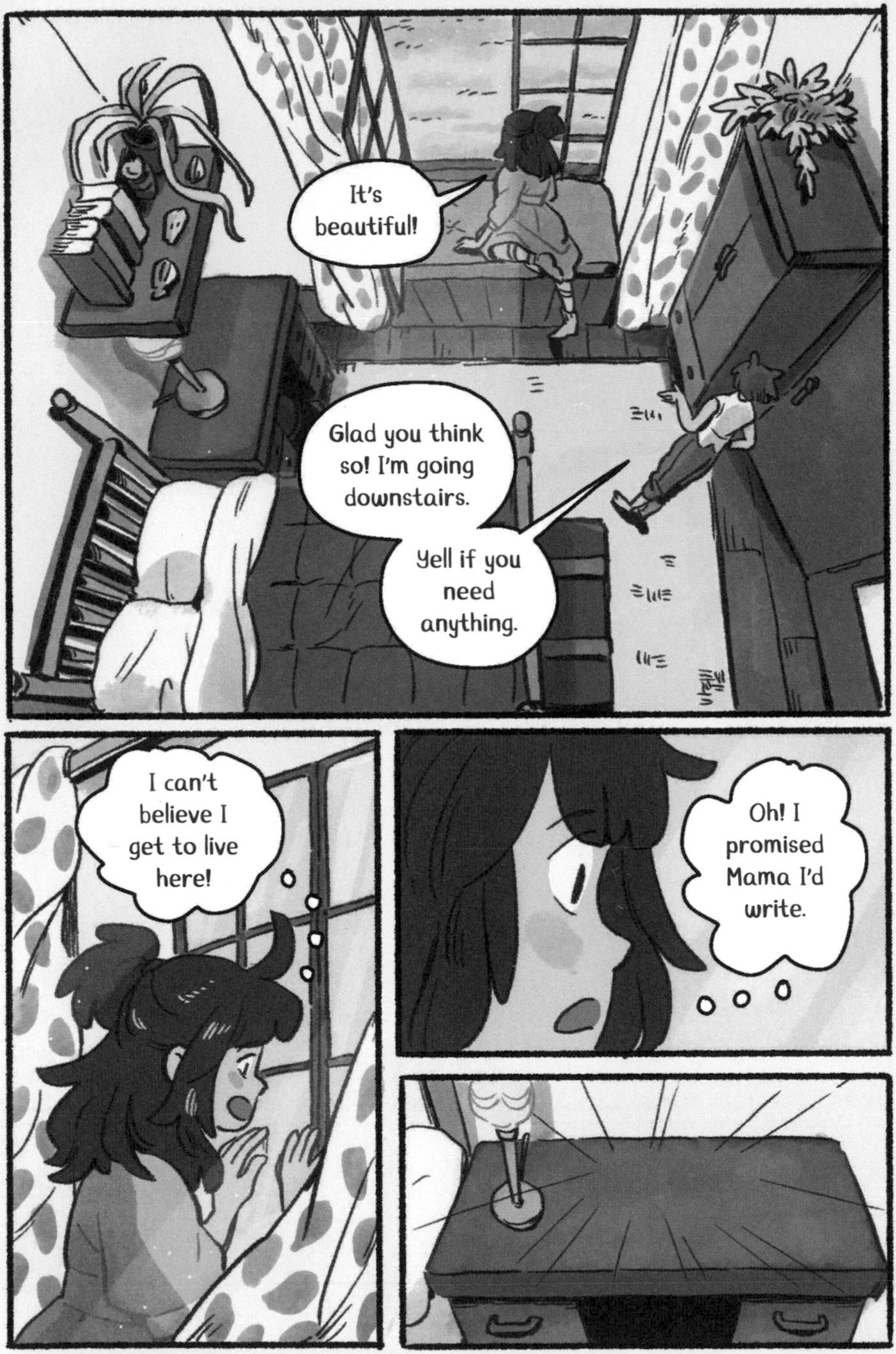
It's beautiful!
Glad you think so! I'm going downstairs.
Yell if you need anything.
I can't believe I get to live here!
Oh! I promised Mama I'd write.

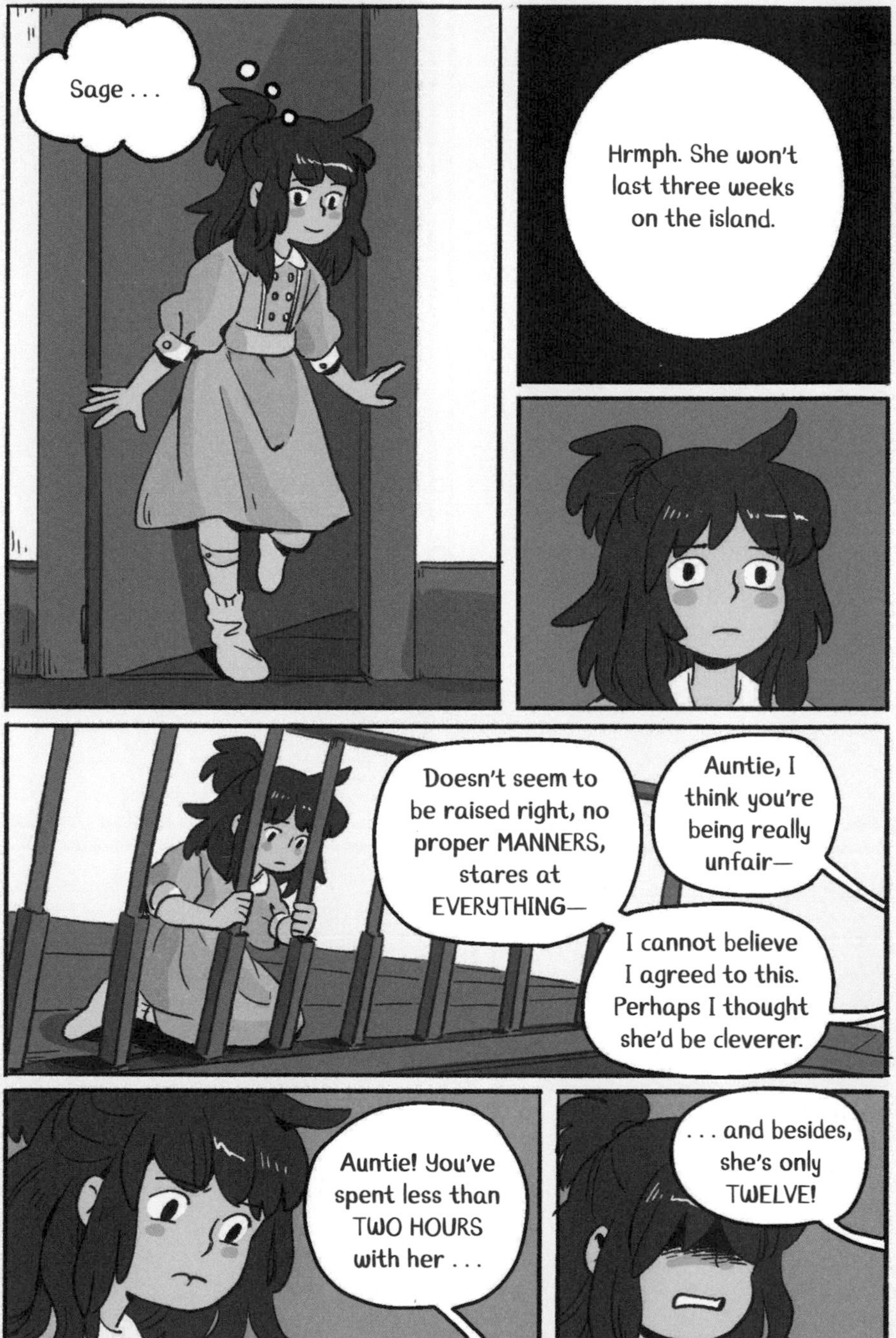
Sage . . .
Hrmph. She won't last three weeks on the island.
Doesn't seem to be raised right, no proper MANNERS, stares at EVERYTHING—
Auntie, I think you're being really unfair—
I cannot believe I agreed to this. Perhaps I thought she'd be cleverer.
Auntie! You've spent less than TWO HOURS with her . . .
. . . and besides, she's only TWELVE!

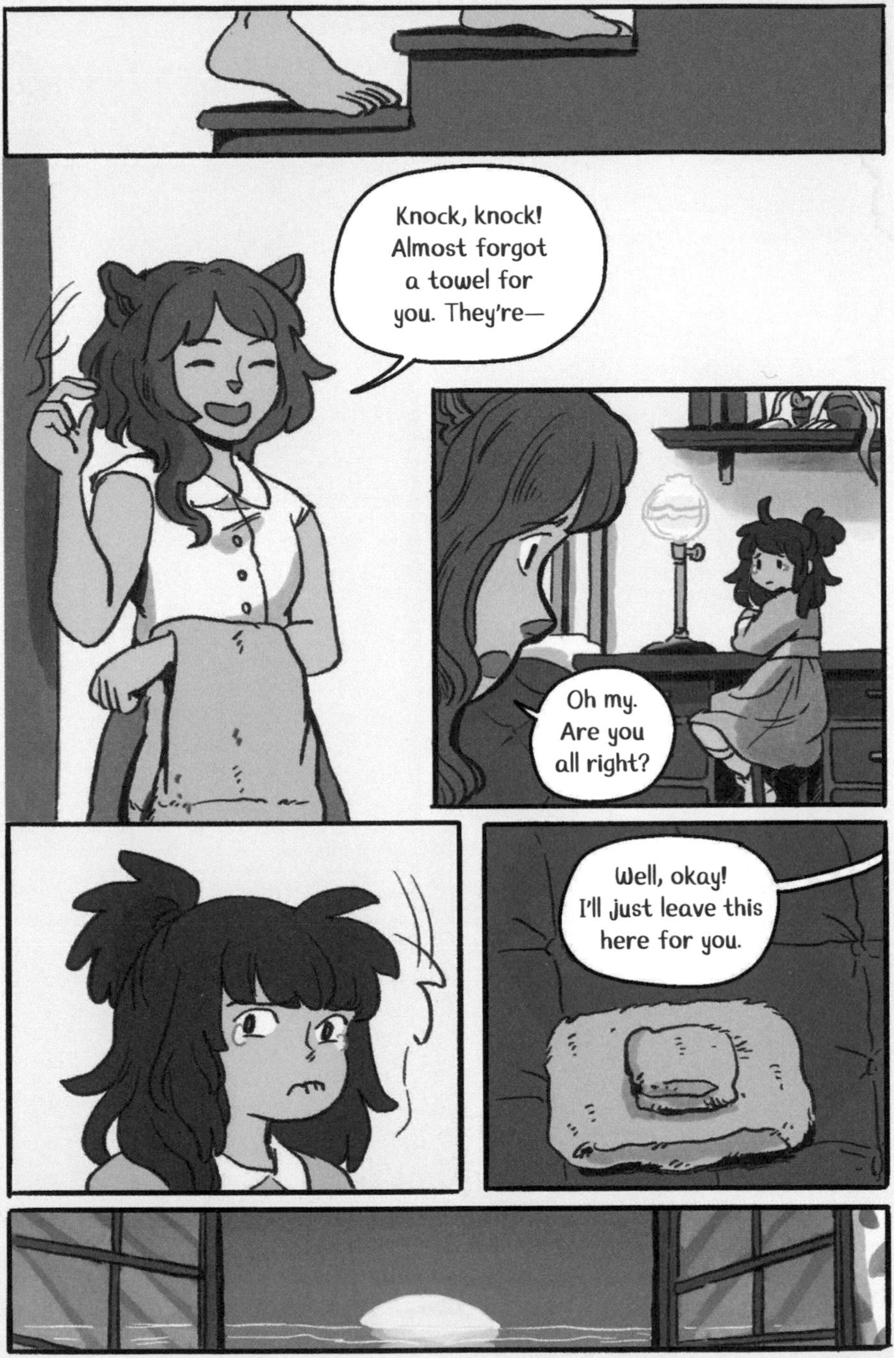
Knock, knock! Almost forgot a towel for you. They're—
Oh my. Are you all right?
Well, okay! I'll just leave this here for you.

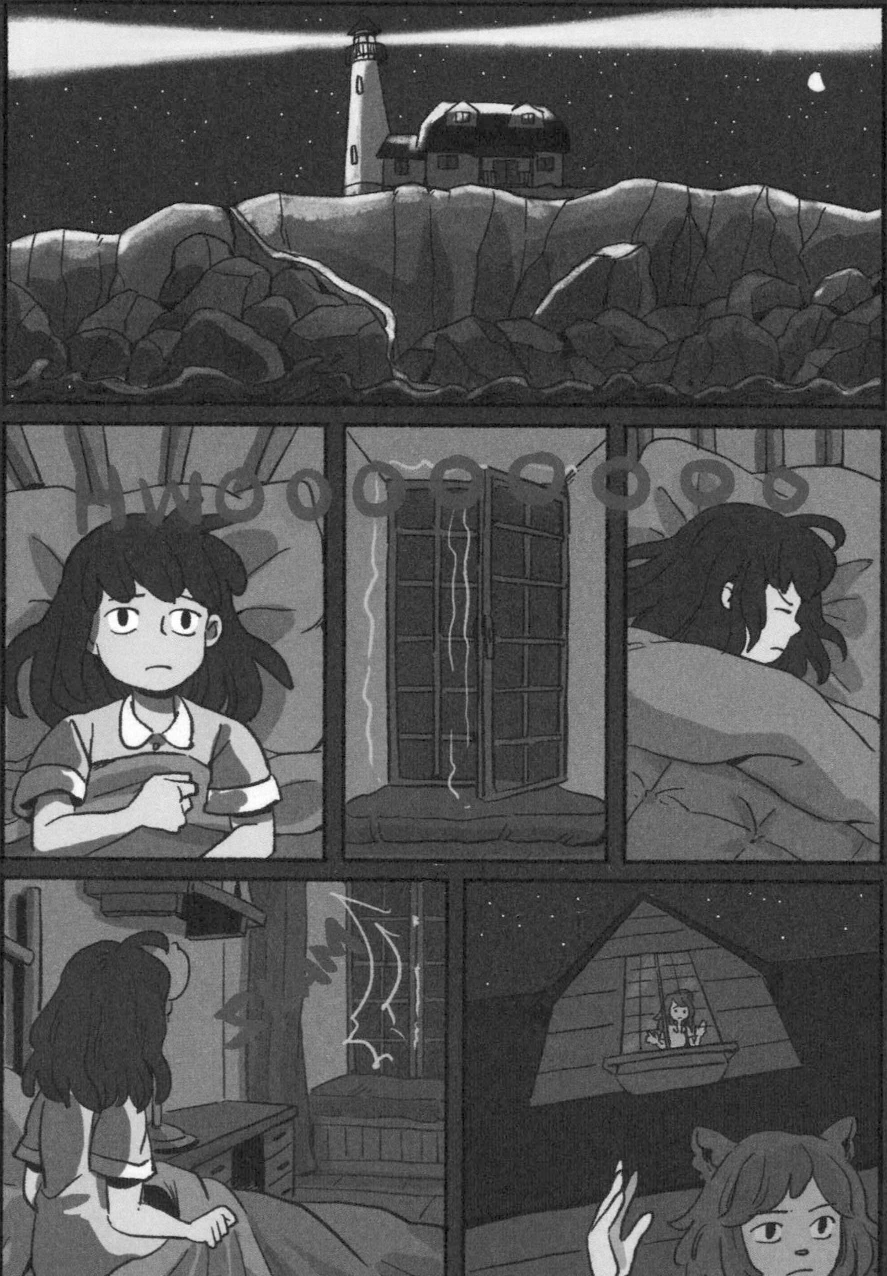
HWOOOOOOOO

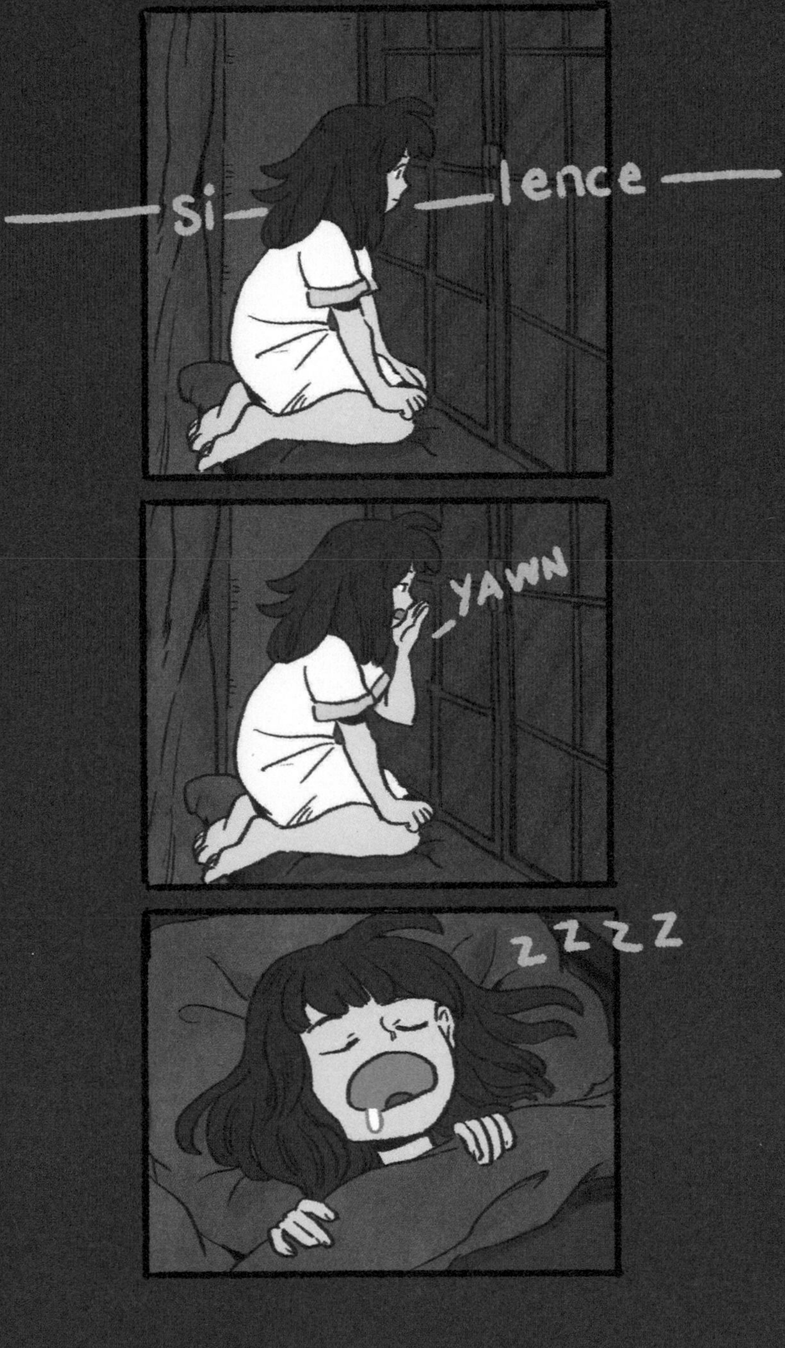
si-
-lence
YAWN
ZZZZ

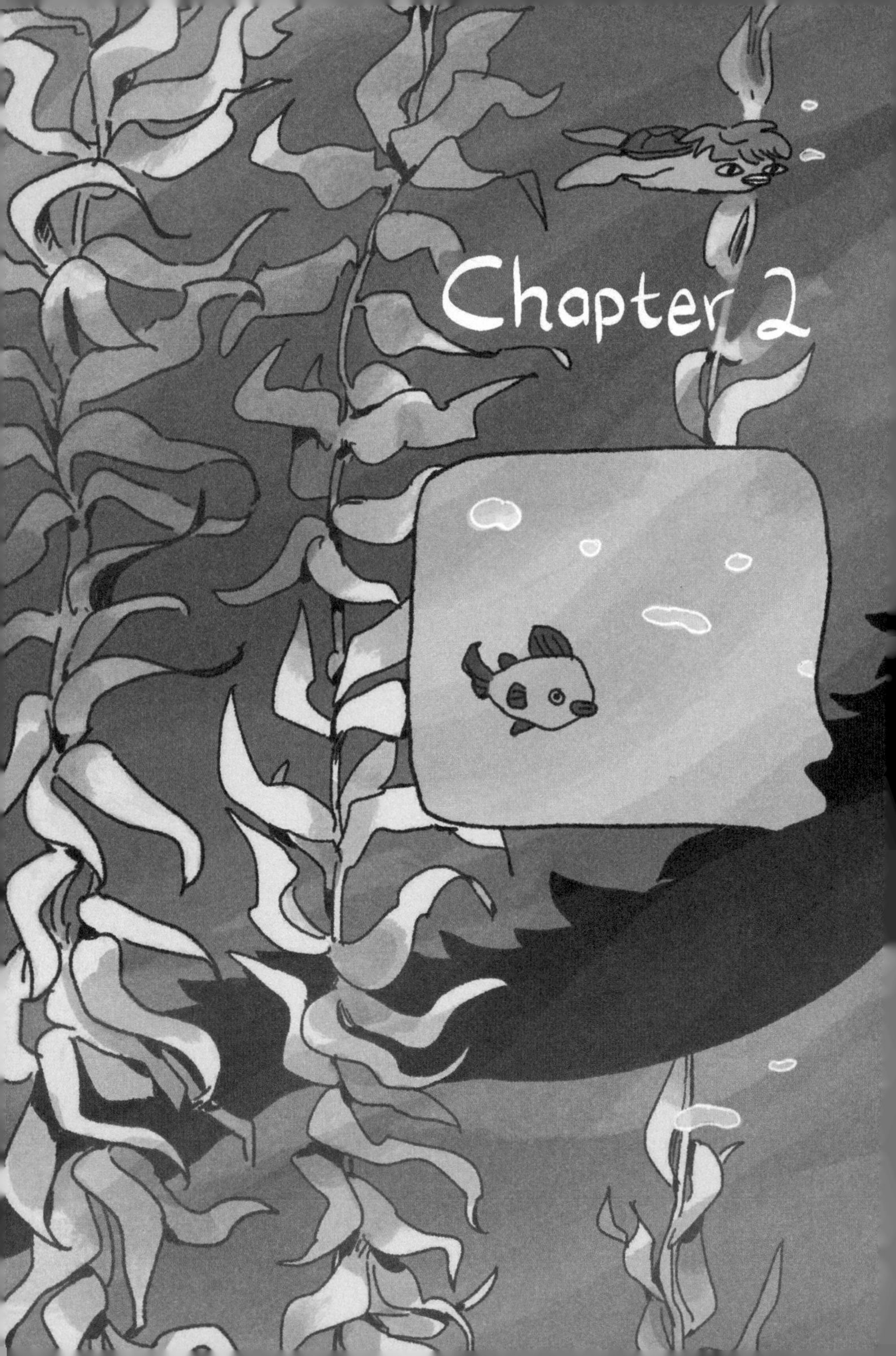
Chapter 2

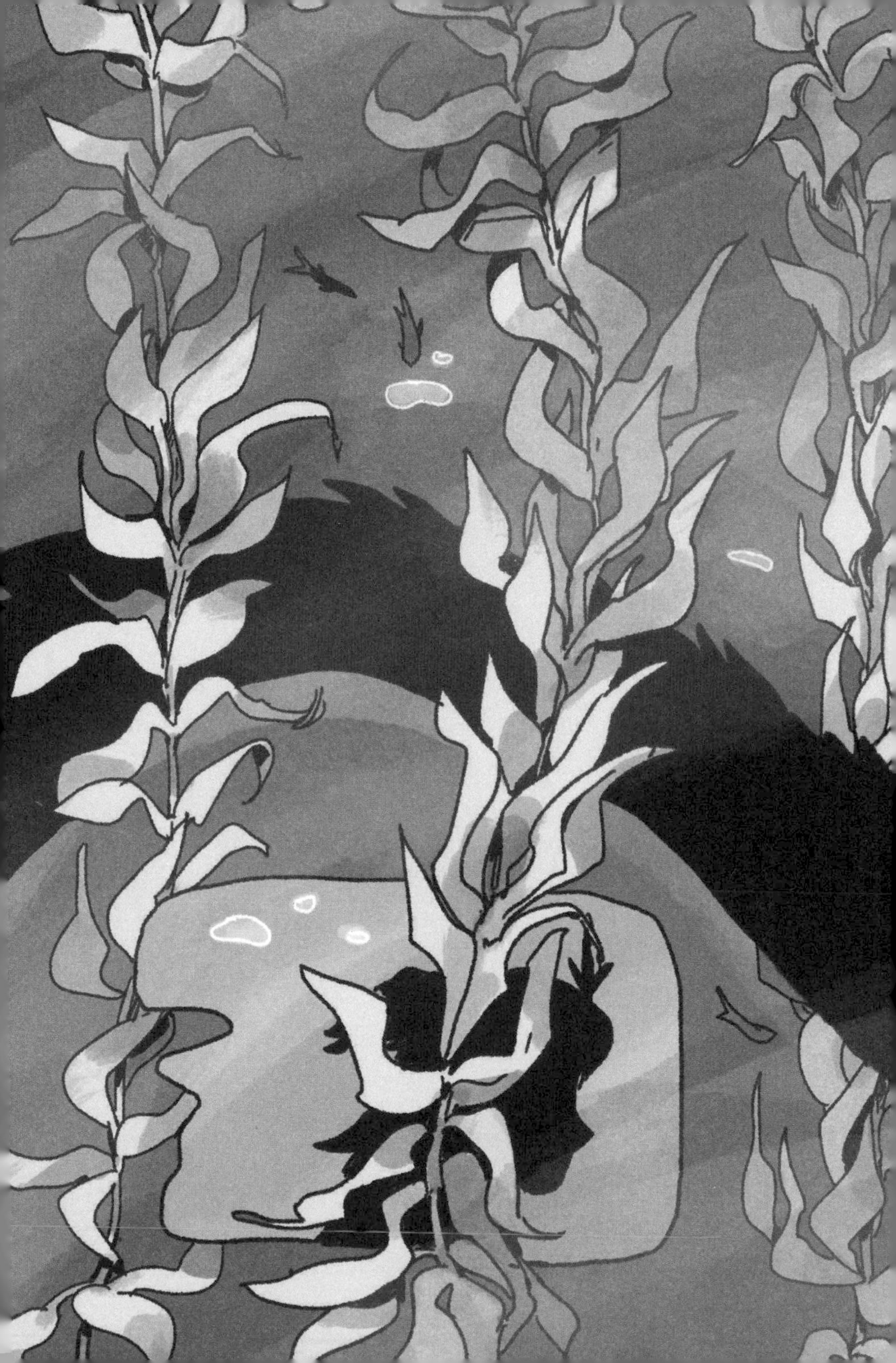

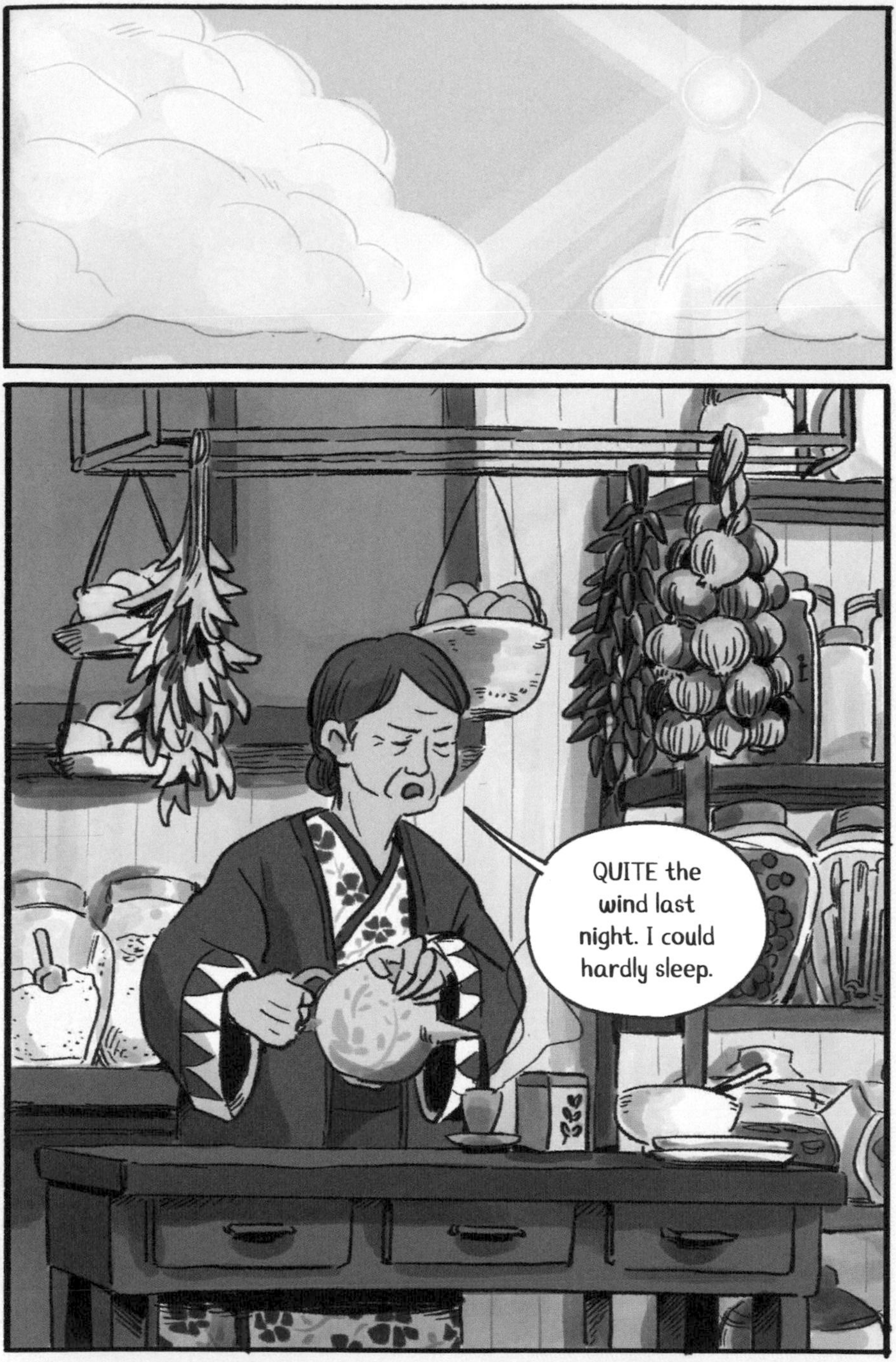
QUITE the wind last night. I could hardly sleep.

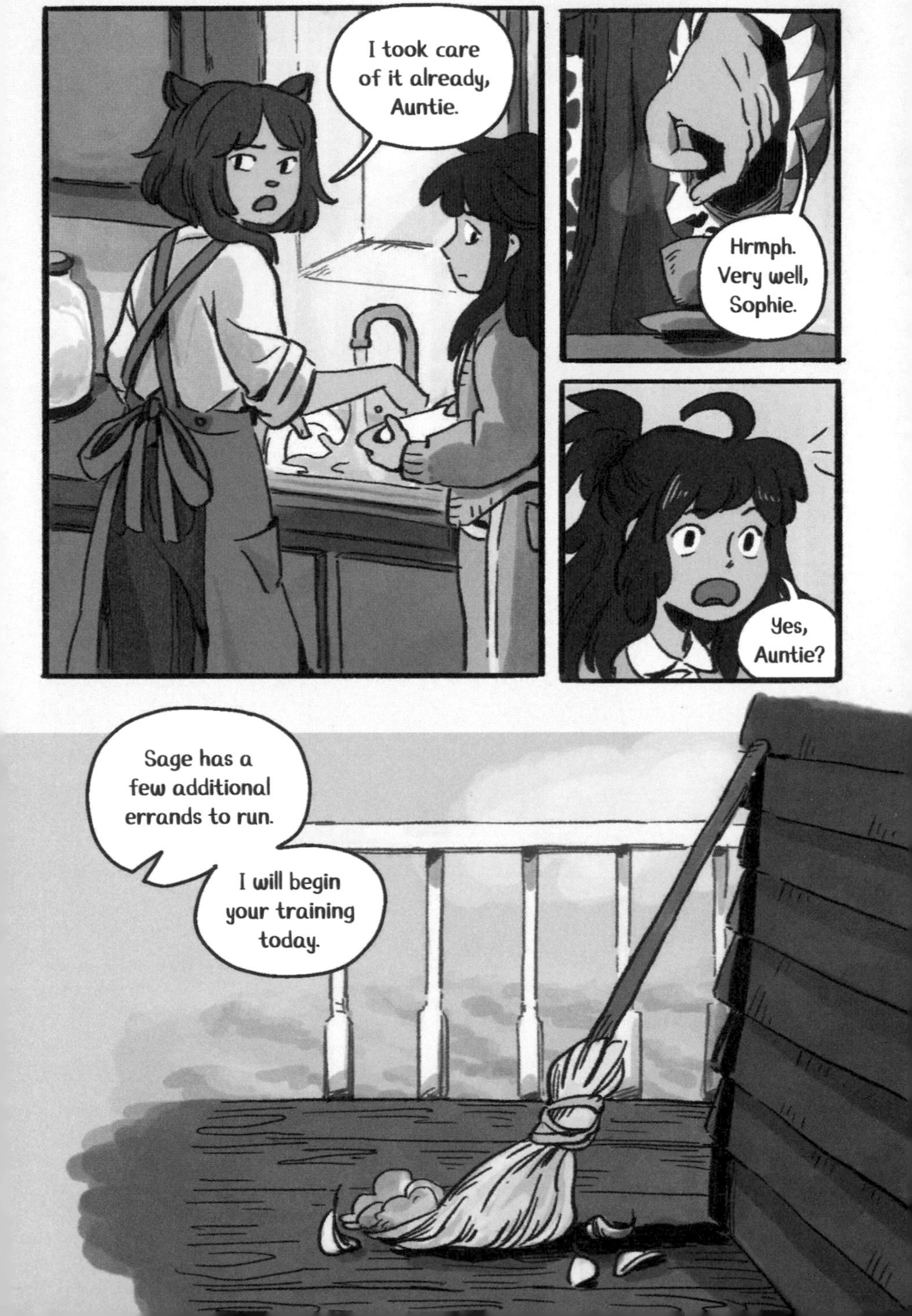
I took care of it already, Auntie.
Hrmph. Very well, Sophie.
Yes, Auntie?
Sage has a few additional errands to run.
I will begin your training today.

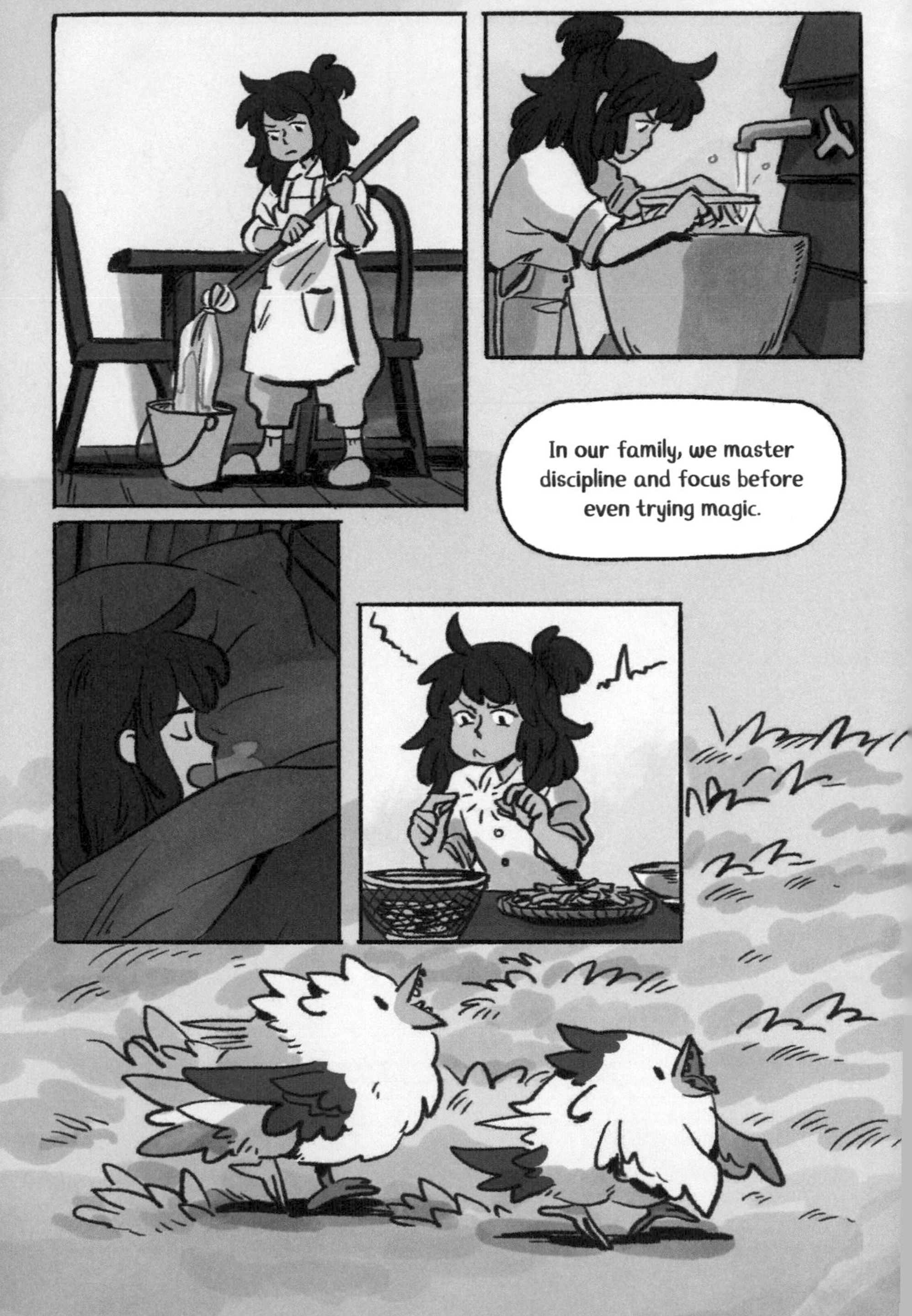
In our family, we master discipline and focus before even trying magic.

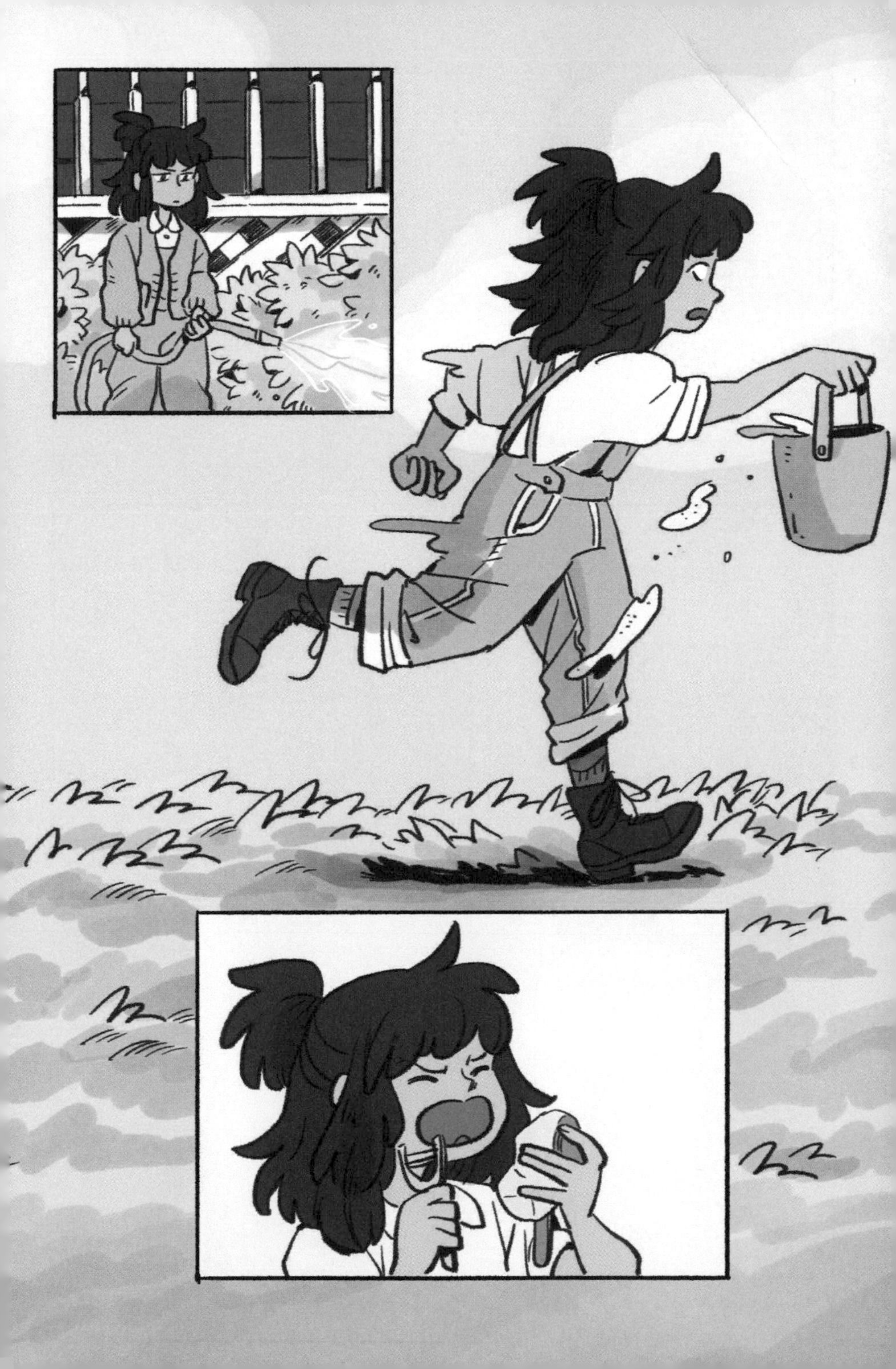

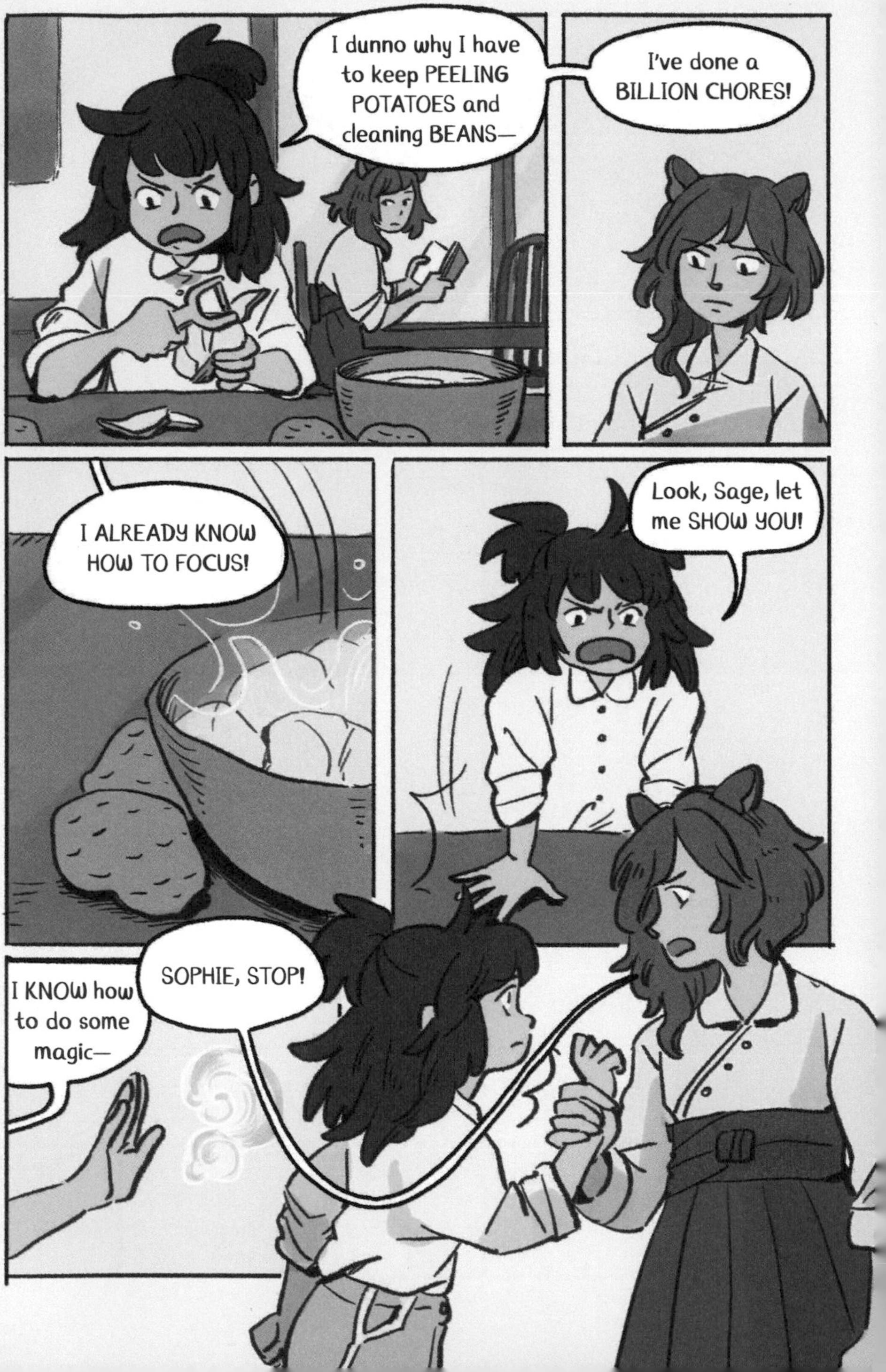
I dunno why I have to keep PEELING POTATOES and cleaning BEANS—
I've done a BILLION CHORES!
I ALREADY KNOW HOW TO FOCUS!
Look, Sage, let me SHOW YOU!
I KNOW how to do some magic—
SOPHIE, STOP!

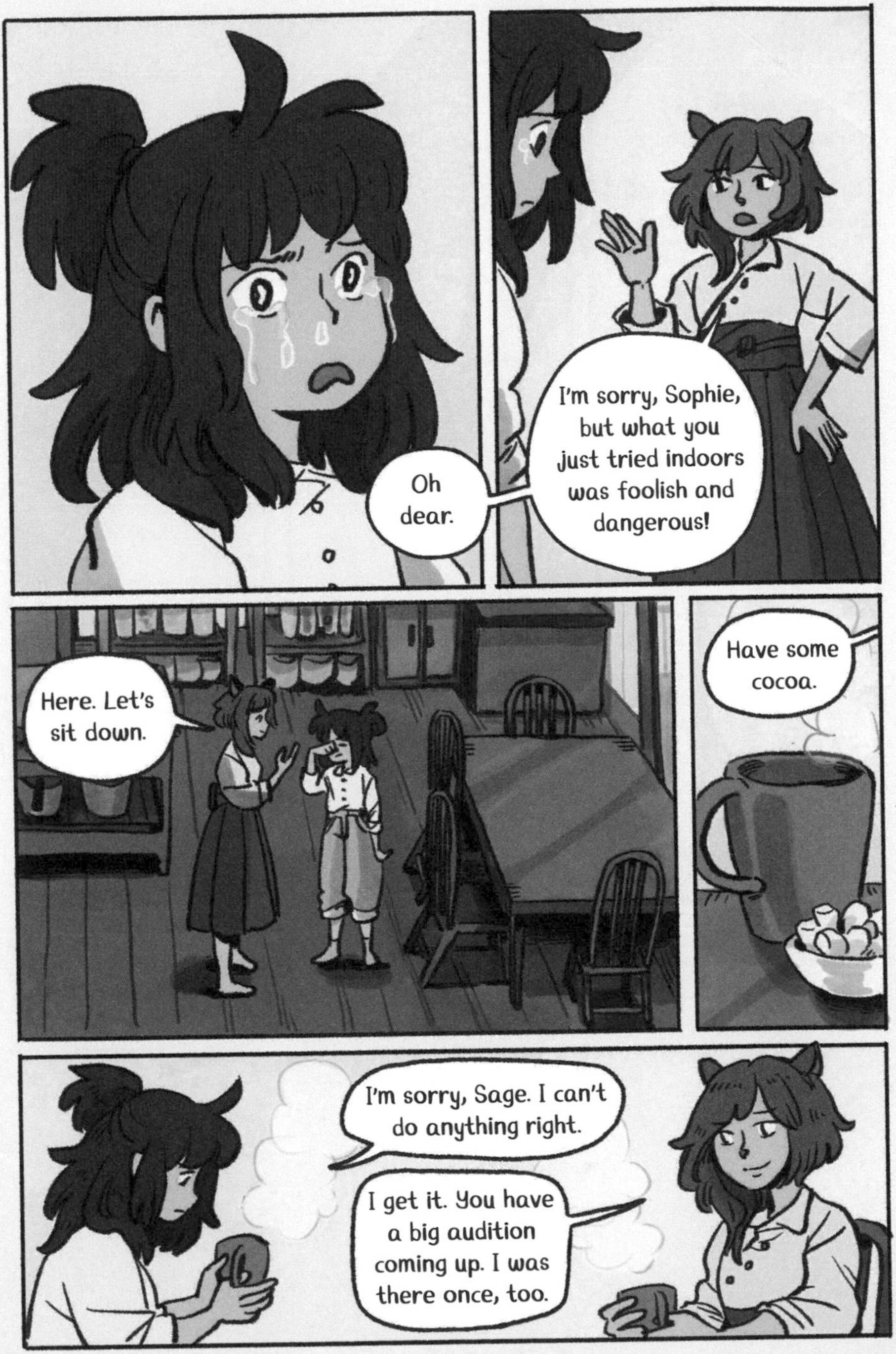
Oh dear.
I'm sorry, Sophie, but what you just tried indoors was foolish and dangerous!
Here. Let's sit down.
Have some cocoa.
I'm sorry, Sage. I can't do anything right.
I get it. You have a big audition coming up. I was there once, too.

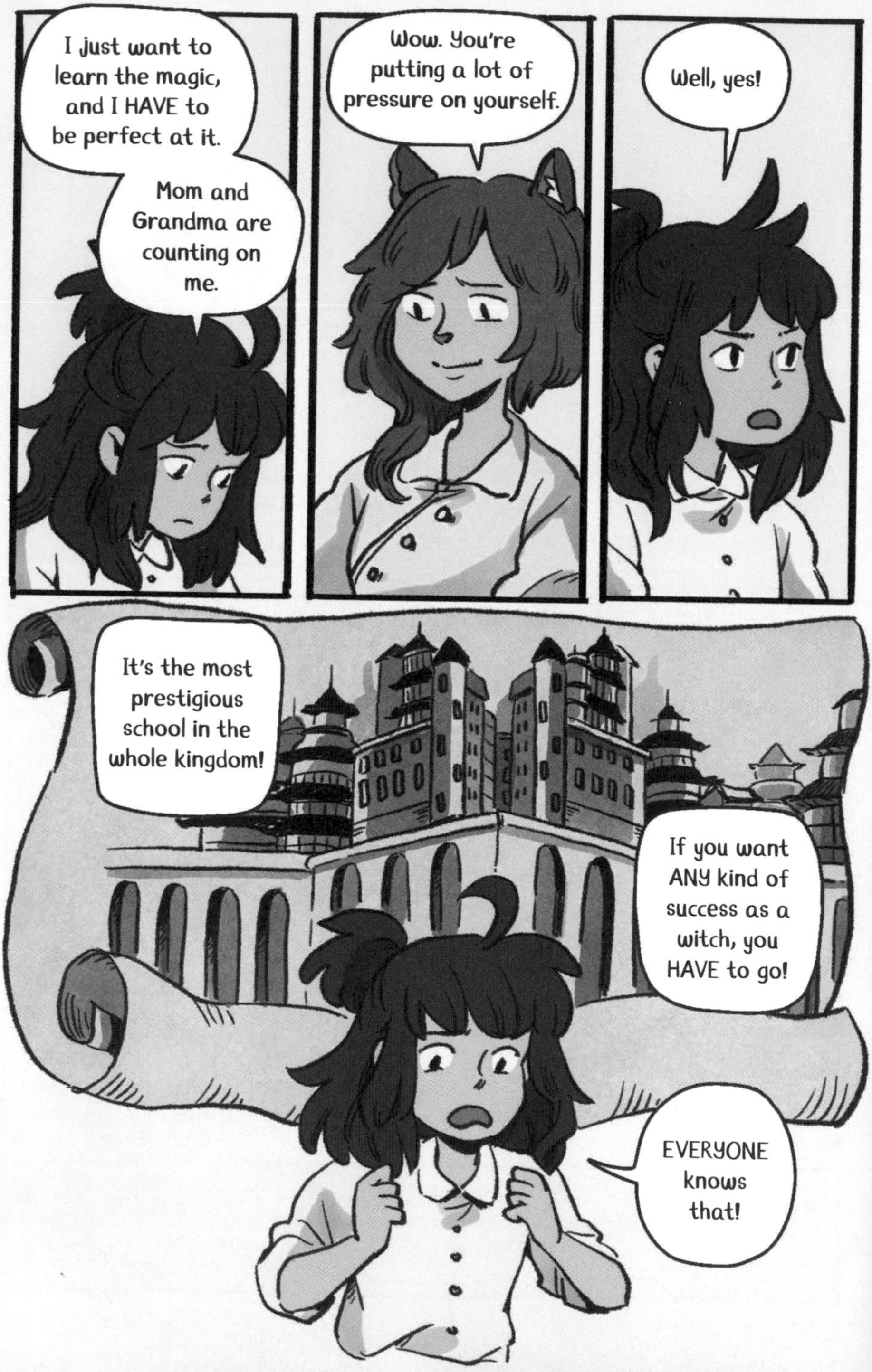

I just want to learn the magic, and I HAVE to be perfect at it.
Mom and Grandma are counting on me.
Wow. You're putting a lot of pressure on yourself.
Well, yes!
It's the most prestigious school in the whole kingdom!
If you want ANY kind of success as a witch, you HAVE to go!
EVERYONE knows that!

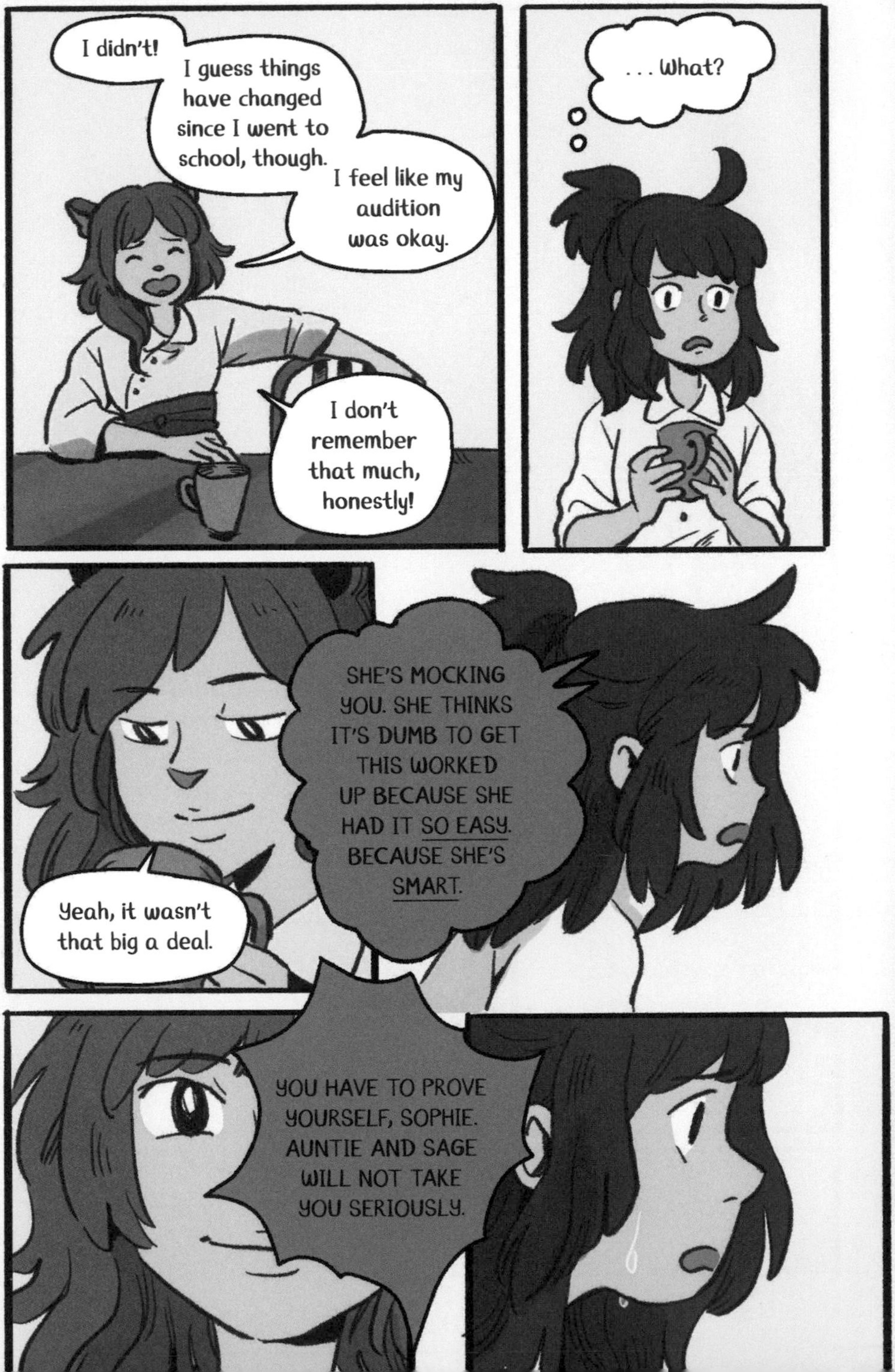
I didn't!
I guess things have changed since I went to school, though.
I feel like my audition was okay.
I don't remember that much, honestly!
. . . What?
SHE'S MOCKING YOU. SHE THINKS IT'S DUMB TO GET THIS WORKED UP BECAUSE SHE HAD IT SO EASY. BECAUSE SHE'S SMART.
Yeah, it wasn't that big a deal.
YOU HAVE TO PROVE YOURSELF, SOPHIE. AUNTIE AND SAGE WILL NOT TAKE YOU SERIOUSLY.

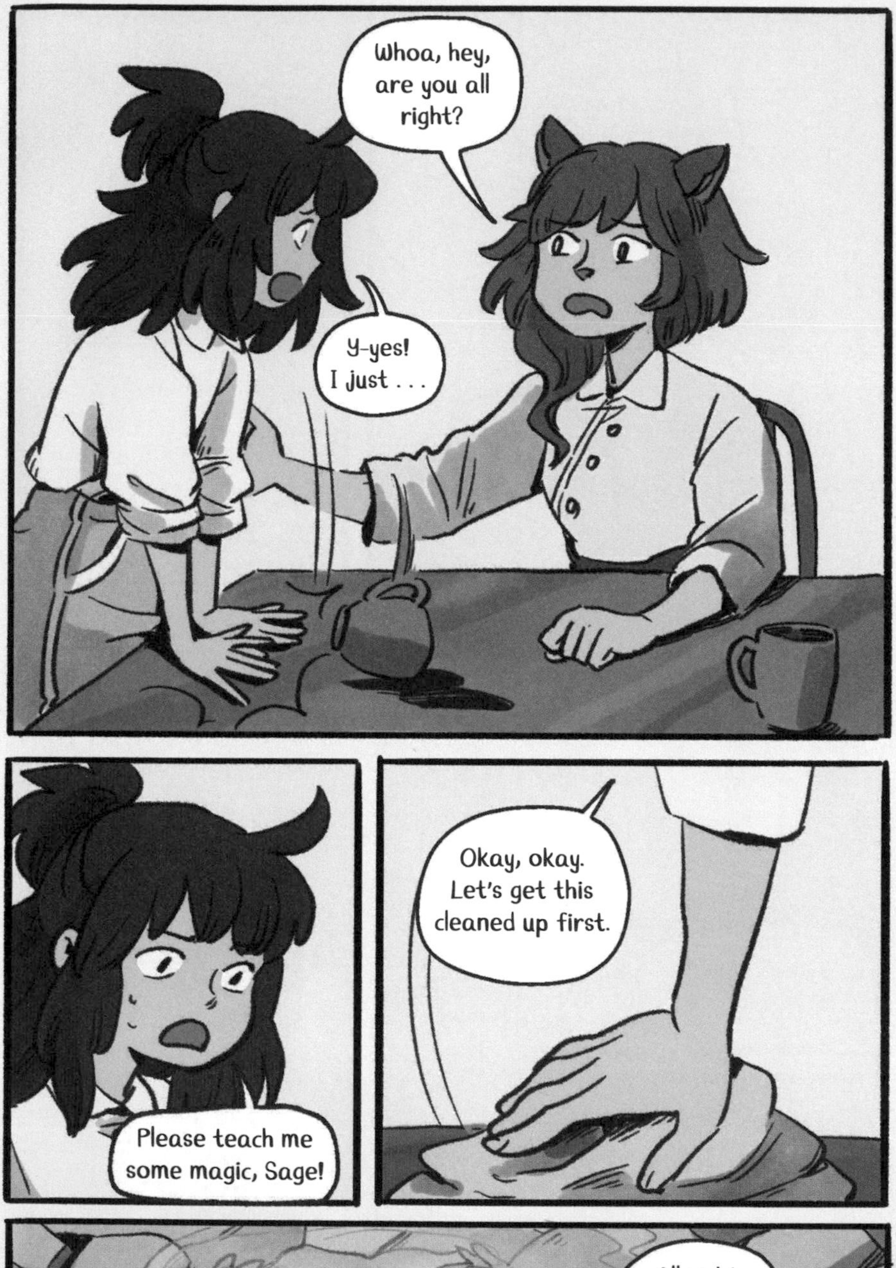

Whoa, hey, are you all right?
Y-yes! I just . . .
Please teach me some magic, Sage!
Okay, okay. Let's get this cleaned up first.
All right, Sophie.

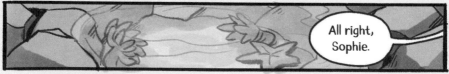

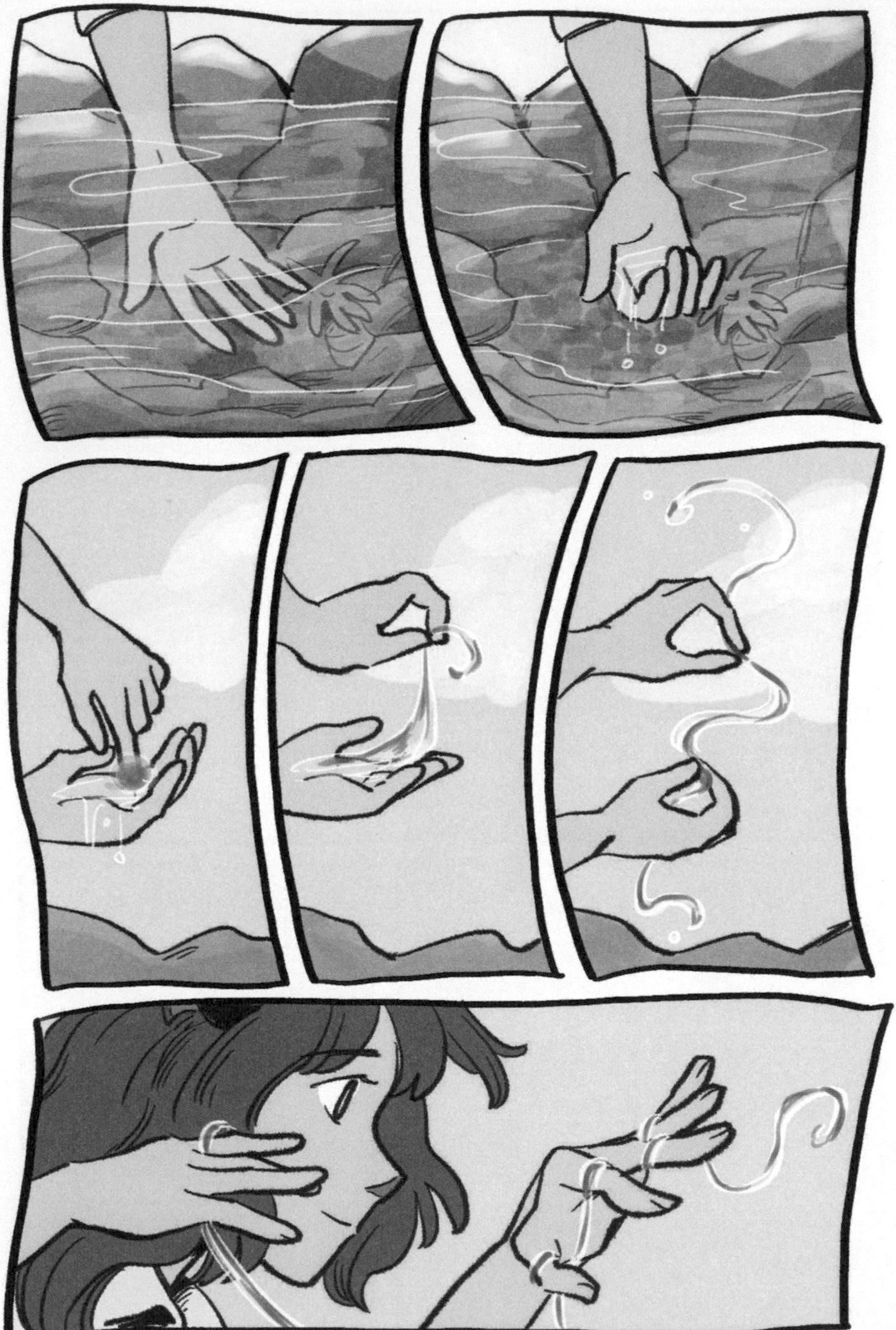

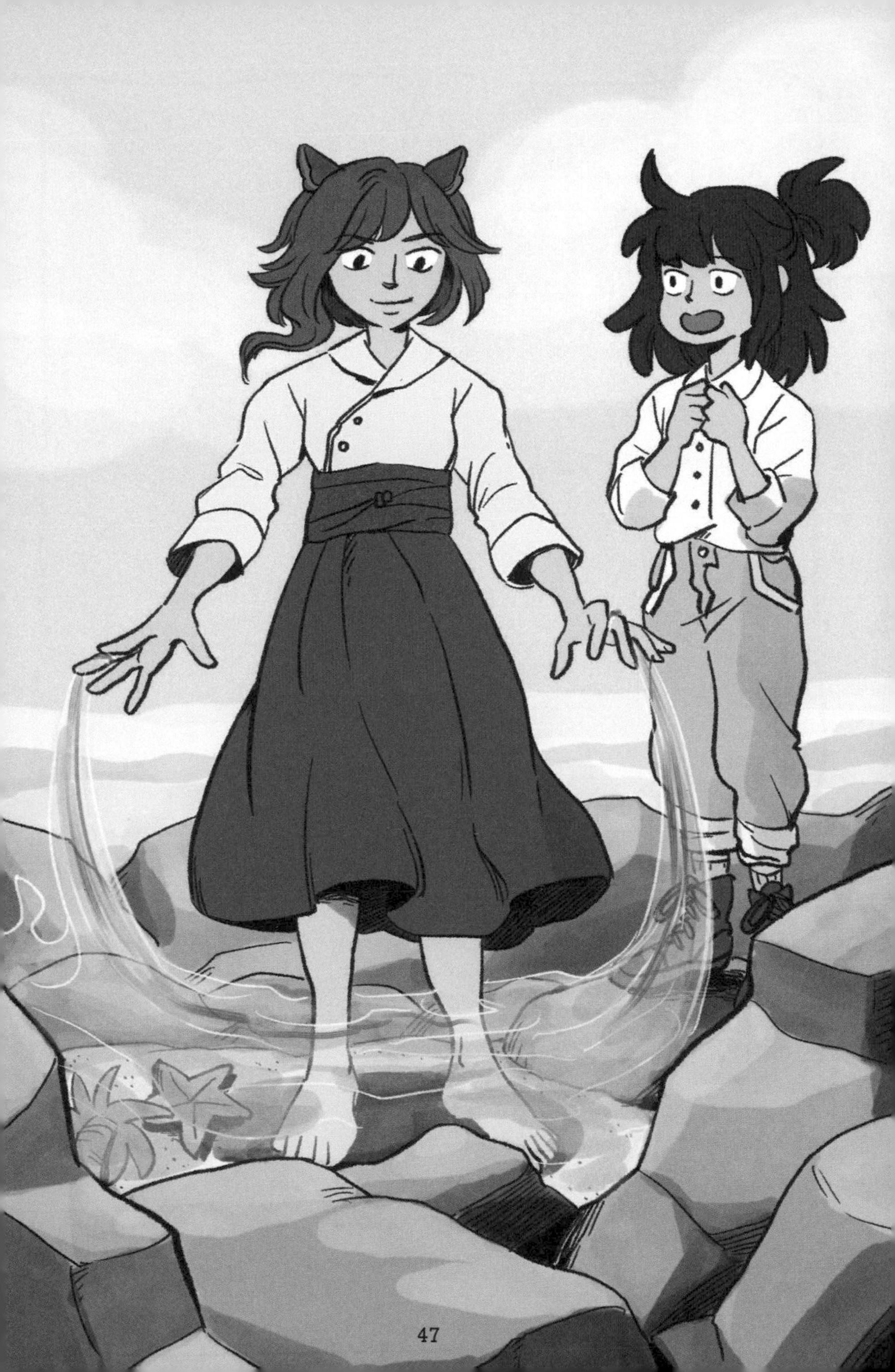

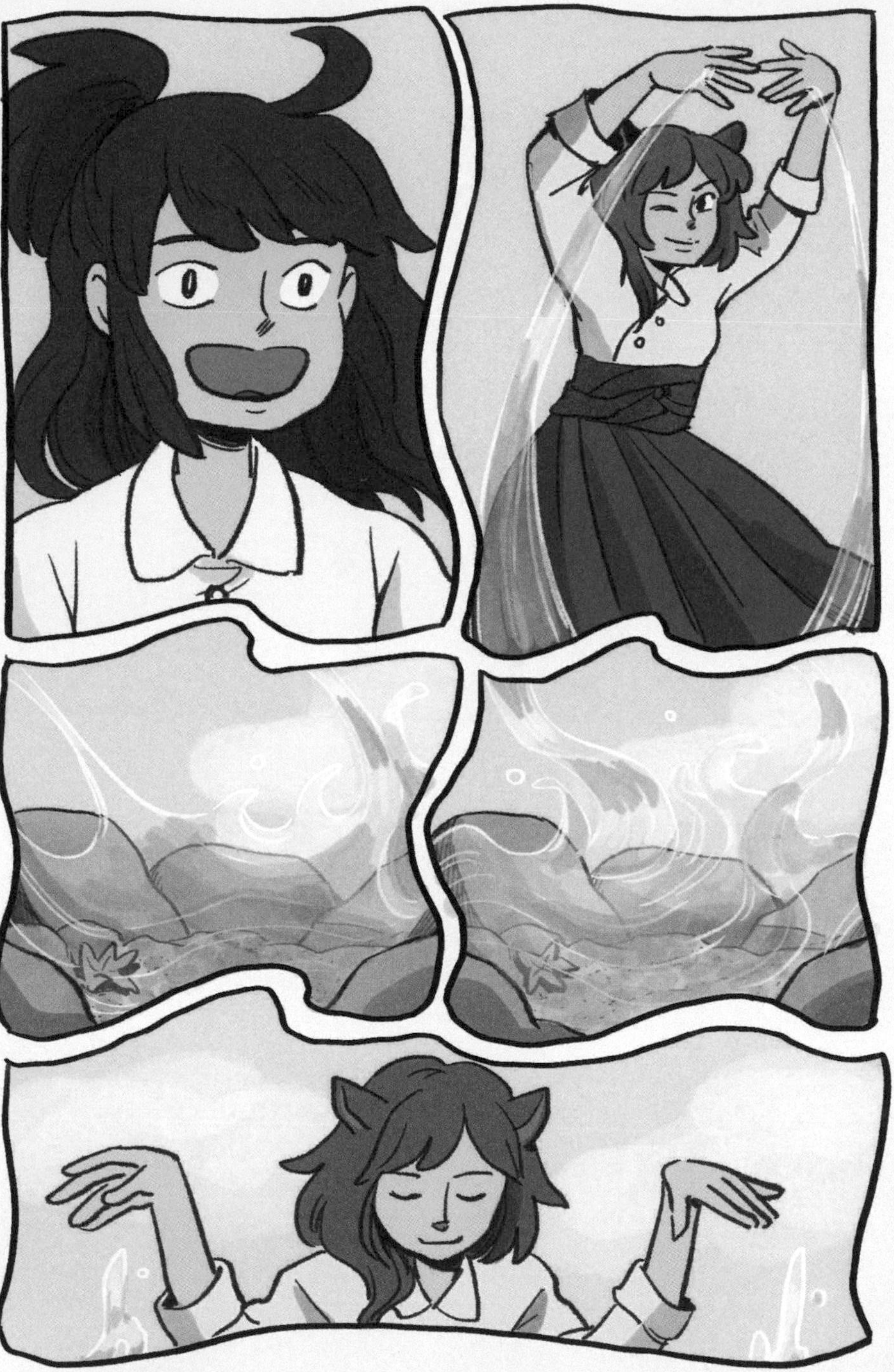

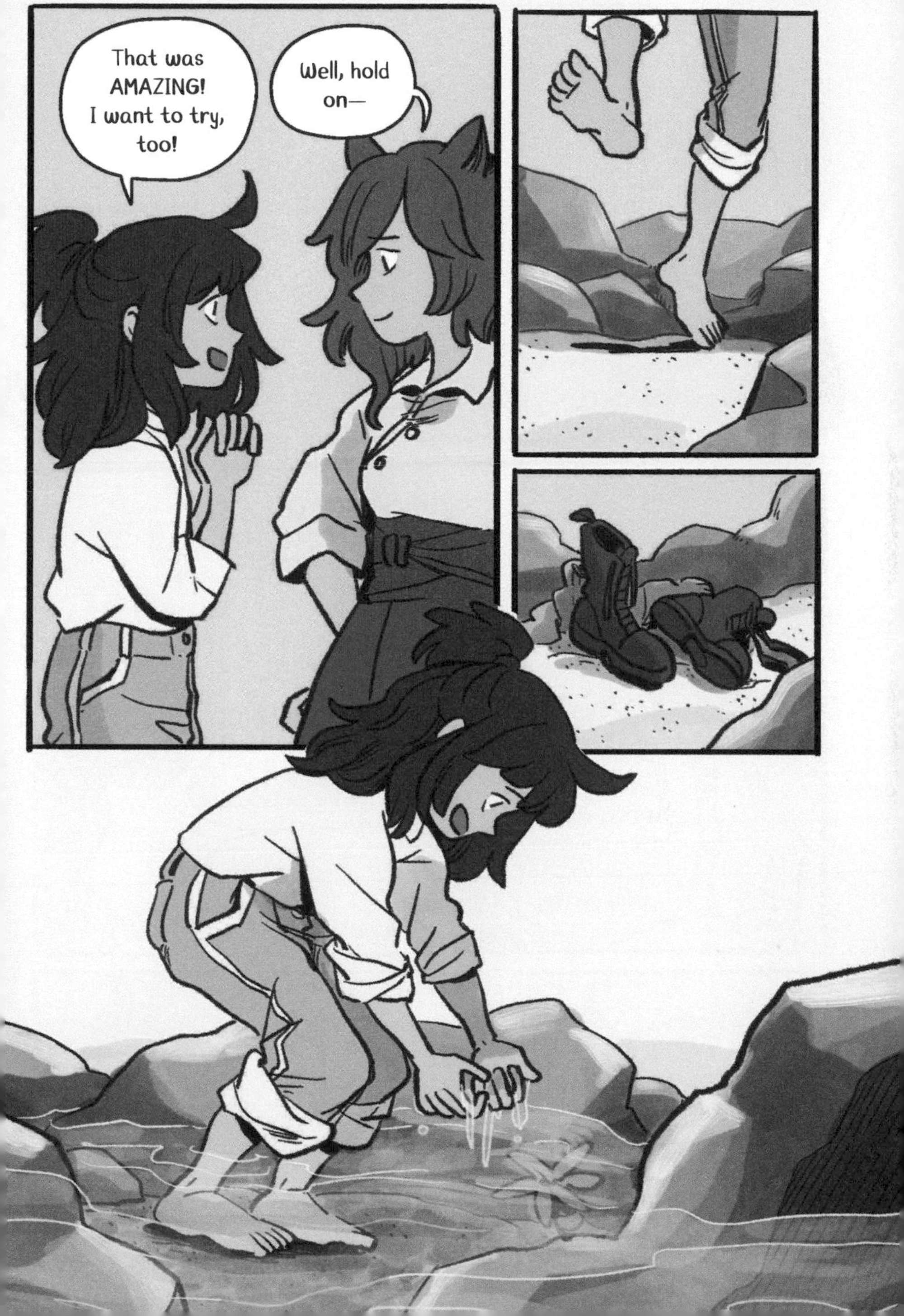
That was AMAZING! I want to try, too!
Well, hold on—

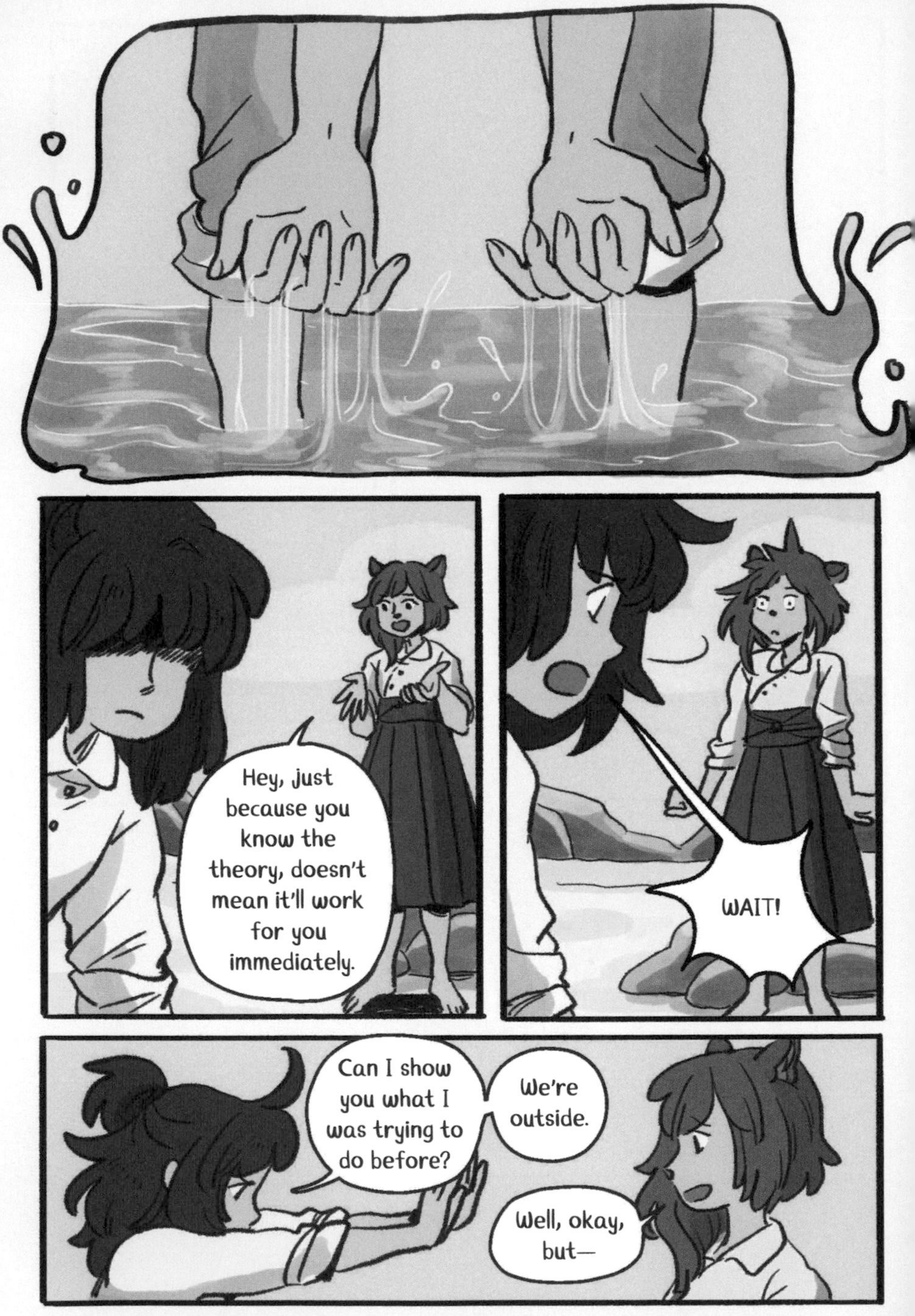
Hey, just because you know the theory, doesn't mean it'll work for you immediately.
WAIT!
Can I show you what I was trying to do before?
We're outside.
Well, okay, but—

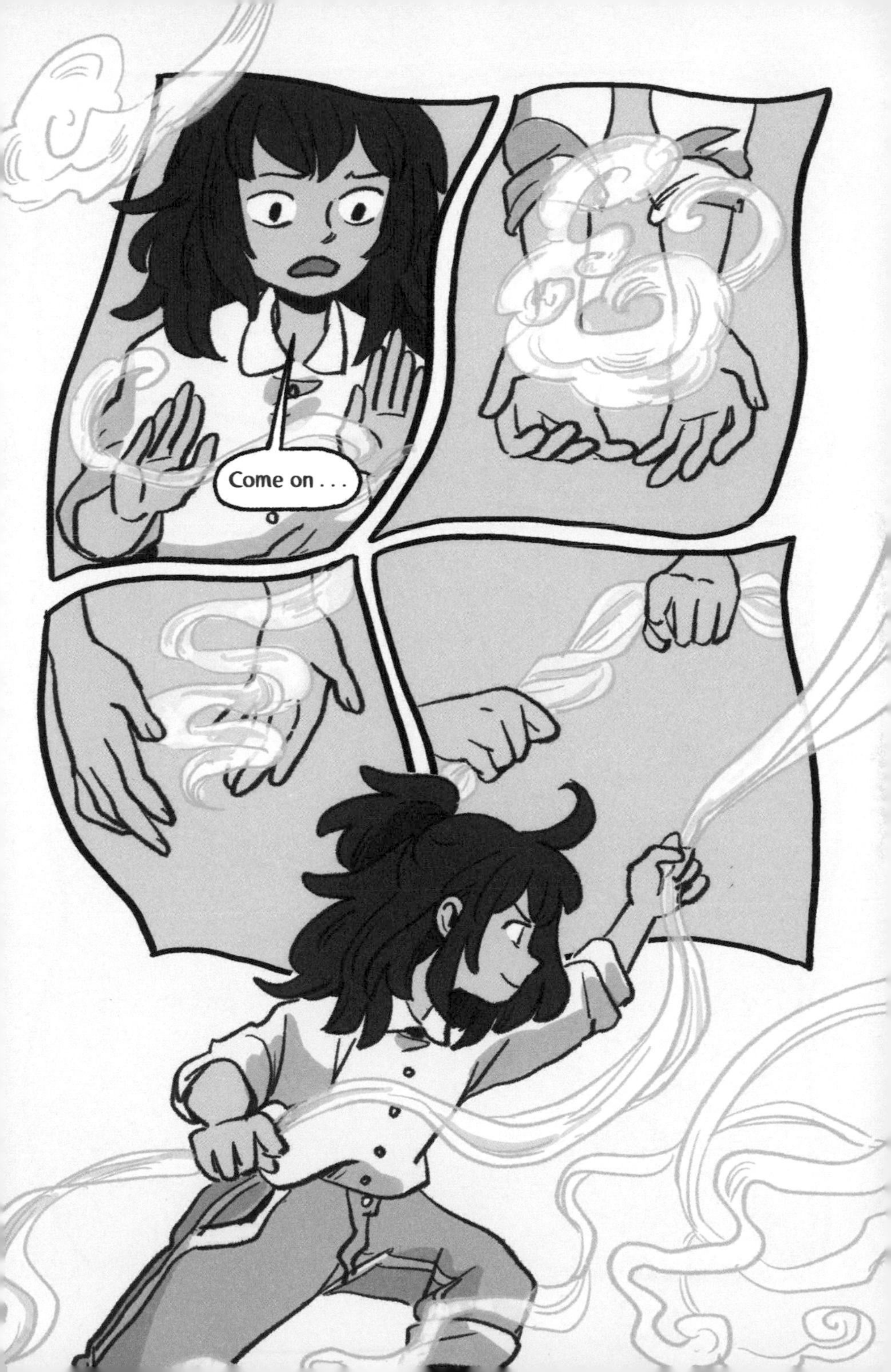
Come on . . .

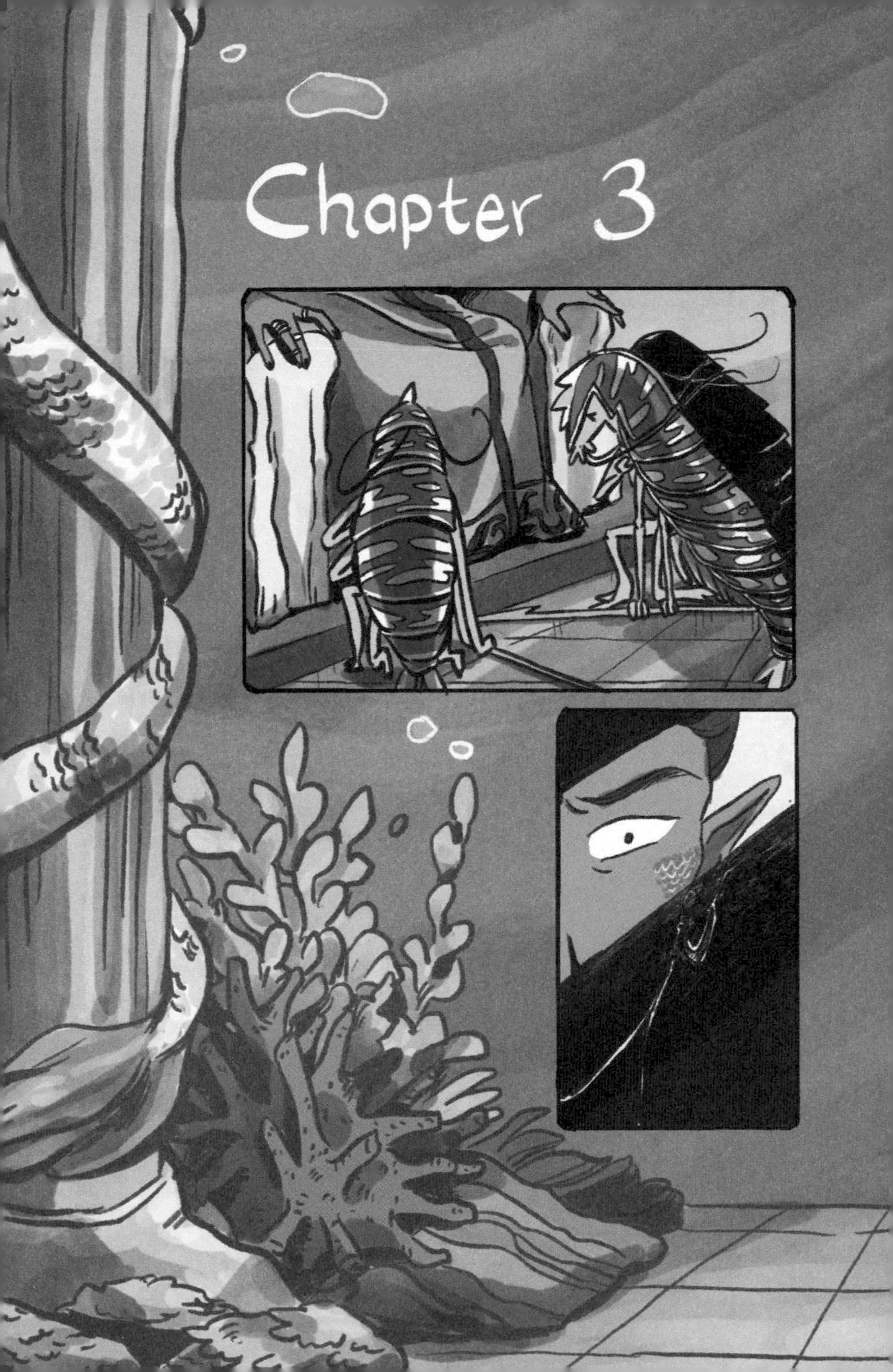
Chapter 3

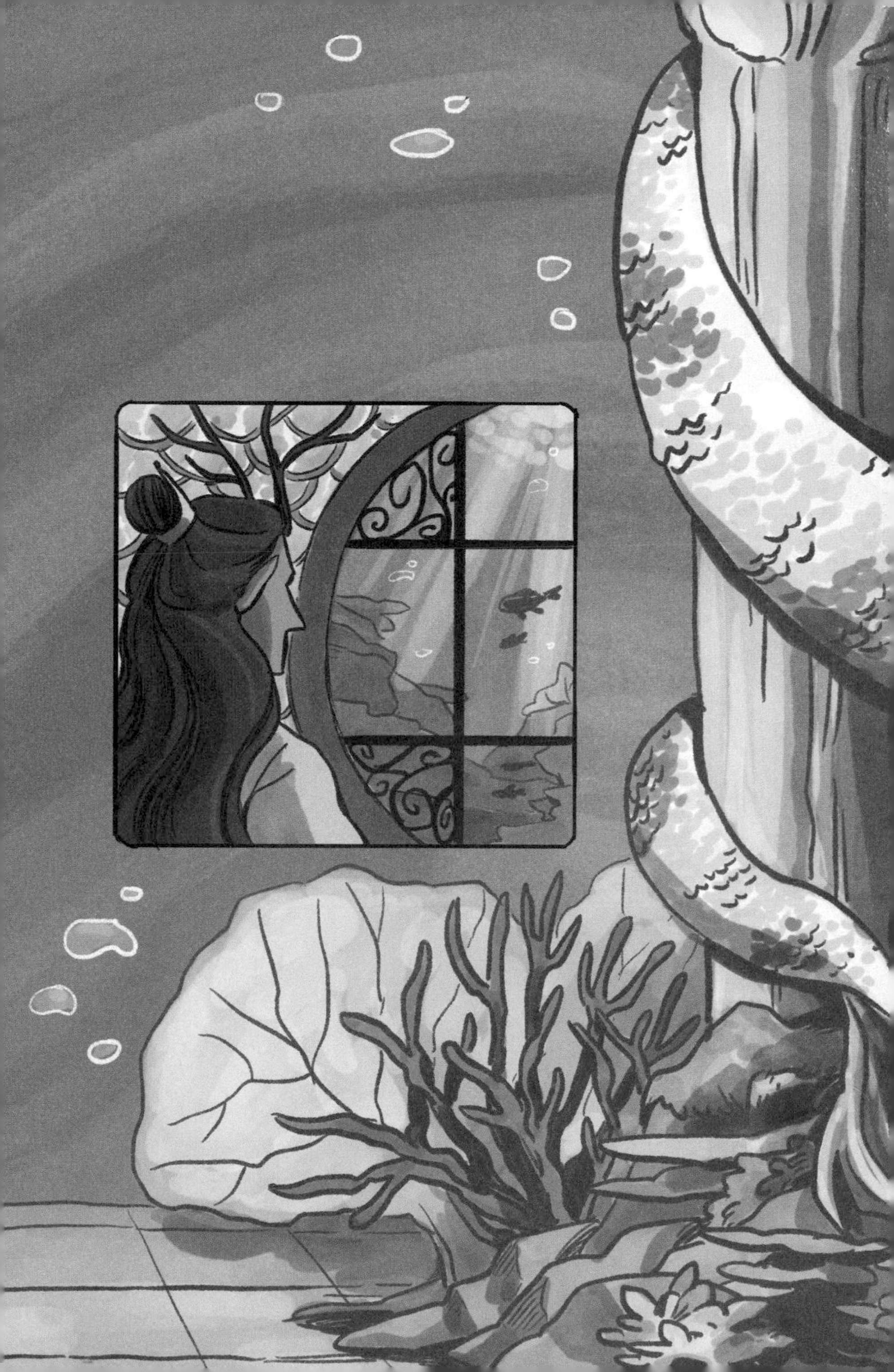

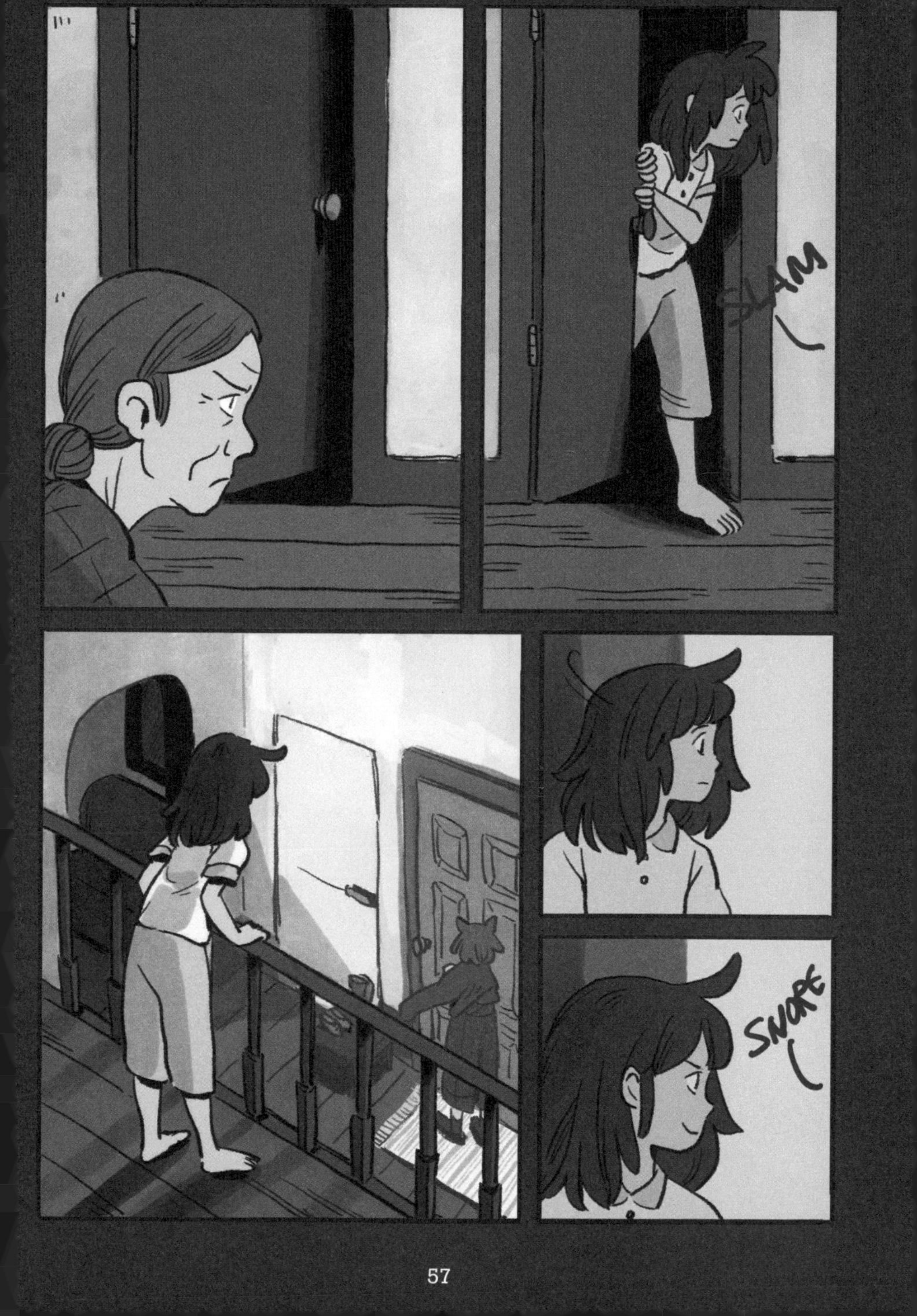
SLAM
SNORE

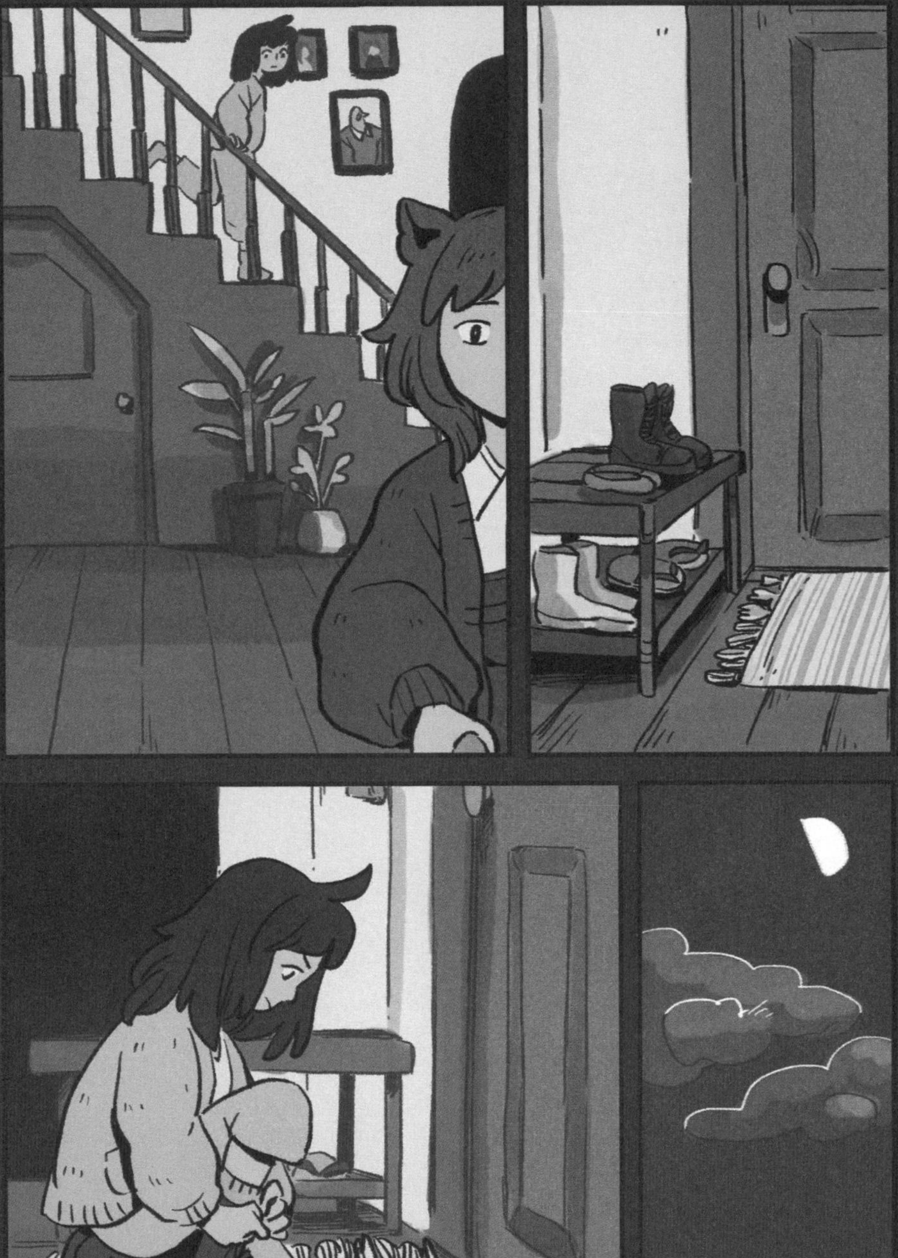

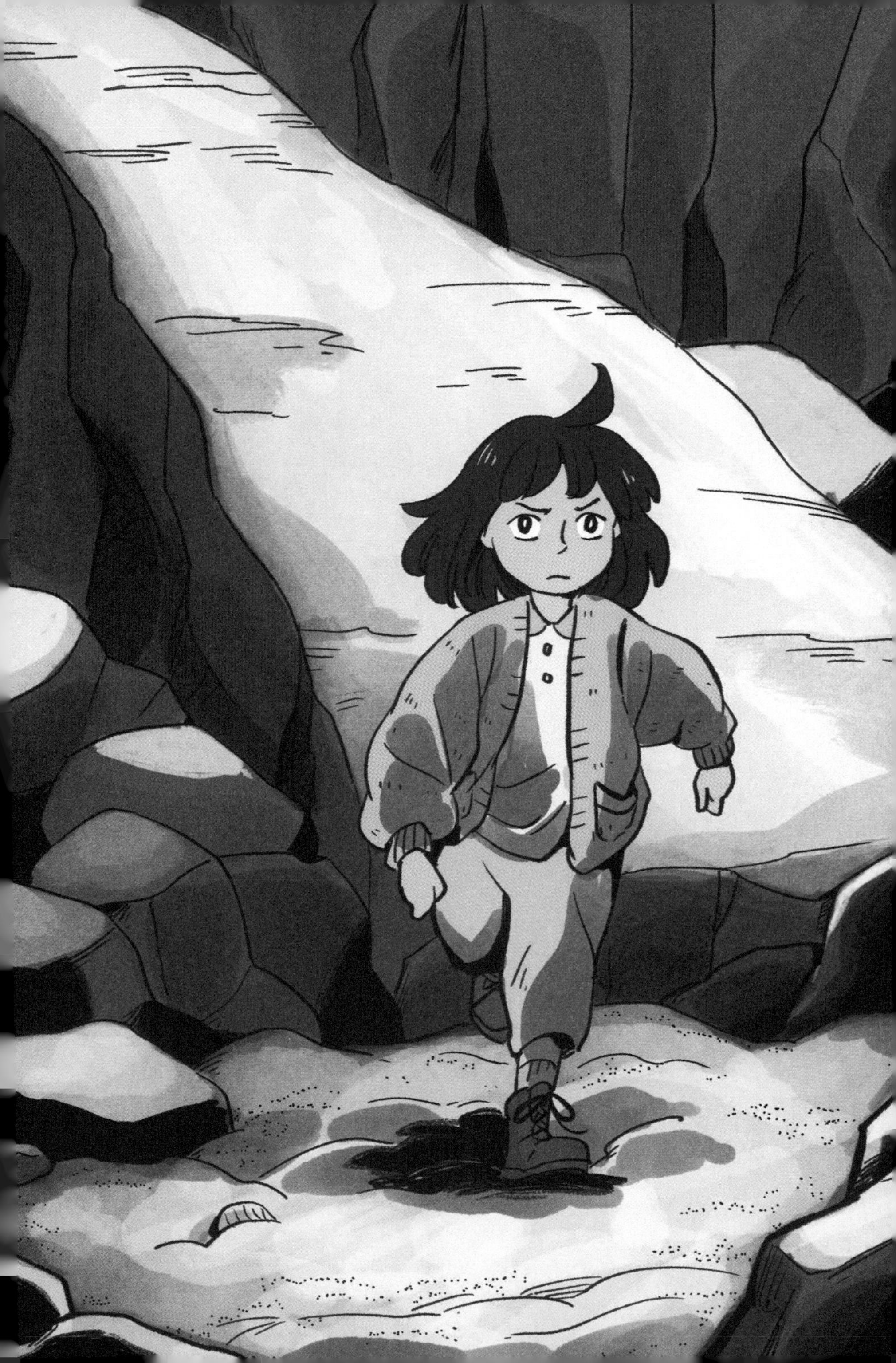

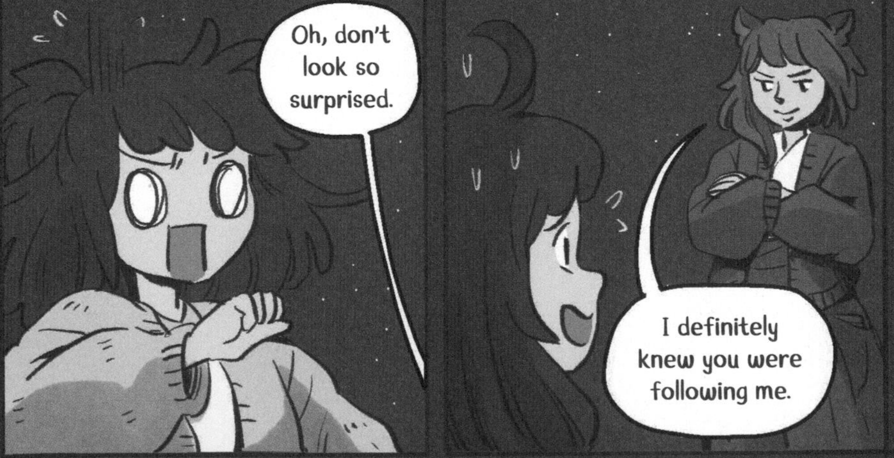
Oh, don't look so surprised.
I definitely knew you were following me.

61

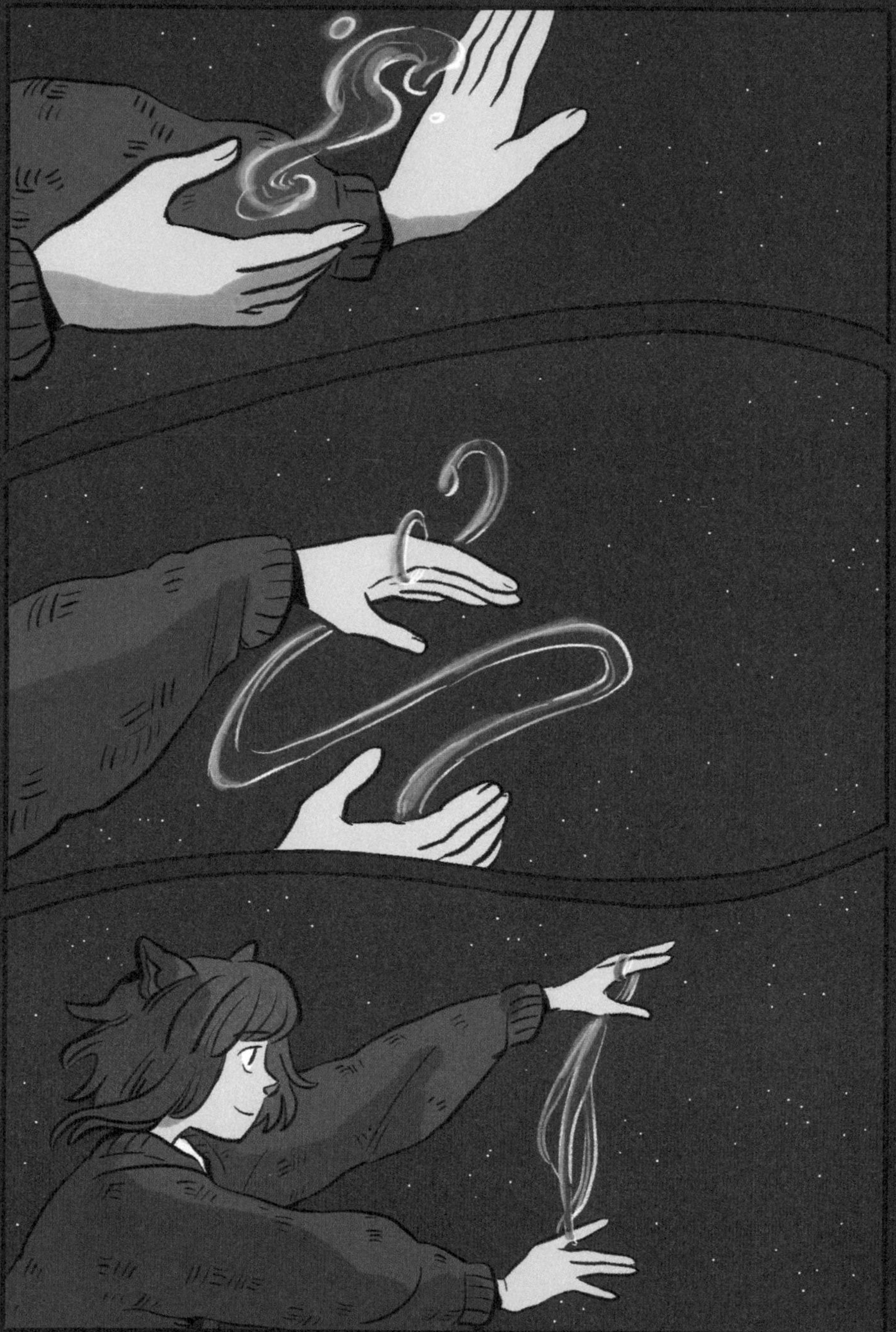

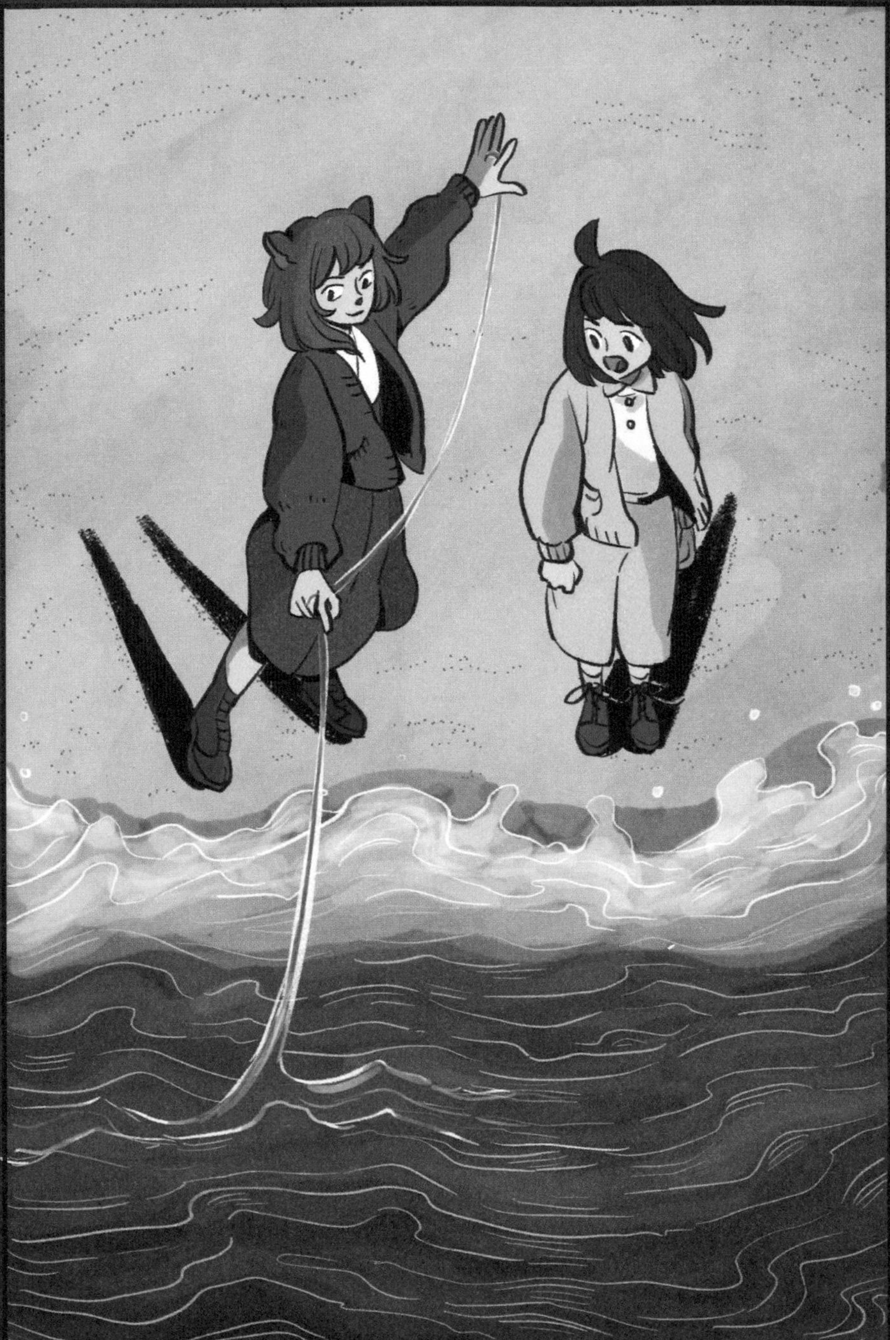

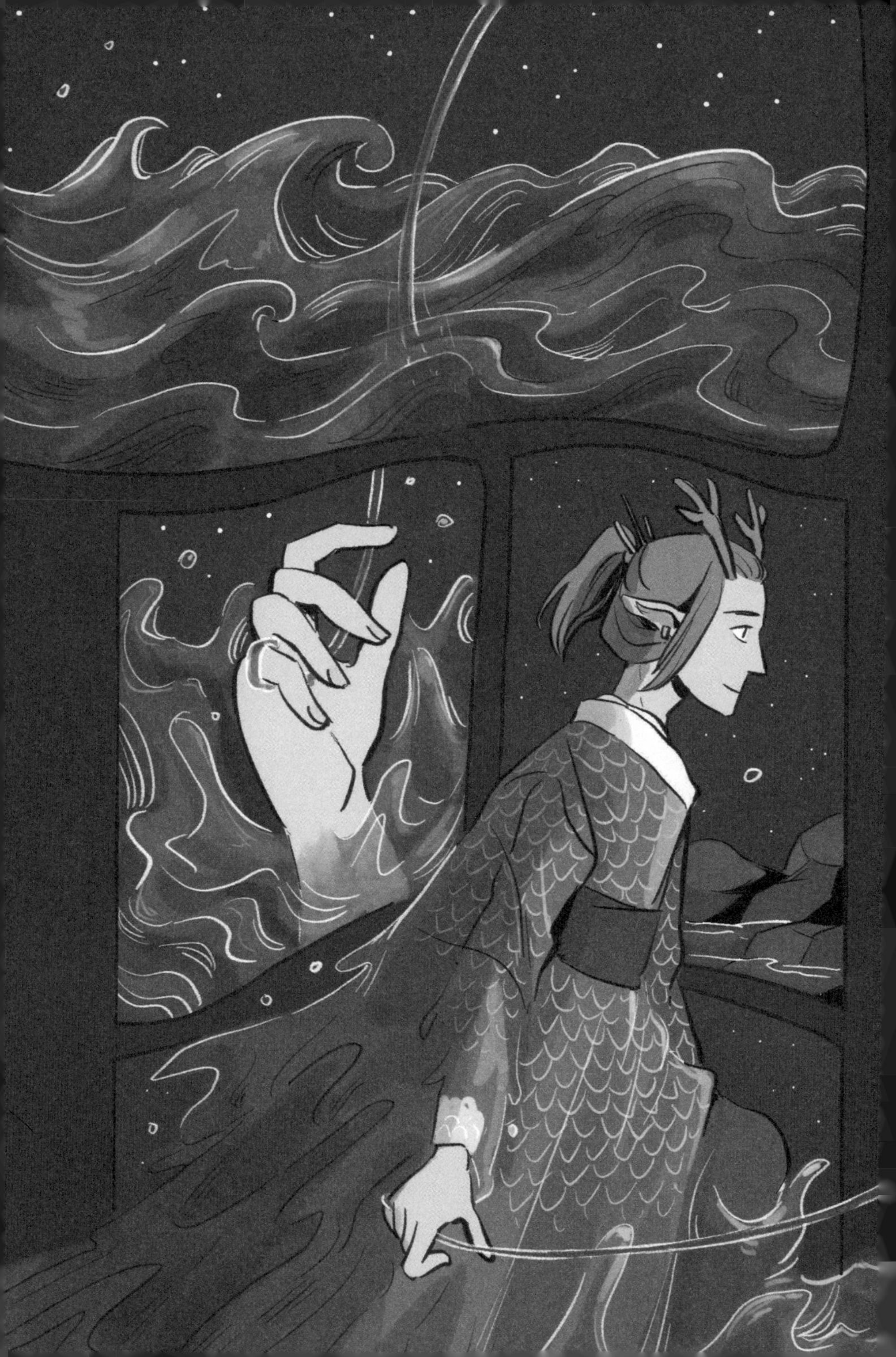

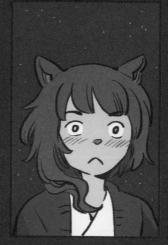

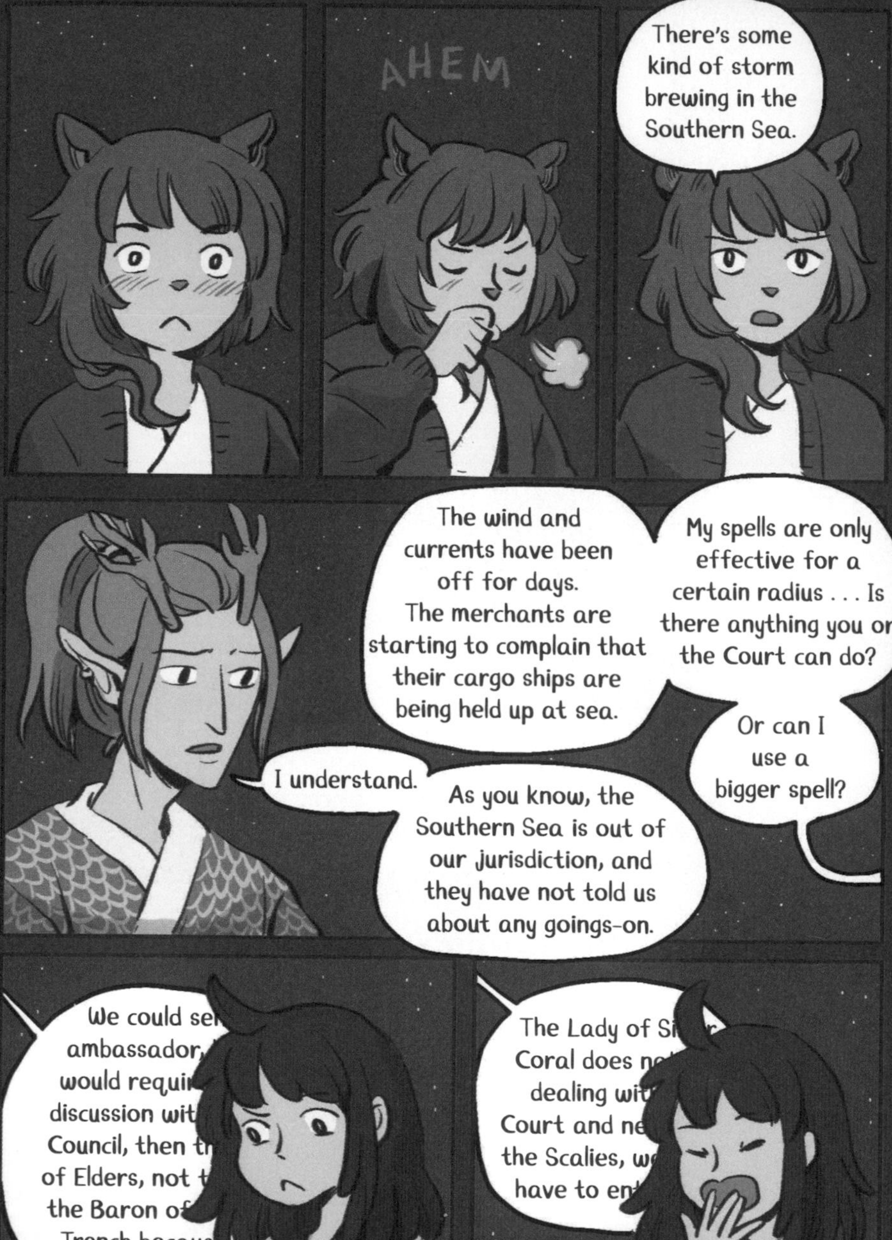
AHEM
There's some kind of storm brewing in the Southern Sea.
The wind and currents have been off for days. The merchants are starting to complain that their cargo ships are being held up at sea.
My spells are only effective for a certain radius . . . Is there anything you or the Court can do?
Or can I use a bigger spell?
I understand.
As you know, the Southern Sea is out of our jurisdiction, and they have not told us about any goings-on.
We could se
ambassador,
would requi
discussion wit
Council, then t
of Elders, not
the Baron o
Trench becaus
be passing thr
doma
The Lady of Si
Coral does n
dealing wit
Court and ne
the Scalies, w
have to en

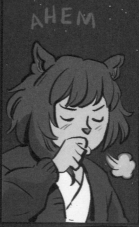

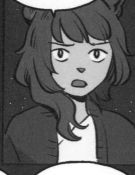

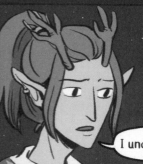

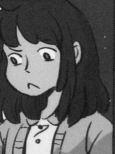

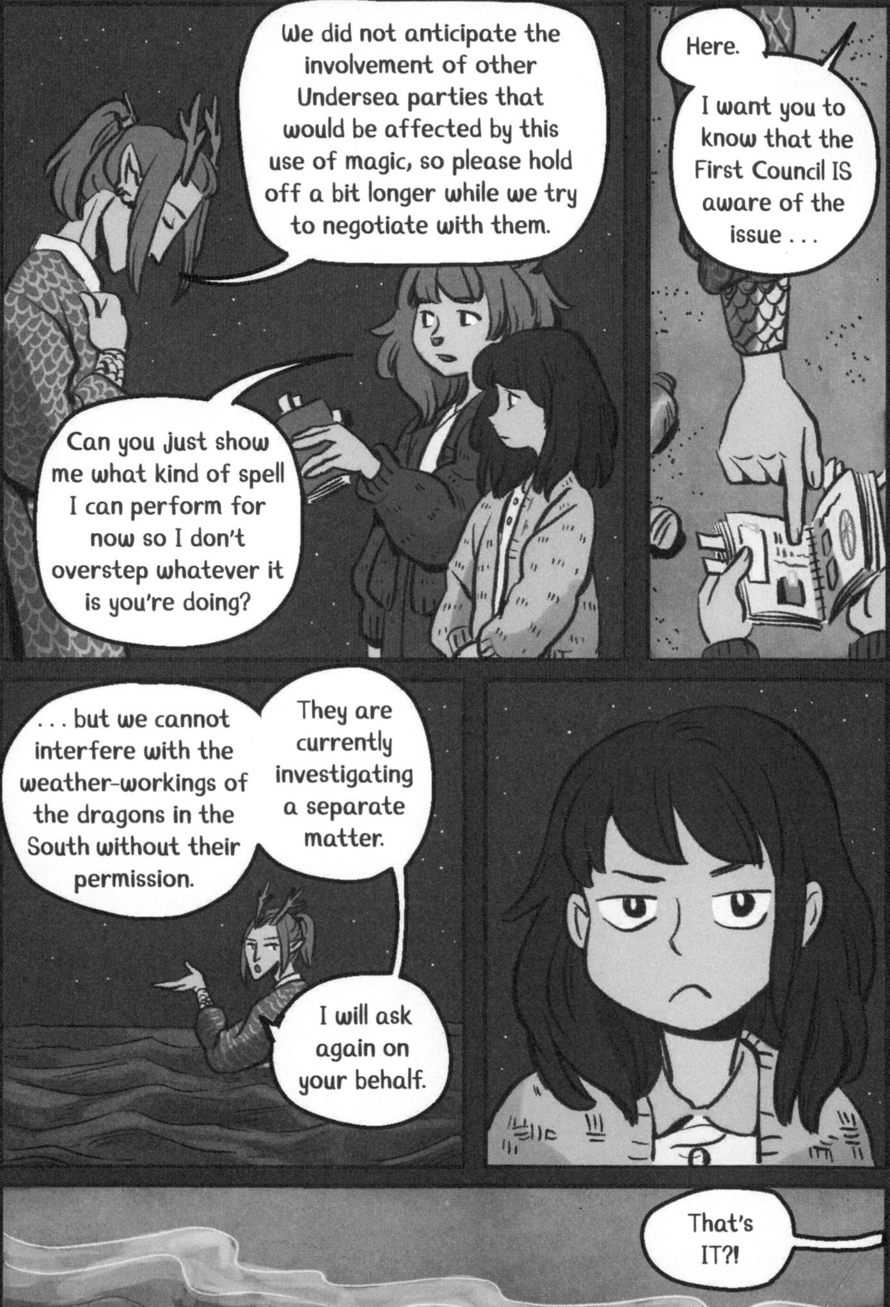
We did not anticipate the involvement of other Undersea parties that would be affected by this use of magic, so please hold off a bit longer while we try to negotiate with them.
Can you just show me what kind of spell I can perform for now so I don't overstep whatever it is you're doing?
Here.
I want you to know that the First Council IS aware of the issue . . .
. . . but we cannot interfere with the weather-workings of the dragons in the South without their permission.
They are currently investigating a separate matter.
I will ask again on your behalf.
That's IT?!

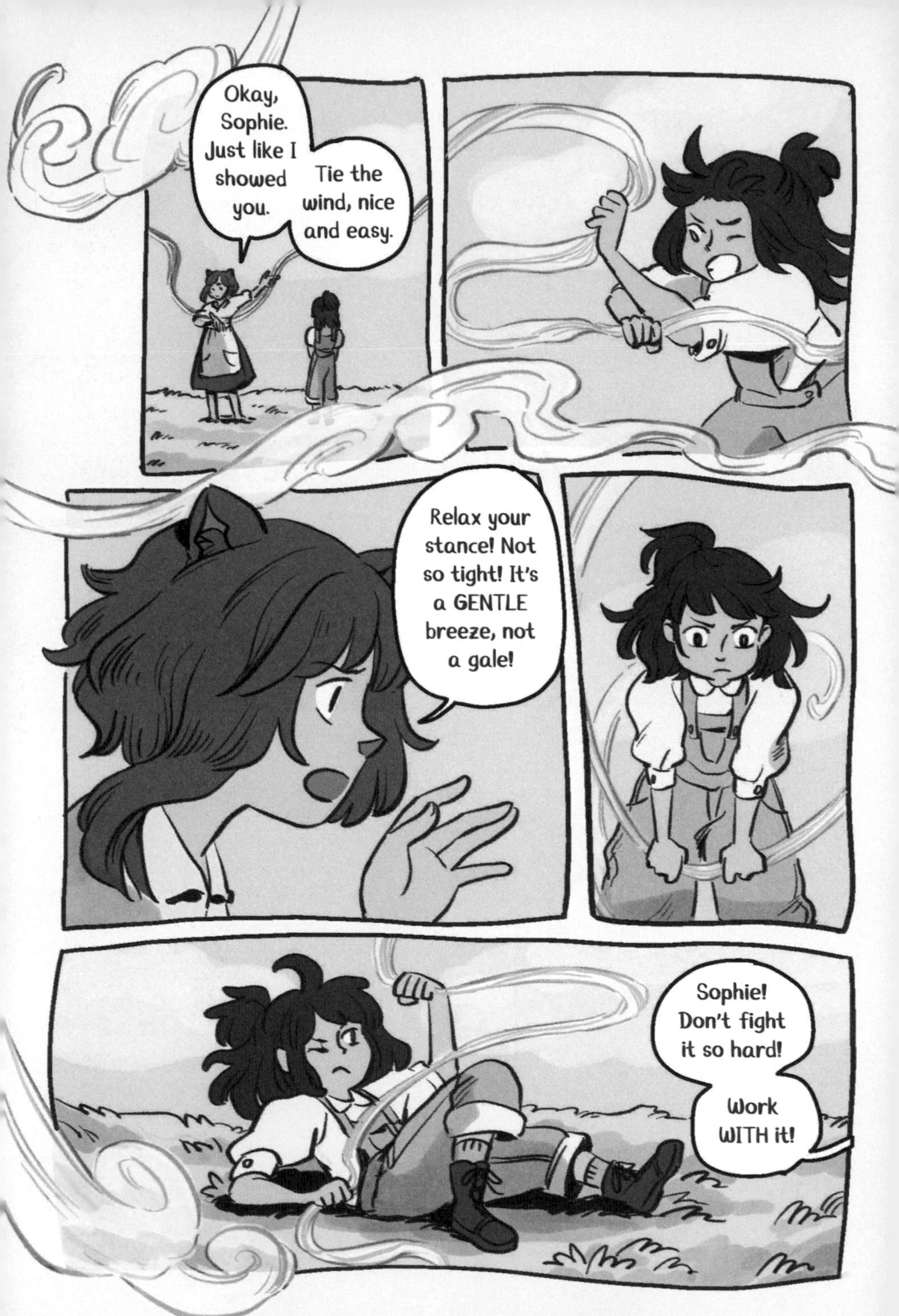
Okay, Sophie. Just like I showed you.
Tie the wind, nice and easy.
Relax your stance! Not so tight! It's a GENTLE breeze, not a gale!
Sophie! Don't fight it so hard!
Work WITH it!

71

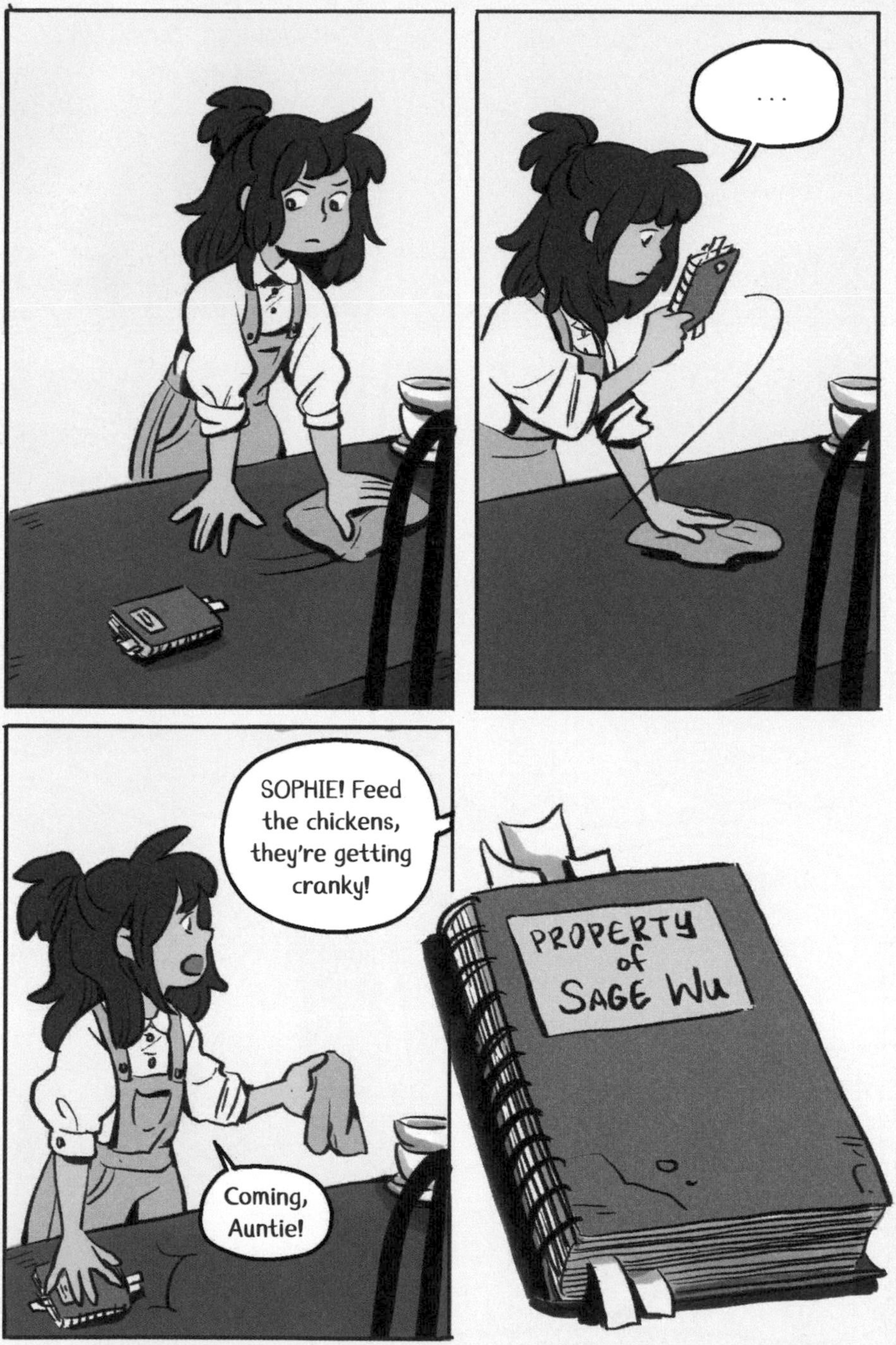
...
SOPHIE! Feed the chickens, they're getting cranky!
Coming, Auntie!
PROPERTY of SAGE WU

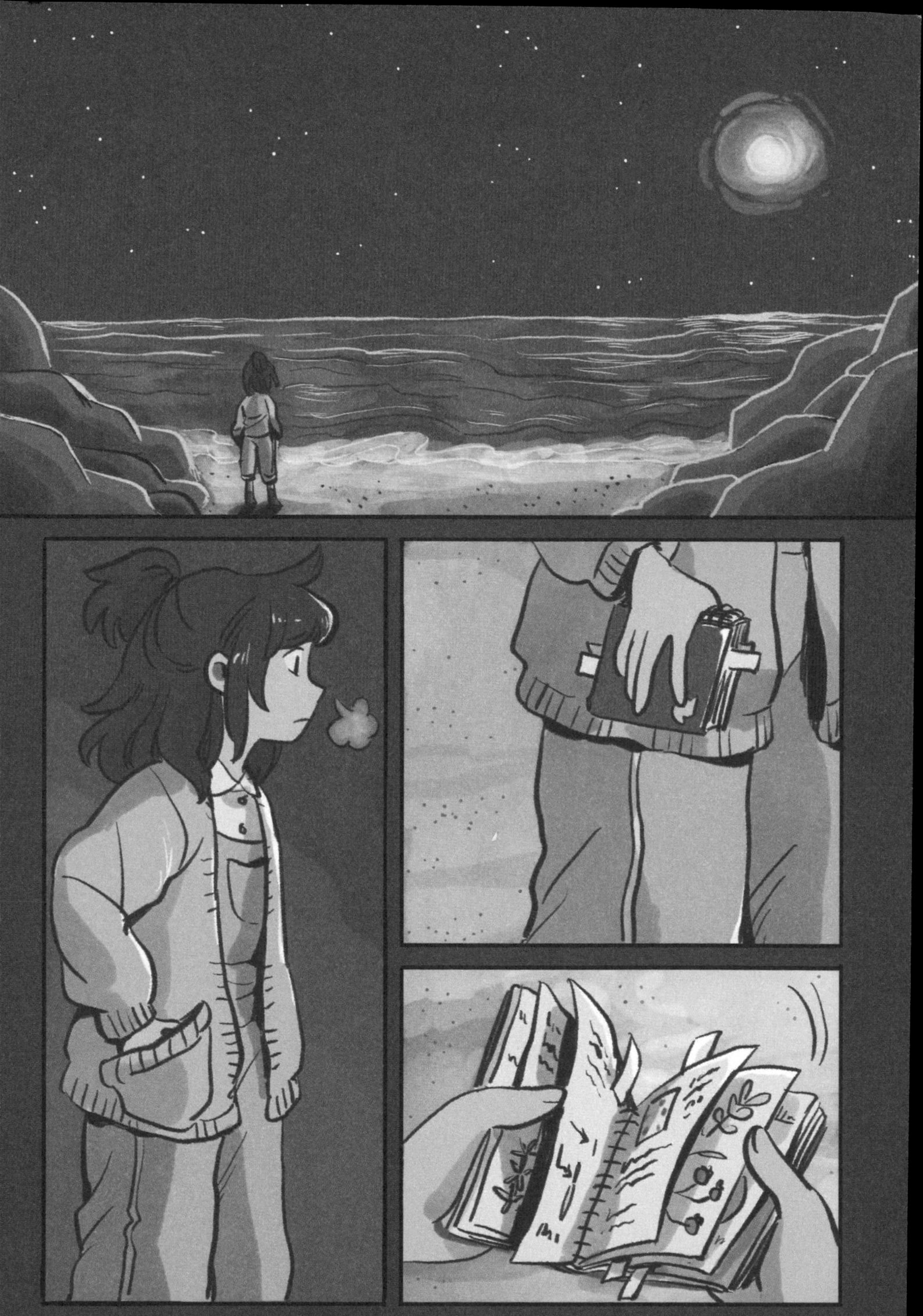

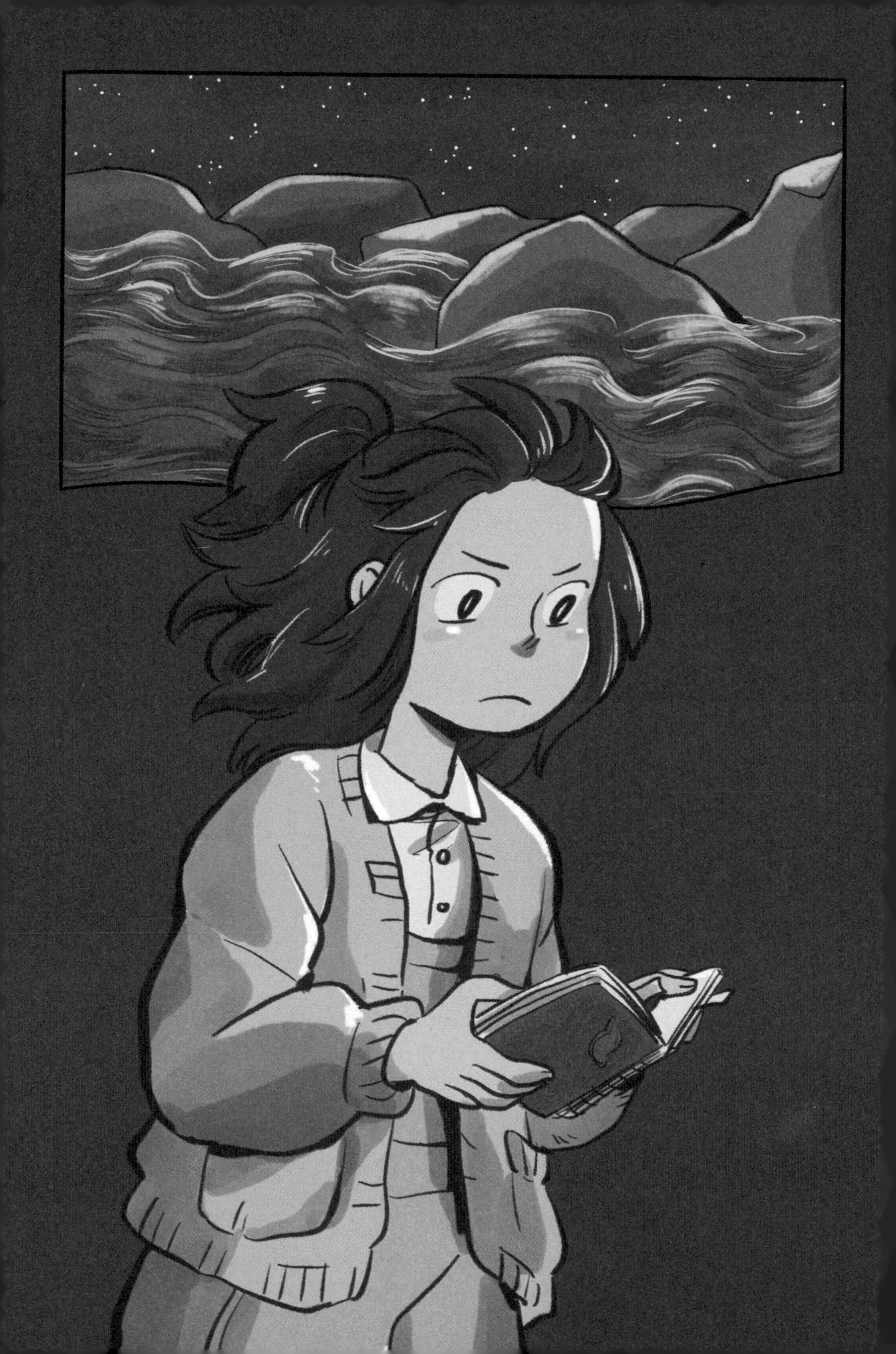

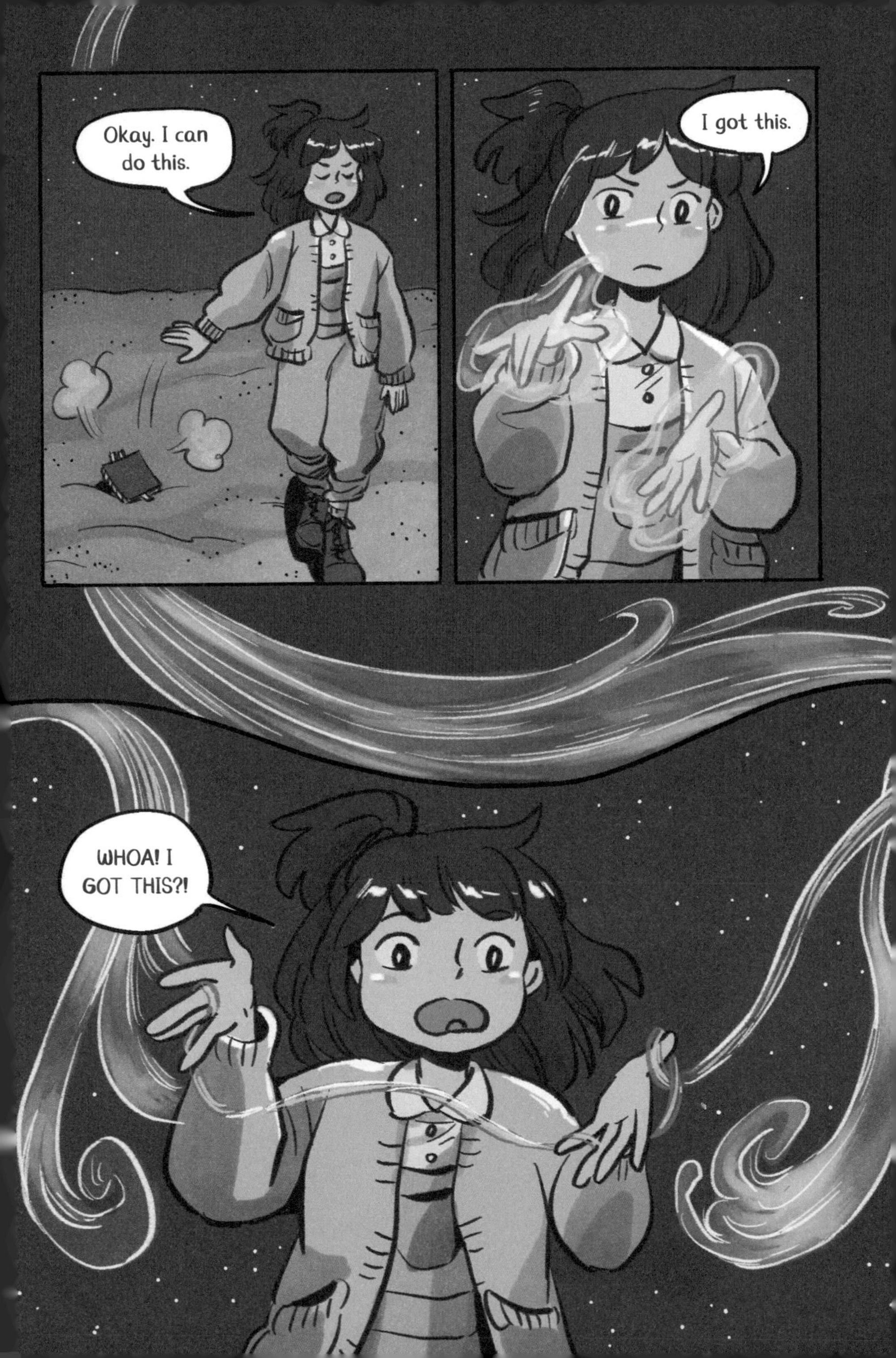
Okay. I can do this.
I got this.
WHOA! I GOT THIS?!

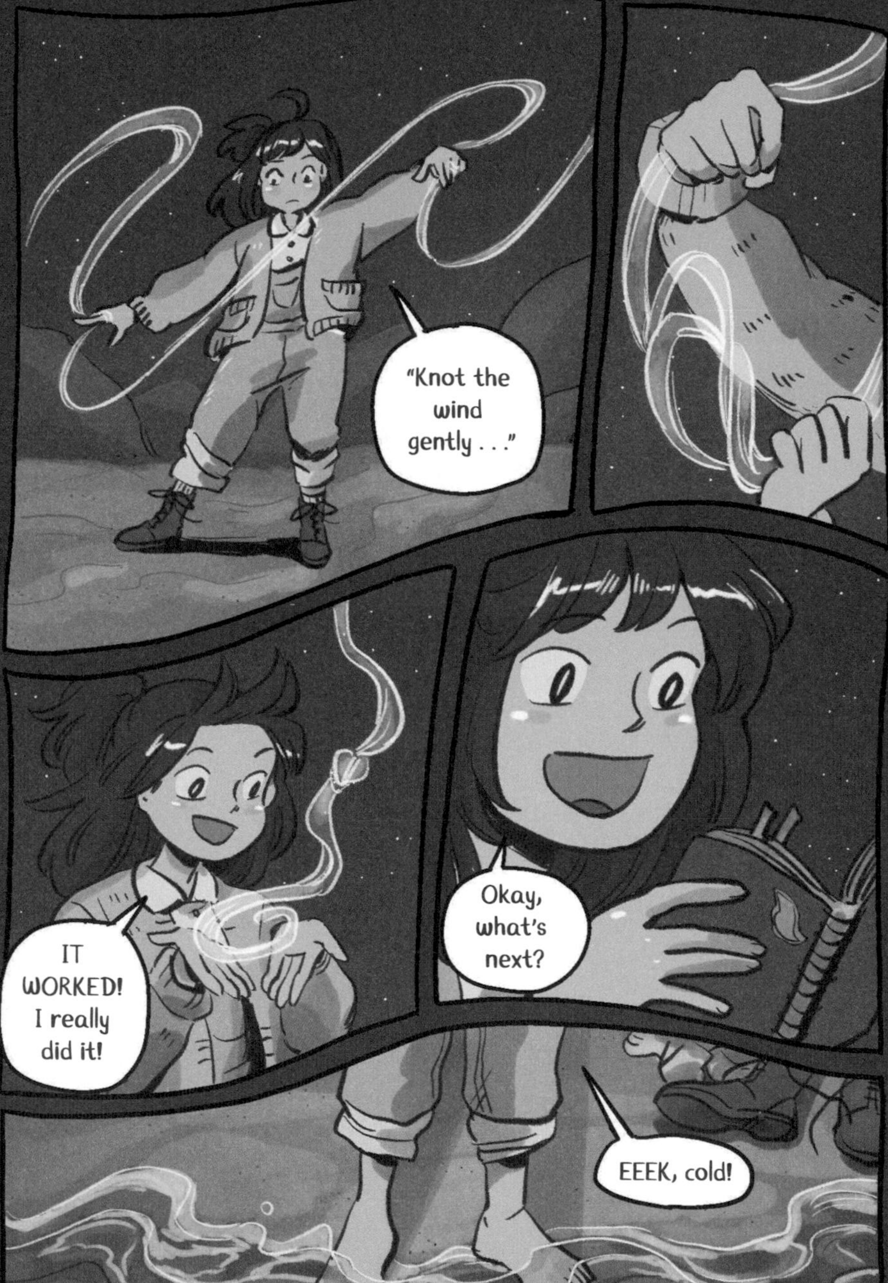
"Knot the wind gently . . ."
IT WORKED! I really did it!
Okay, what's next?
EEEK, cold!

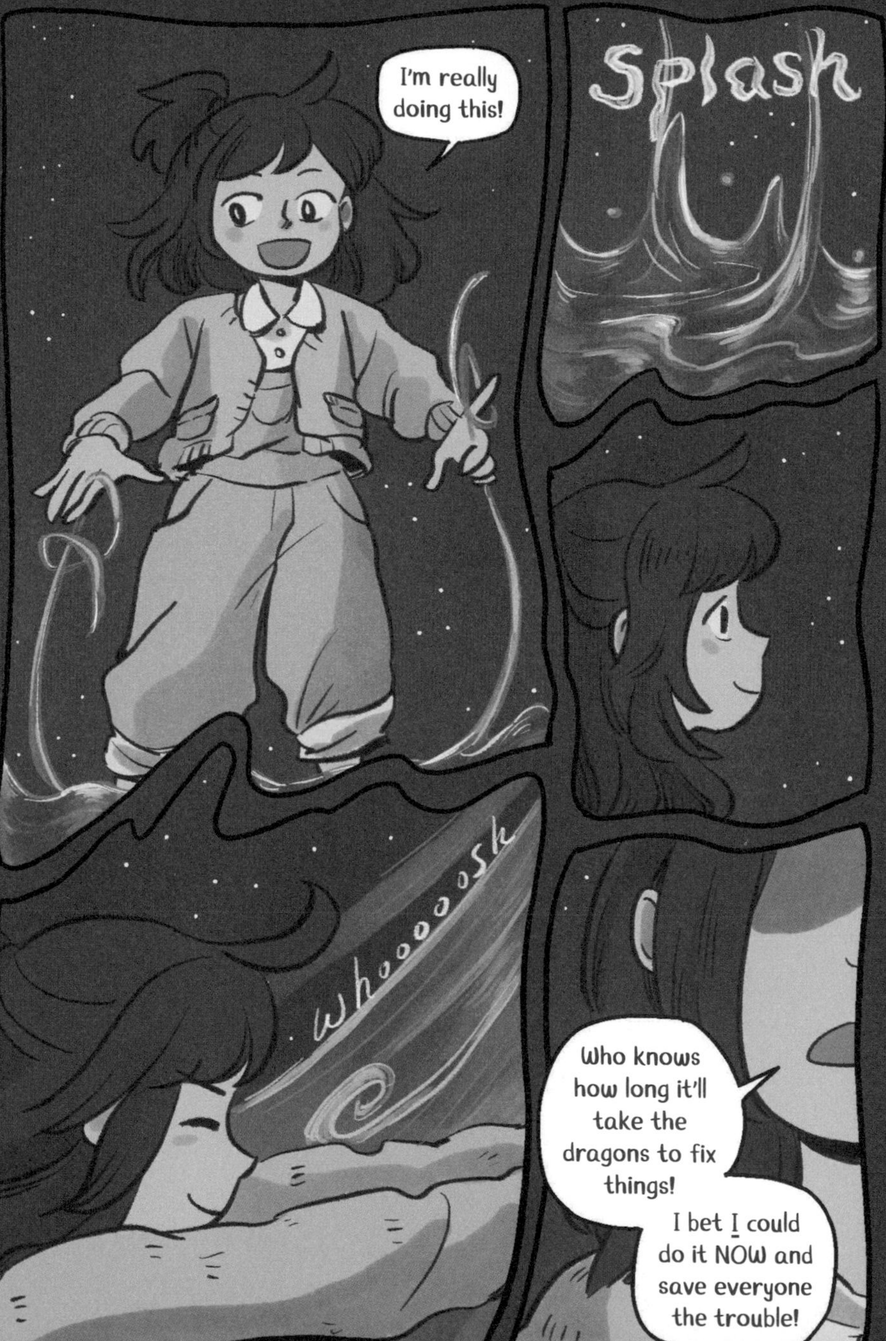
I'm really doing this!
Splash
Whoooooosh
Who knows how long it'll take the dragons to fix things!
I bet I could do it NOW and save everyone the trouble!

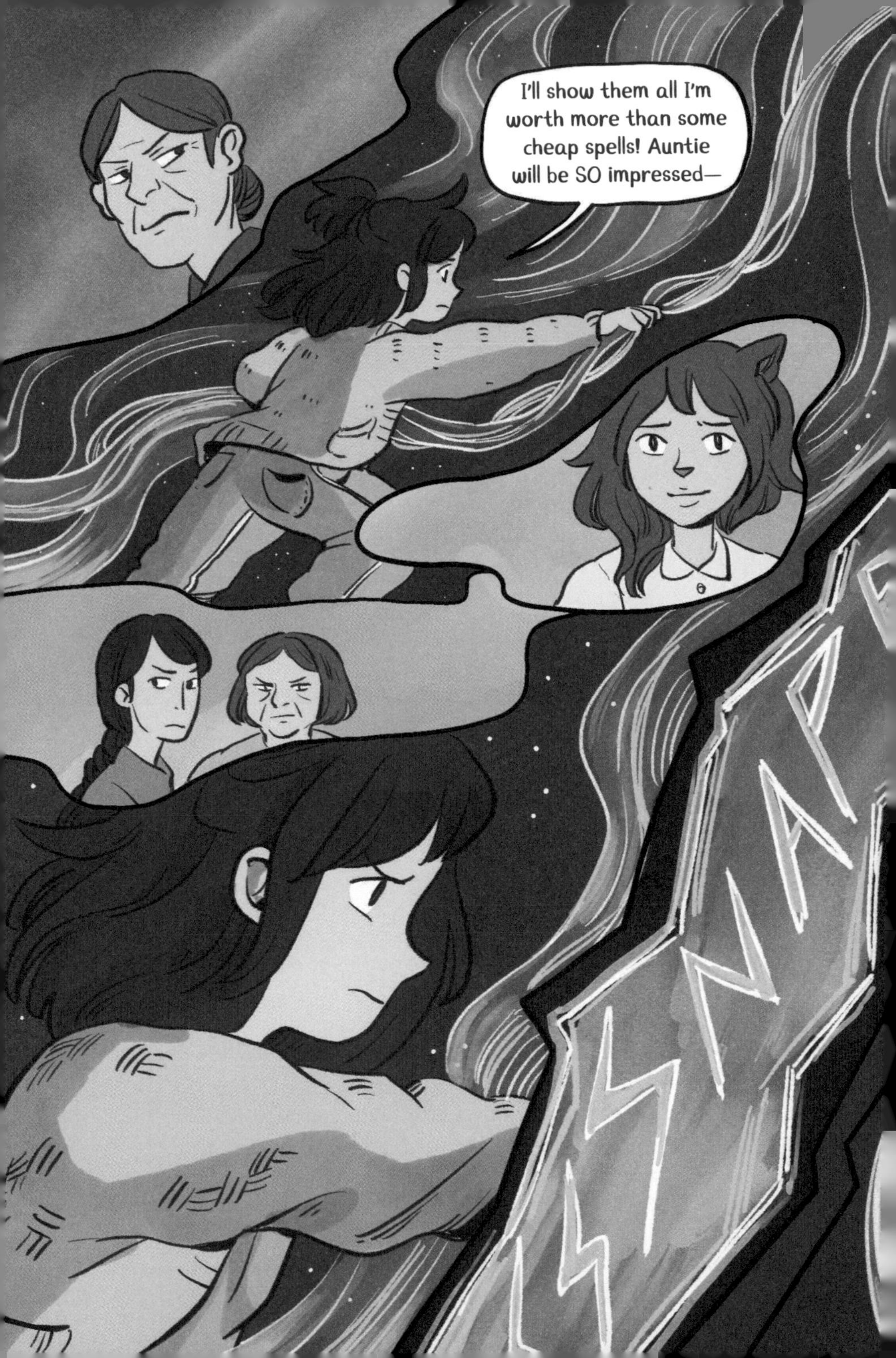
I'll show them all I'm worth more than some cheap spells! Auntie will be SO impressed—
SNAP

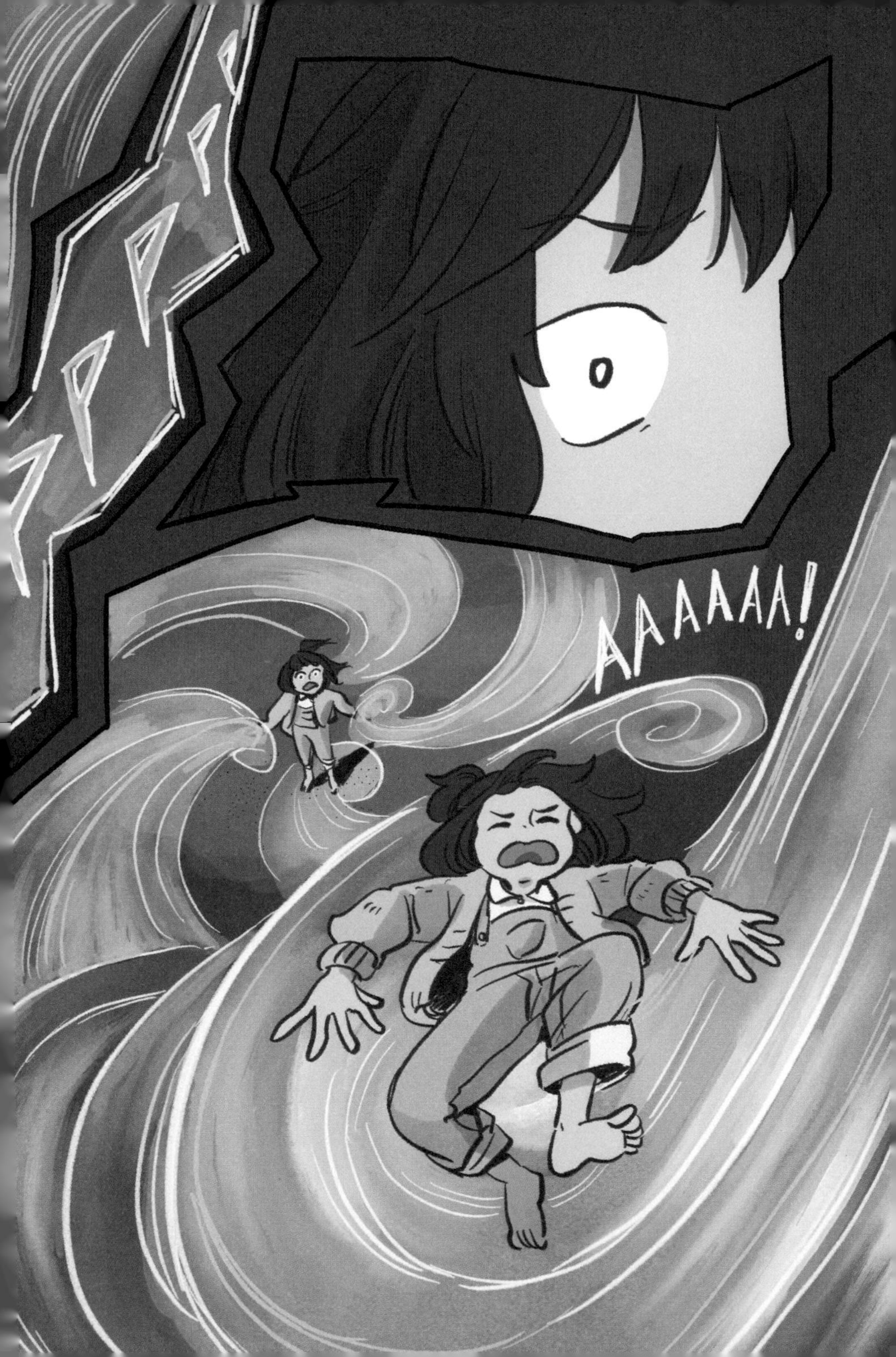
AAAAAA!

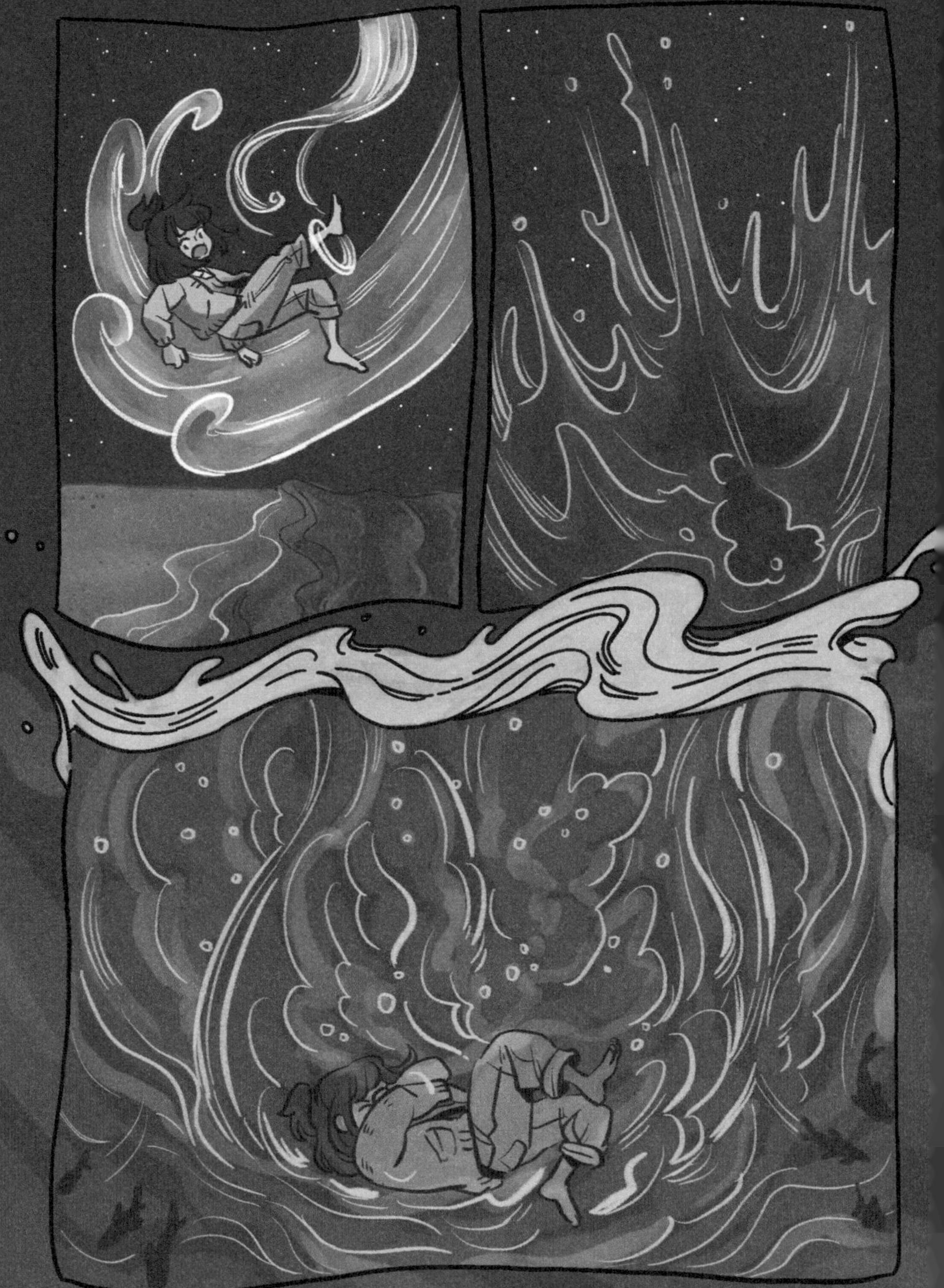

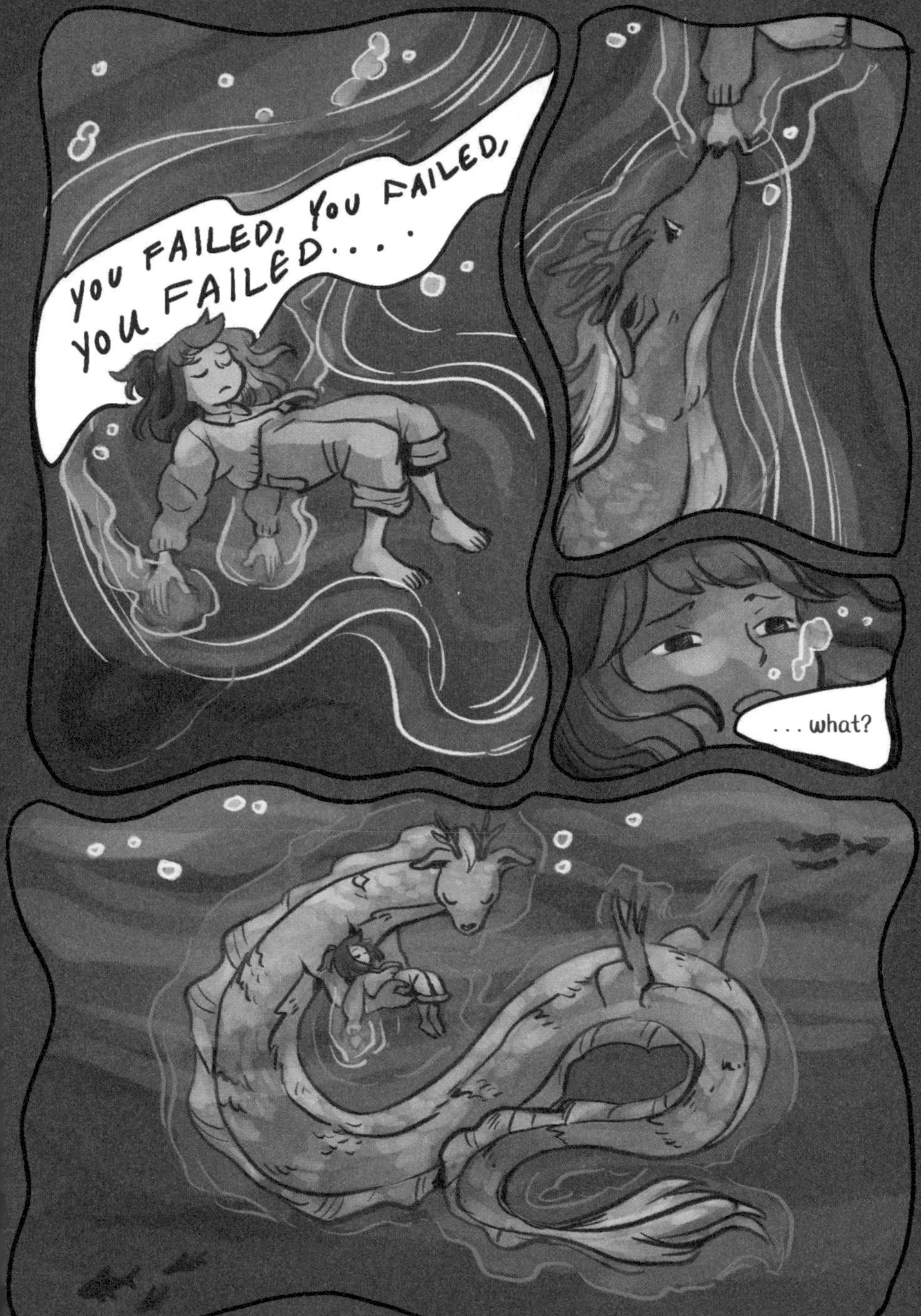
YOU FAILED, YOU FAILED, YOU FAILED. . . .
. . . what?

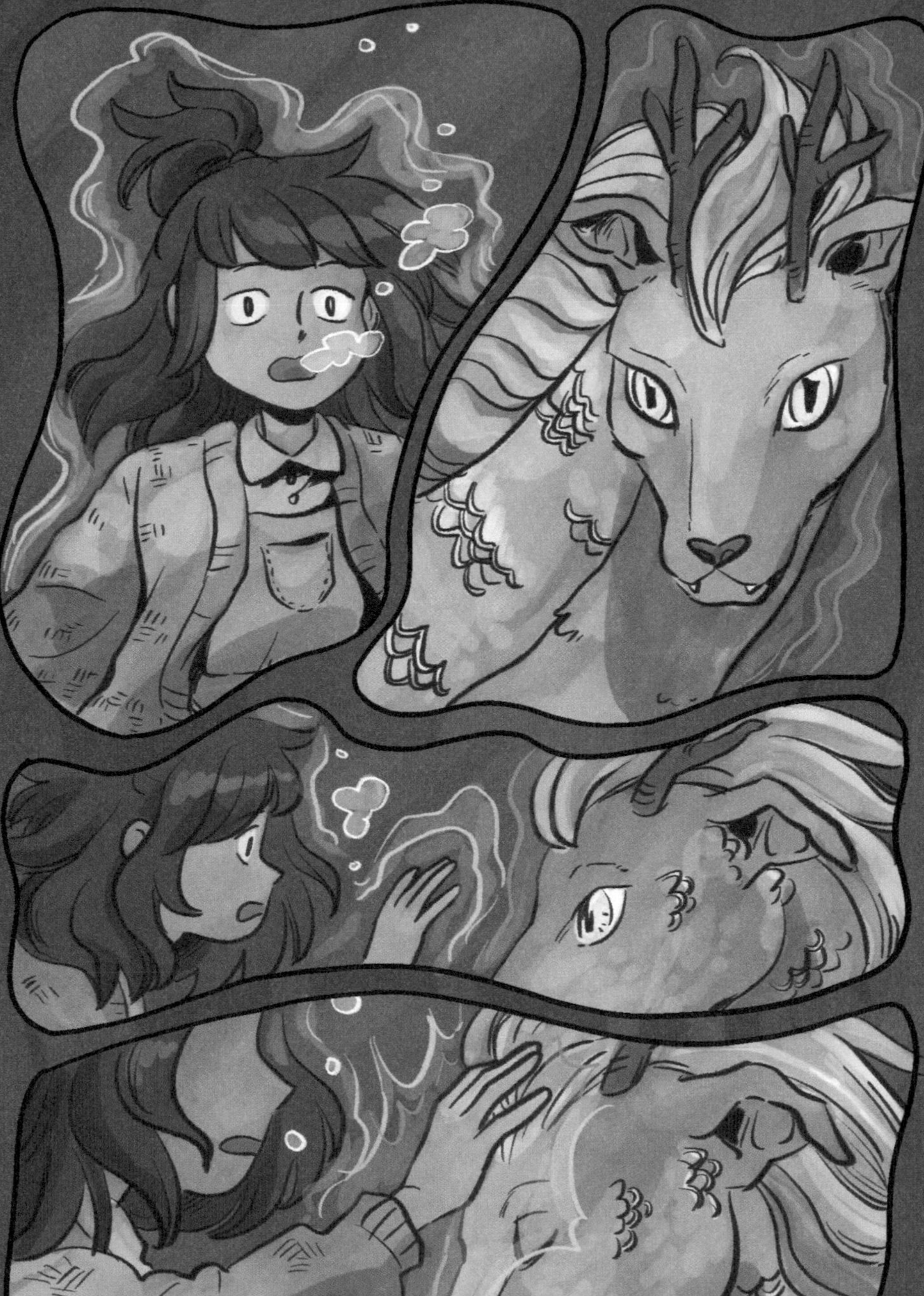

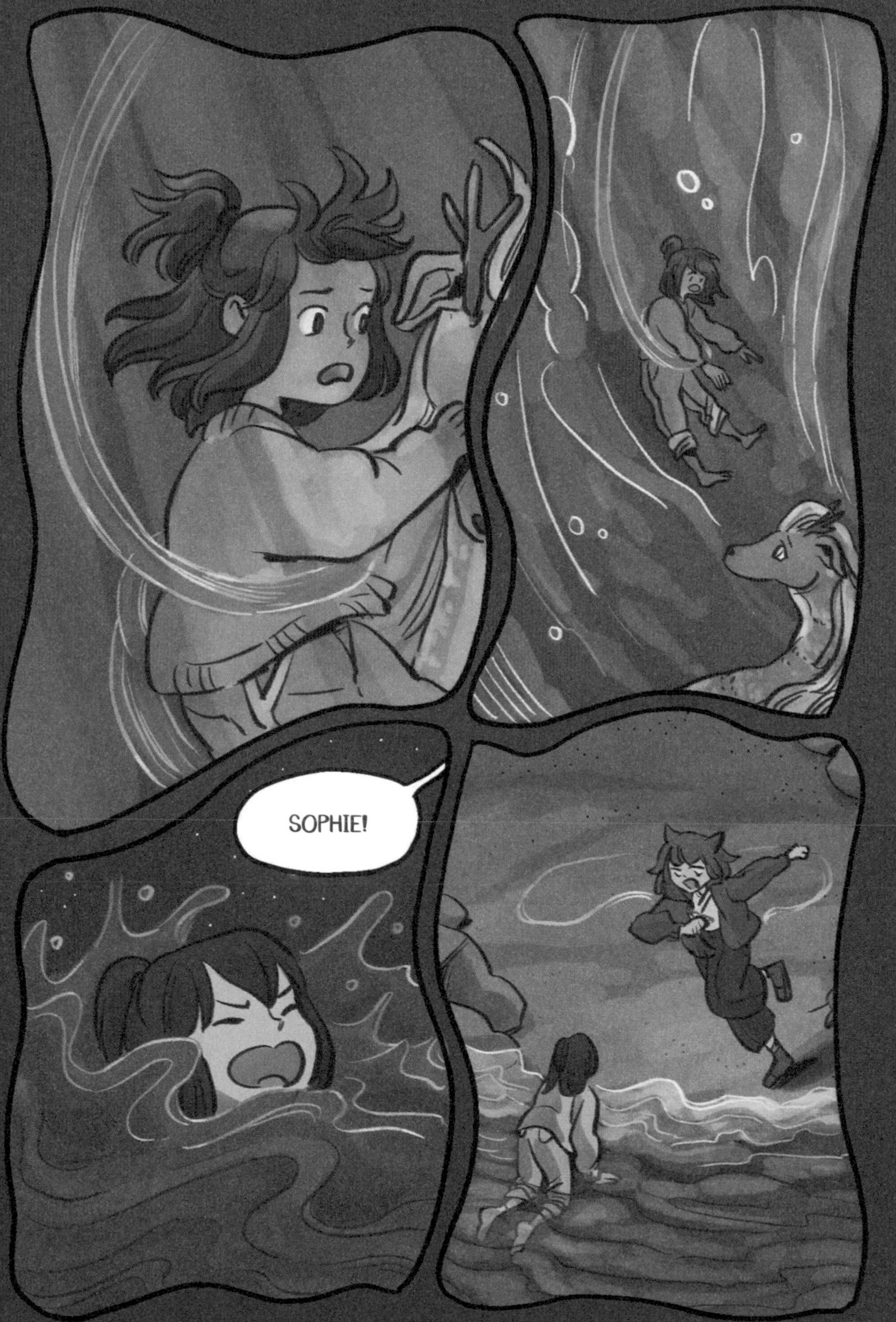
SOPHIE!

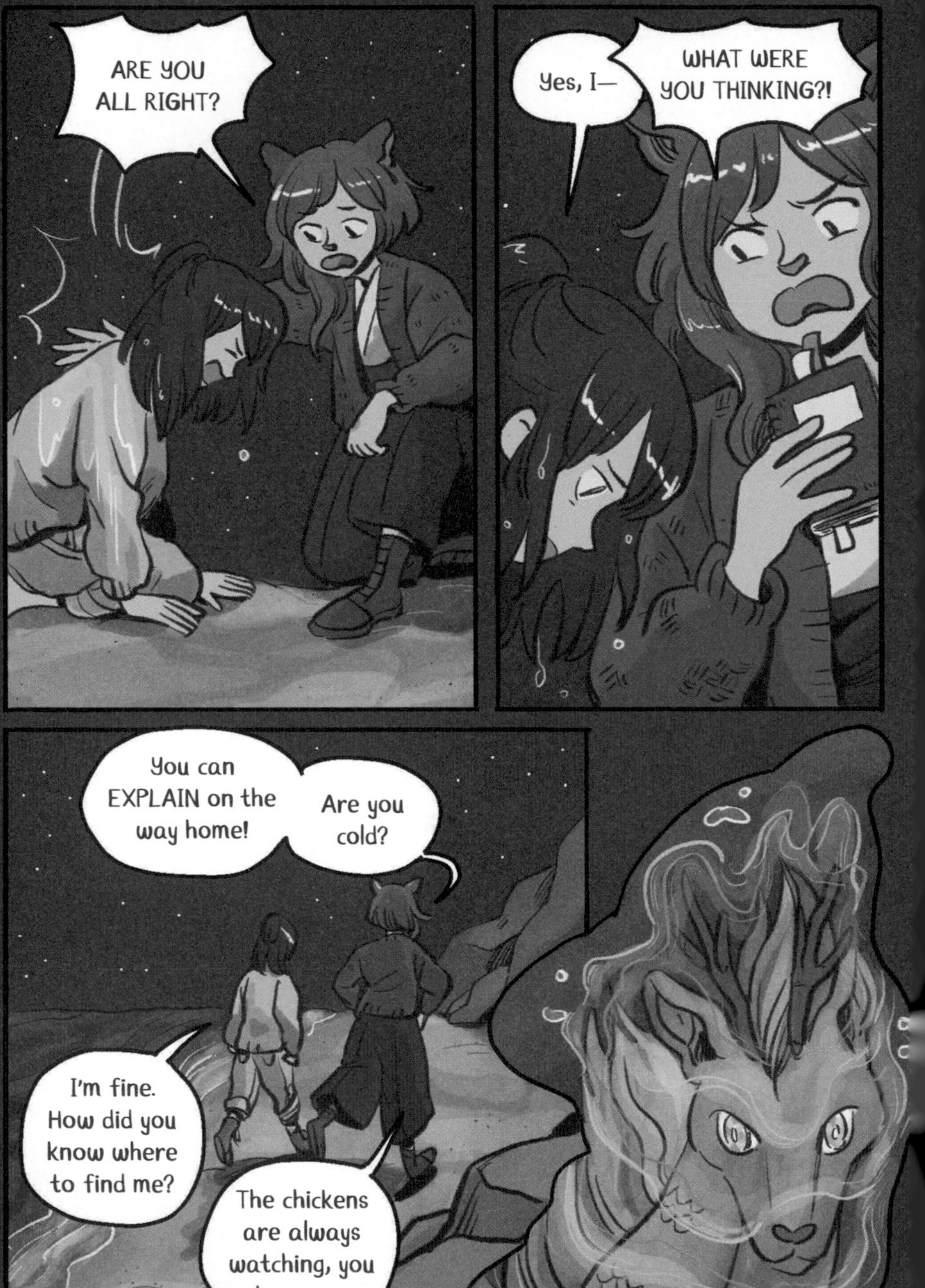

ARE YOU ALL RIGHT?
Yes, I—
WHAT WERE YOU THINKING?!
You can EXPLAIN on the way home!
Are you cold?
I'm fine. How did you know where to find me?
The chickens are always watching, you know . . .

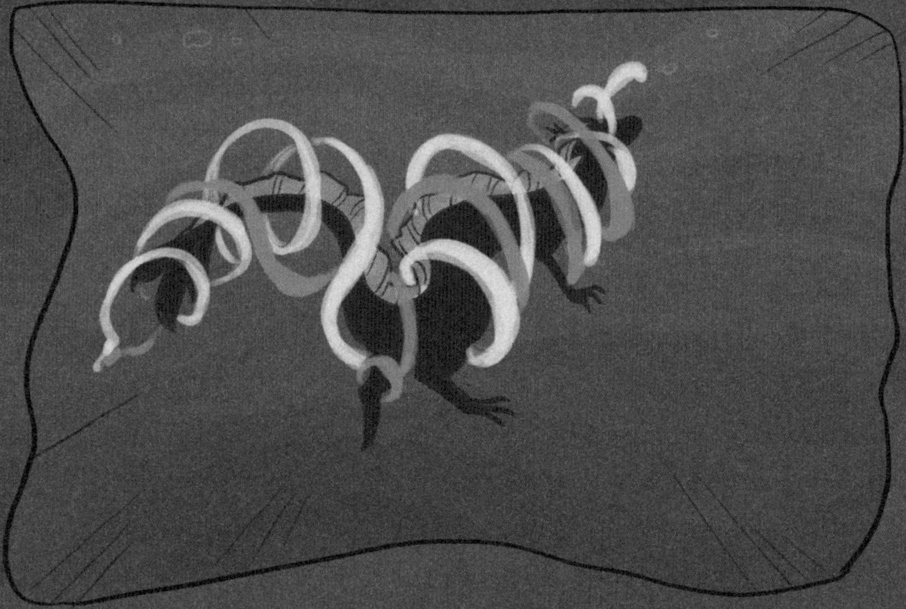

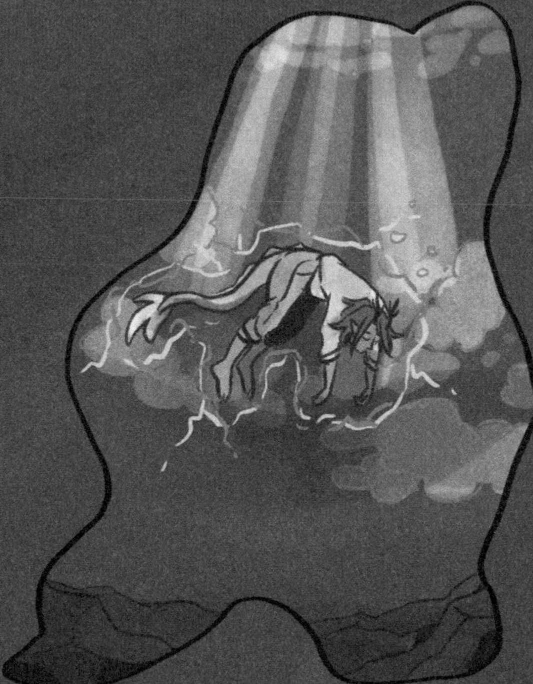

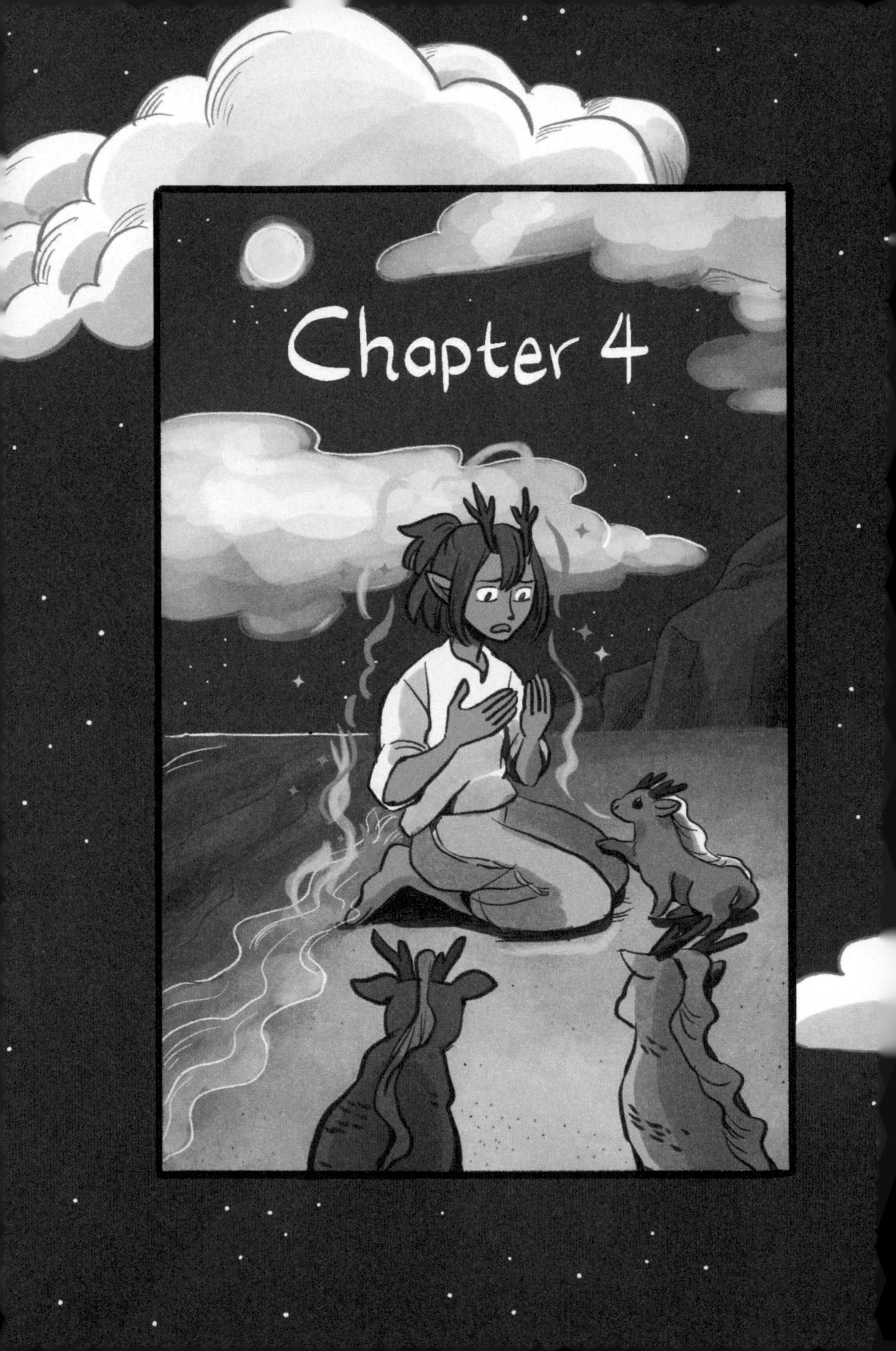
Chapter 4

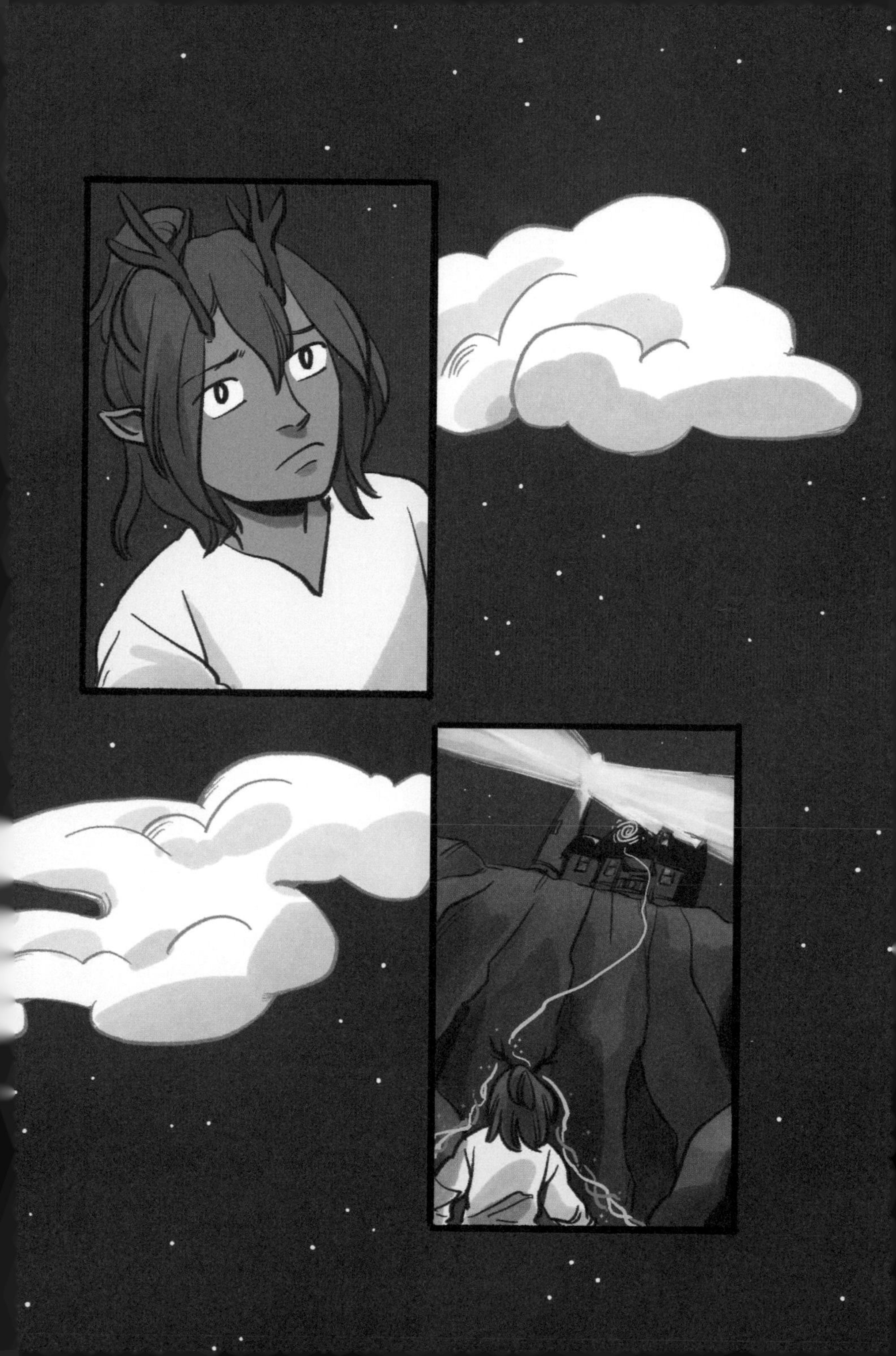

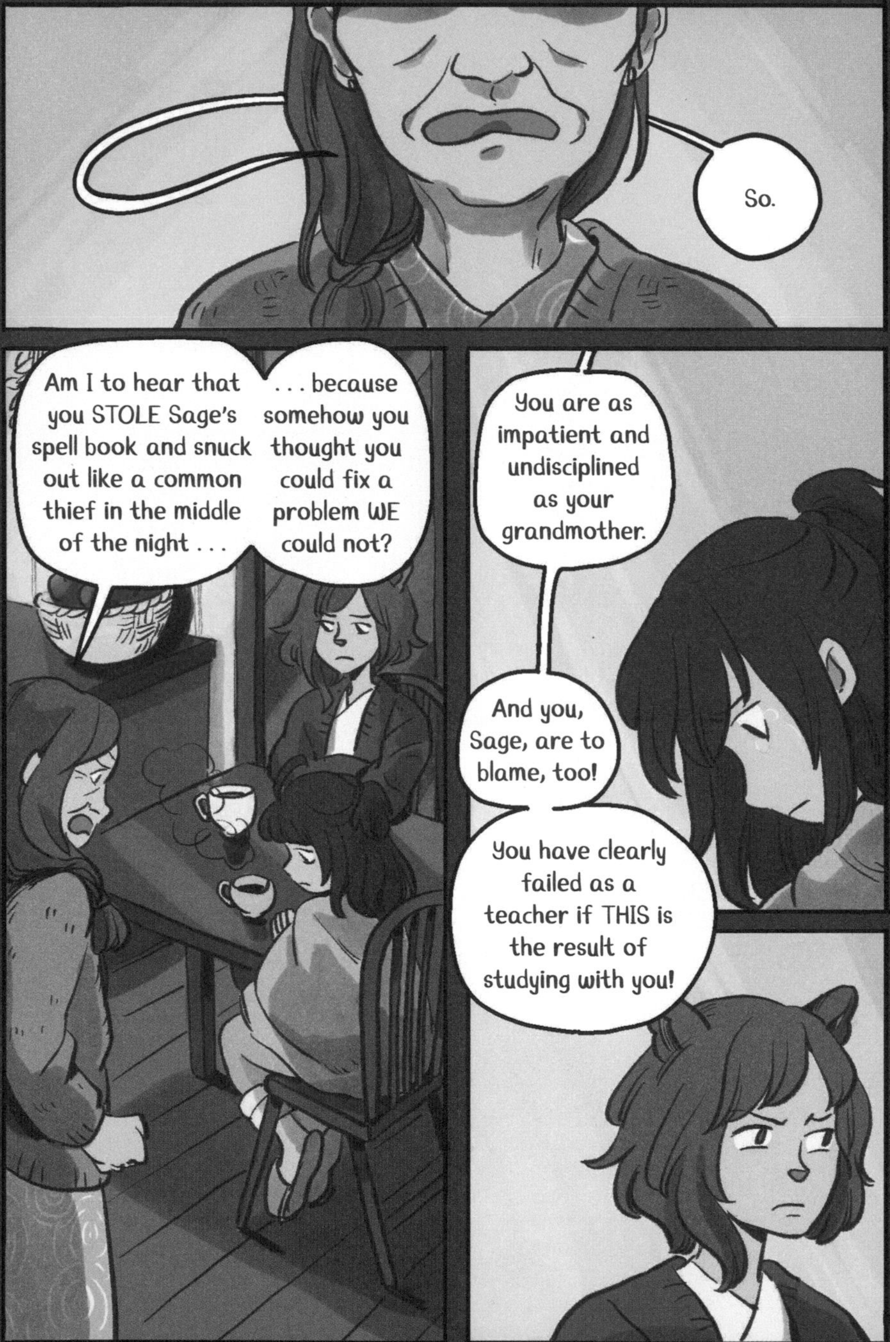
So.
Am I to hear that you STOLE Sage's spell book and snuck out like a common thief in the middle of the night . . .
. . . because somehow you thought you could fix a problem WE could not?
You are as impatient and undisciplined as your grandmother.
And you, Sage, are to blame, too!
You have clearly failed as a teacher if THIS is the result of studying with you!

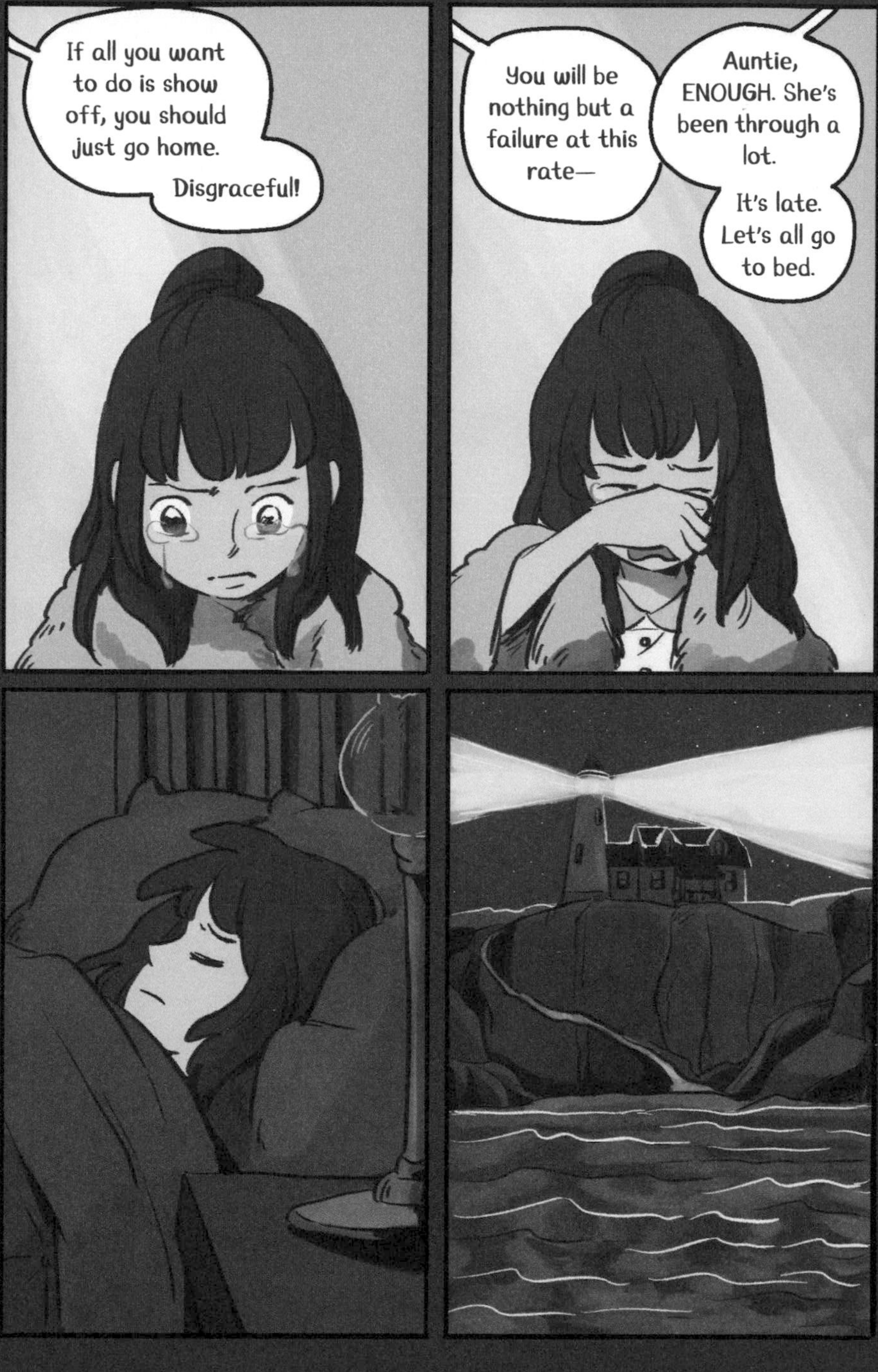
If all you want to do is show off, you should just go home.
Disgraceful!
You will be nothing but a failure at this rate—
Auntie, ENOUGH. She's been through a lot.
It's late. Let's all go to bed.

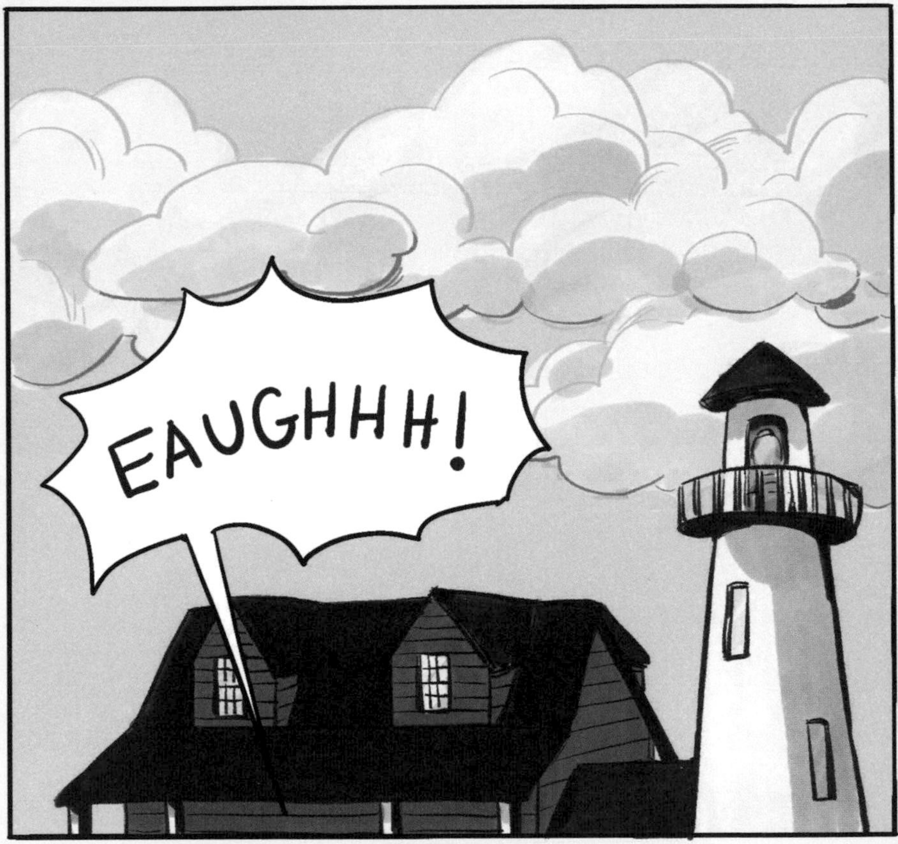
EAUGHHH!

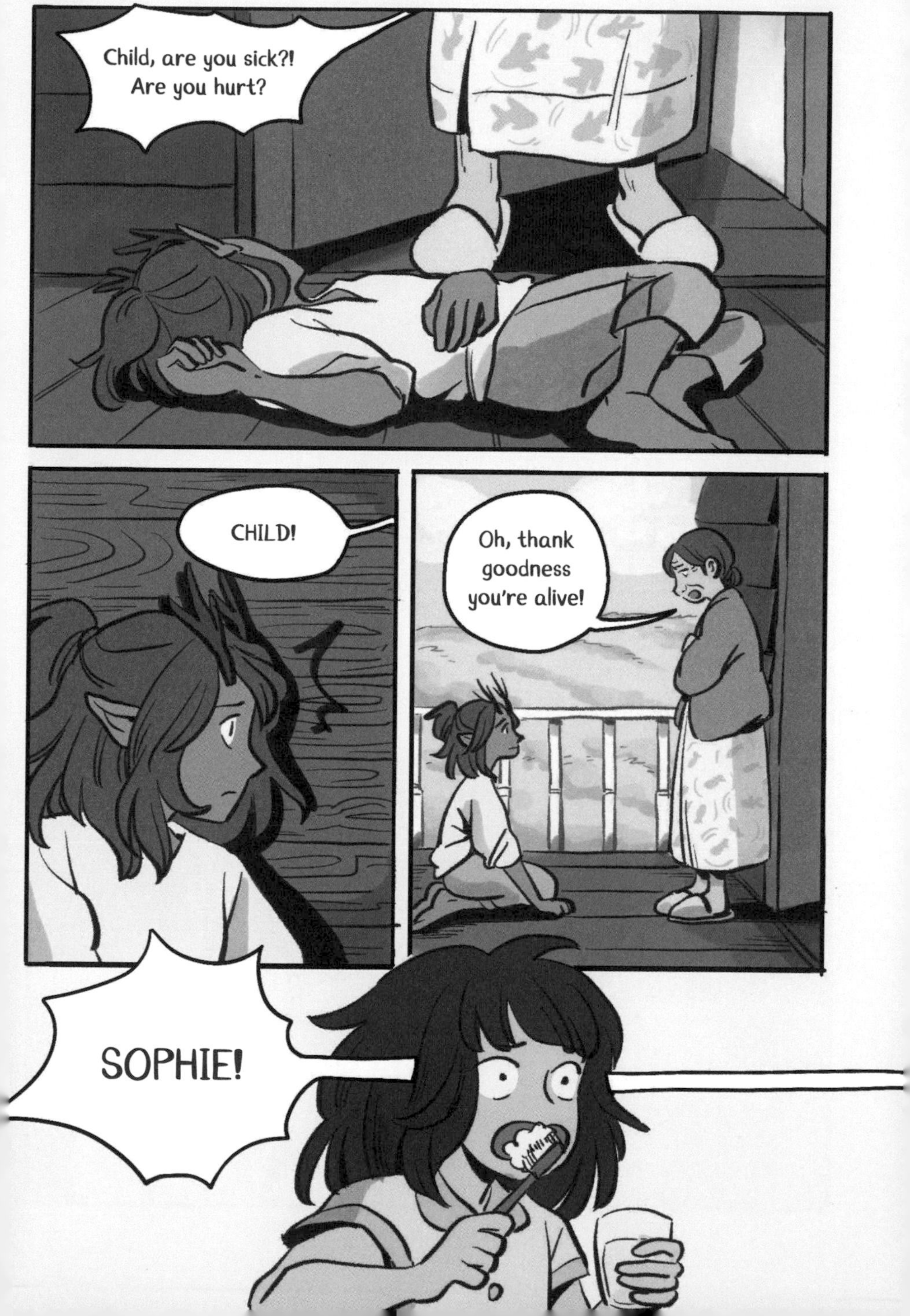
Child, are you sick?! Are you hurt?
CHILD!
Oh, thank goodness you're alive!
SOPHIE!

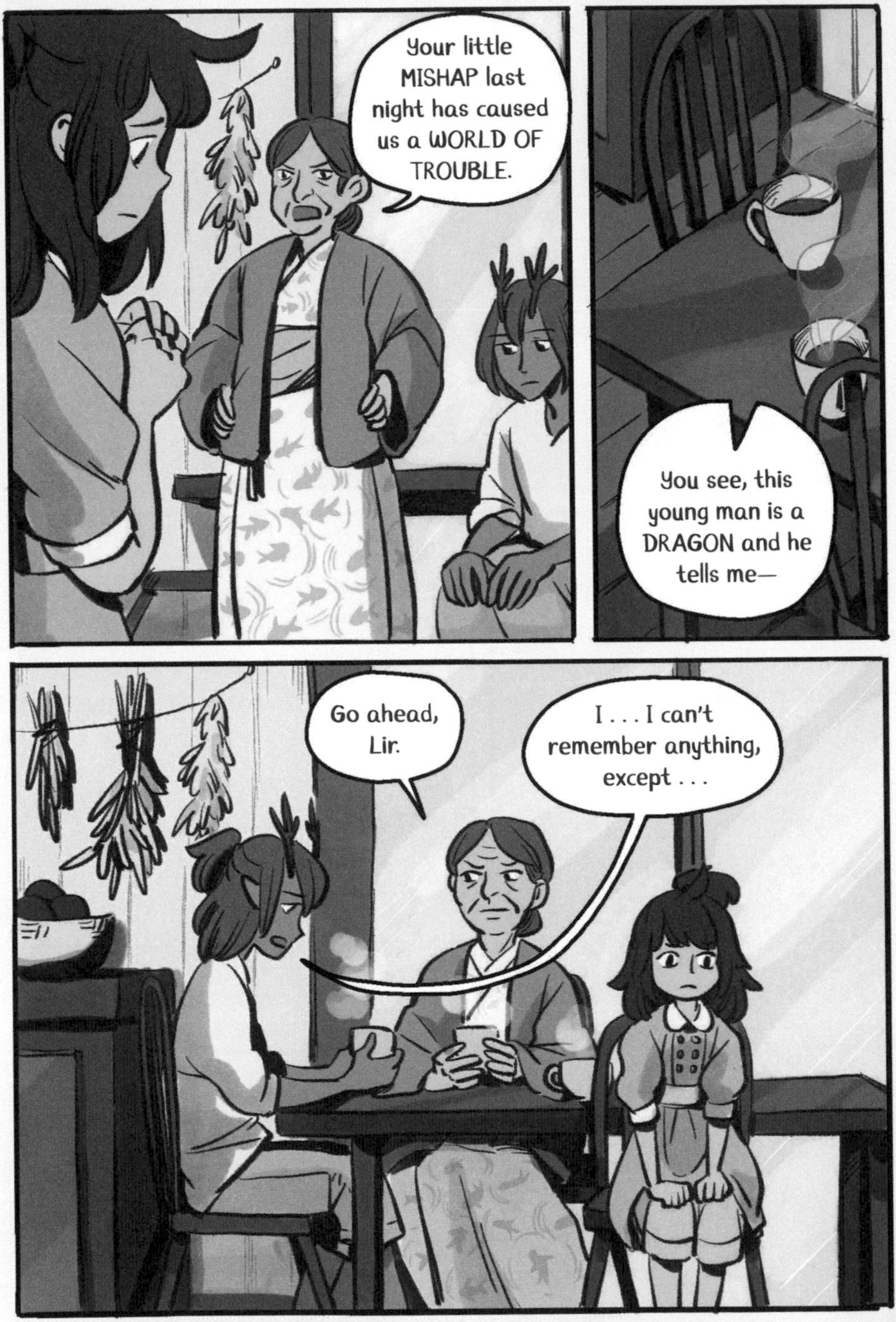
Your little MISHAP last night has caused us a WORLD OF TROUBLE.
You see, this young man is a DRAGON and he tells me—
Go ahead, Lir.
I . . . I can't remember anything, except . . .

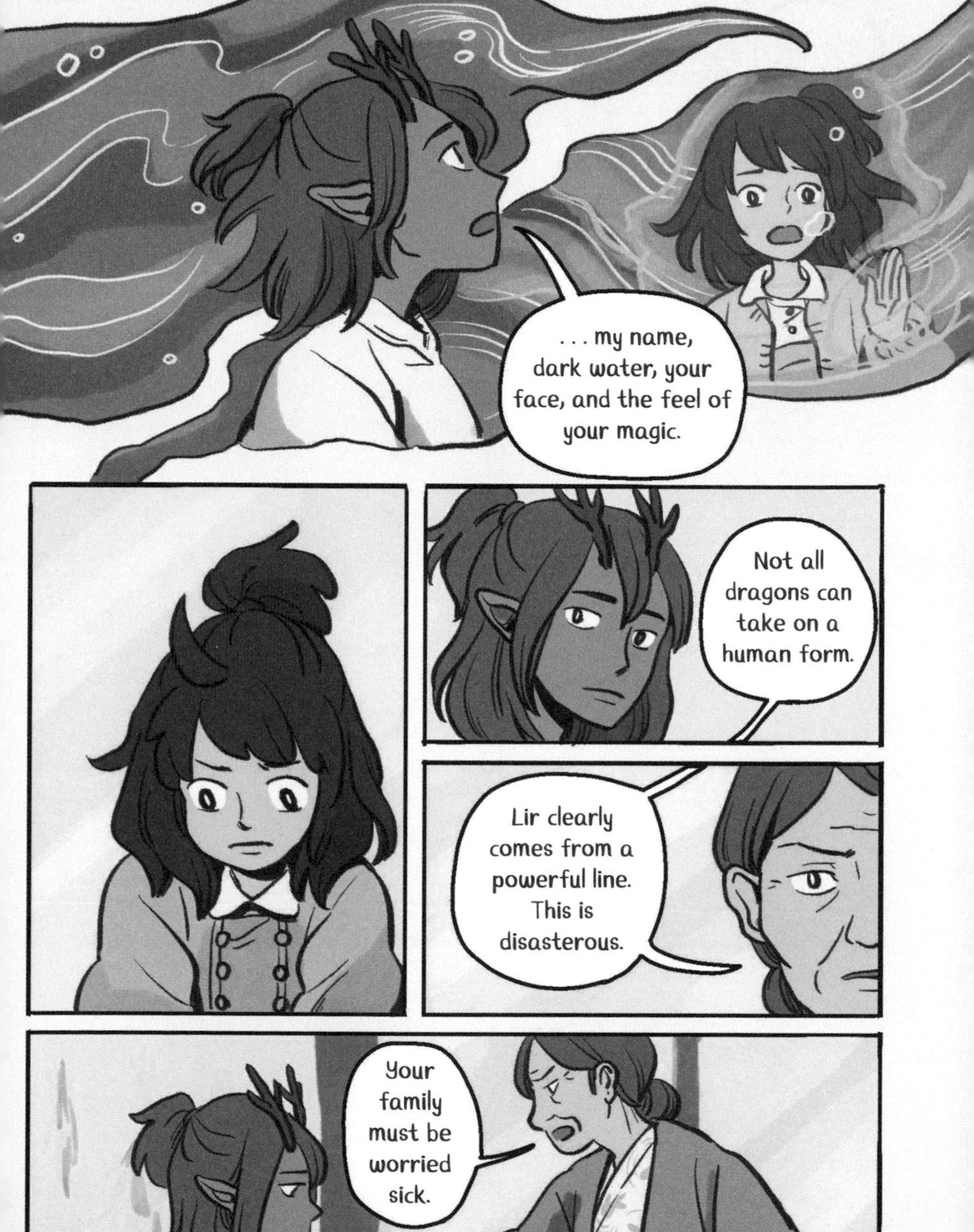
. . . my name, dark water, your face, and the feel of your magic.
Not all dragons can take on a human form.
Lir clearly comes from a powerful line. This is disasterous.
Your family must be worried sick.

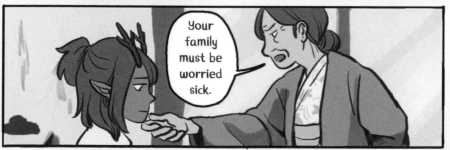

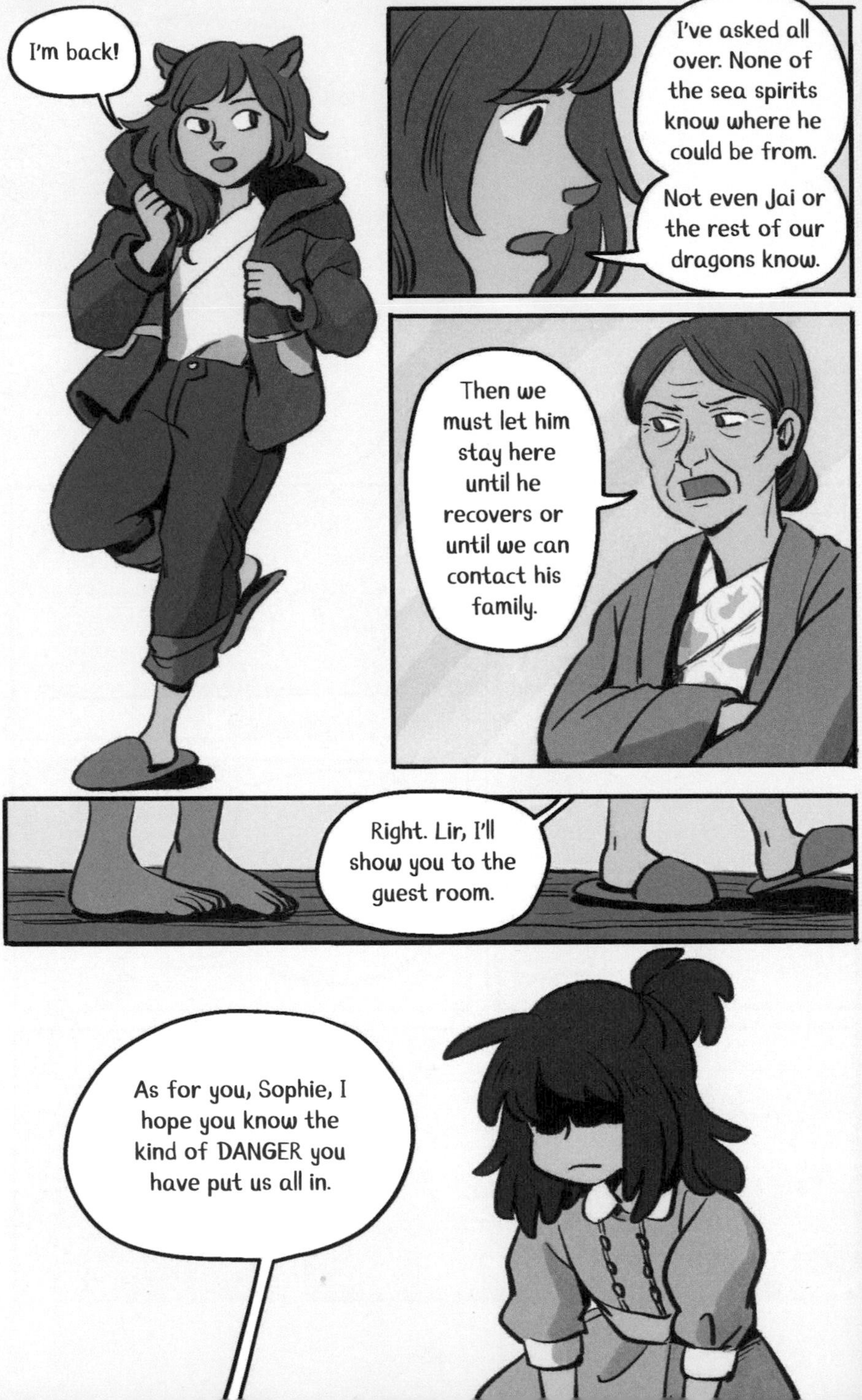
I'm back!
I've asked all over. None of the sea spirits know where he could be from.
Not even Jai or the rest of our dragons know.
Then we must let him stay here until he recovers or until we can contact his family.
Right. Lir, I'll show you to the guest room.
As for you, Sophie, I hope you know the kind of DANGER you have put us all in.

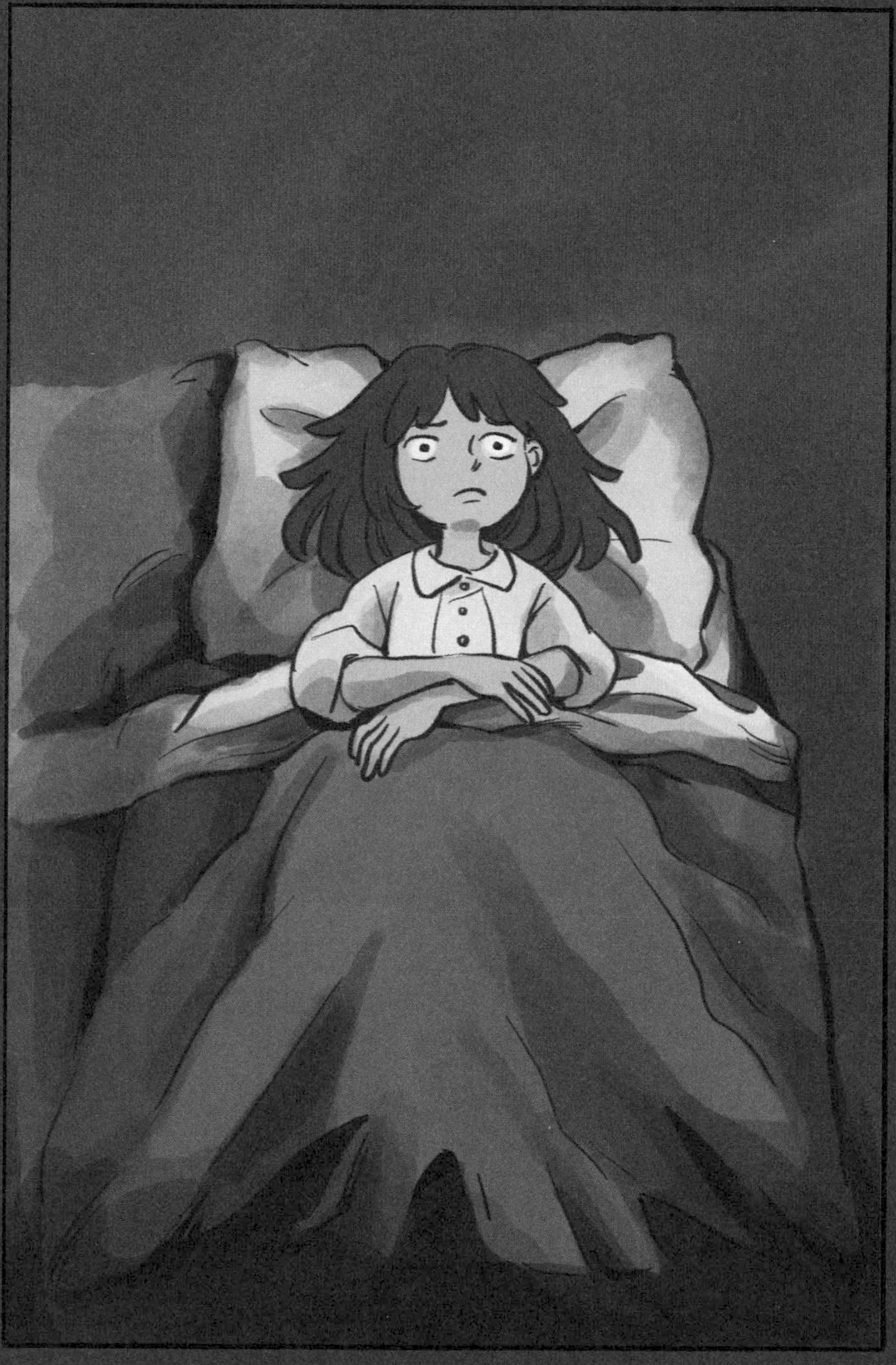

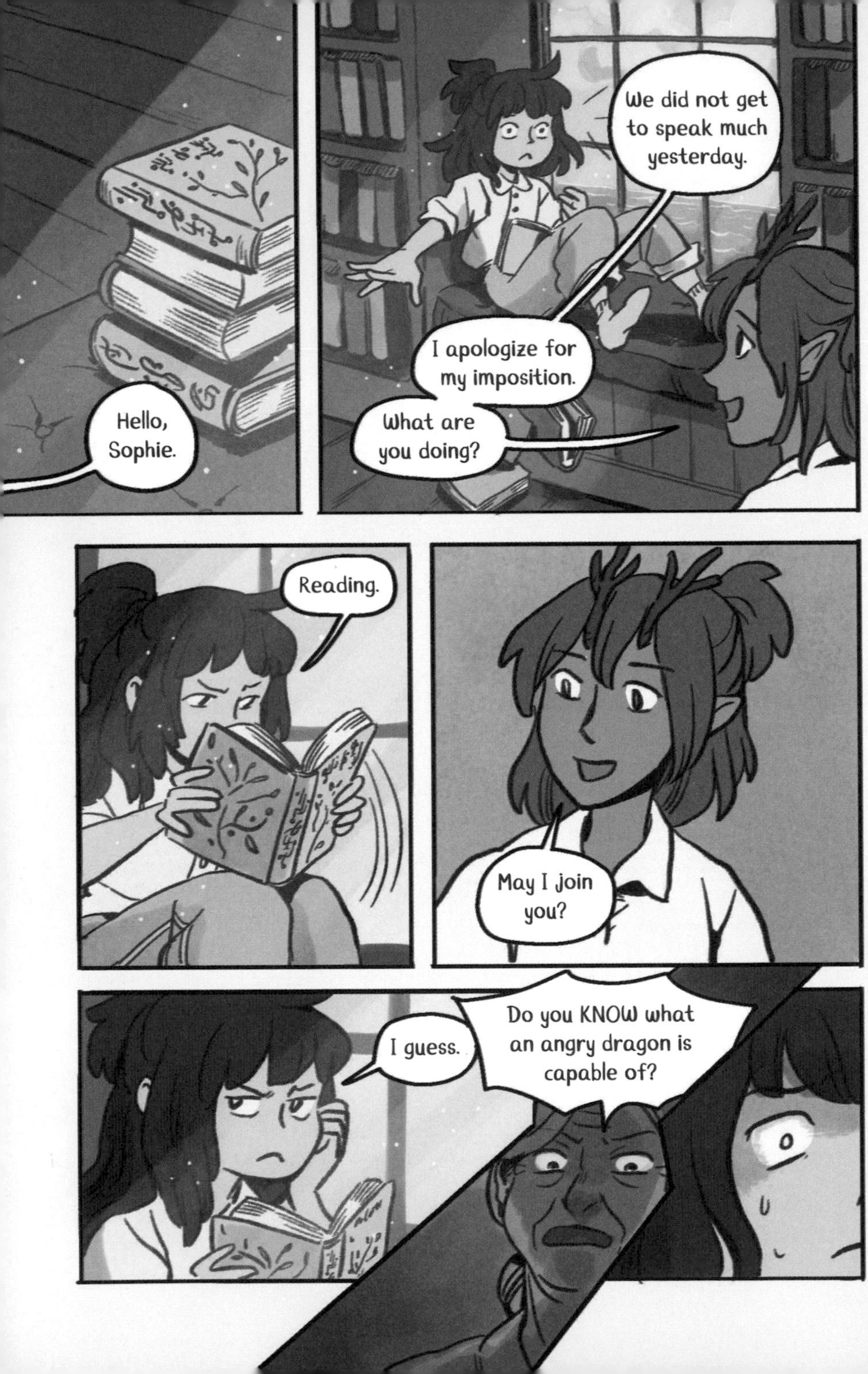
Hello, Sophie.
We did not get to speak much yesterday.
I apologize for my imposition.
What are you doing?
Reading.
May I join you?
I guess.
Do you KNOW what an angry dragon is capable of?

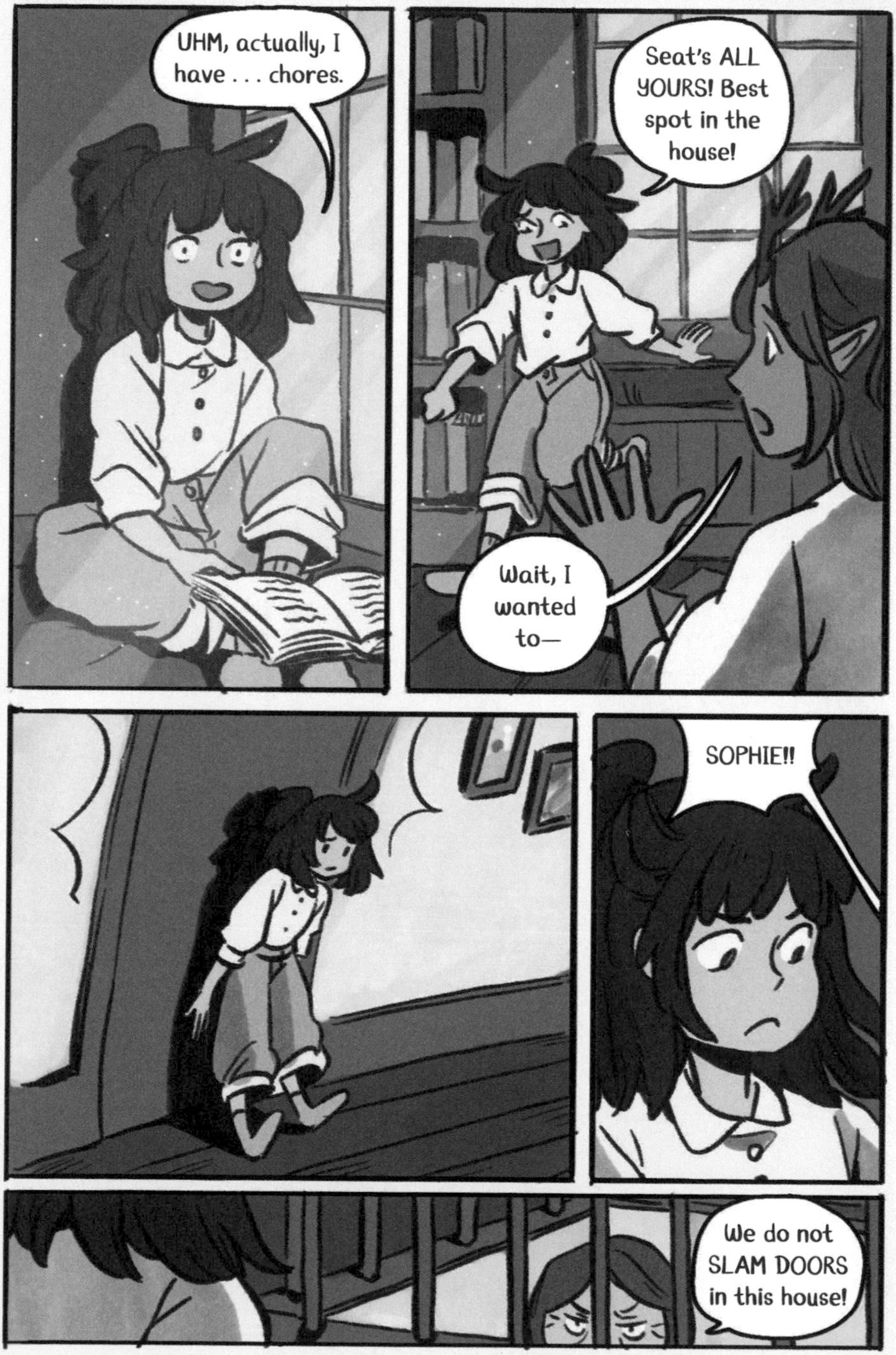
UHM, actually, I have . . . chores.
Seat's ALL YOURS! Best spot in the house!
Wait, I wanted to—
SOPHIE!!
We do not SLAM DOORS in this house!

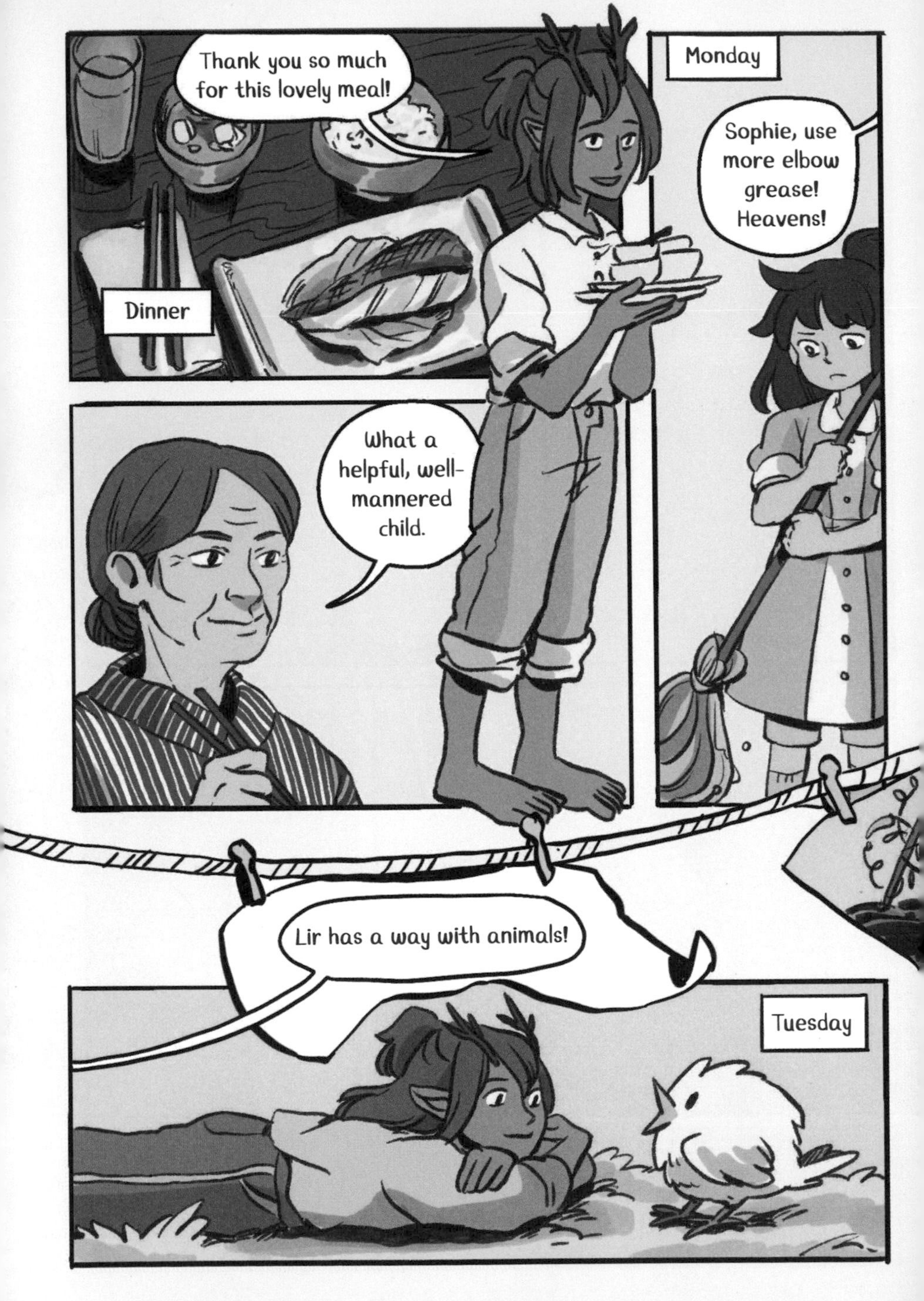
Dinner
Thank you so much for this lovely meal!
What a helpful, well-mannered child.
Monday
Sophie, use more elbow grease! Heavens!
Lir has a way with animals!
Tuesday

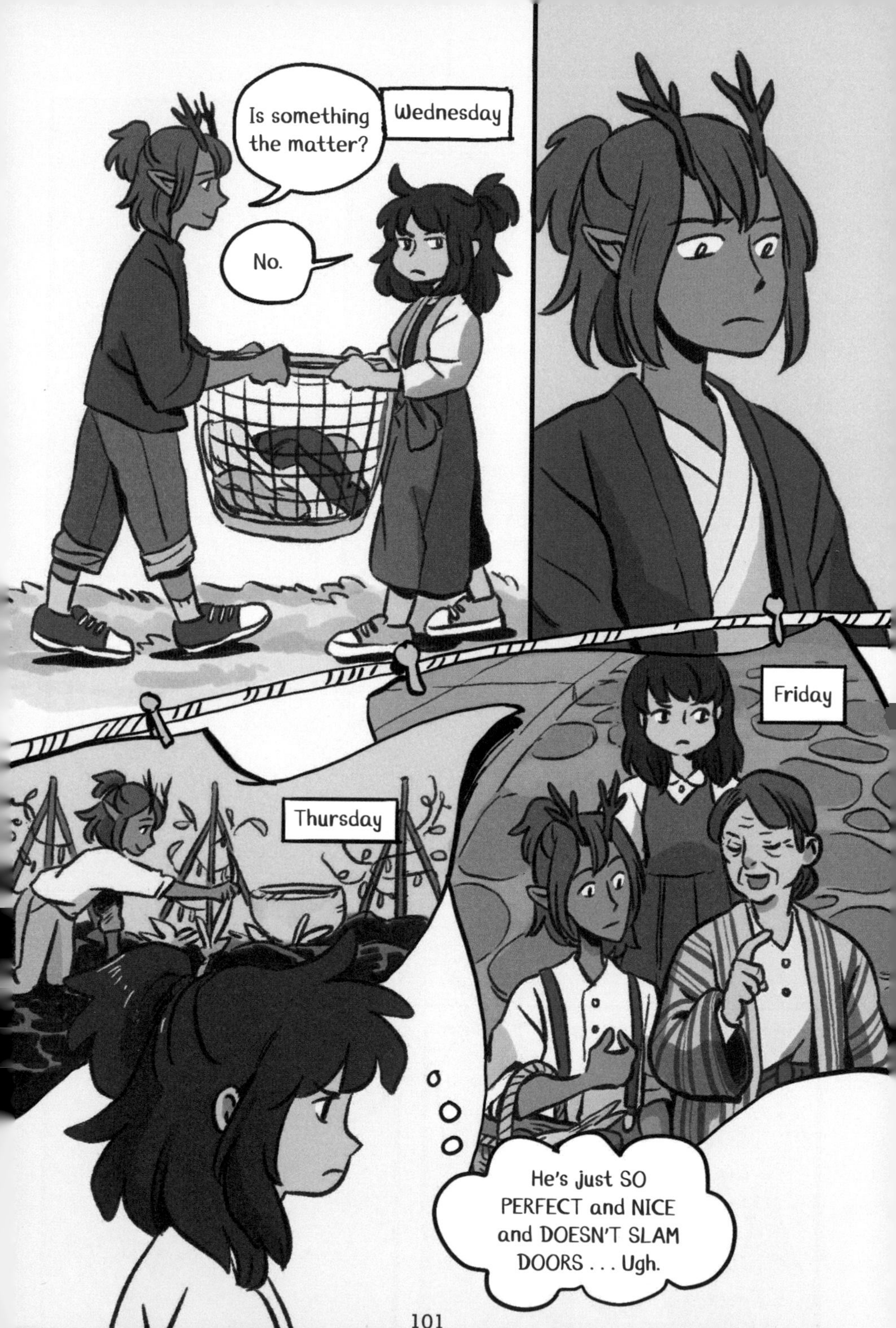
Wednesday
Is something the matter?
No.
Thursday
Friday
He's just SO PERFECT and NICE and DOESN'T SLAM DOORS . . . Ugh.

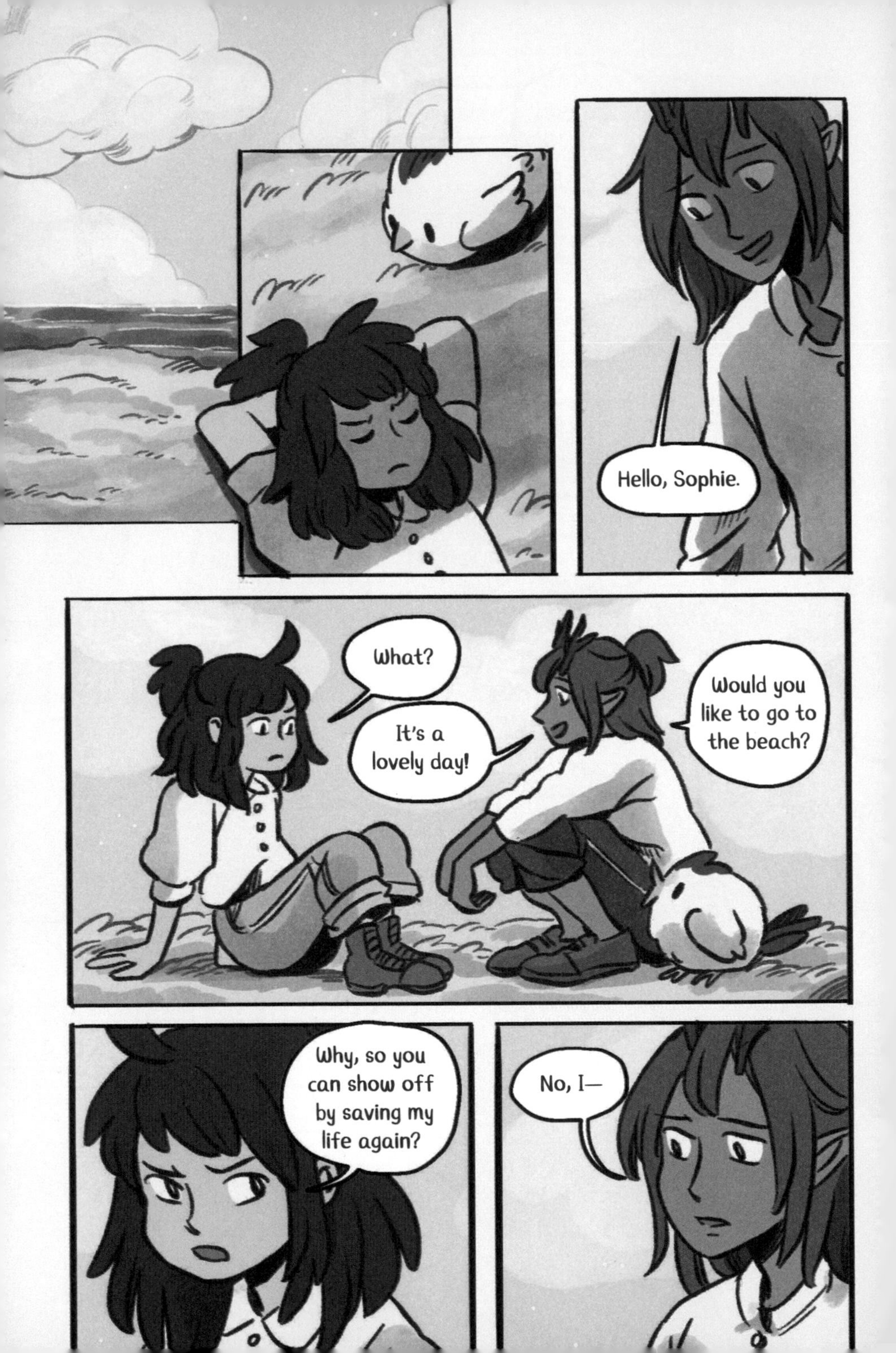

Hello, Sophie.
What?
It's a lovely day!
Would you like to go to the beach?
Why, so you can show off by saving my life again?
No, I—

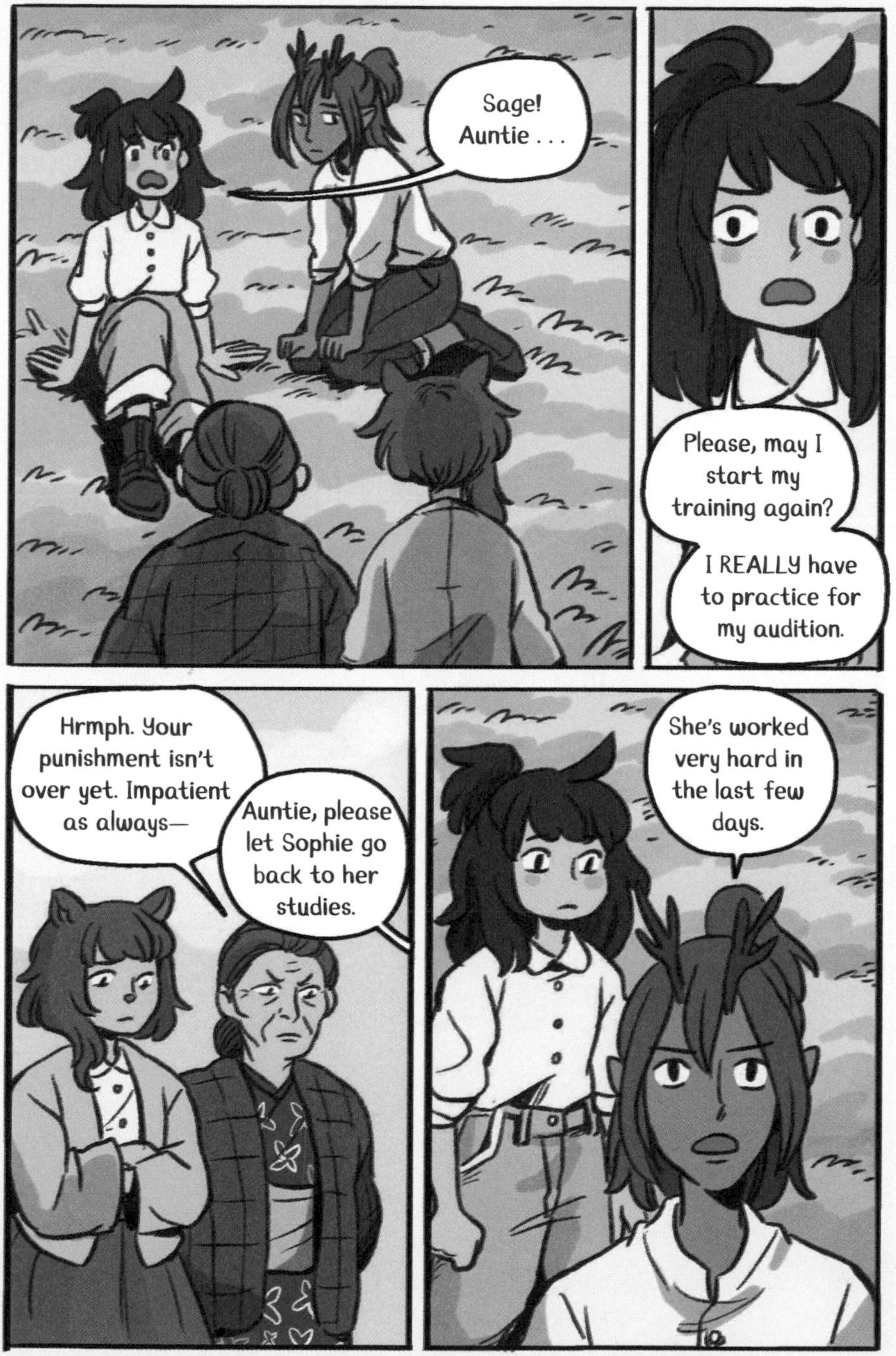
Sage! Auntie . . .
Please, may I start my training again?
I REALLY have to practice for my audition.
Hrmph. Your punishment isn't over yet. Impatient as always—
Auntie, please let Sophie go back to her studies.
She's worked very hard in the last few days.

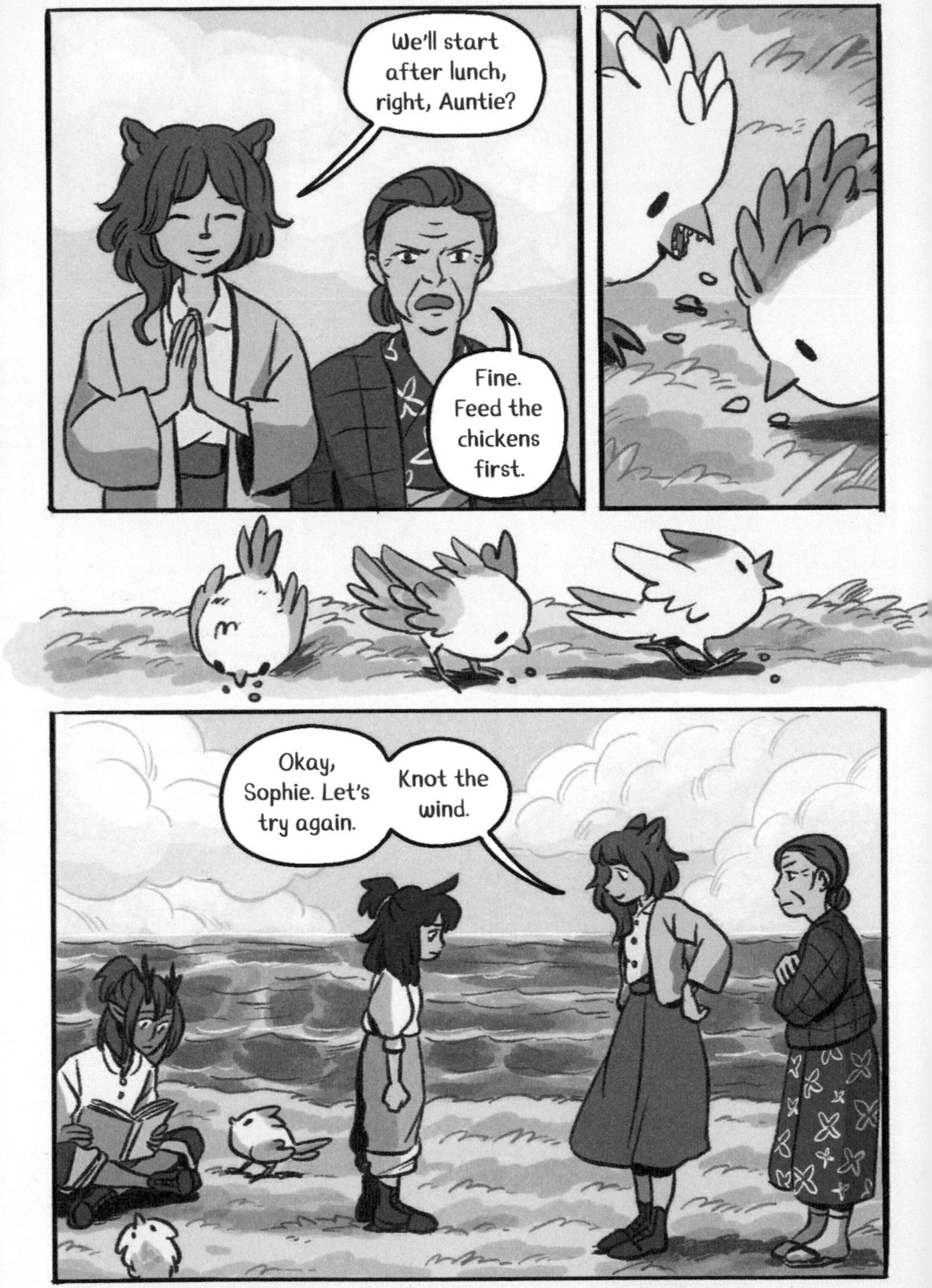
We'll start after lunch, right, Auntie?
Fine. Feed the chickens first.
Okay, Sophie. Let's try again.
Knot the wind.

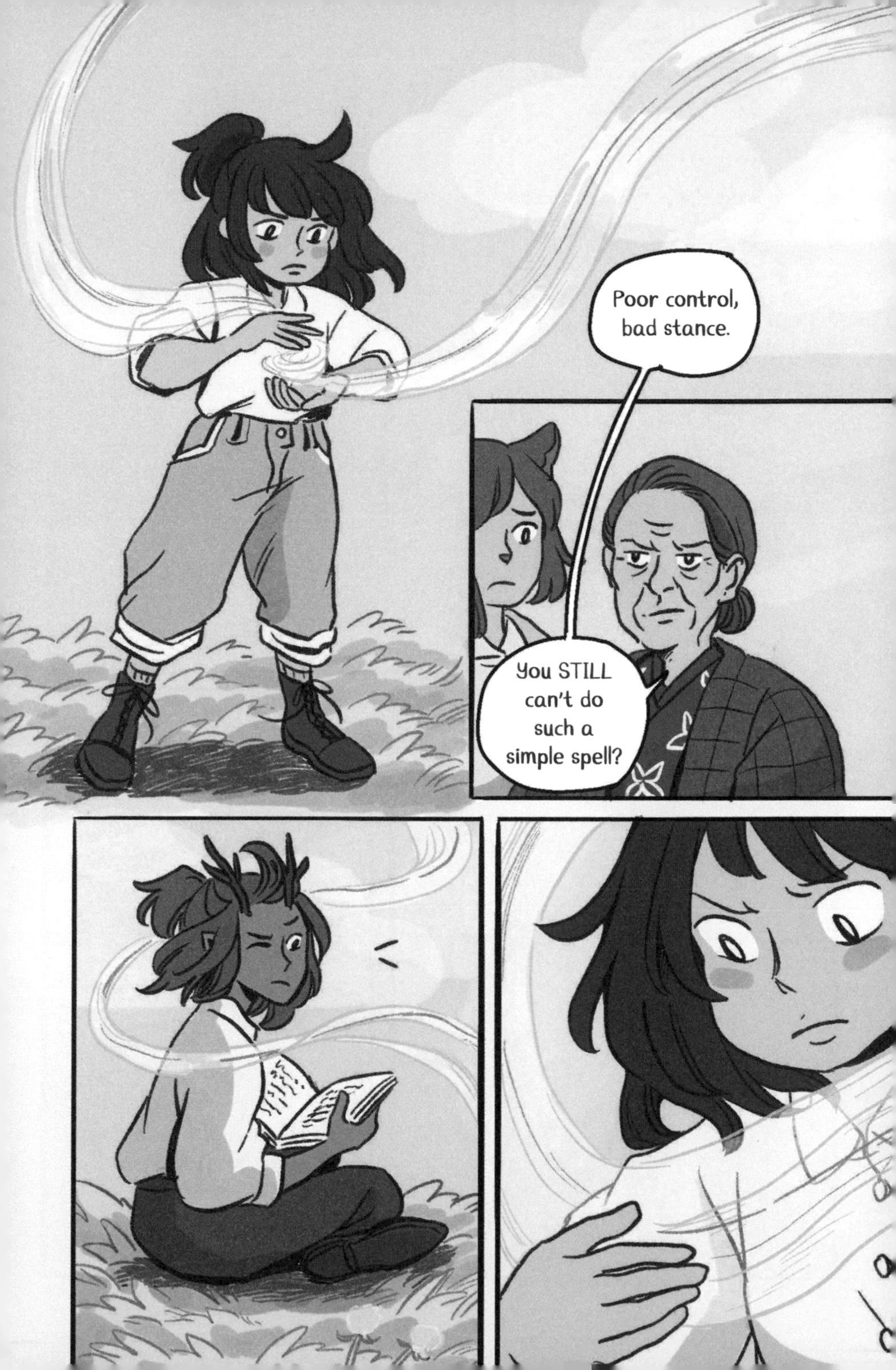
Poor control, bad stance.
You STILL can't do such a simple spell?

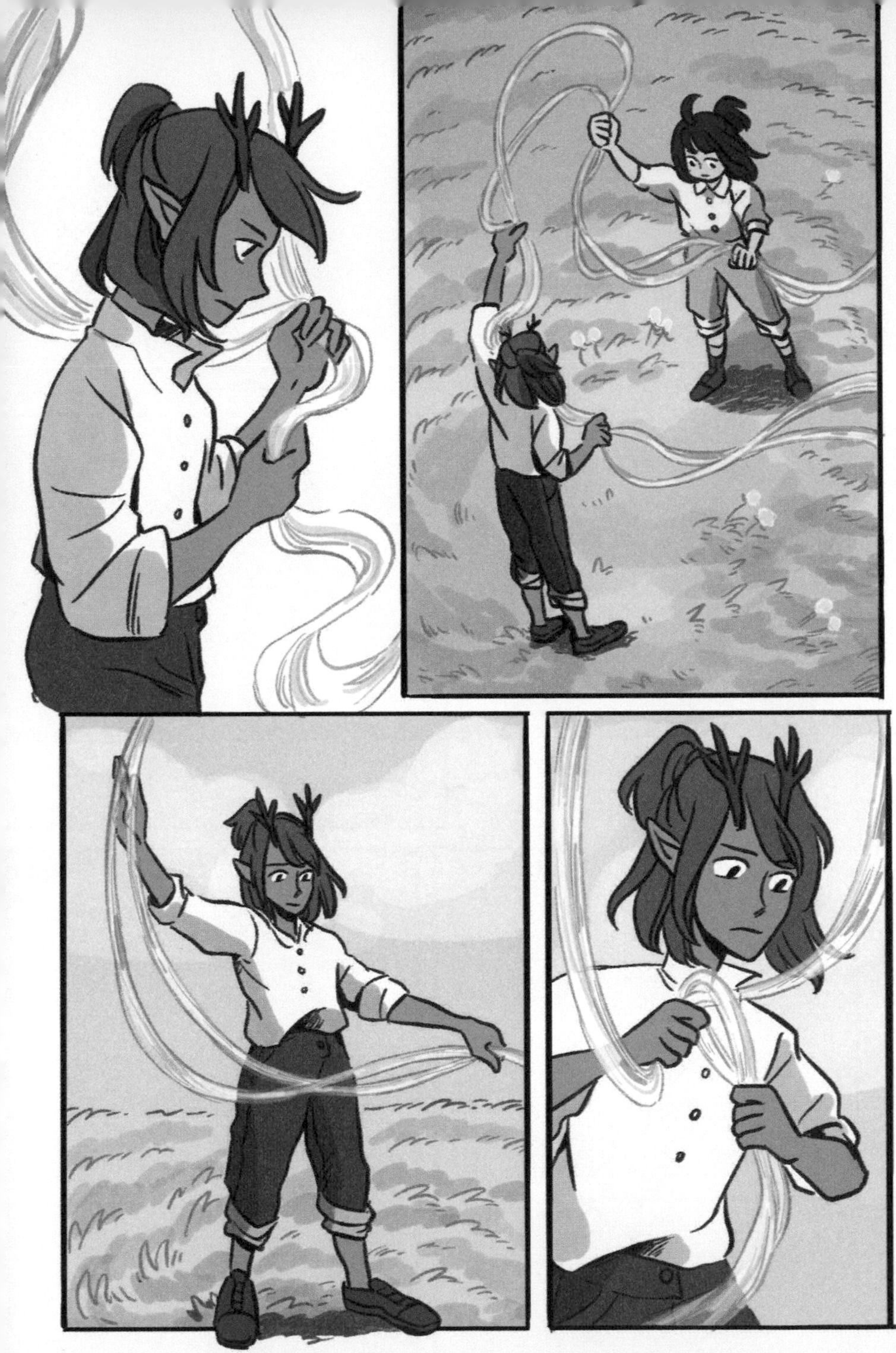

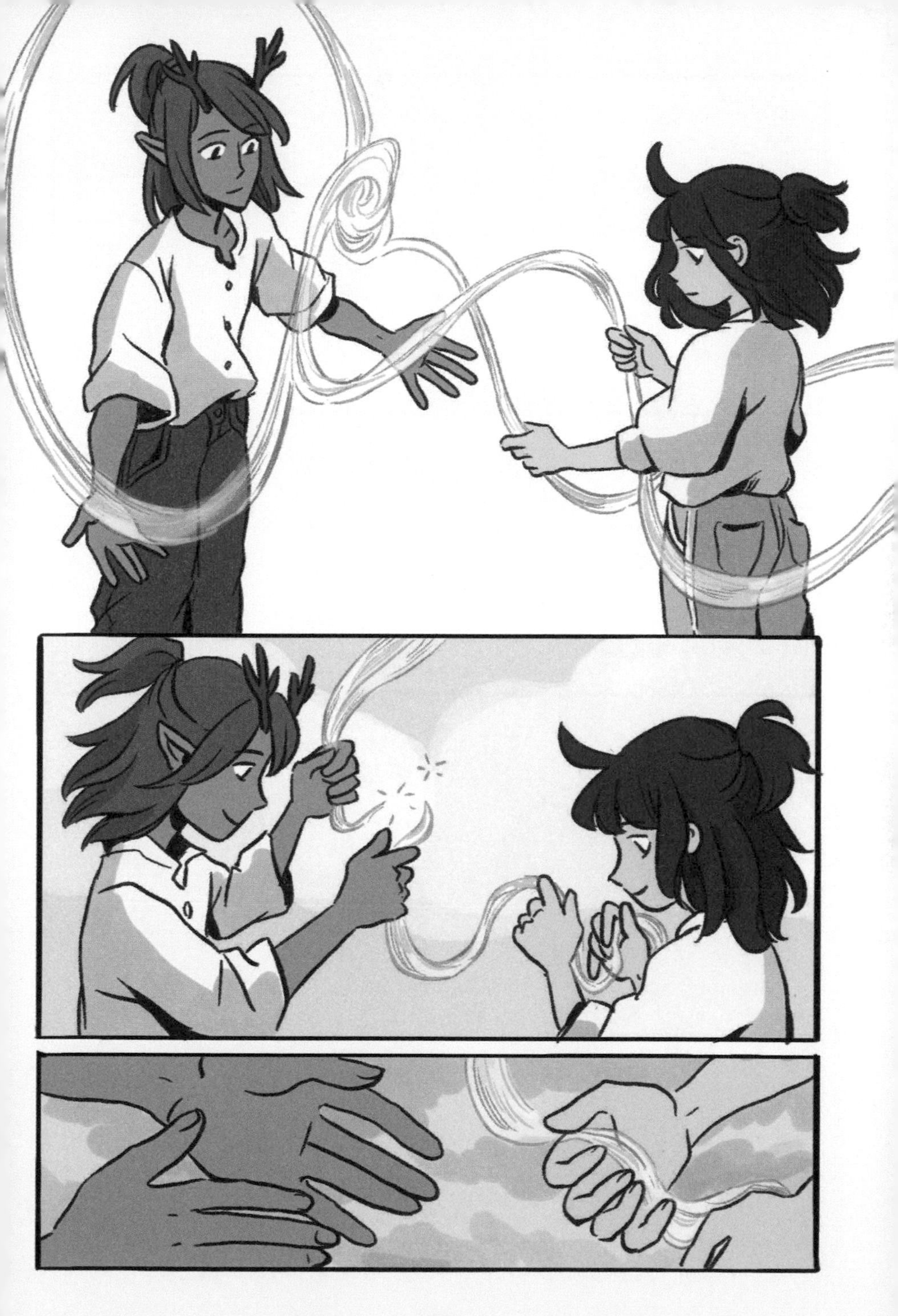

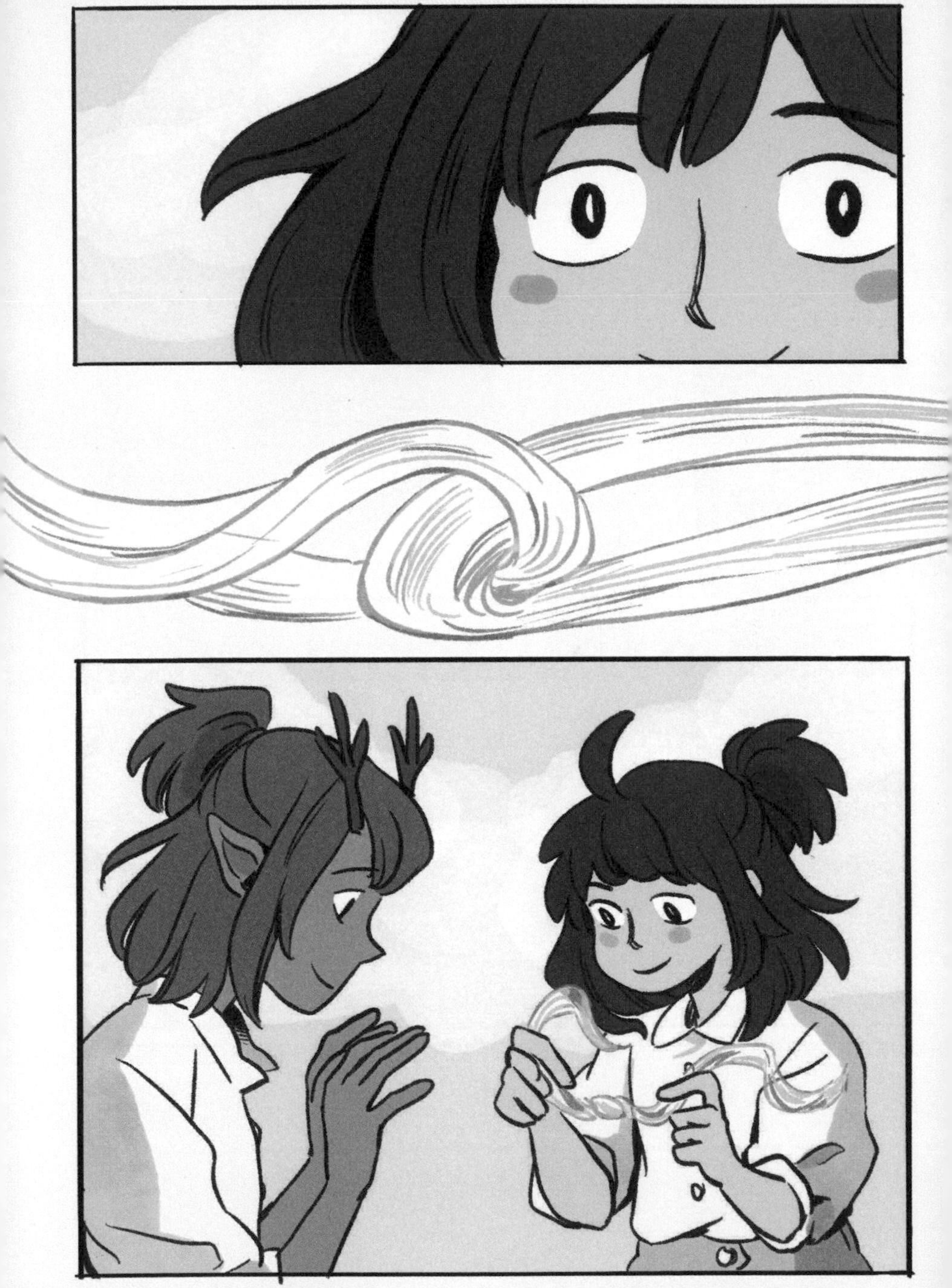

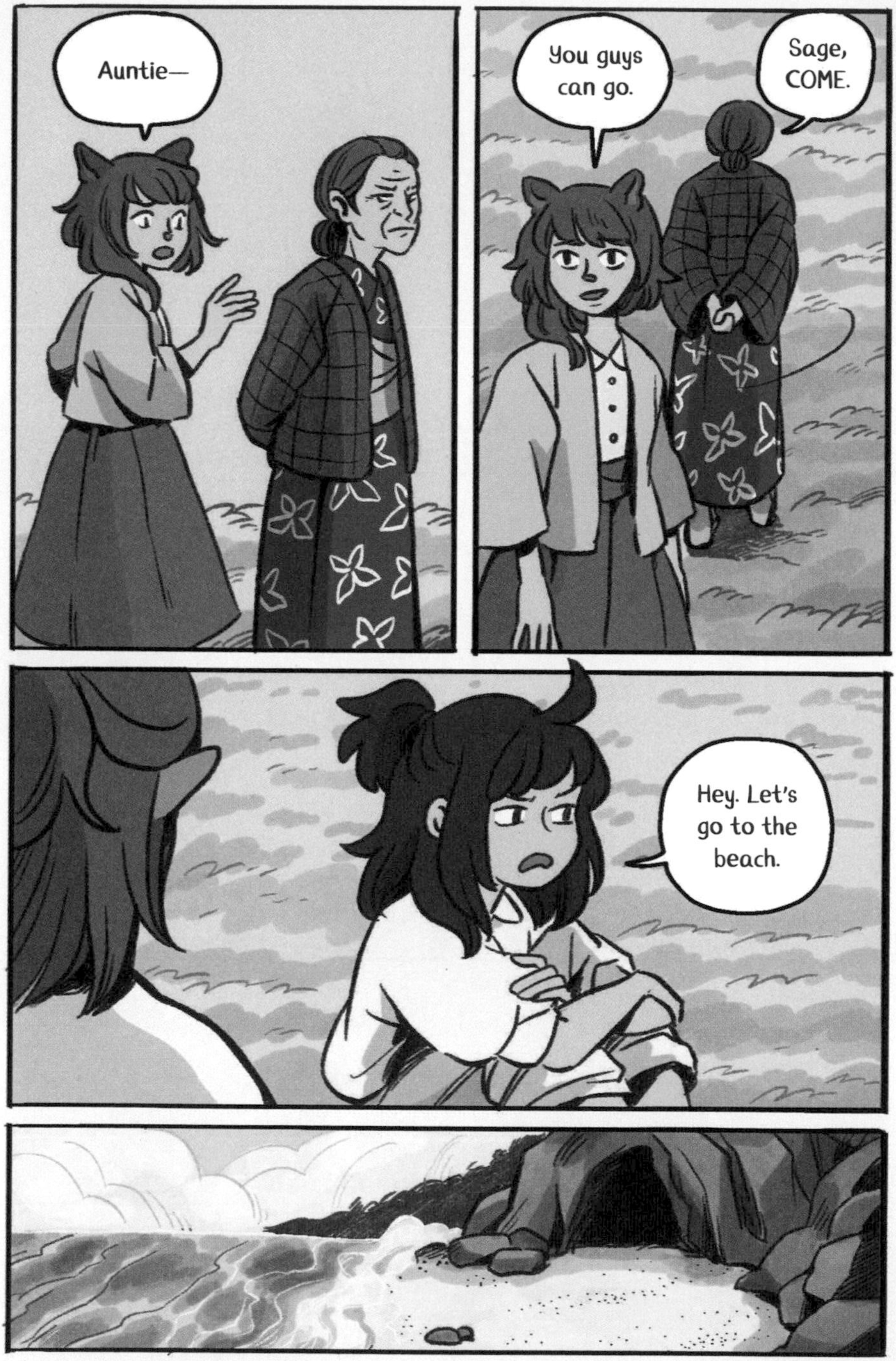
Auntie—
You guys can go.
Sage, COME.
Hey. Let's go to the beach.

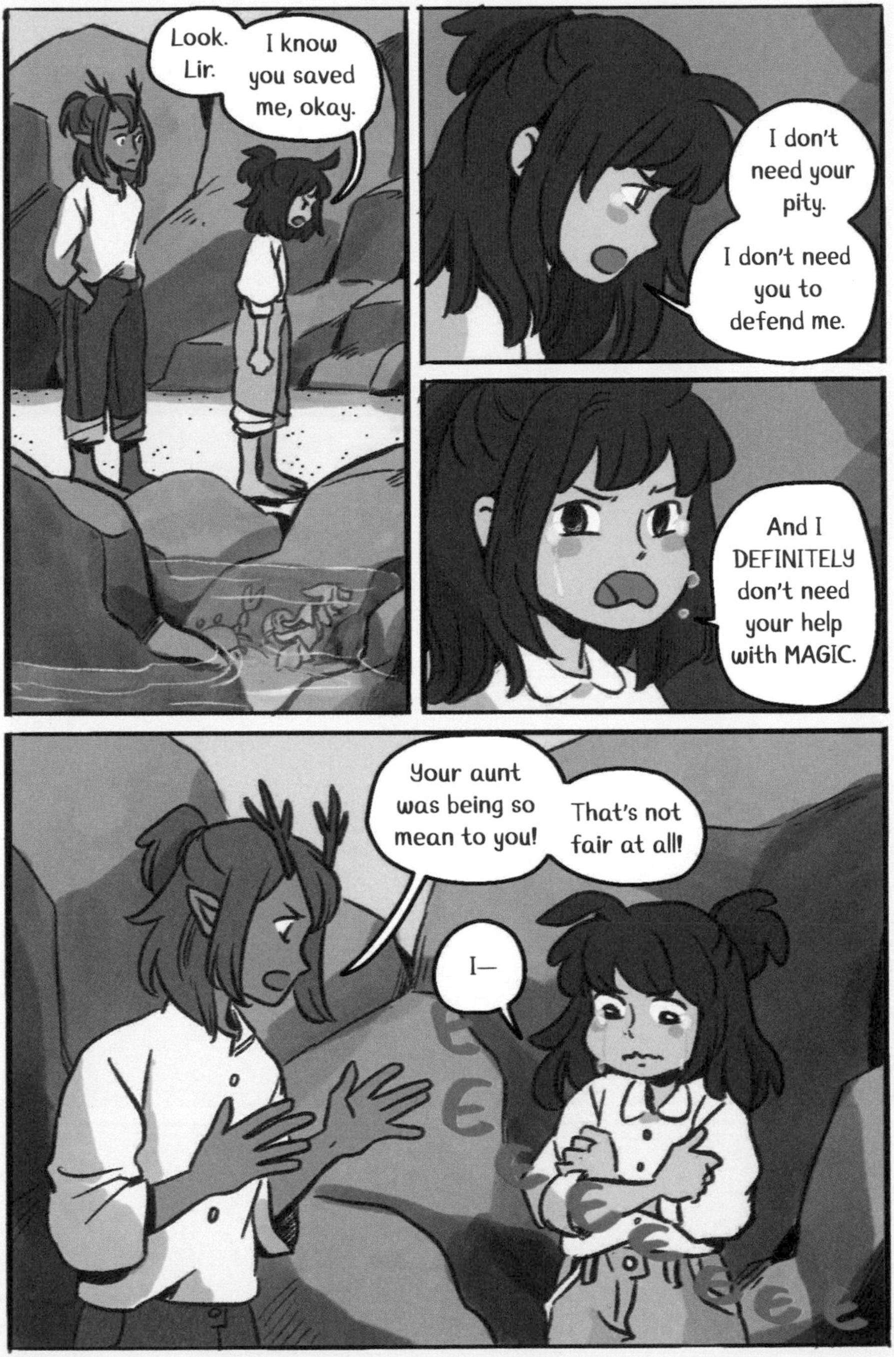
Look. Lir.
I know you saved me, okay.
I don't need your pity.
I don't need you to defend me.
And I DEFINITELY don't need your help with MAGIC.
Your aunt was being so mean to you!
That's not fair at all!
I—

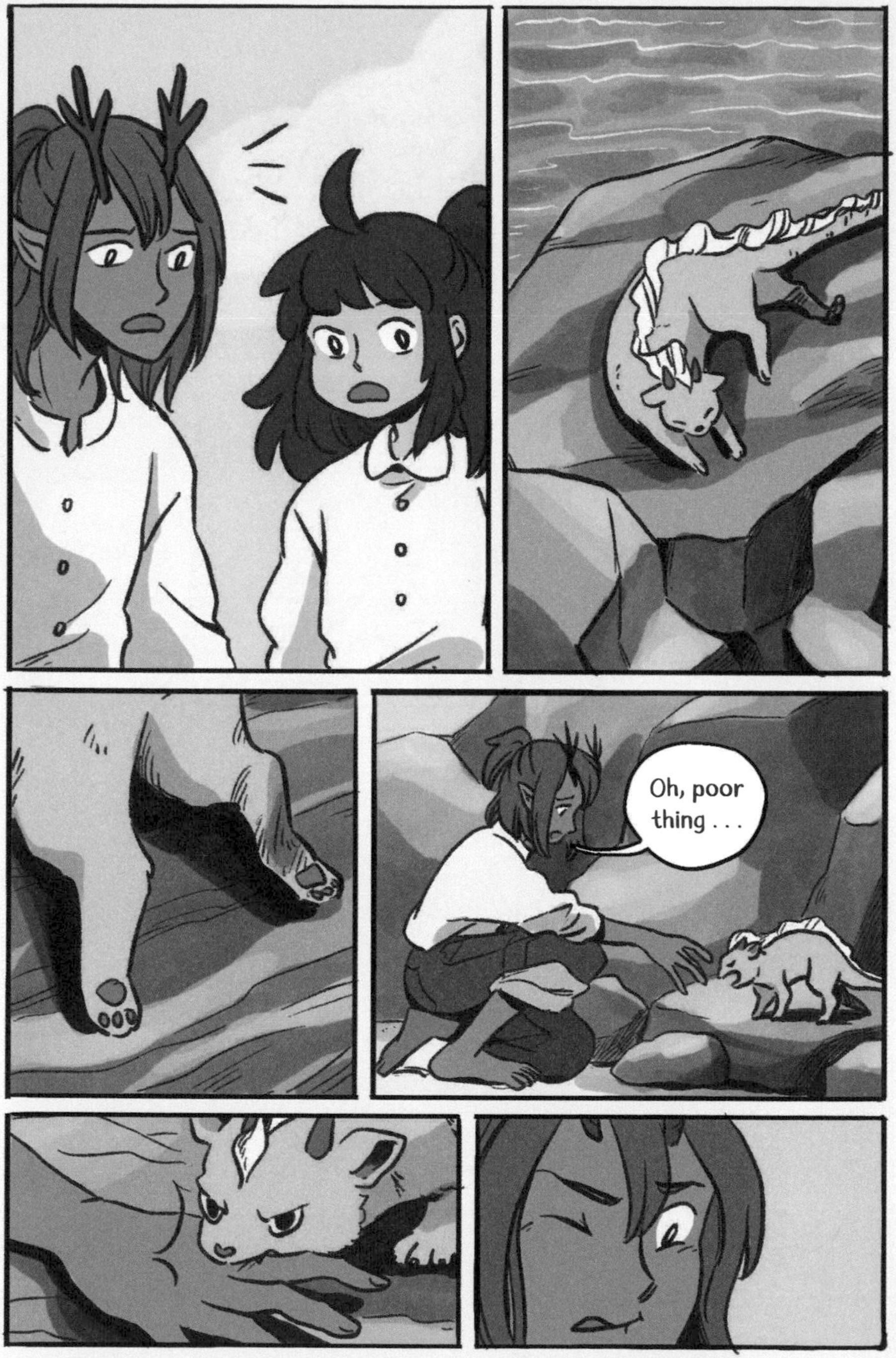
Oh, poor thing . . .

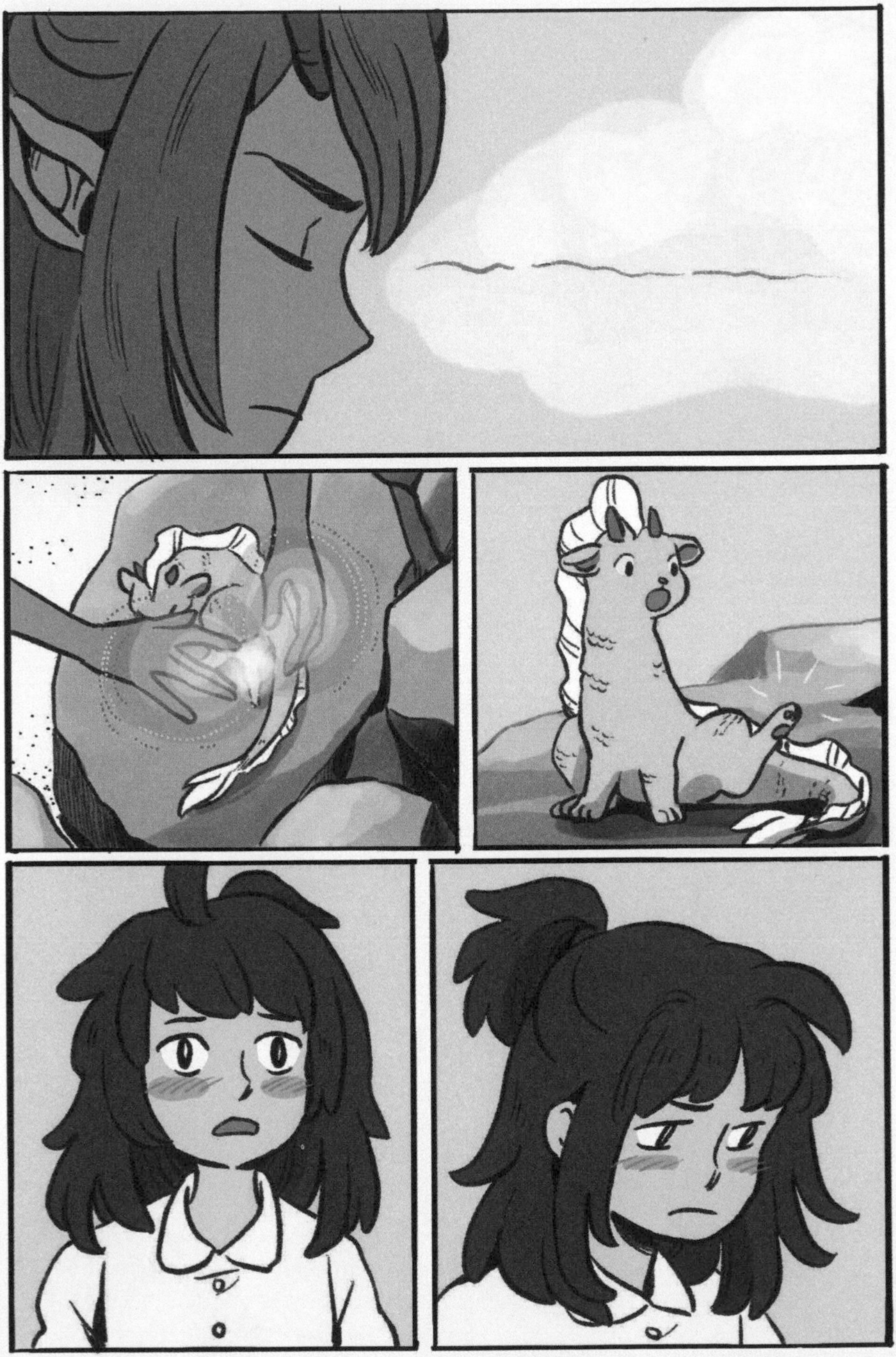

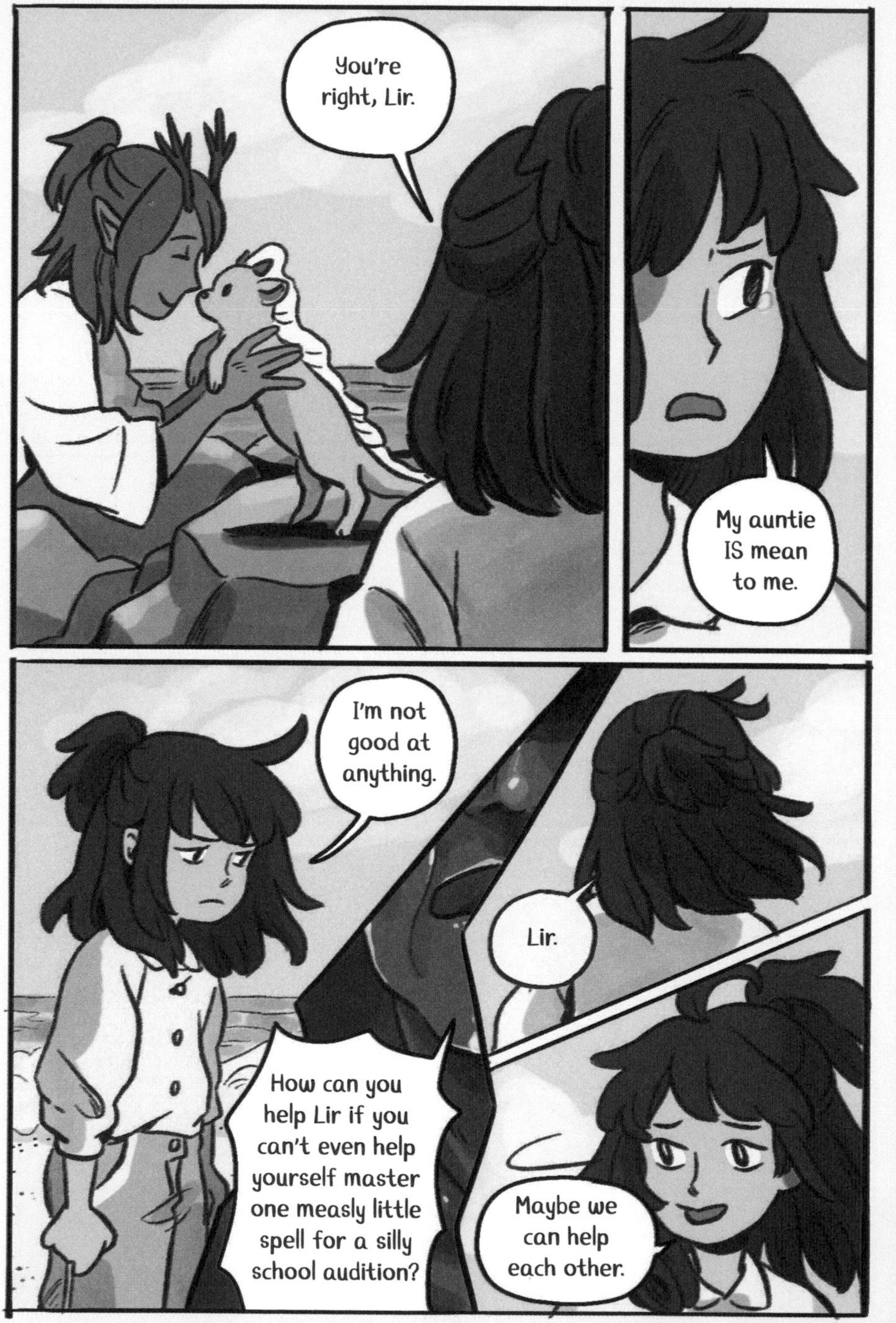
You're right, Lir.
My auntie IS mean to me.
I'm not good at anything.
Lir.
How can you help Lir if you can't even help yourself master one measly little spell for a silly school audition?
Maybe we can help each other.

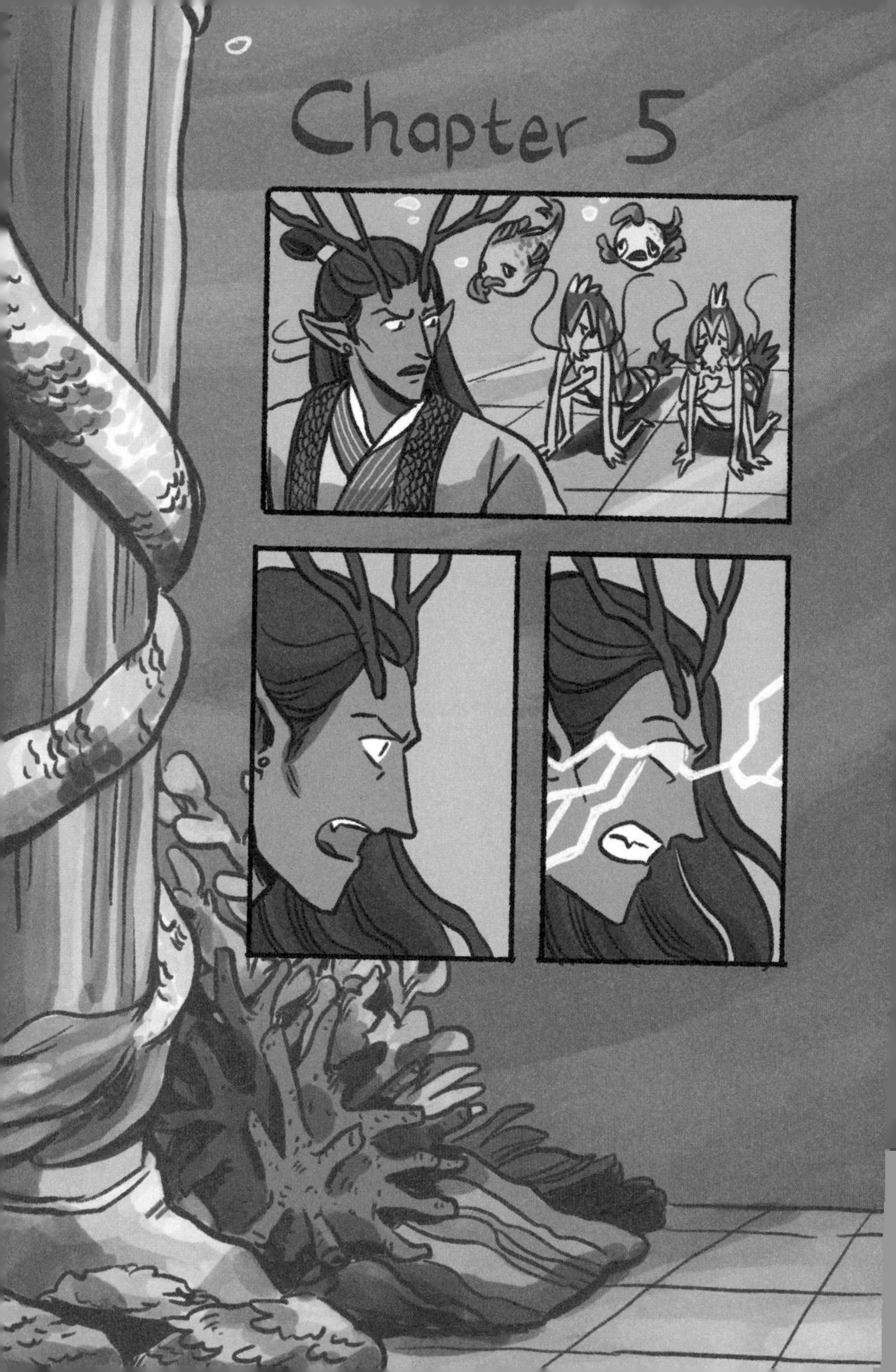
Chapter 5

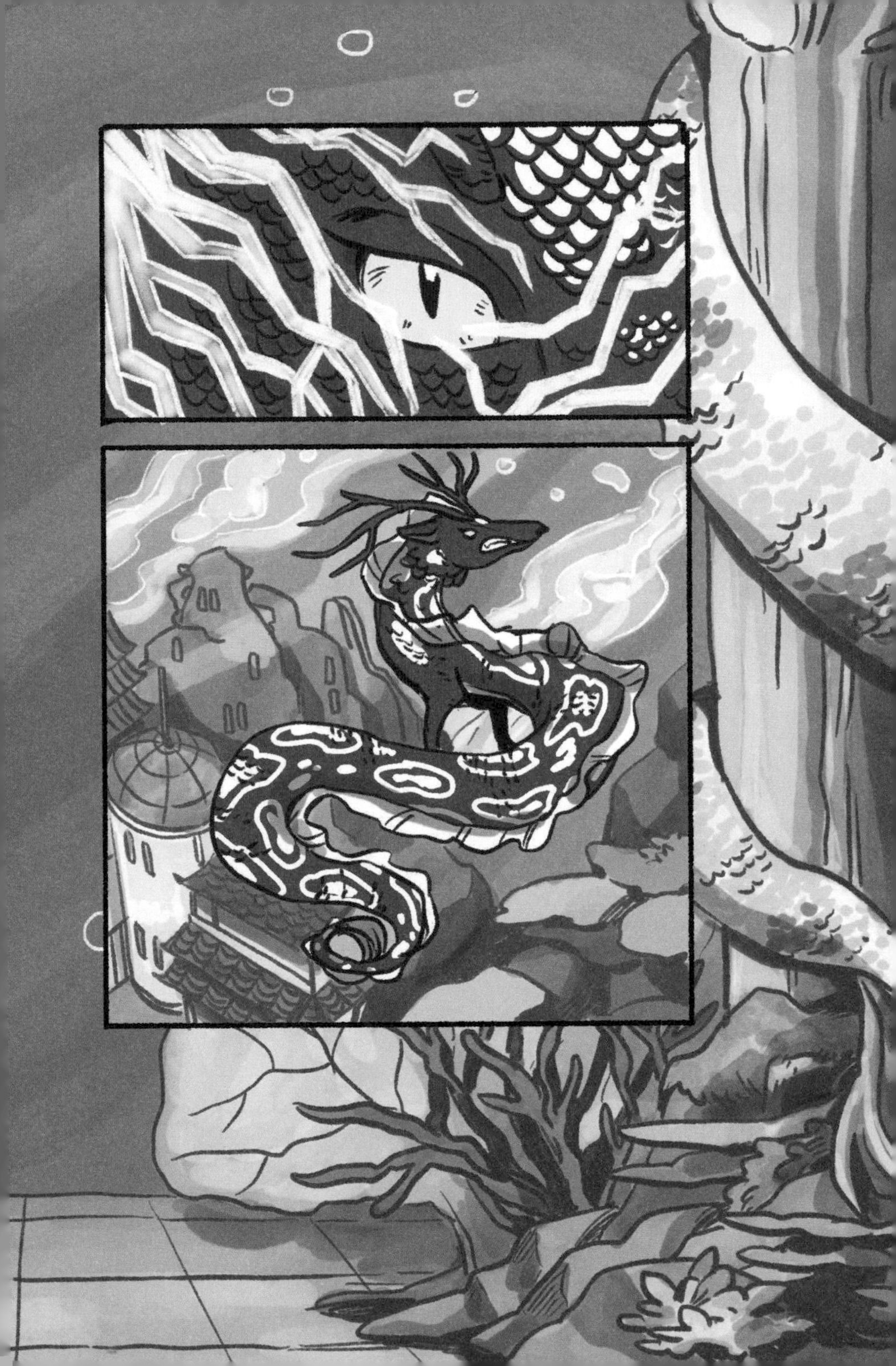

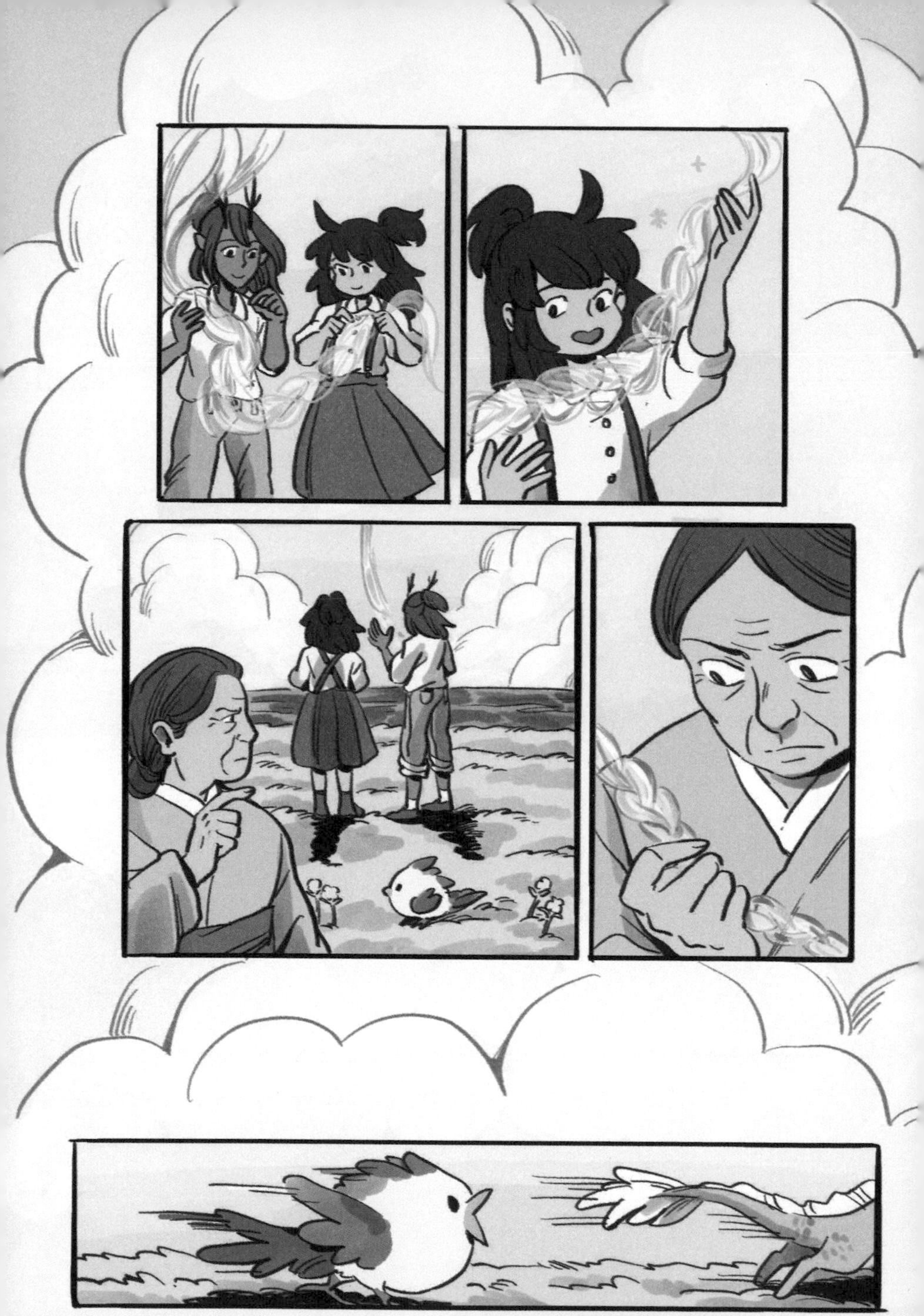

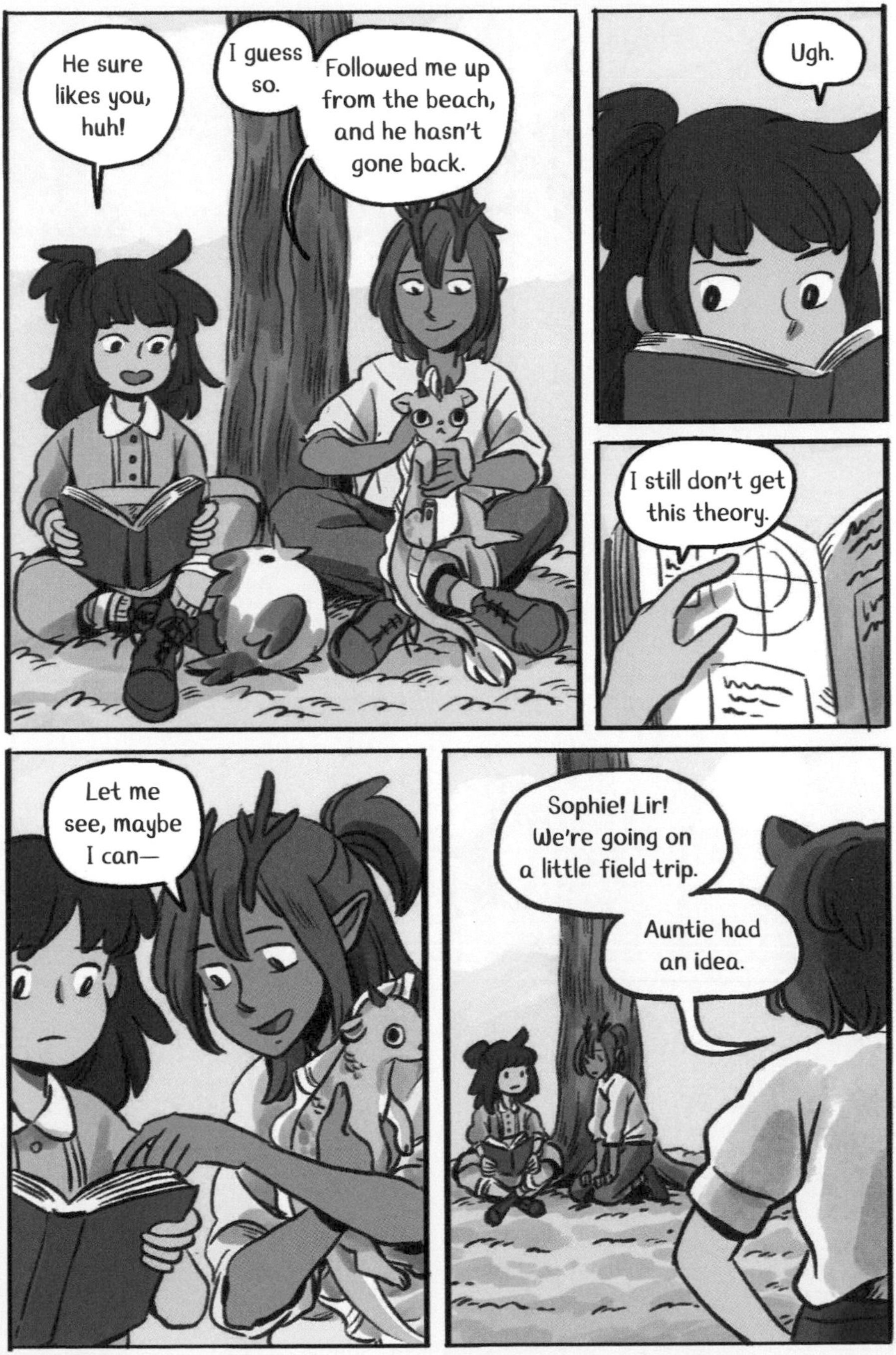
He sure likes you, huh!
I guess so.
Followed me up from the beach, and he hasn't gone back.
Ugh.
I still don't get this theory.
Let me see, maybe I can—
Sophie! Lir! We're going on a little field trip.
Auntie had an idea.

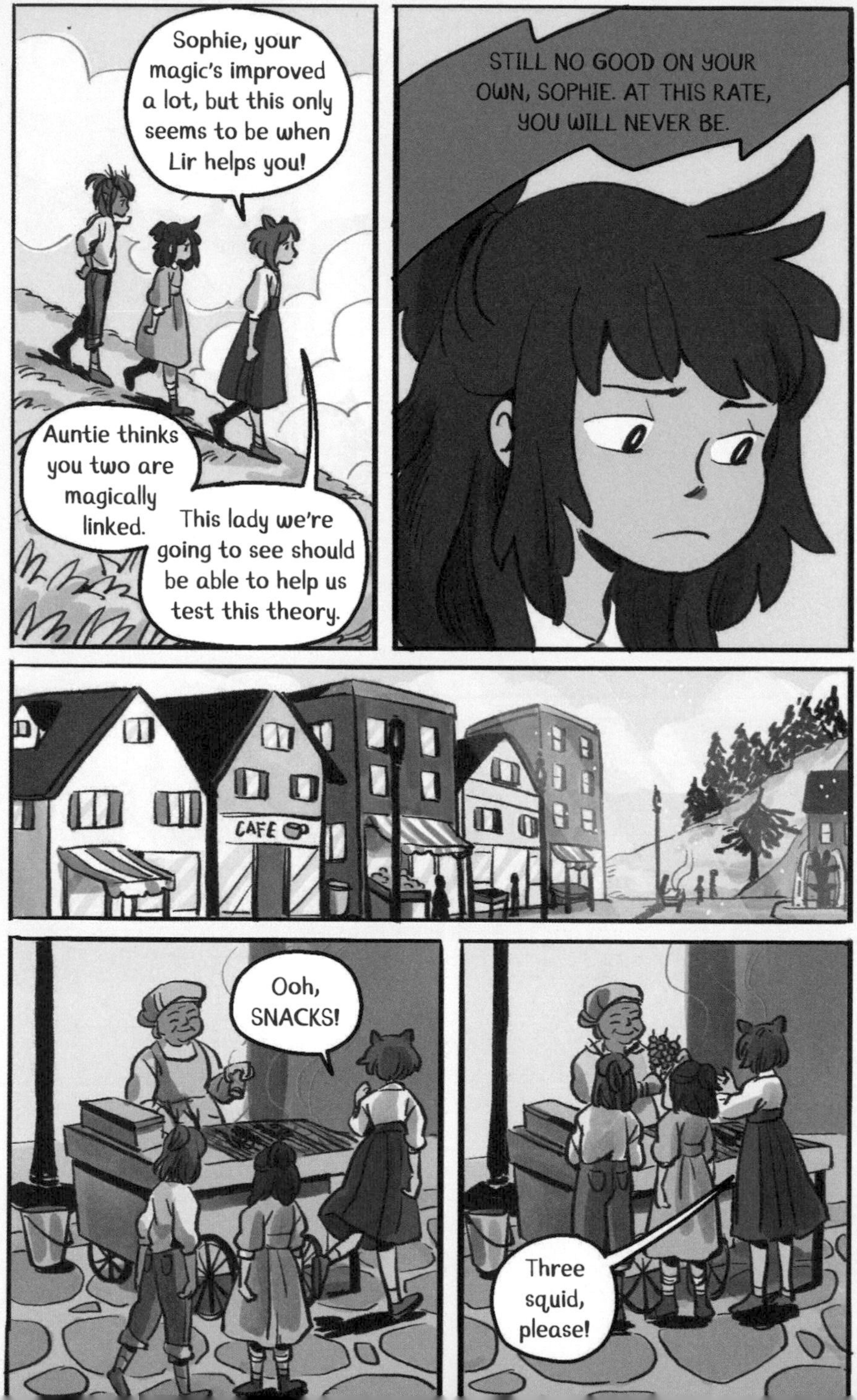
Sophie, your magic's improved a lot, but this only seems to be when Lir helps you!
Auntie thinks you two are magically linked.
This lady we're going to see should be able to help us test this theory.
STILL NO GOOD ON YOUR OWN, SOPHIE. AT THIS RATE, YOU WILL NEVER BE.
CAFE
Ooh, SNACKS!
Three squid, please!

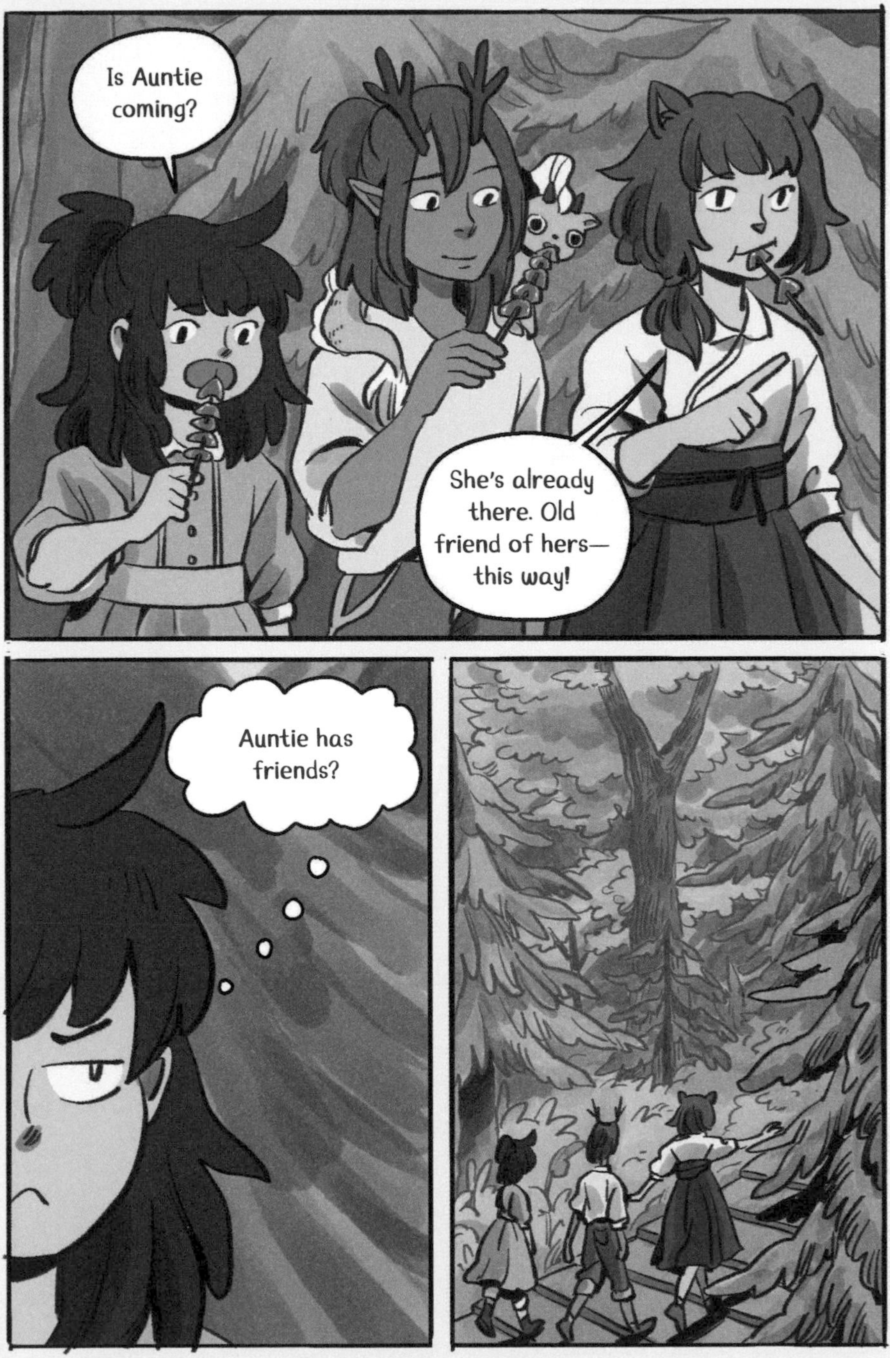
Is Auntie coming?
She's already there. Old friend of hers—this way!
Auntie has friends?

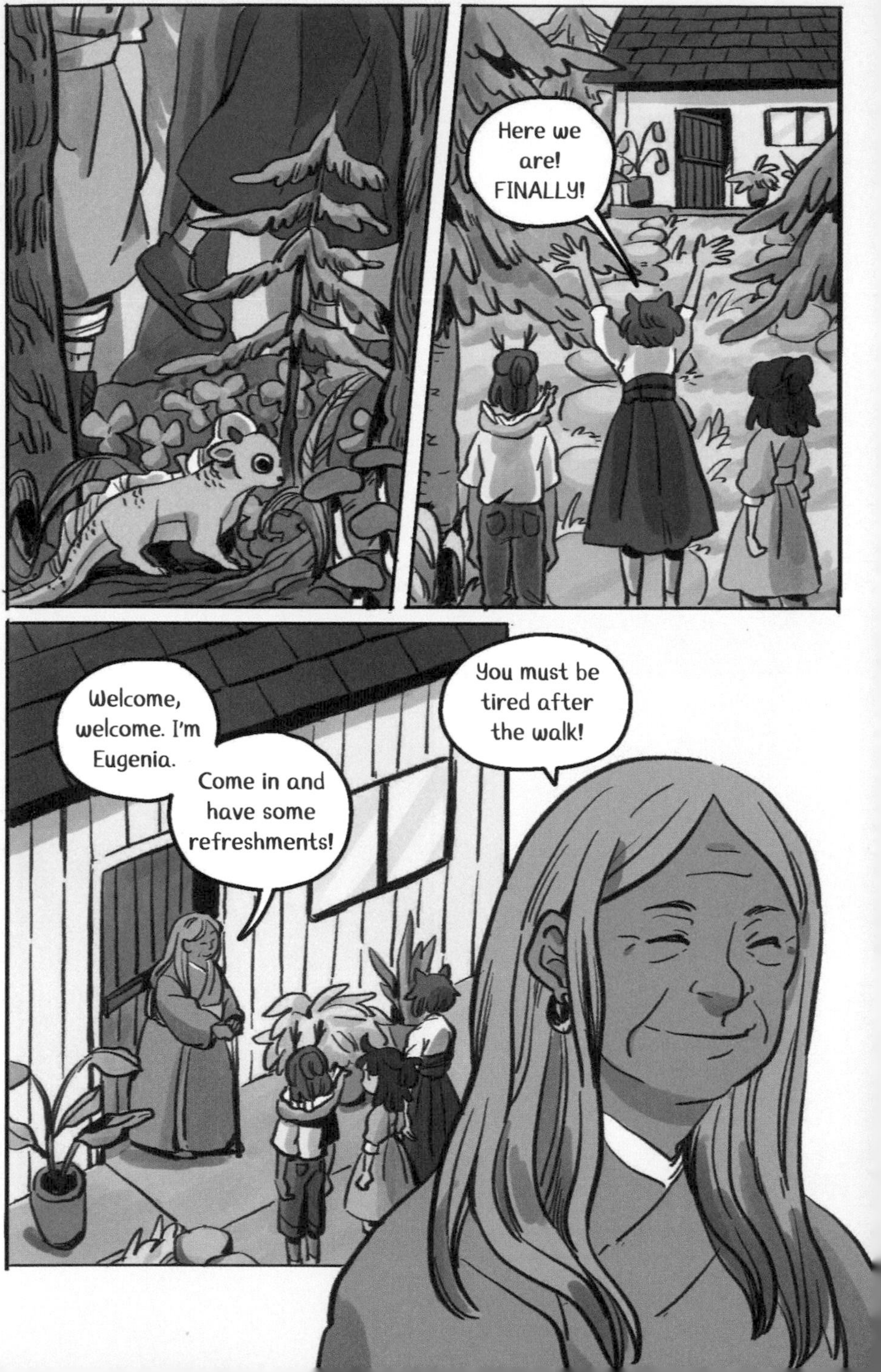
Here we are! FINALLY!
Welcome, welcome. I'm Eugenia.
Come in and have some refreshments!
You must be tired after the walk!

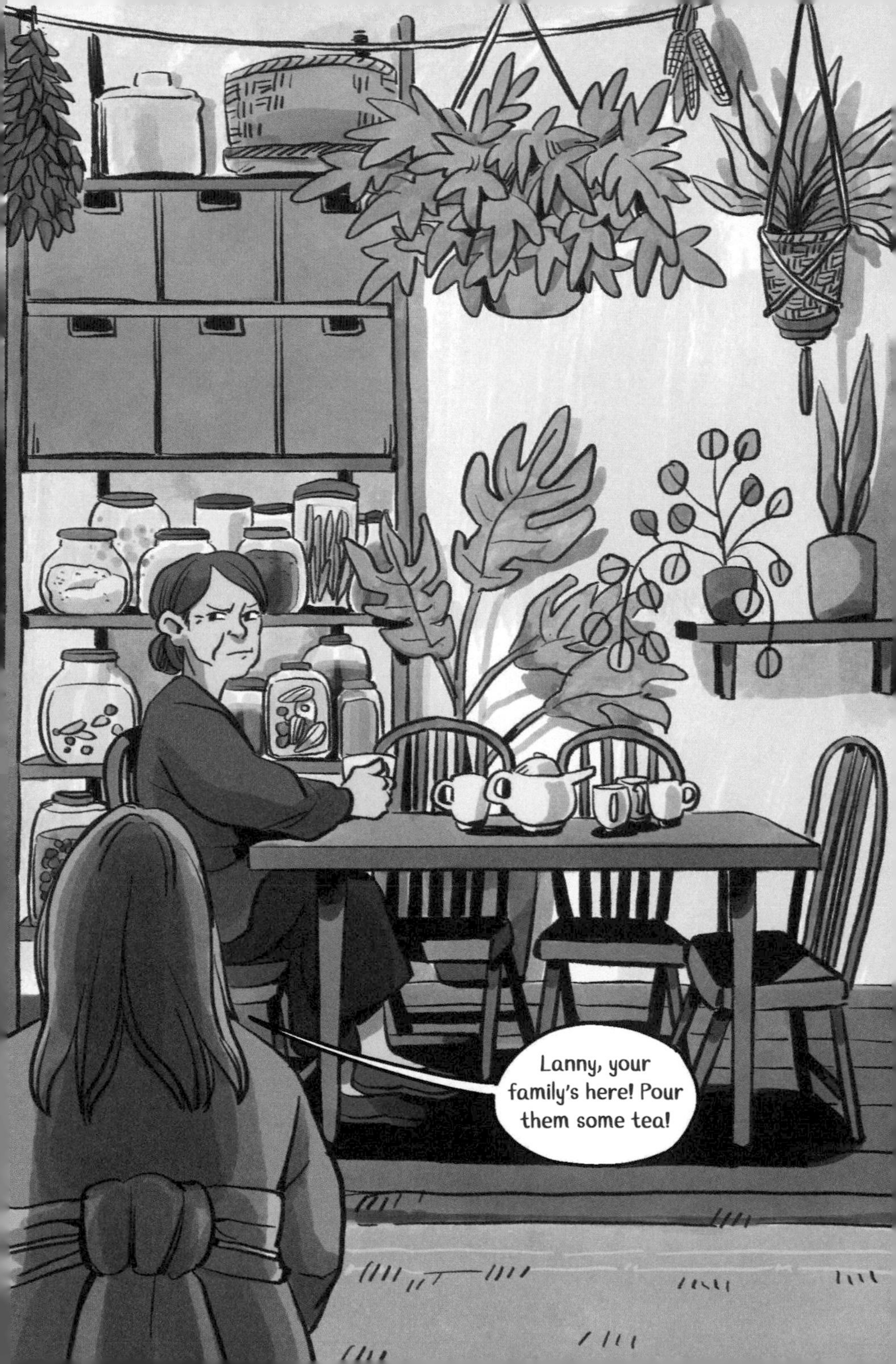
Lanny, your family's here! Pour them some tea!

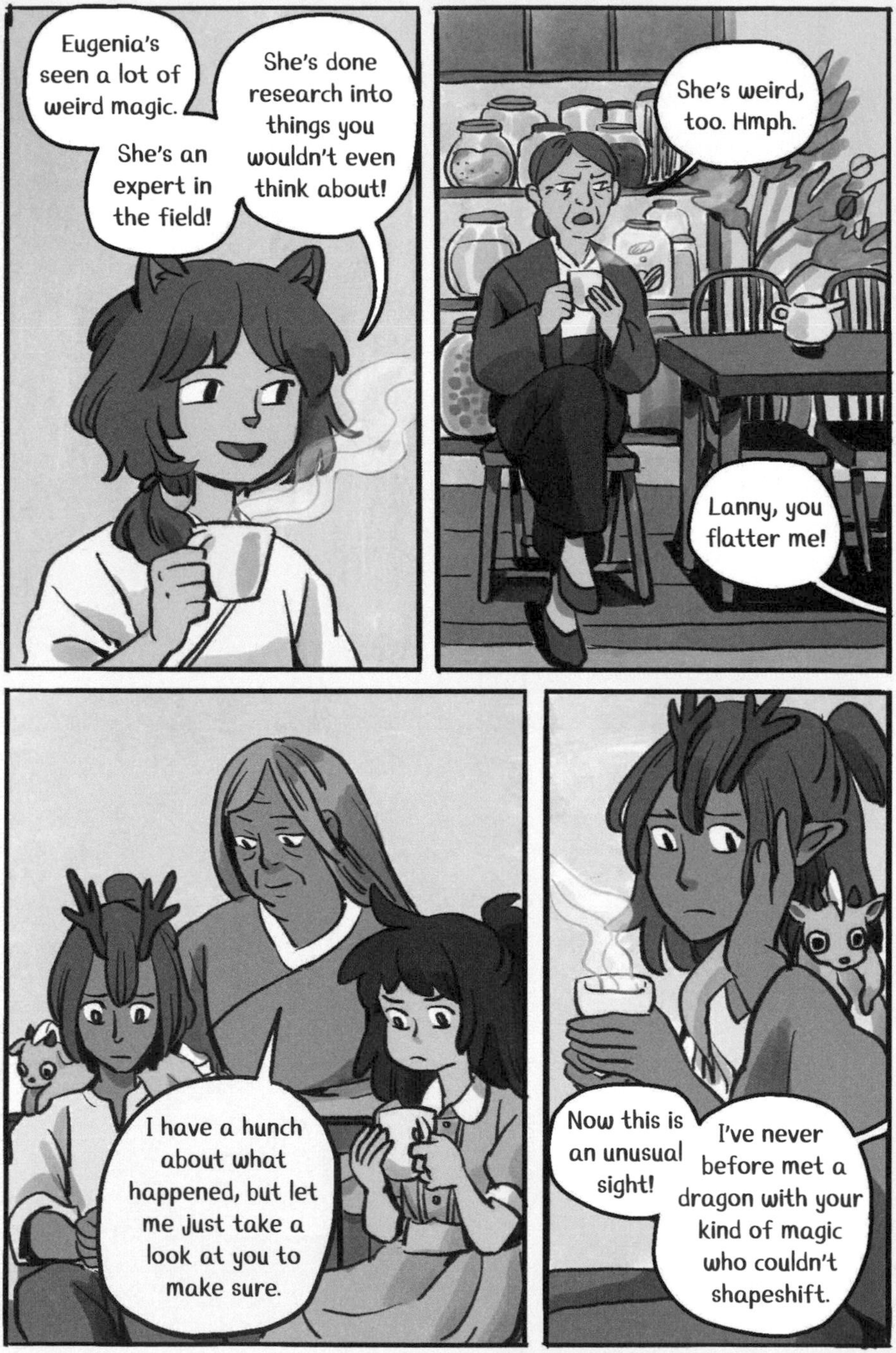
Eugenia's seen a lot of weird magic.
She's an expert in the field!
She's done research into things you wouldn't even think about!
She's weird, too. Hmph.
Lanny, you flatter me!
I have a hunch about what happened, but let me just take a look at you to make sure.
Now this is an unusual sight!
I've never before met a dragon with your kind of magic who couldn't shapeshift.

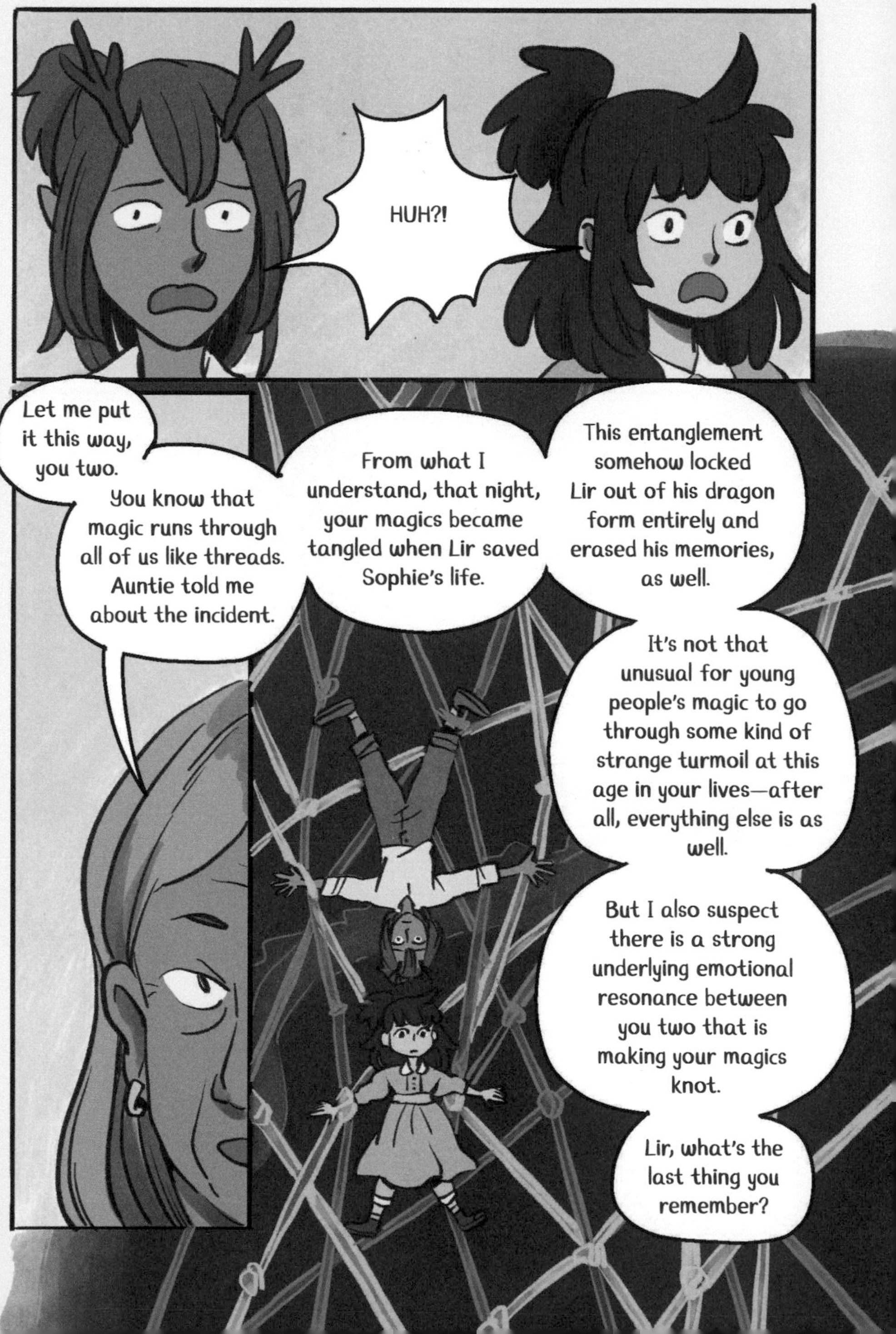
HUH?!
Let me put it this way, you two.
You know that magic runs through all of us like threads. Auntie told me about the incident.
From what I understand, that night, your magics became tangled when Lir saved Sophie's life.
This entanglement somehow locked Lir out of his dragon form entirely and erased his memories, as well.
It's not that unusual for young people's magic to go through some kind of strange turmoil at this age in your lives—after all, everything else is as well.
But I also suspect there is a strong underlying emotional resonance between you two that is making your magics knot.
Lir, what's the last thing you remember?

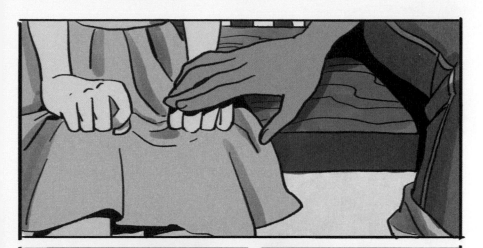

Lir . . . even though he's stuck here, he still wants to comfort me . . .

Ah, found it!

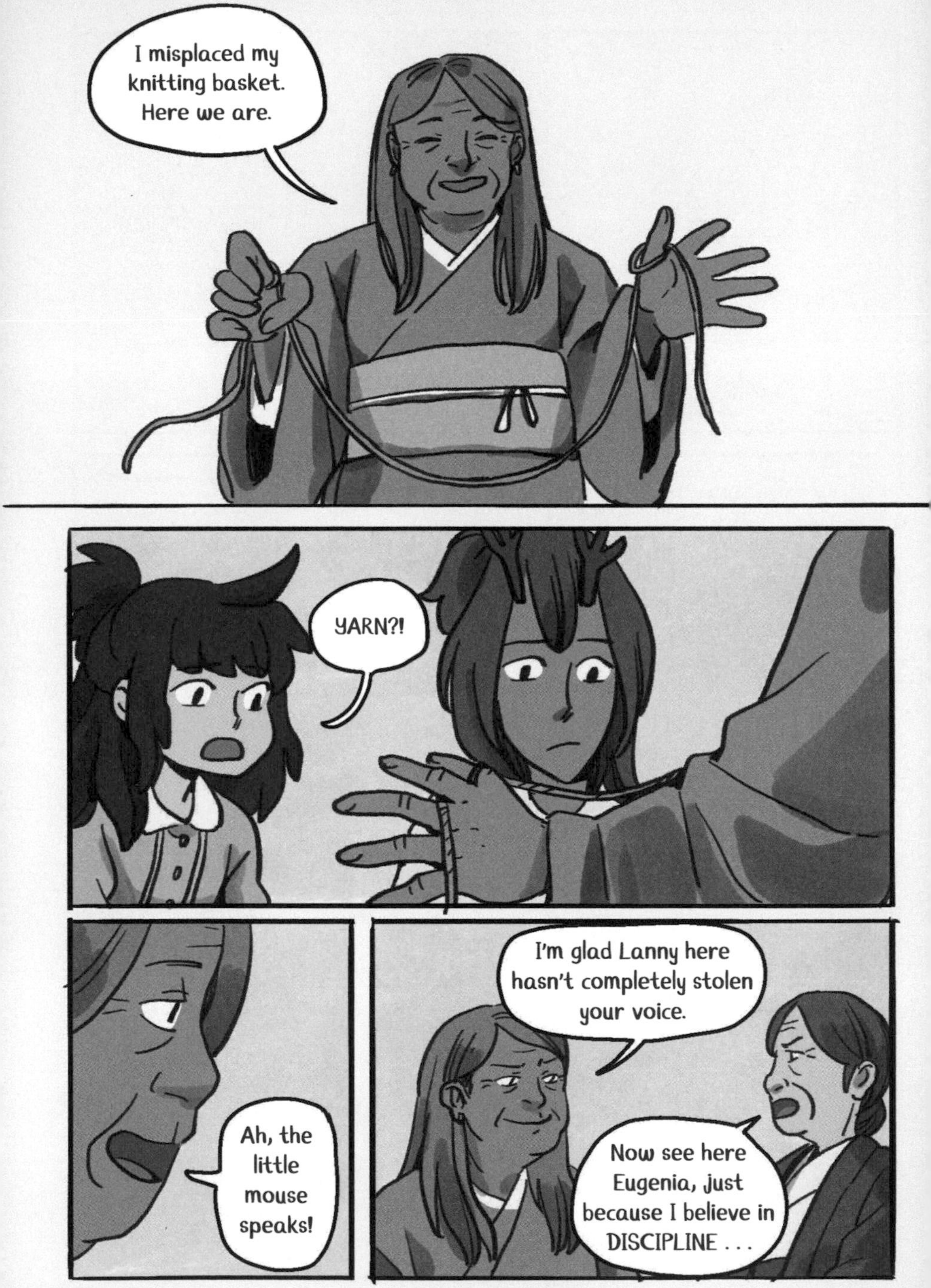
I misplaced my knitting basket. Here we are.
YARN?!
Ah, the little mouse speaks!
I'm glad Lanny here hasn't completely stolen your voice.
Now see here Eugenia, just because I believe in DISCIPLINE . . .

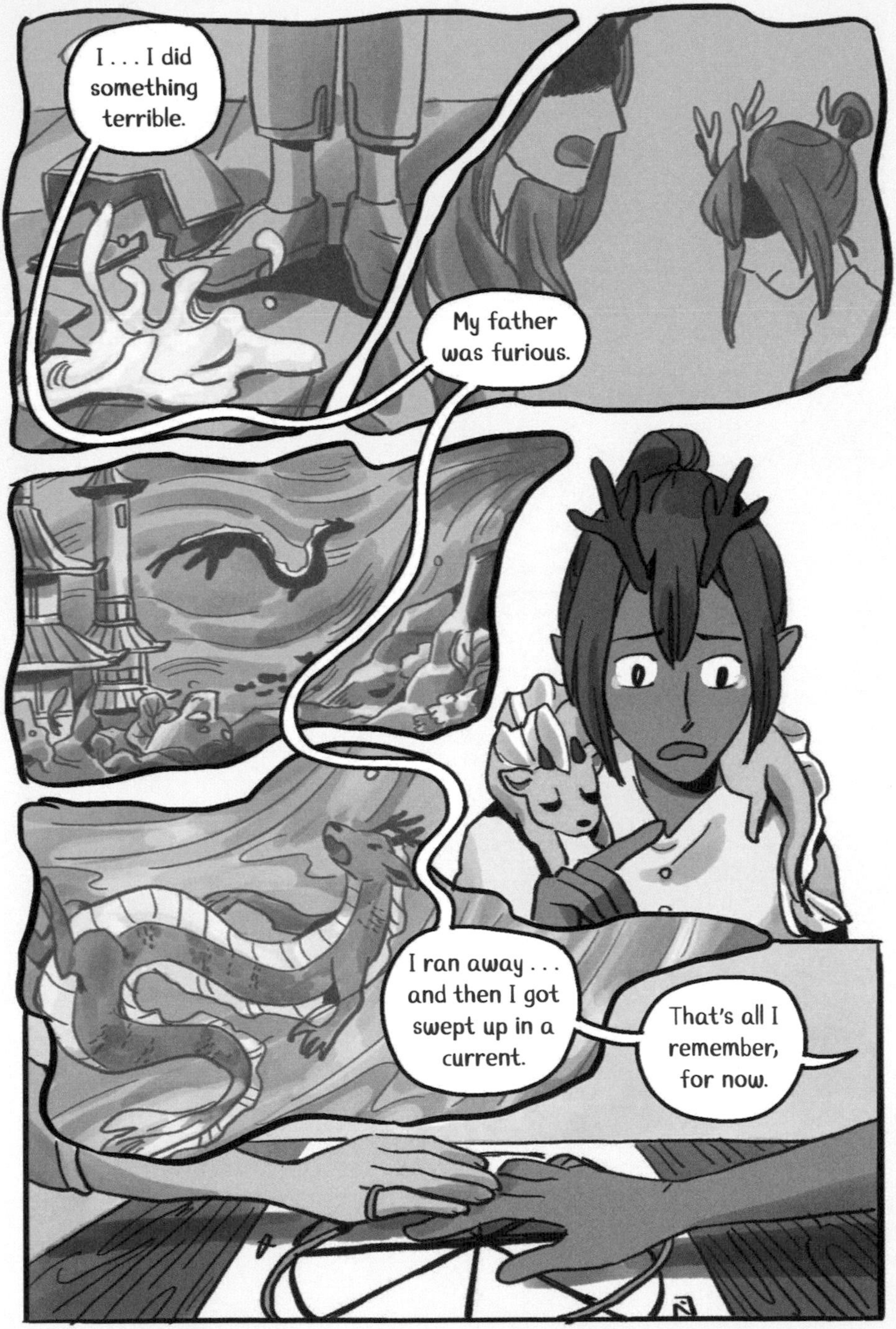
I . . . I did something terrible.
My father was furious.
I ran away . . . and then I got swept up in a current.
That's all I remember, for now.

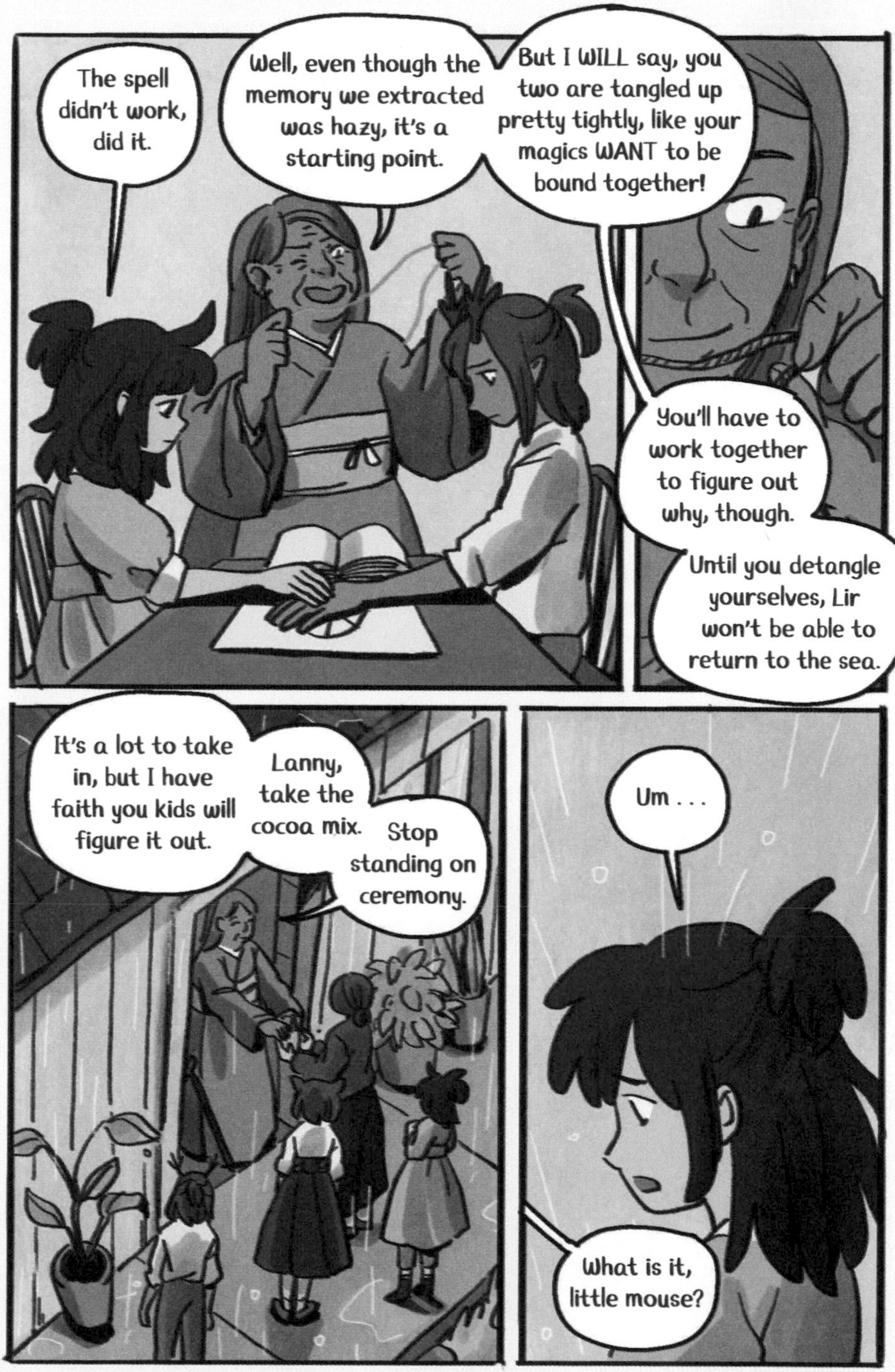
The spell didn't work, did it.
Well, even though the memory we extracted was hazy, it's a starting point.
But I WILL say, you two are tangled up pretty tightly, like your magics WANT to be bound together!
You'll have to work together to figure out why, though.
Until you detangle yourselves, Lir won't be able to return to the sea.
It's a lot to take in, but I have faith you kids will figure it out.
Lanny, take the cocoa mix.
Stop standing on ceremony.
Um . . .
What is it, little mouse?

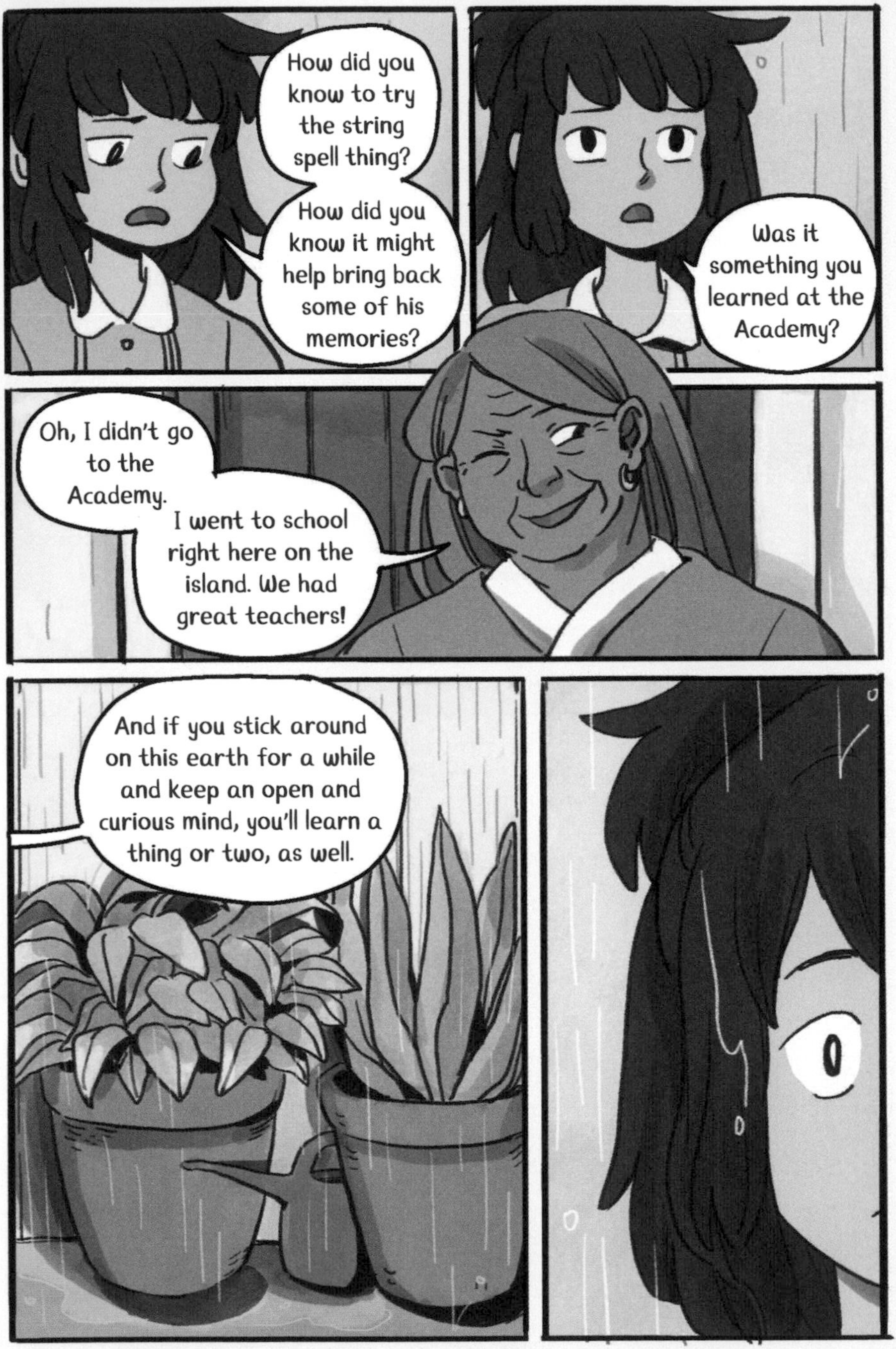
How did you know to try the string spell thing?
How did you know it might help bring back some of his memories?
Was it something you learned at the Academy?
Oh, I didn't go to the Academy.
I went to school right here on the island. We had great teachers!
And if you stick around on this earth for a while and keep an open and curious mind, you'll learn a thing or two, as well.

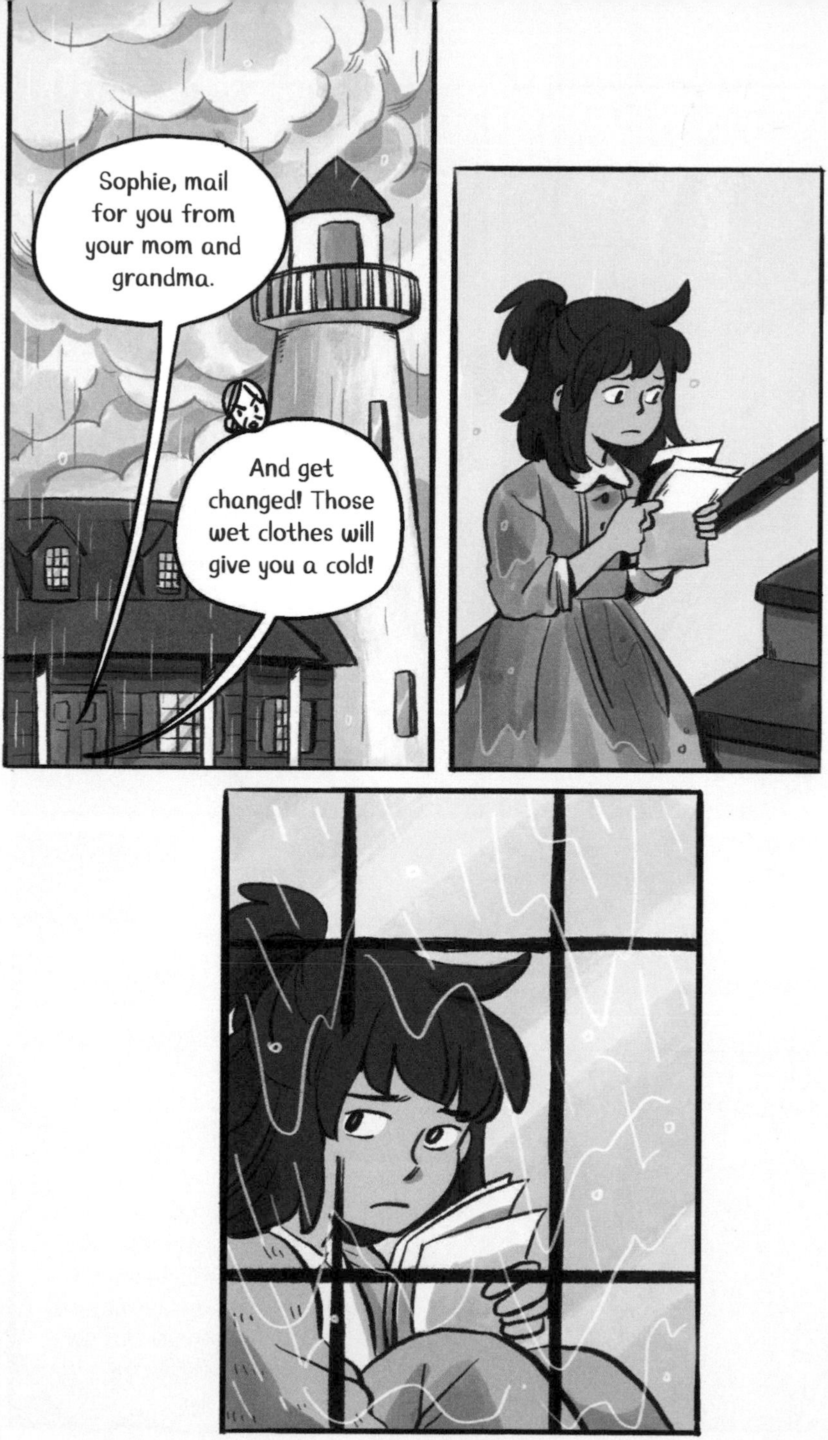
Sophie, mail for you from your mom and grandma.
And get changed! Those wet clothes will give you a cold!

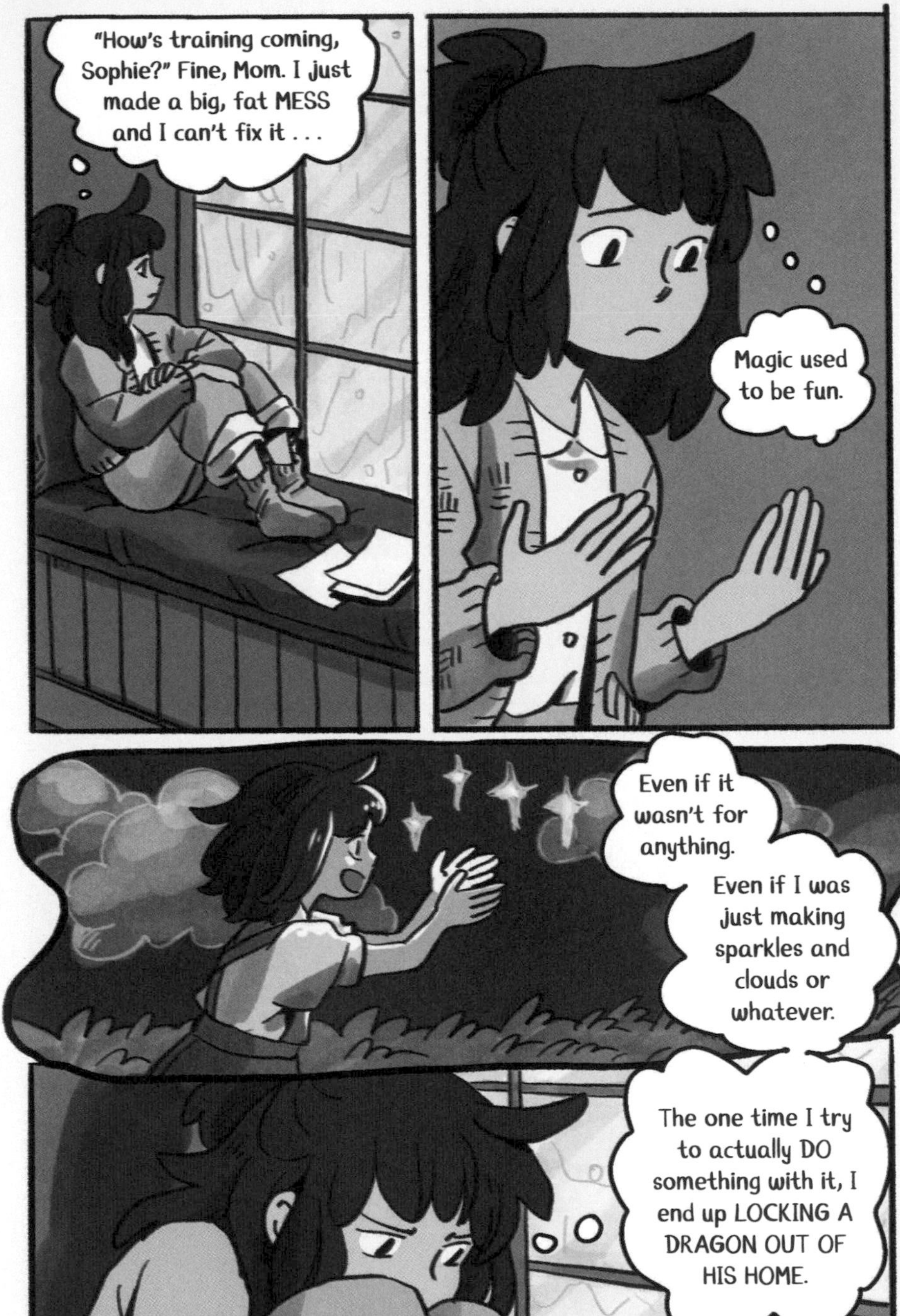

"How's training coming, Sophie?" Fine, Mom. I just made a big, fat MESS and I can't fix it . . .
Magic used to be fun.
Even if it wasn't for anything.
Even if I was just making sparkles and clouds or whatever.
The one time I try to actually DO something with it, I end up LOCKING A DRAGON OUT OF HIS HOME.

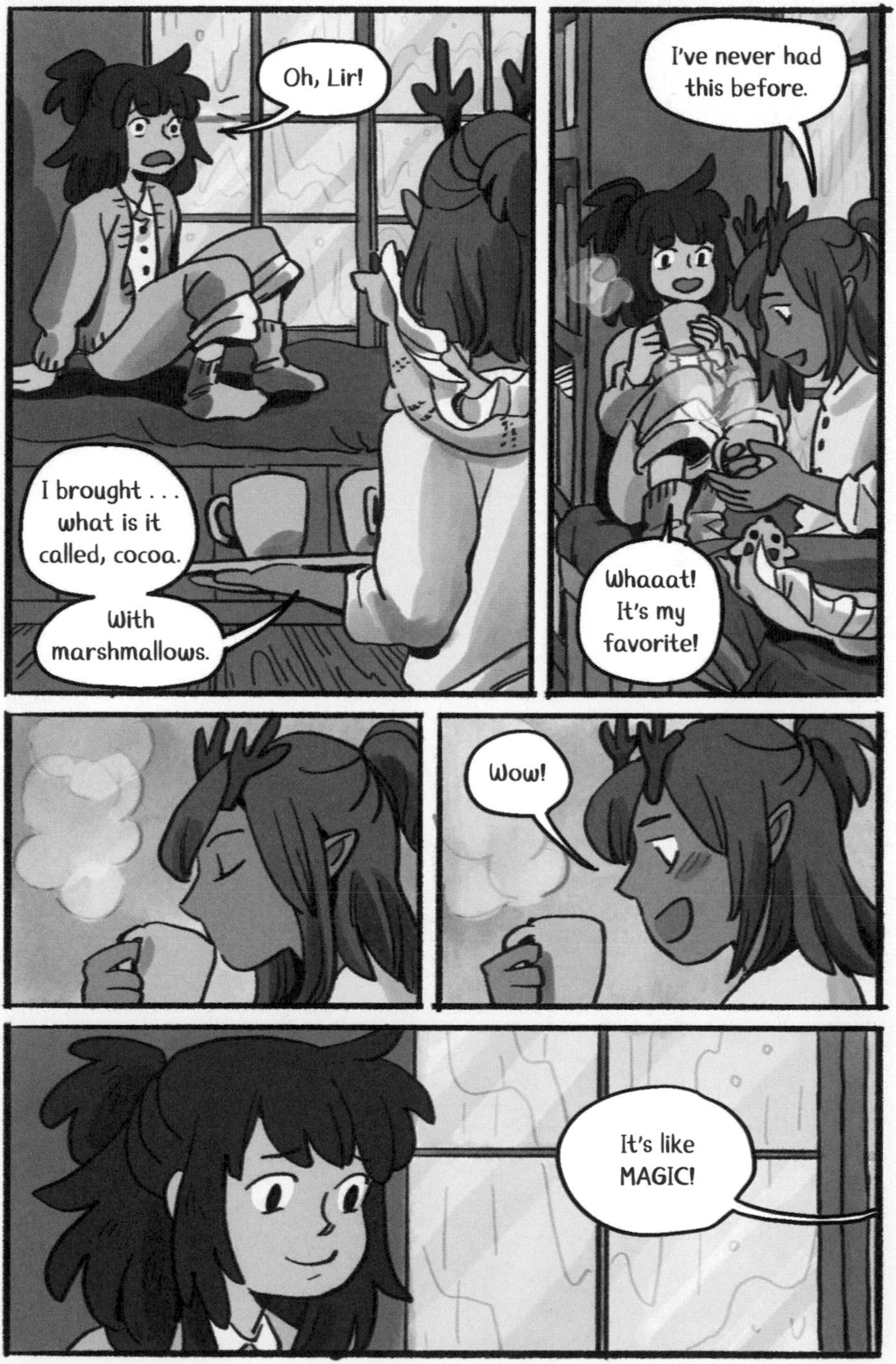
Oh, Lir!
I brought . . . what is it called, cocoa.
With marshmallows.
I've never had this before.
Whaaat! It's my favorite!
Wow!
It's like MAGIC!

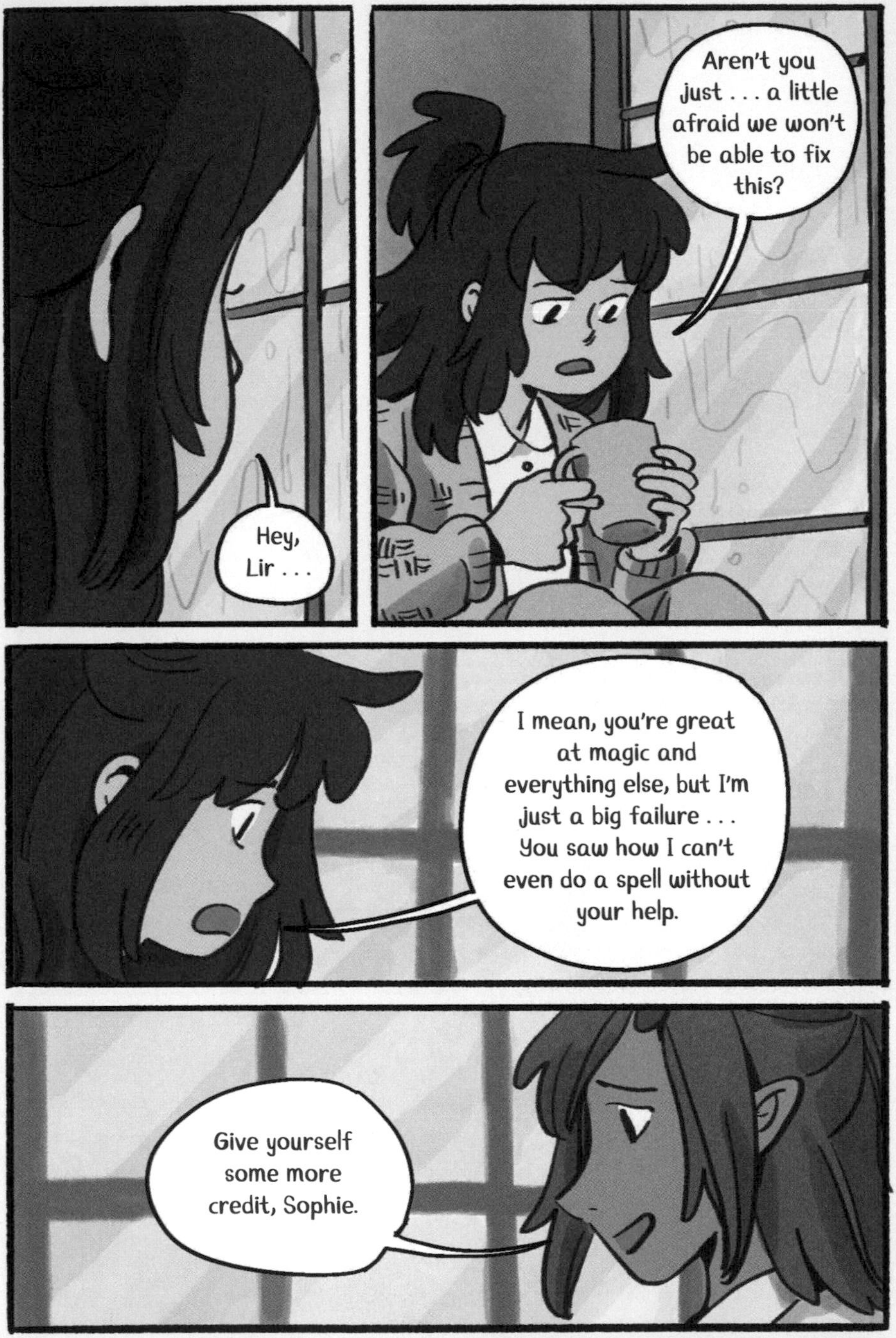
Hey, Lir . . .
Aren't you just . . . a little afraid we won't be able to fix this?
I mean, you're great at magic and everything else, but I'm just a big failure . . . You saw how I can't even do a spell without your help.
Give yourself some more credit, Sophie.

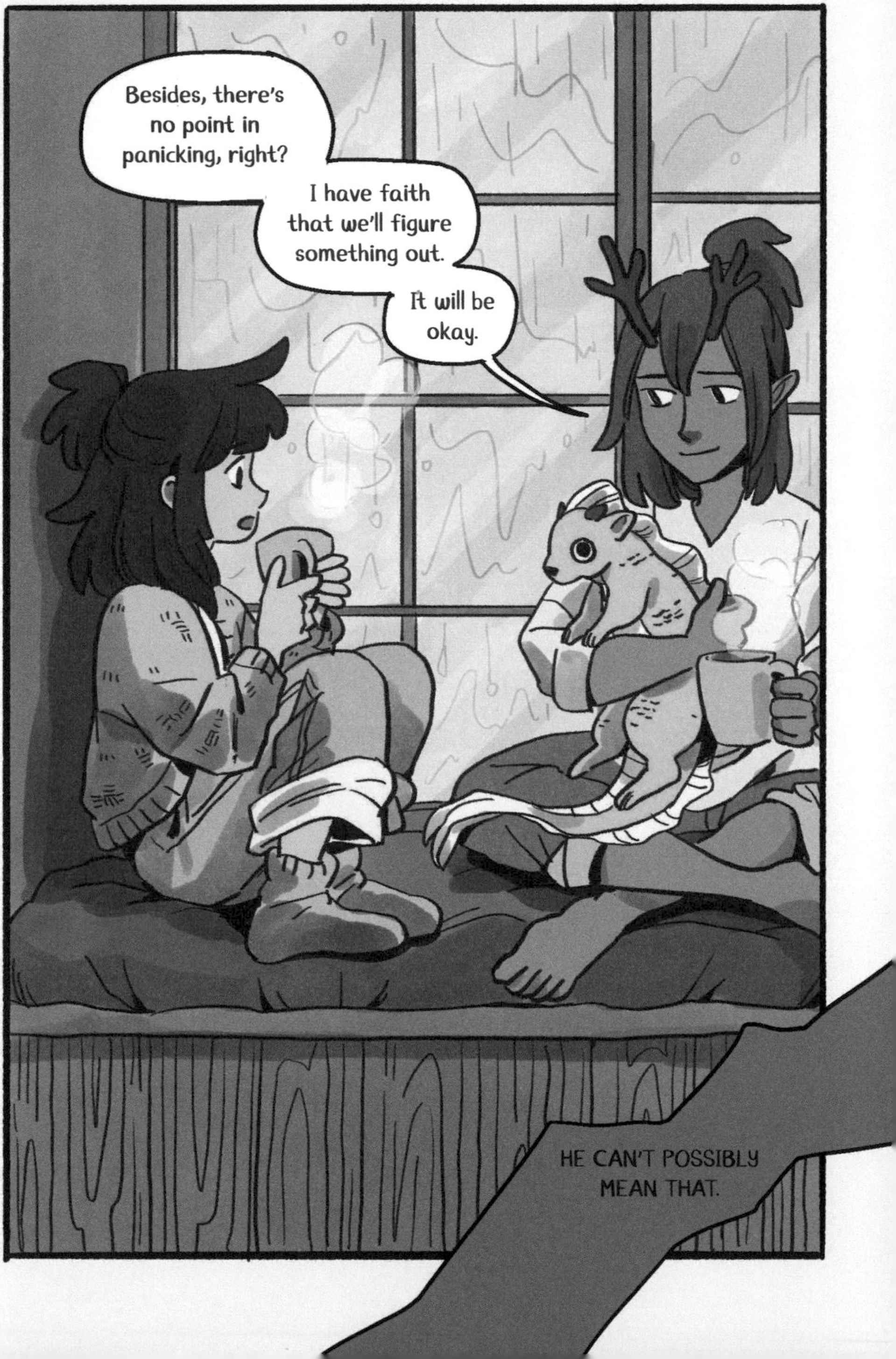
Besides, there's no point in panicking, right?
I have faith that we'll figure something out.
It will be okay.
HE CAN'T POSSIBLY MEAN THAT.

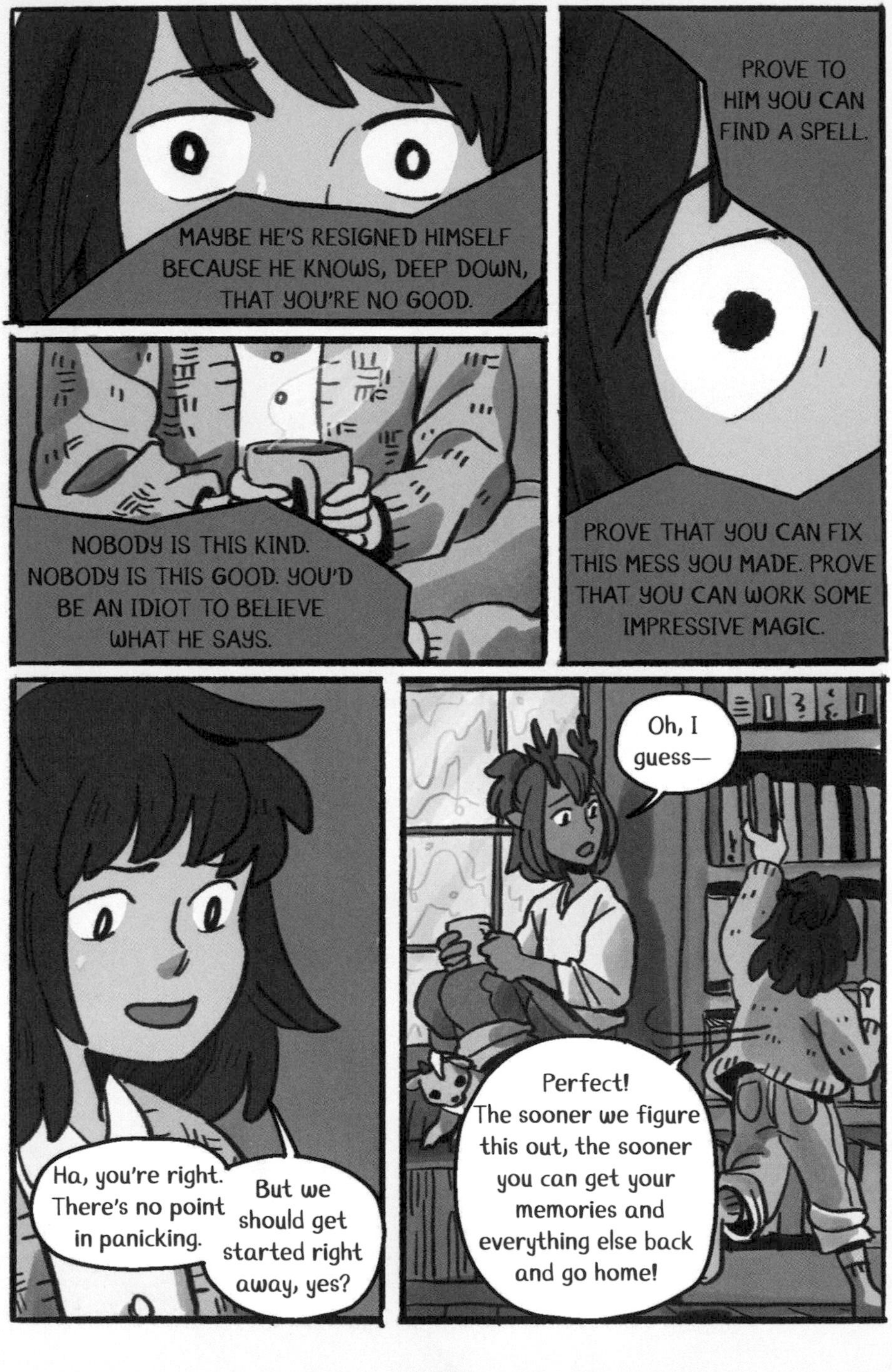
MAYBE HE'S RESIGNED HIMSELF BECAUSE HE KNOWS, DEEP DOWN, THAT YOU'RE NO GOOD.
PROVE TO HIM YOU CAN FIND A SPELL.
NOBODY IS THIS KIND. NOBODY IS THIS GOOD. YOU'D BE AN IDIOT TO BELIEVE WHAT HE SAYS.
PROVE THAT YOU CAN FIX THIS MESS YOU MADE. PROVE THAT YOU CAN WORK SOME IMPRESSIVE MAGIC.
Ha, you're right. There's no point in panicking.
But we should get started right away, yes?
Oh, I guess—
Perfect! The sooner we figure this out, the sooner you can get your memories and everything else back and go home!

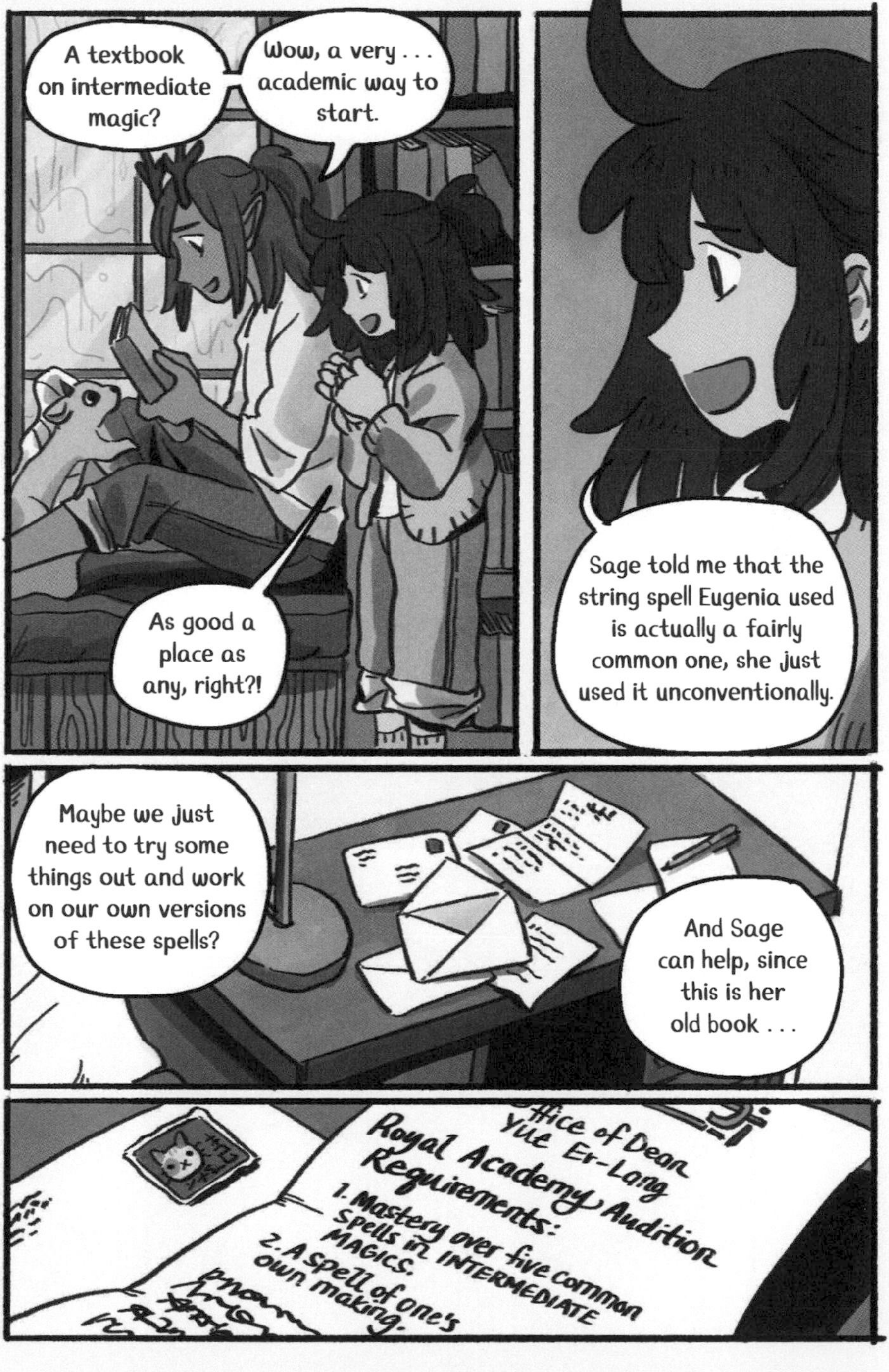
A textbook on intermediate magic?
Wow, a very . . . academic way to start.
As good a place as any, right?!
Sage told me that the string spell Eugenia used is actually a fairly common one, she just used it unconventionally.
Maybe we just need to try some things out and work on our own versions of these spells?
And Sage can help, since this is her old book . . .
Office of Dean
Yue Er-Lang
Royal Academy Audition
Requirements:
1. Mastery over five common Spells in INTERMEDIATE MAGICS.
2. A Spell of one's own making.

Chapter 6

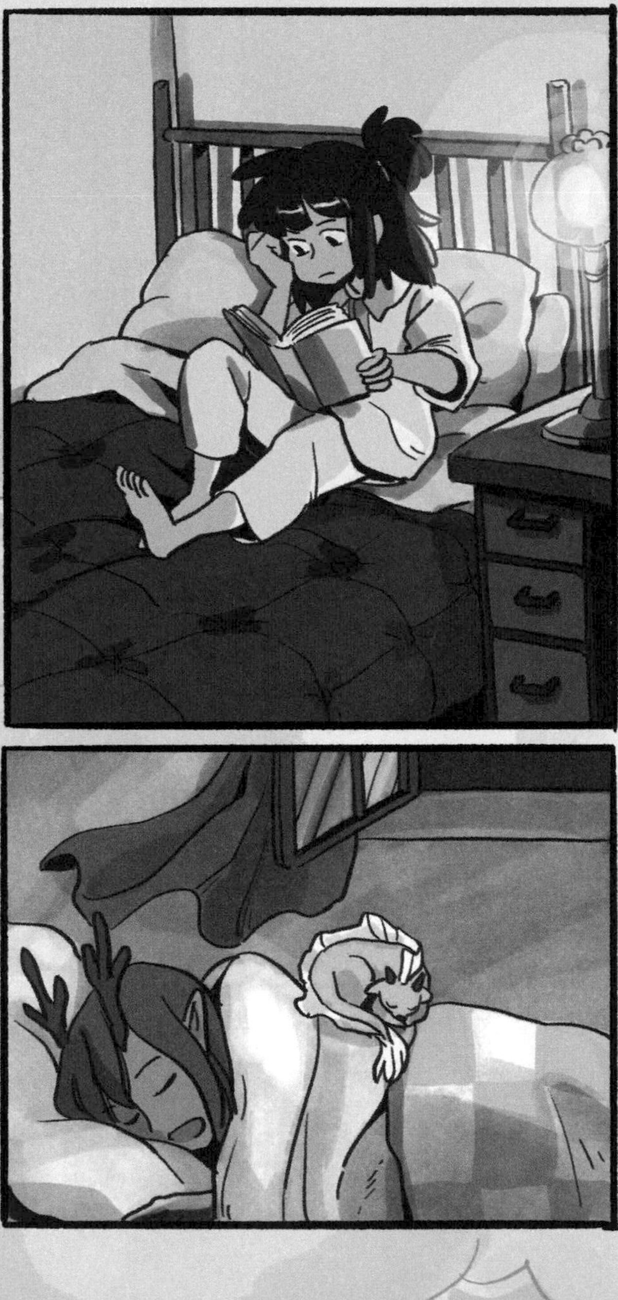

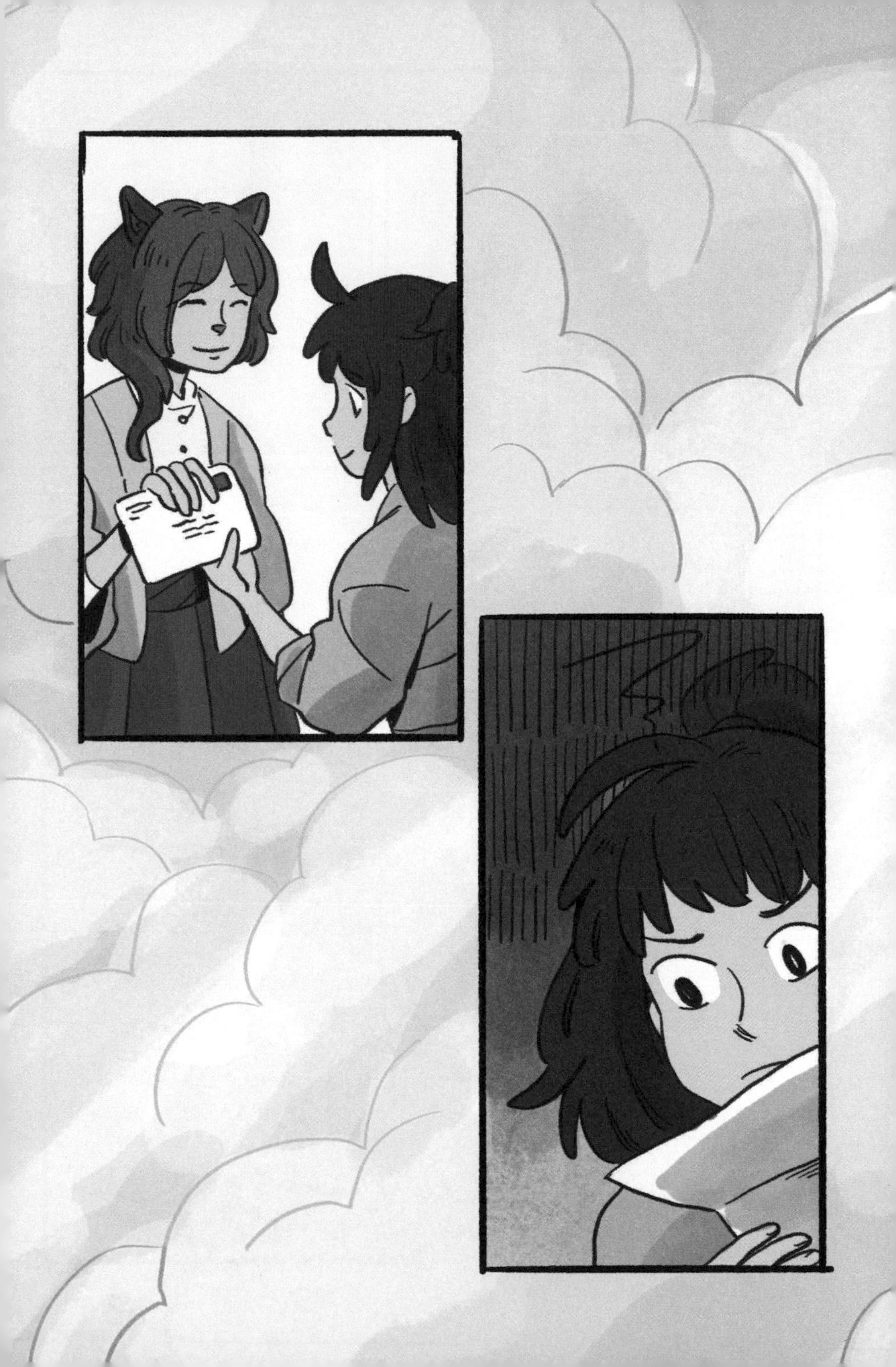

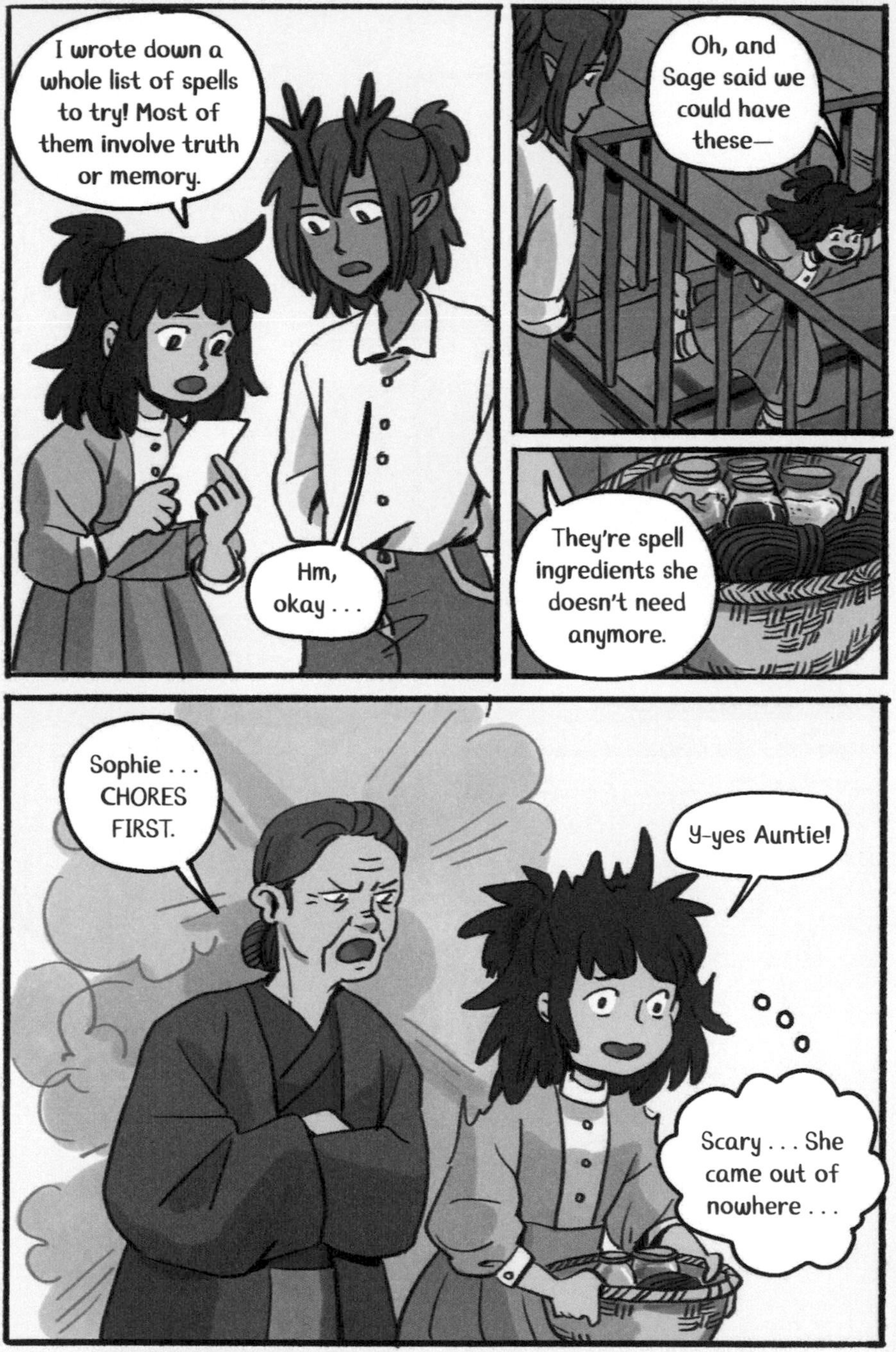

I wrote down a whole list of spells to try! Most of them involve truth or memory.
Hm, okay . . .
Oh, and Sage said we could have these—
They're spell ingredients she doesn't need anymore.
Sophie . . . CHORES FIRST.
Y-yes Auntie!
Scary . . . She came out of nowhere . . .

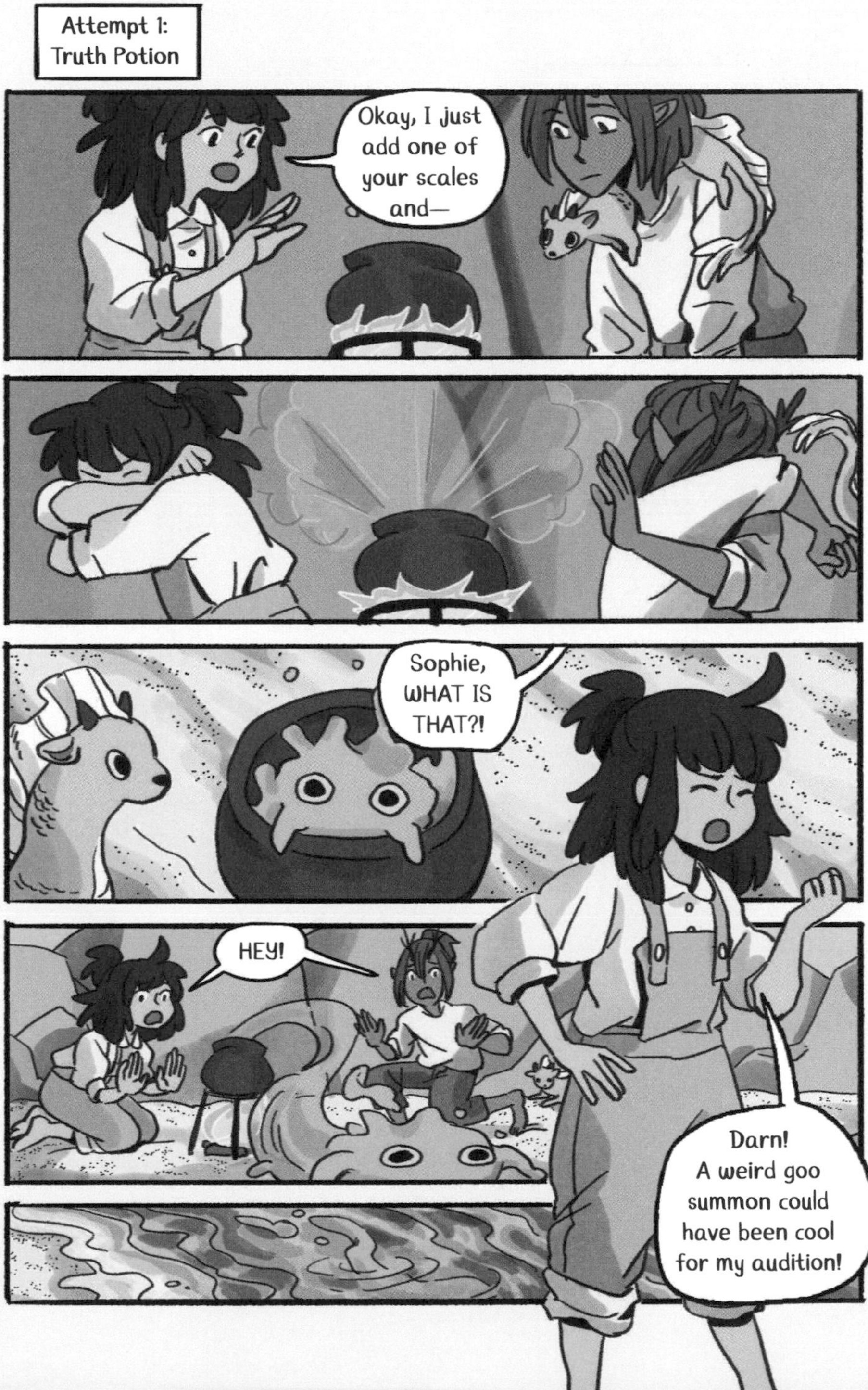
Attempt 1:
Truth Potion
Okay, I just add one of your scales and—
Sophie, WHAT IS THAT?!
HEY!
Darn! A weird goo summon could have been cool for my audition!

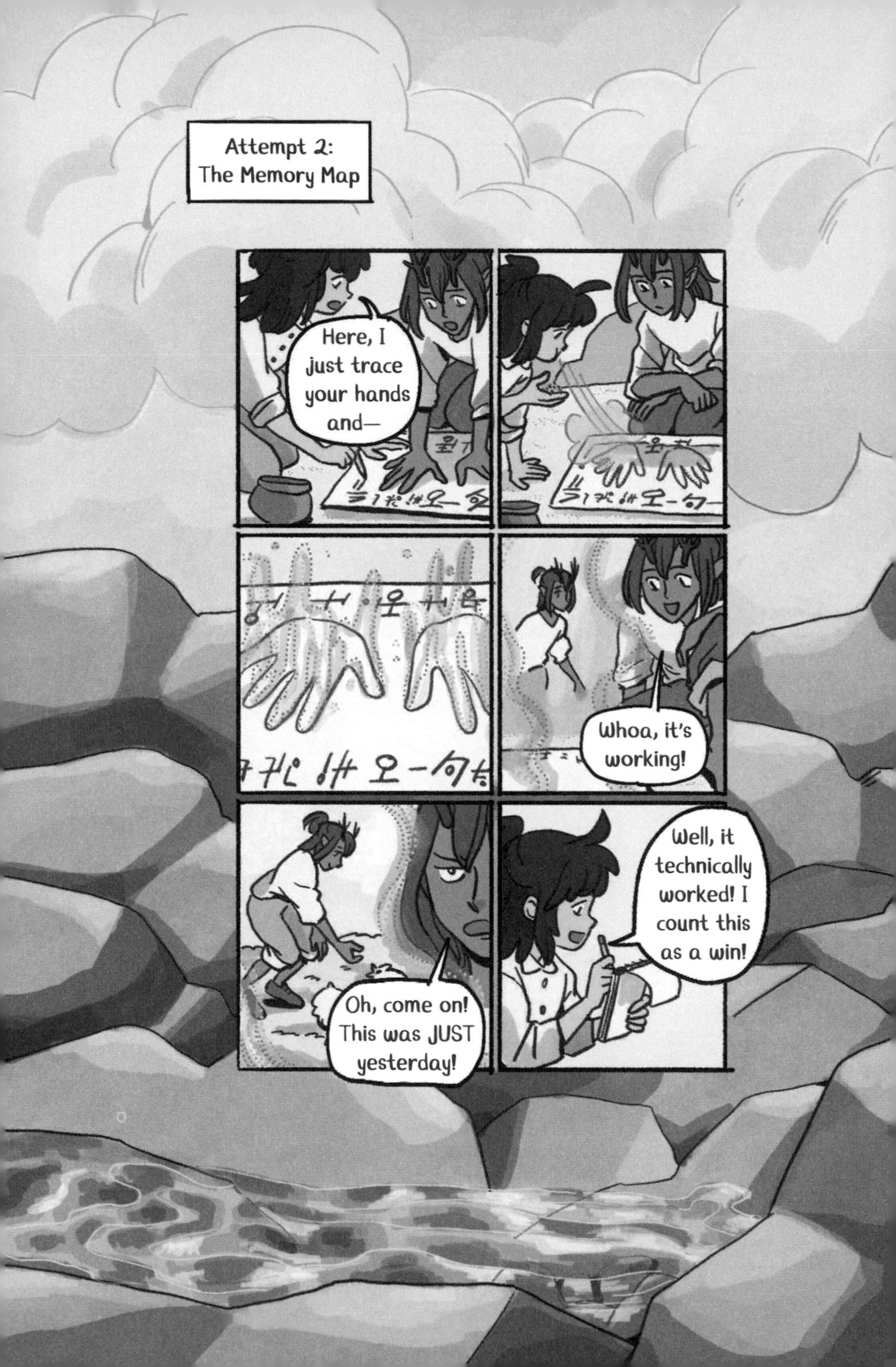

Attempt 2: The Memory Map
Here, I just trace your hands and—
Whoa, it's working!
Oh, come on! This was JUST yesterday!
Well, it technically worked! I count this as a win!

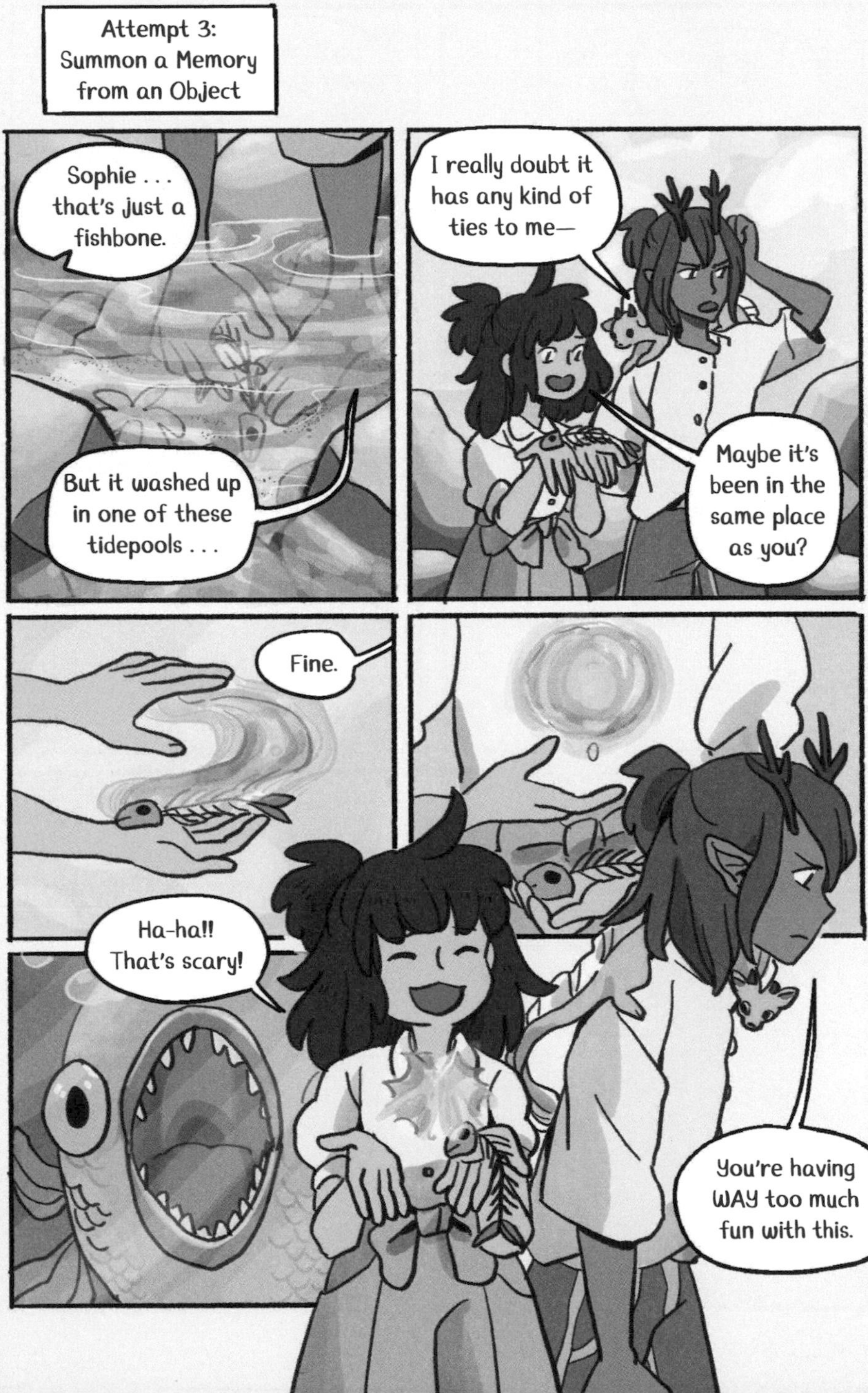

Attempt 3:
Summon a Memory from an Object
Sophie . . . that's just a fishbone.
But it washed up in one of these tidepools . . .
I really doubt it has any kind of ties to me—
Maybe it's been in the same place as you?
Fine.
Ha-ha!! That's scary!
You're having WAY too much fun with this.

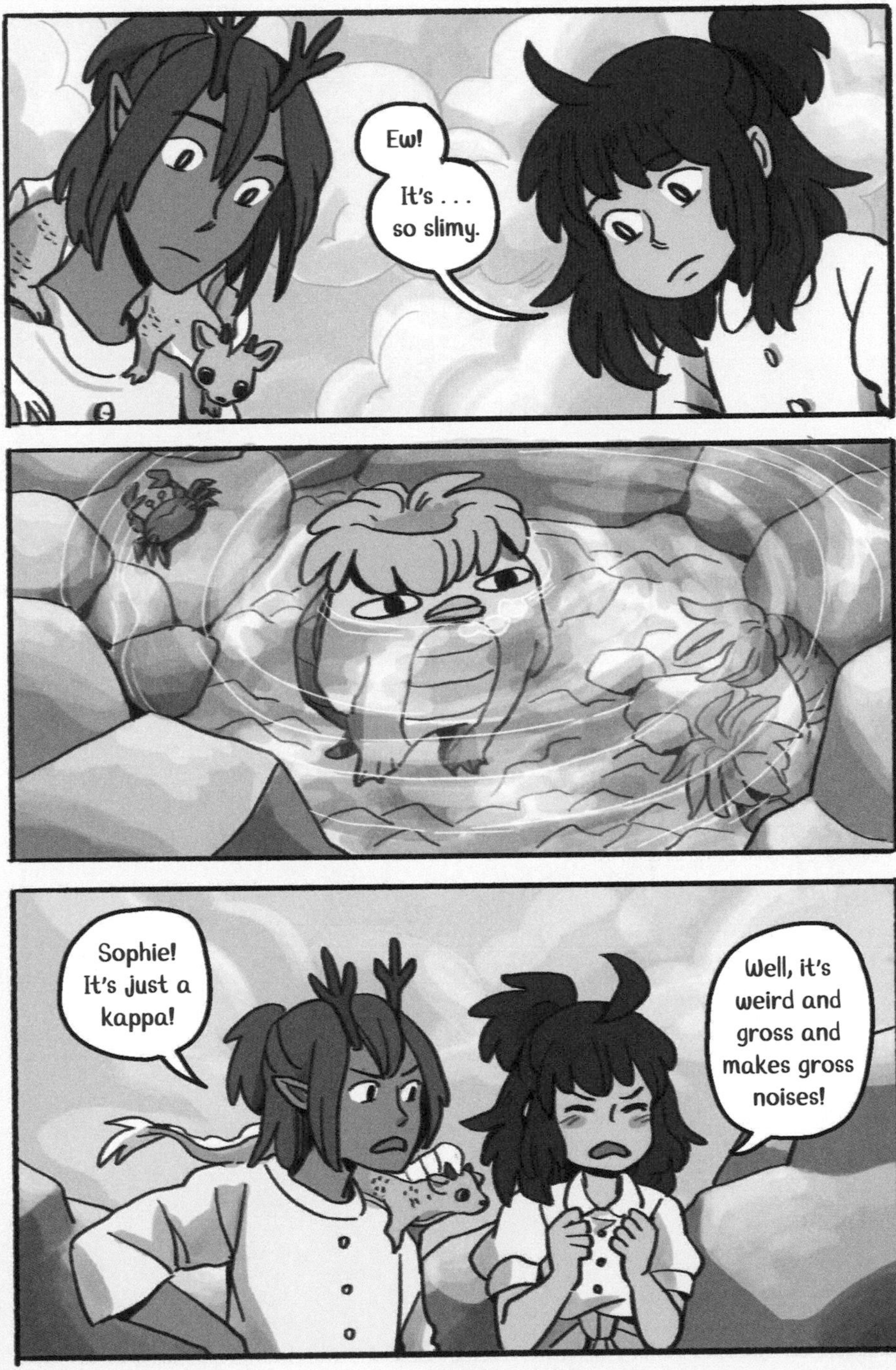
Ew!
It's . . . so slimy.
Sophie! It's just a kappa!
Well, it's weird and gross and makes gross noises!

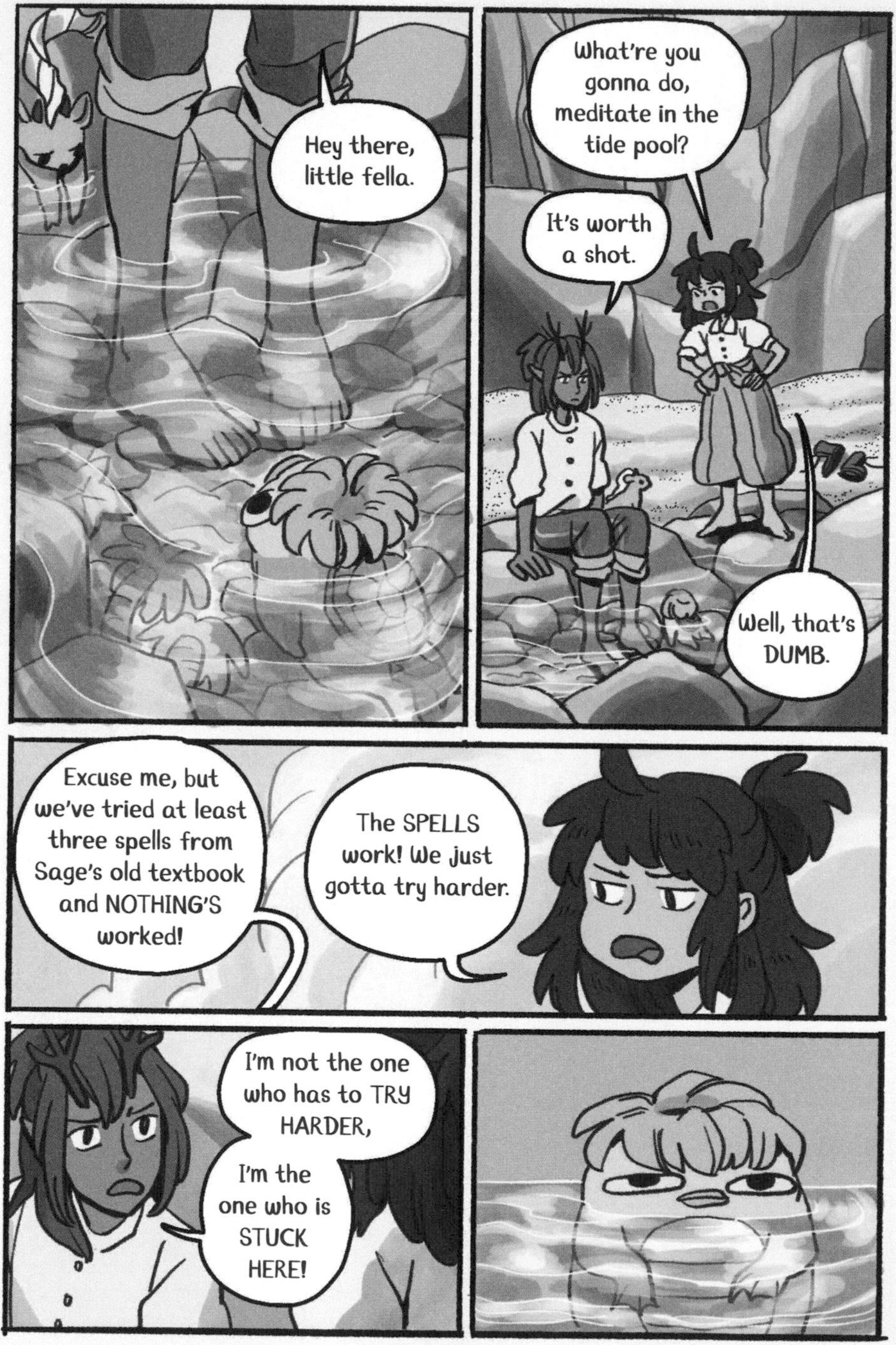
Hey there, little fella.
What're you gonna do, meditate in the tide pool?
It's worth a shot.
Well, that's DUMB.
Excuse me, but we've tried at least three spells from Sage's old textbook and NOTHING'S worked!
The SPELLS work! We just gotta try harder.
I'm not the one who has to TRY HARDER,
I'm the one who is STUCK HERE!

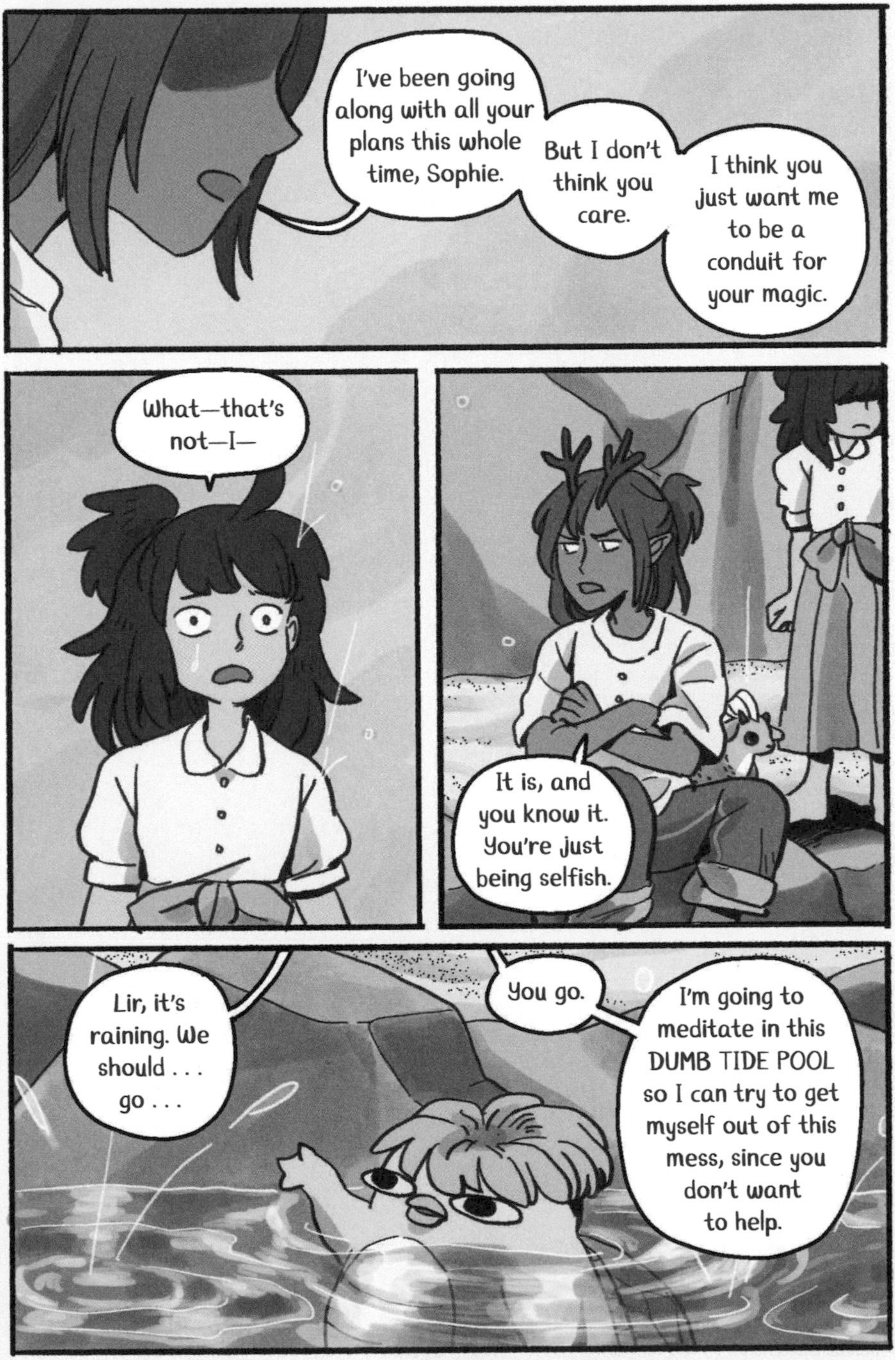
I've been going along with all your plans this whole time, Sophie.
But I don't think you care.
I think you just want me to be a conduit for your magic.
What—that's not—I—
It is, and you know it. You're just being selfish.
Lir, it's raining. We should . . . go . . .
You go.
I'm going to meditate in this DUMB TIDE POOL so I can try to get myself out of this mess, since you don't want to help.

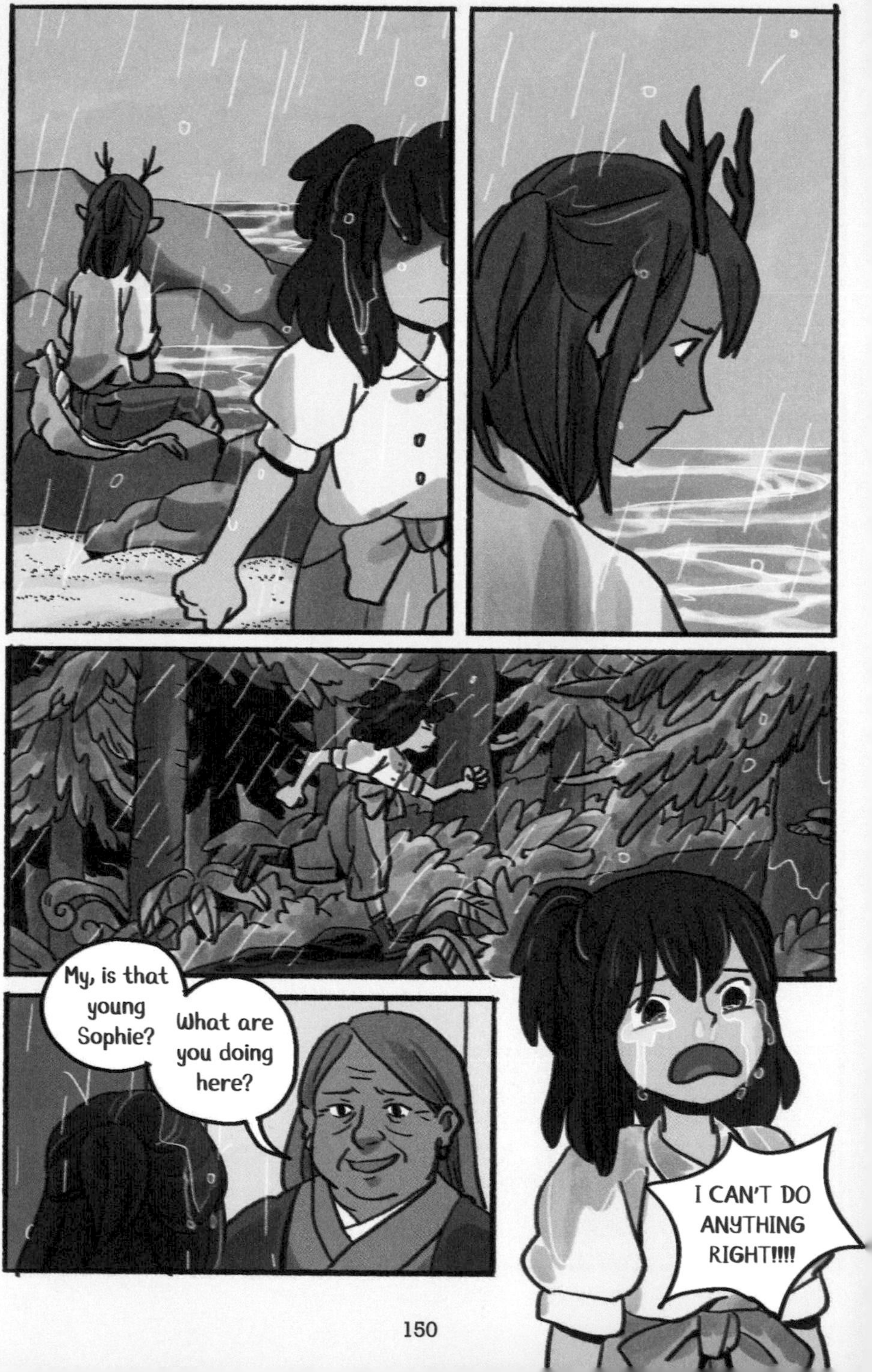
My, is that young Sophie?
What are you doing here?
I CAN'T DO ANYTHING RIGHT!!!!

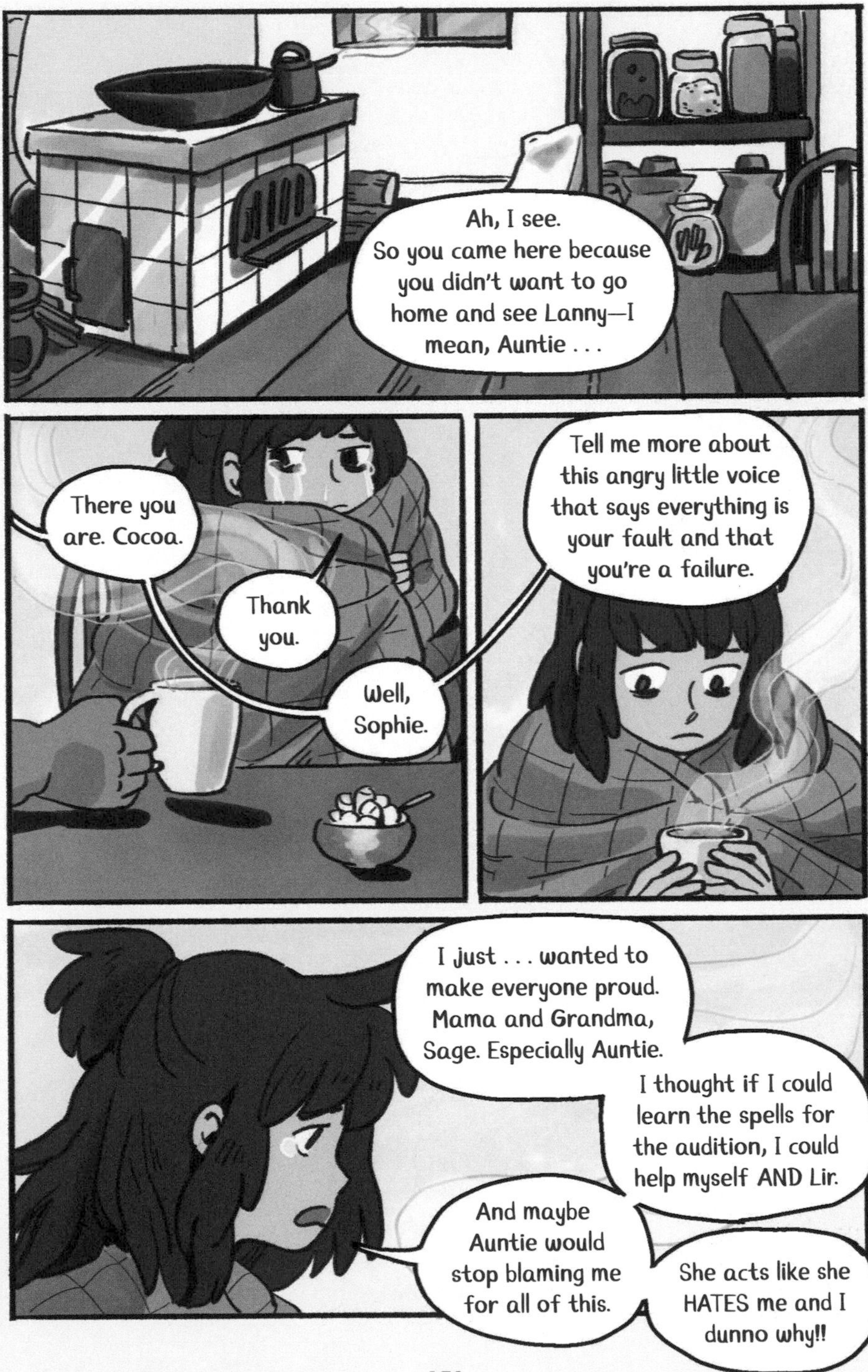
Ah, I see.
So you came here because you didn't want to go home and see Lanny—I mean, Auntie . . .
There you are. Cocoa.
Thank you.
Well, Sophie.
Tell me more about this angry little voice that says everything is your fault and that you're a failure.
I just . . . wanted to make everyone proud. Mama and Grandma, Sage. Especially Auntie.
I thought if I could learn the spells for the audition, I could help myself AND Lir.
And maybe Auntie would stop blaming me for all of this.
She acts like she HATES me and I dunno why!!

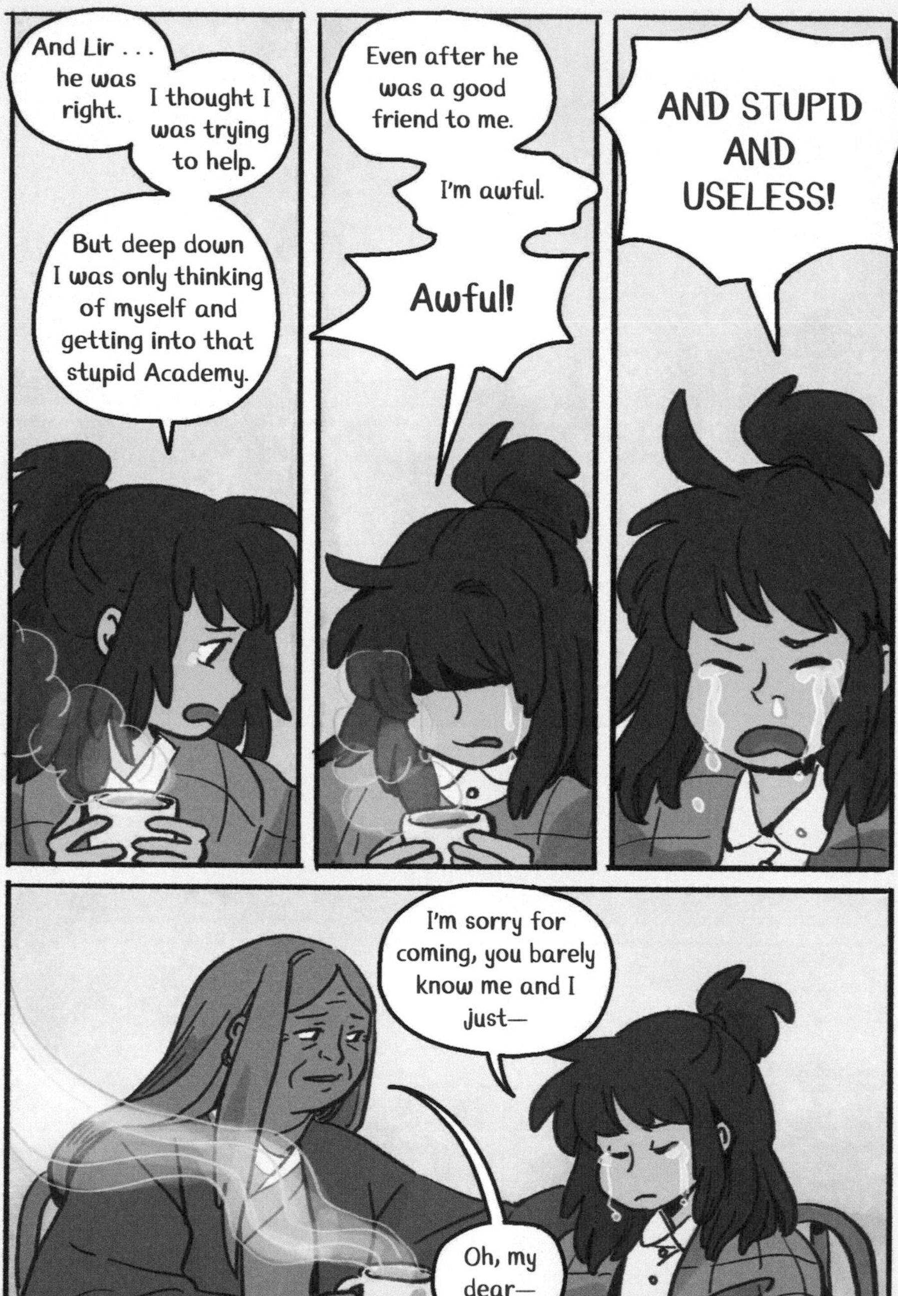
And Lir . . . he was right.
I thought I was trying to help.
But deep down I was only thinking of myself and getting into that stupid Academy.
Even after he was a good friend to me.
I'm awful.
Awful!
AND STUPID AND USELESS!
I'm sorry for coming, you barely know me and I just—
Oh, my dear—

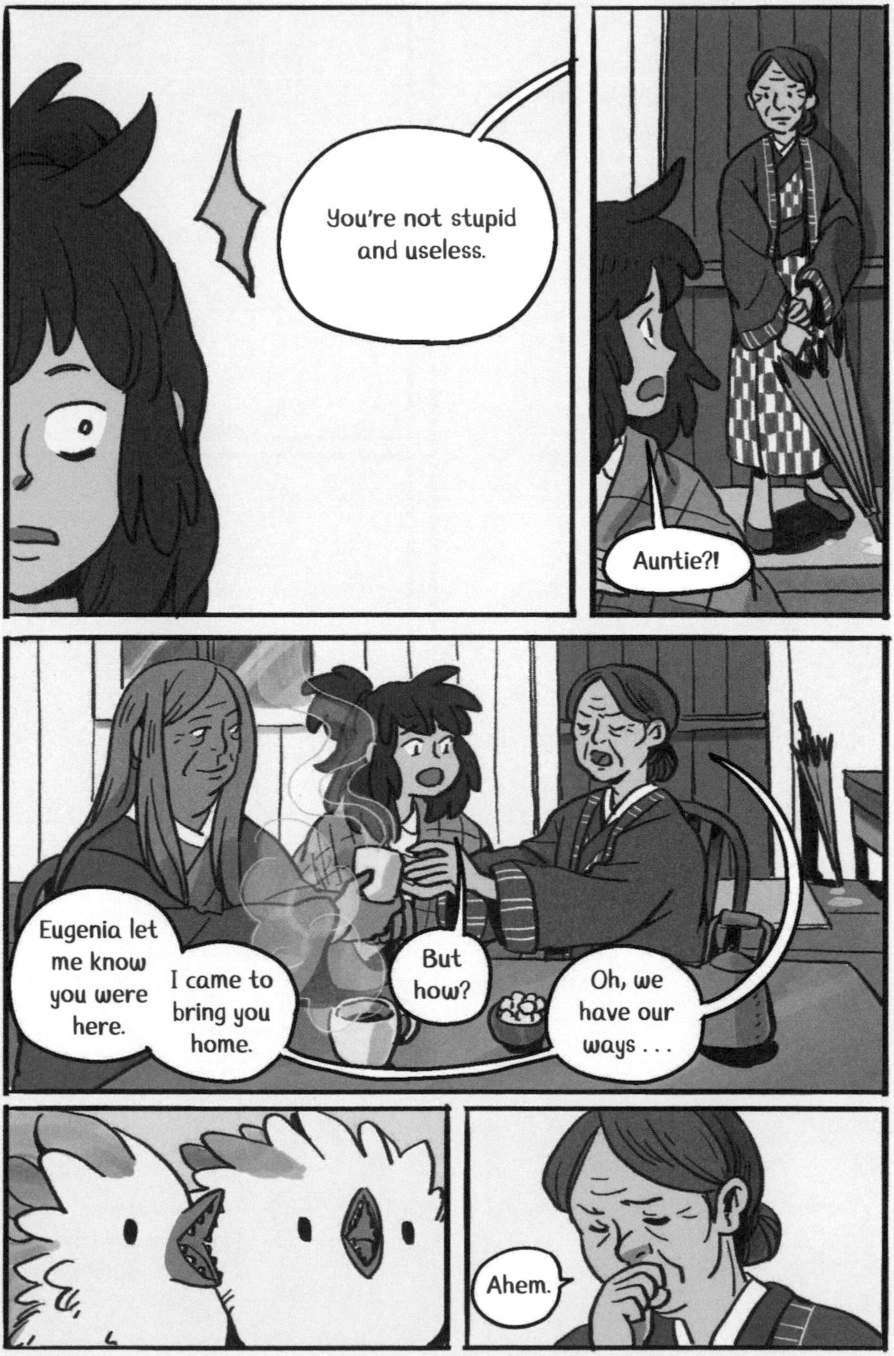
You're not stupid and useless.
Auntie?!
Eugenia let me know you were here.
I came to bring you home.
But how?
Oh, we have our ways . . .
Ahem.

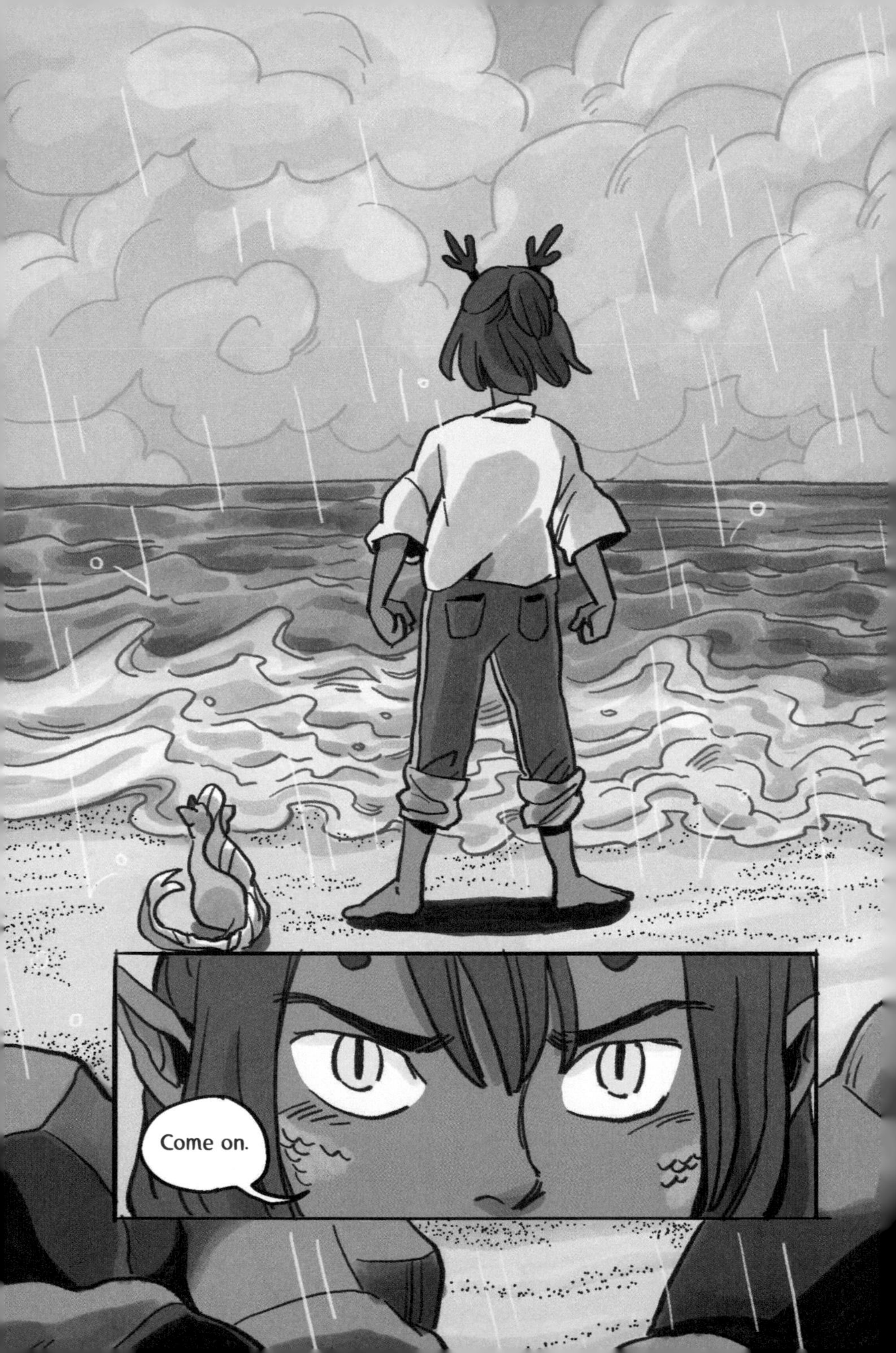
Come on.

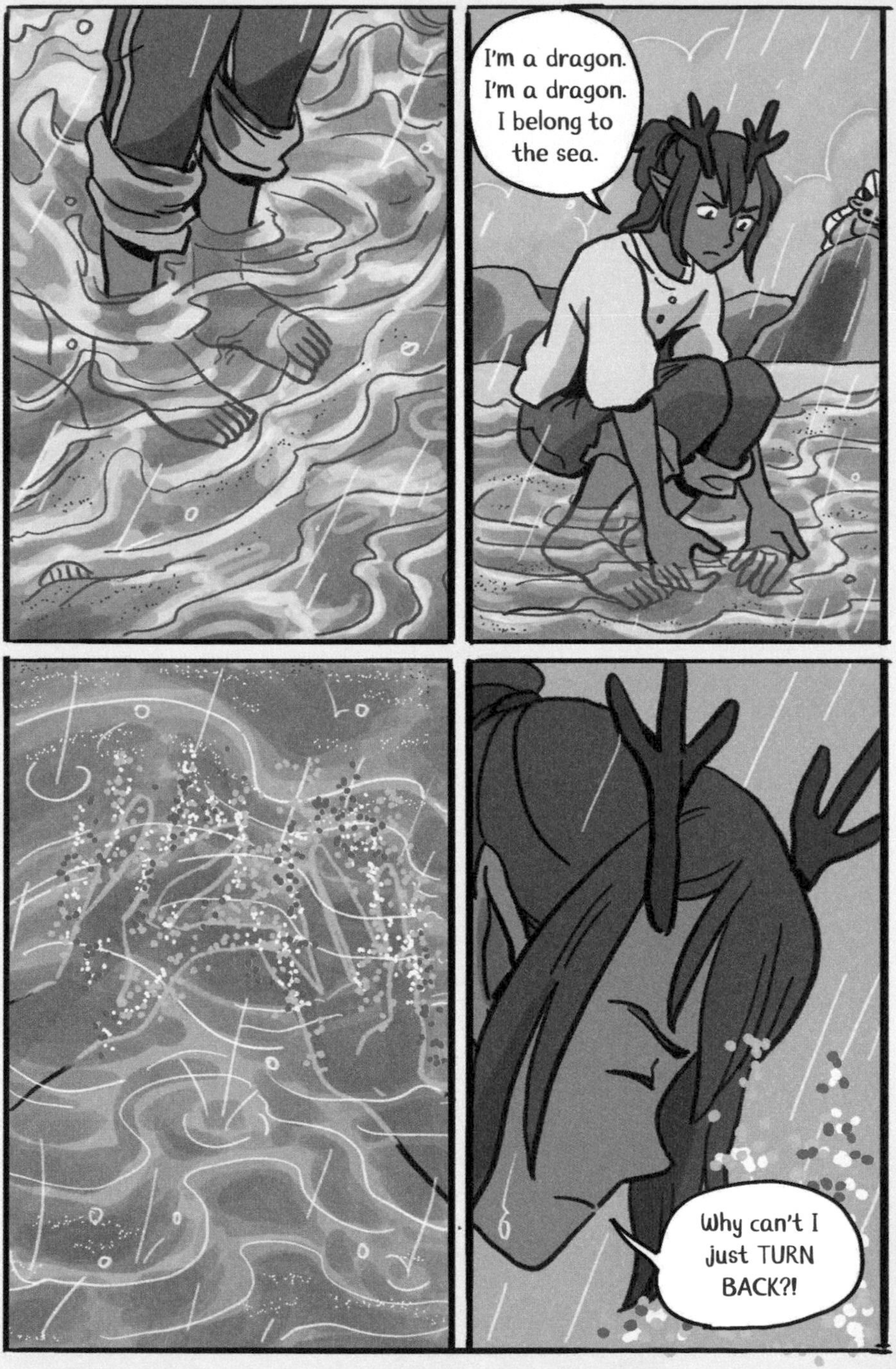
I'm a dragon. I'm a dragon. I belong to the sea.
Why can't I just TURN BACK?!

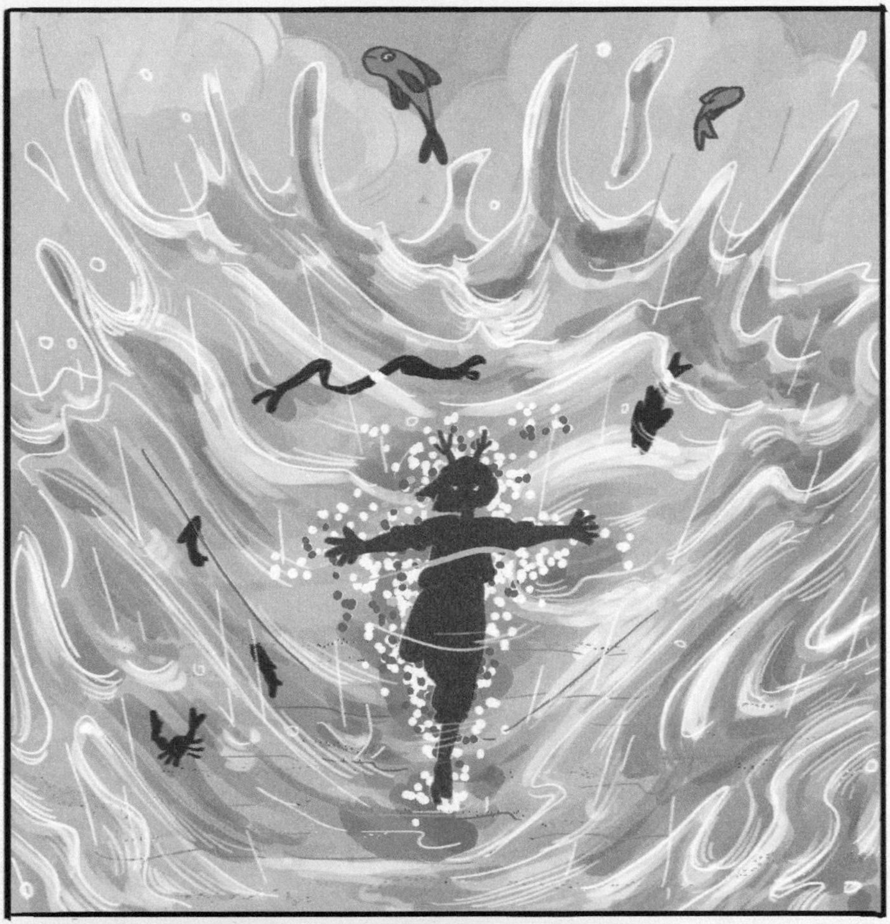

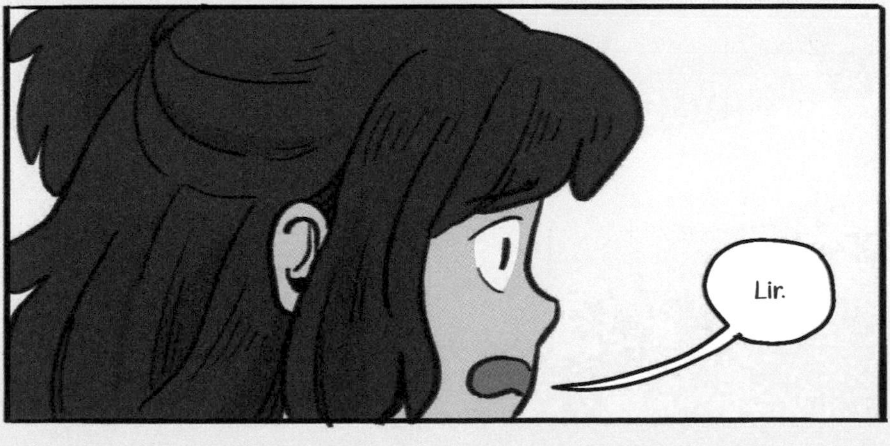
Lir.

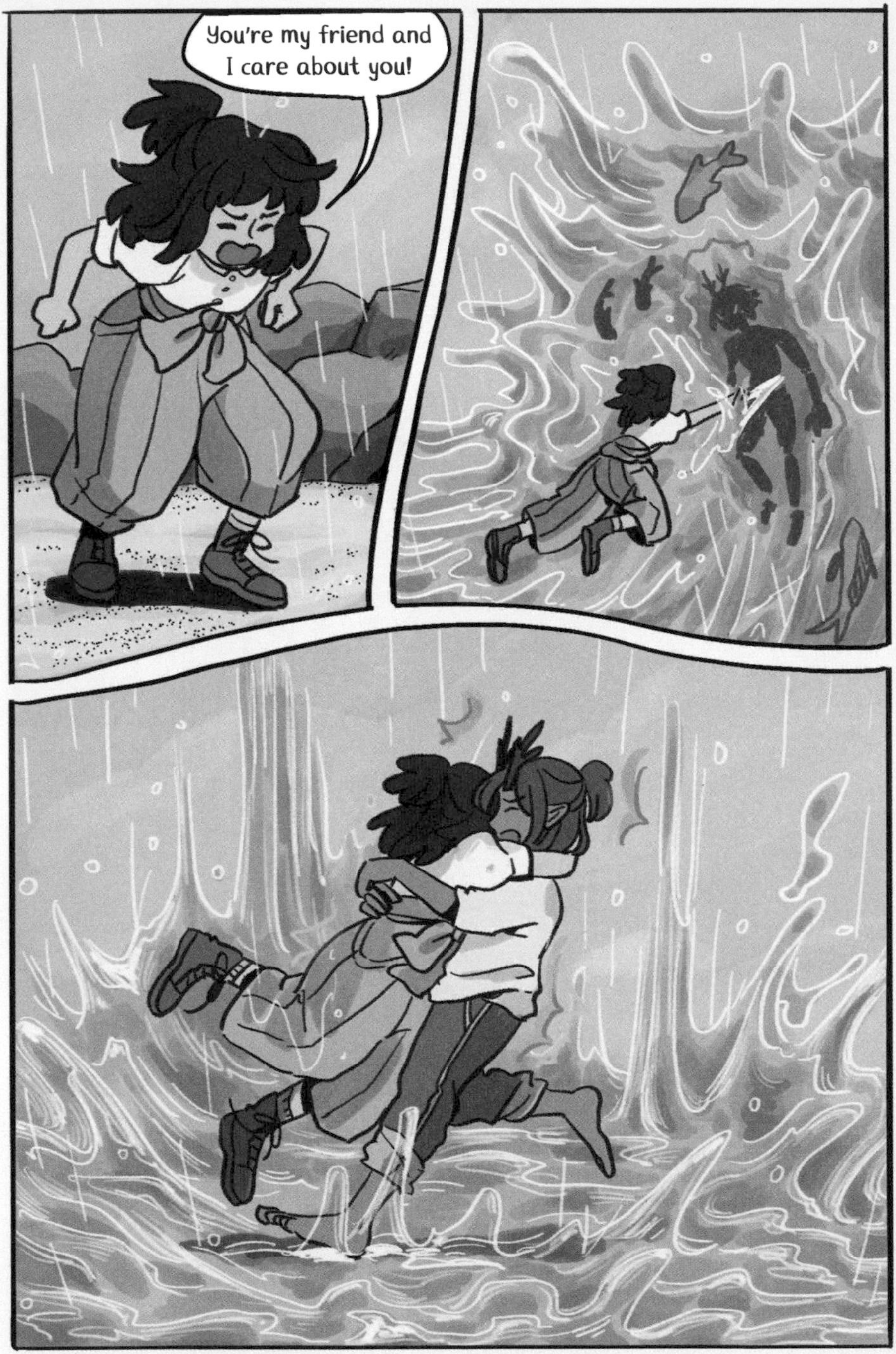
You're my friend and
I care about you!

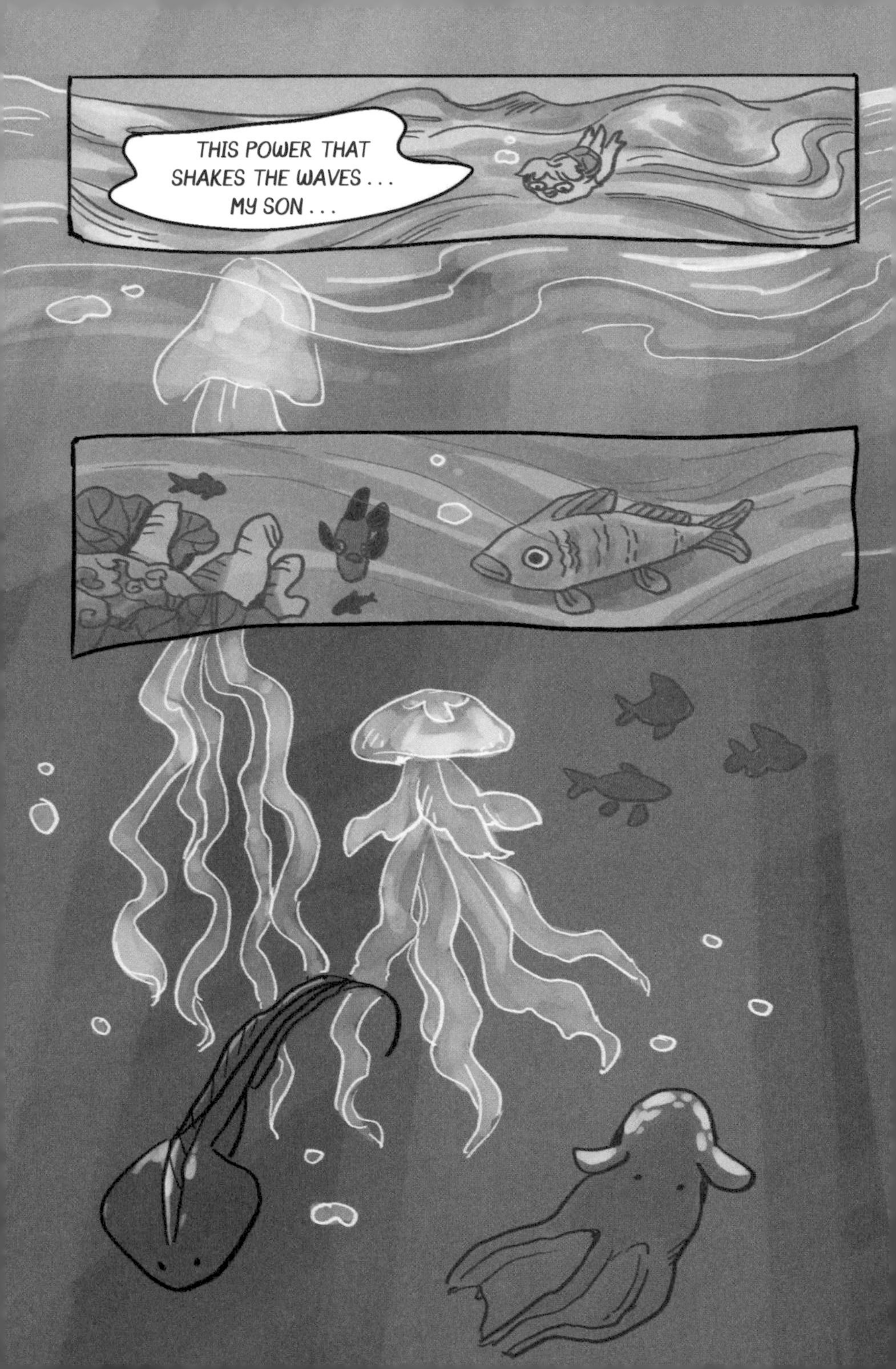
THIS POWER THAT SHAKES THE WAVES . . . MY SON . . .

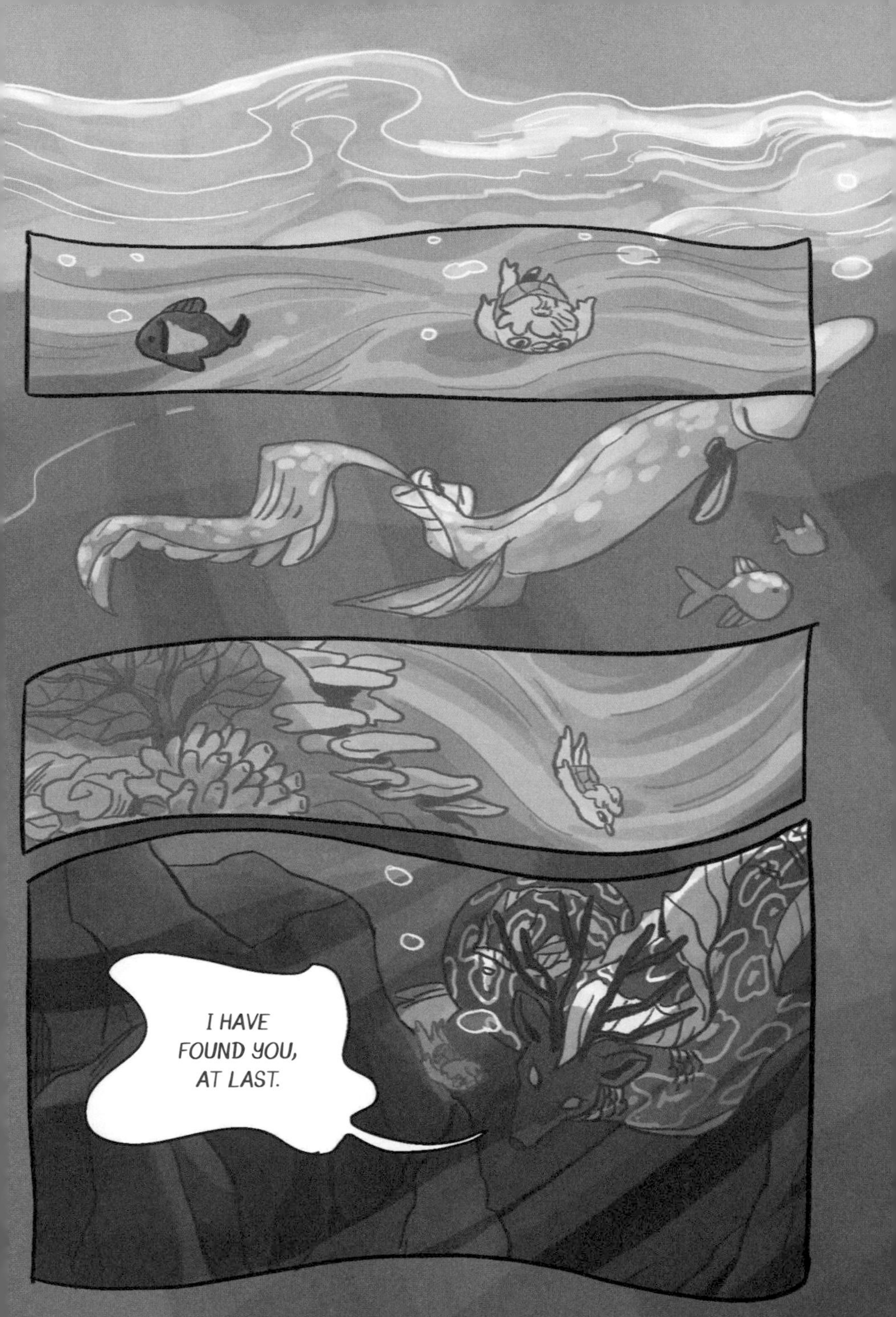
I HAVE FOUND YOU, AT LAST.

Chapter 7

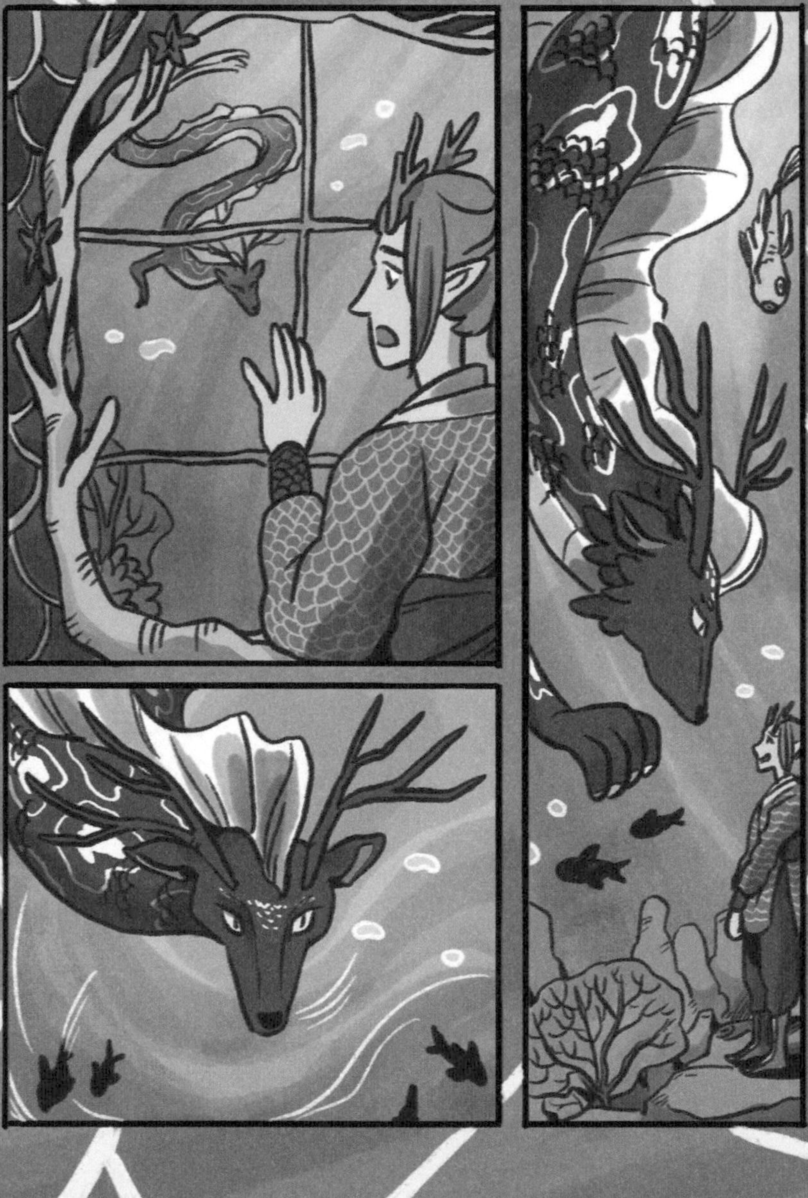

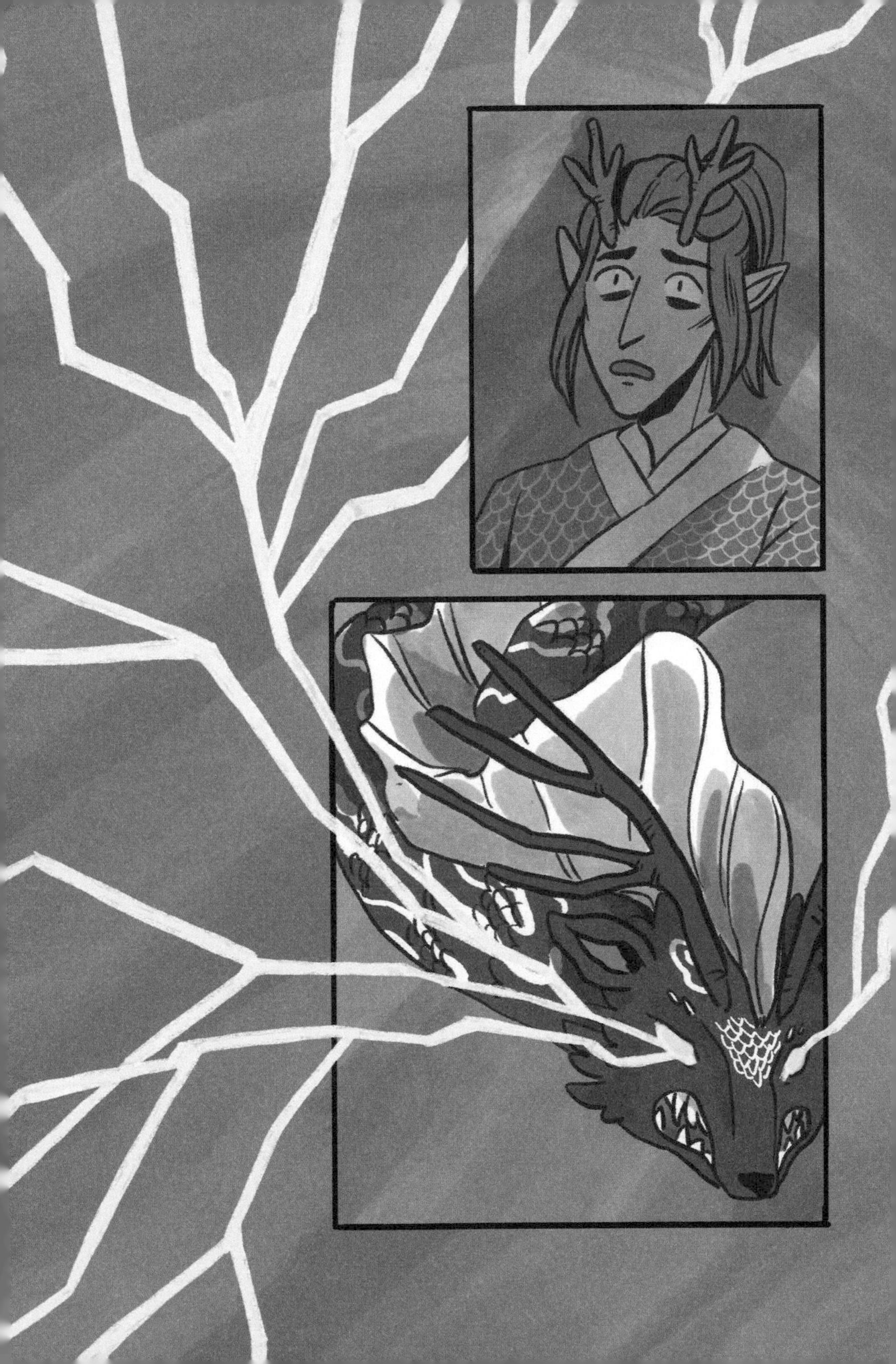

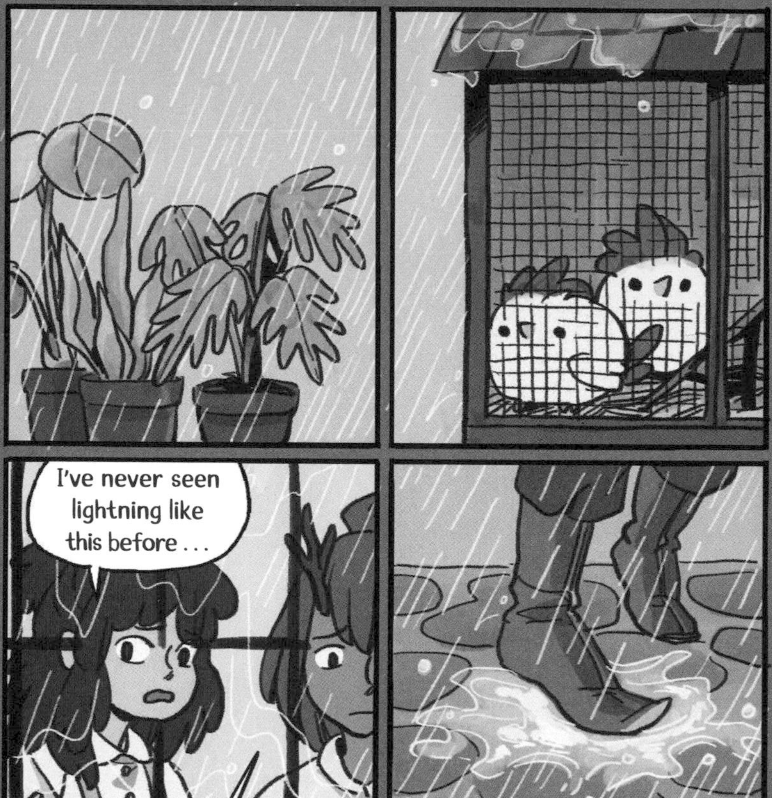
I've never seen lightning like this before . . .
. . .

Jai, I was just about to contact you—this storm, it's—

We have an emergency on our hands.

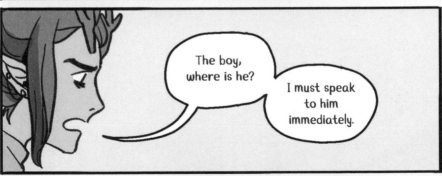

The boy, where is he?

I must speak to him immediately.

No flowery greetings?

It must be bad!

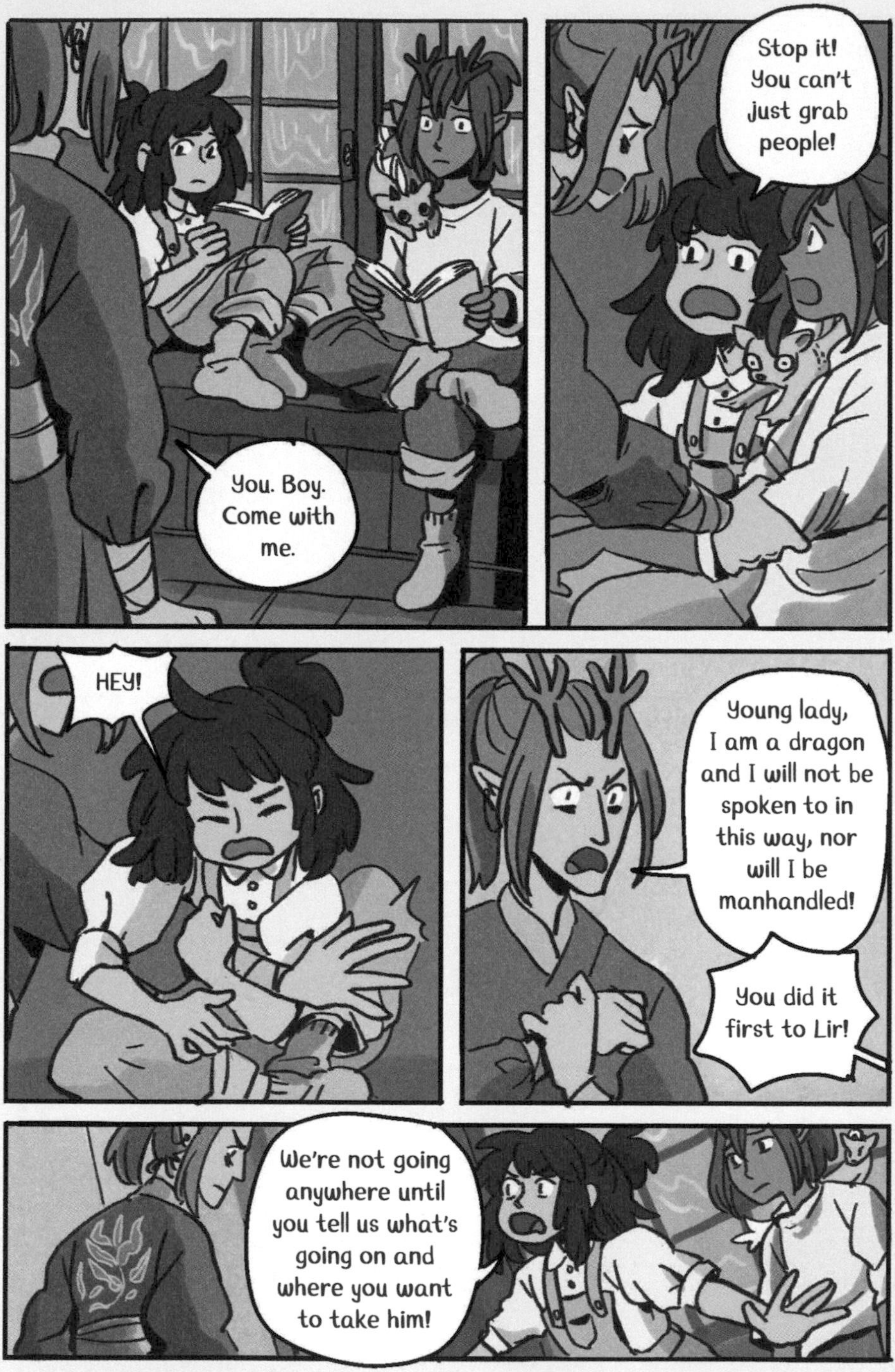
You. Boy. Come with me.
Stop it! You can't just grab people!
HEY!
Young lady, I am a dragon and I will not be spoken to in this way, nor will I be manhandled!
You did it first to Lir!
We're not going anywhere until you tell us what's going on and where you want to take him!

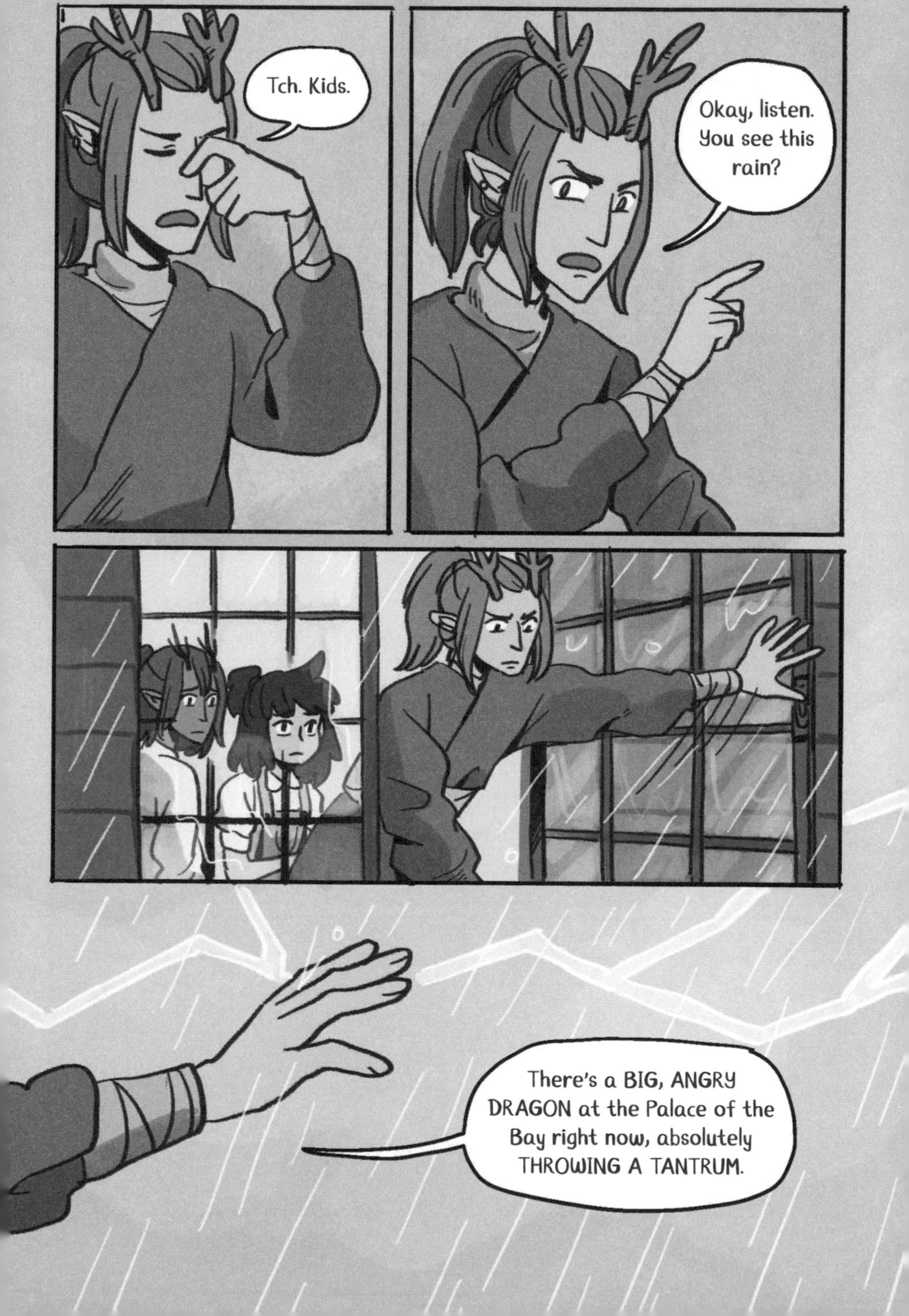
Tch. Kids.
Okay, listen. You see this rain?
There's a BIG, ANGRY DRAGON at the Palace of the Bay right now, absolutely THROWING A TANTRUM.

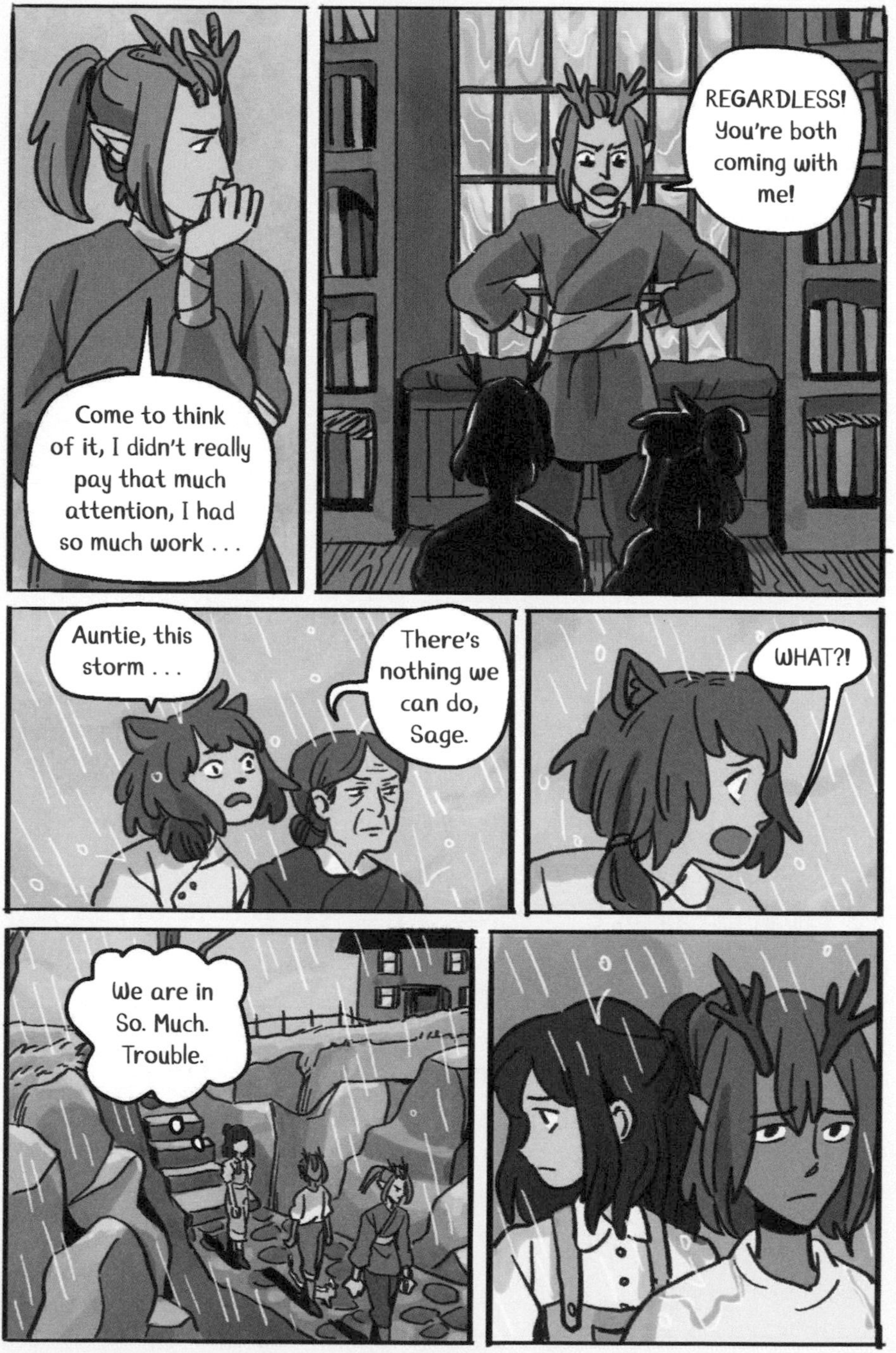
Come to think of it, I didn't really pay that much attention, I had so much work . . .
REGARDLESS! You're both coming with me!
Auntie, this storm . . .
There's nothing we can do, Sage.
WHAT?!
We are in So. Much. Trouble.

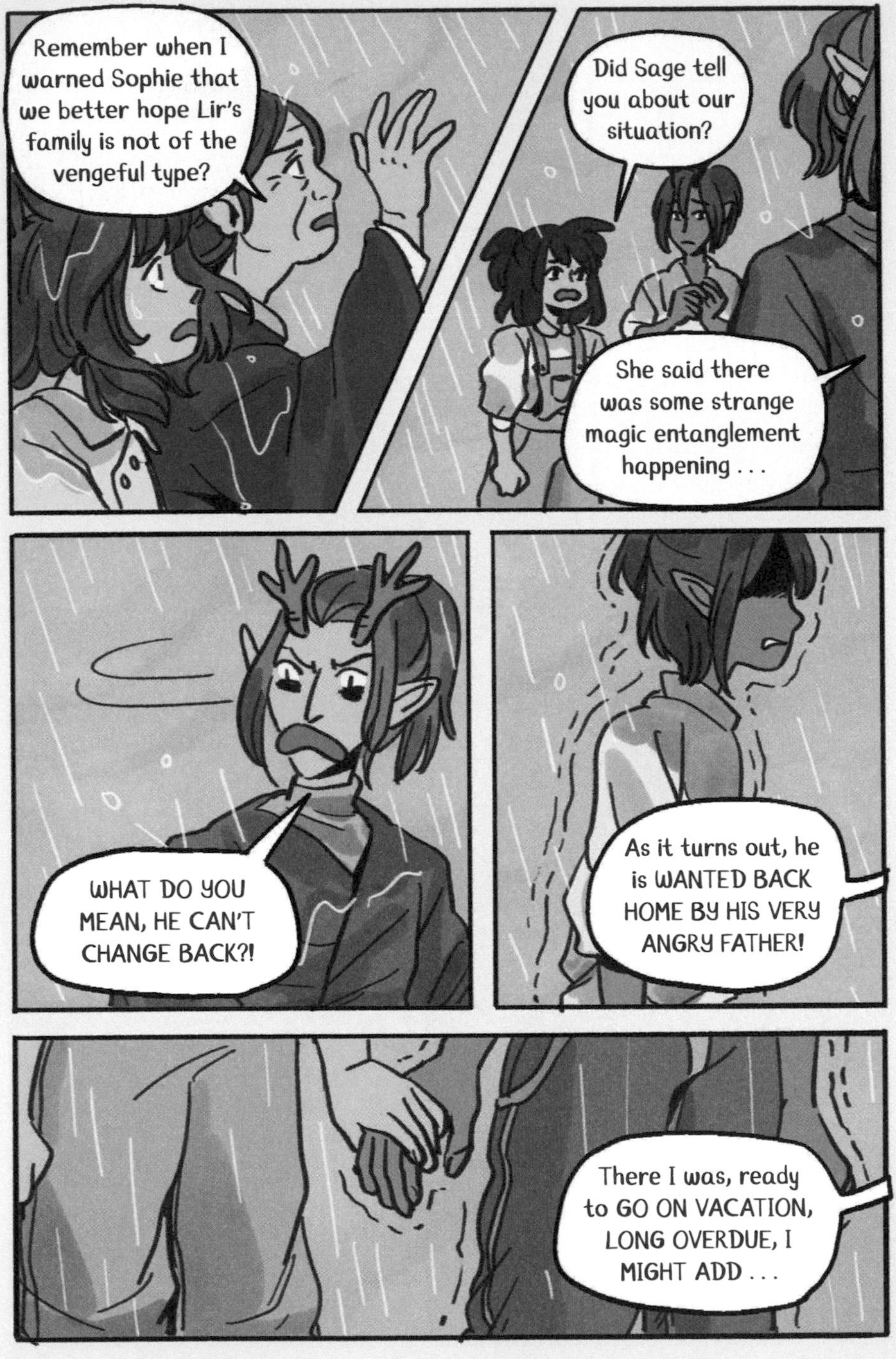
Remember when I warned Sophie that we better hope Lir's family is not of the vengeful type?
Did Sage tell you about our situation?
She said there was some strange magic entanglement happening . . .
WHAT DO YOU MEAN, HE CAN'T CHANGE BACK?!
As it turns out, he is WANTED BACK HOME BY HIS VERY ANGRY FATHER!
There I was, ready to GO ON VACATION, LONG OVERDUE, I MIGHT ADD . . .

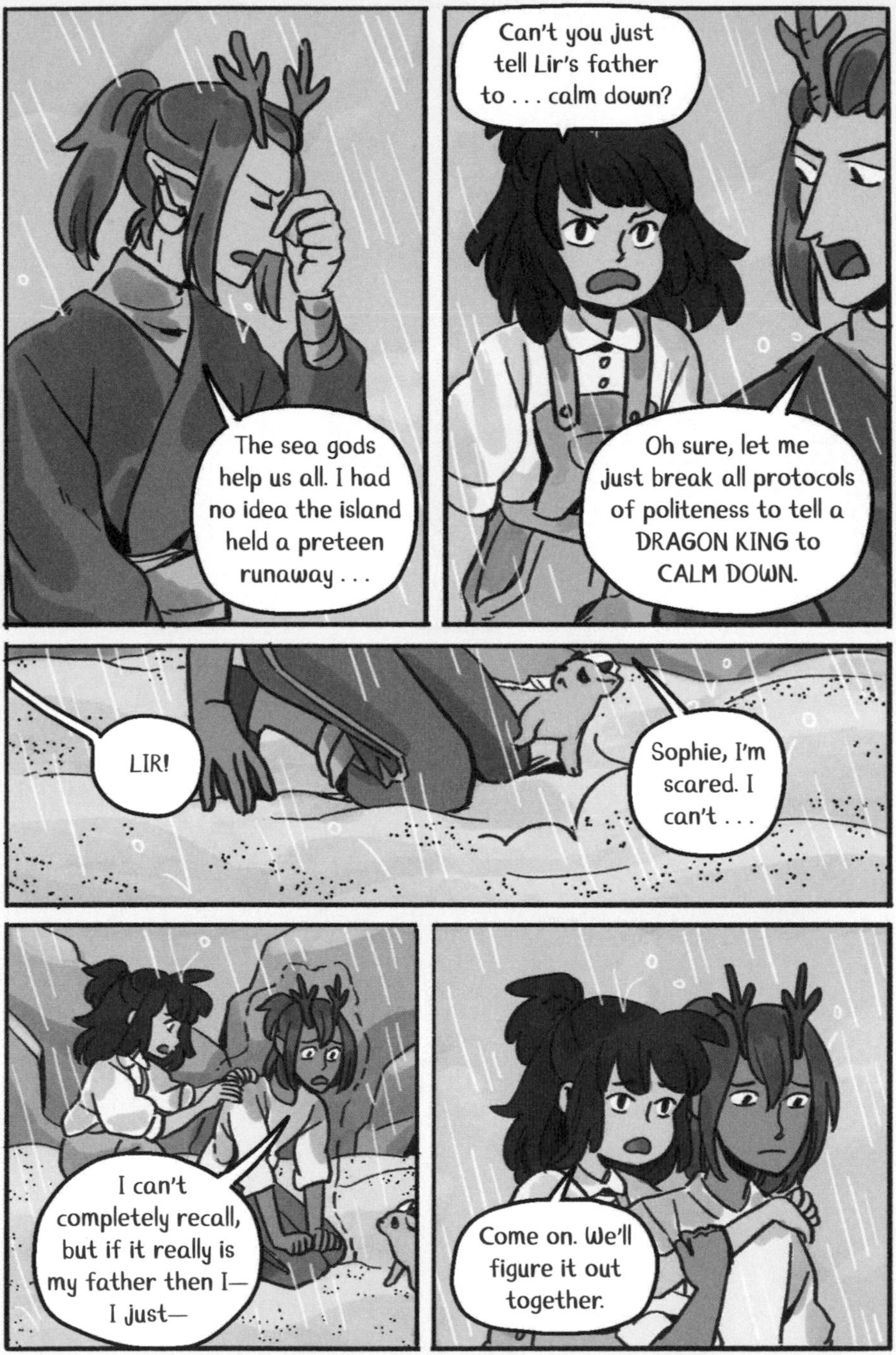

The sea gods help us all. I had no idea the island held a preteen runaway . . .
Can't you just tell Lir's father to . . . calm down?
Oh sure, let me just break all protocols of politeness to tell a DRAGON KING to CALM DOWN.
LIR!
Sophie, I'm scared. I can't . . .
I can't completely recall, but if it really is my father then I— I just—
Come on. We'll figure it out together.

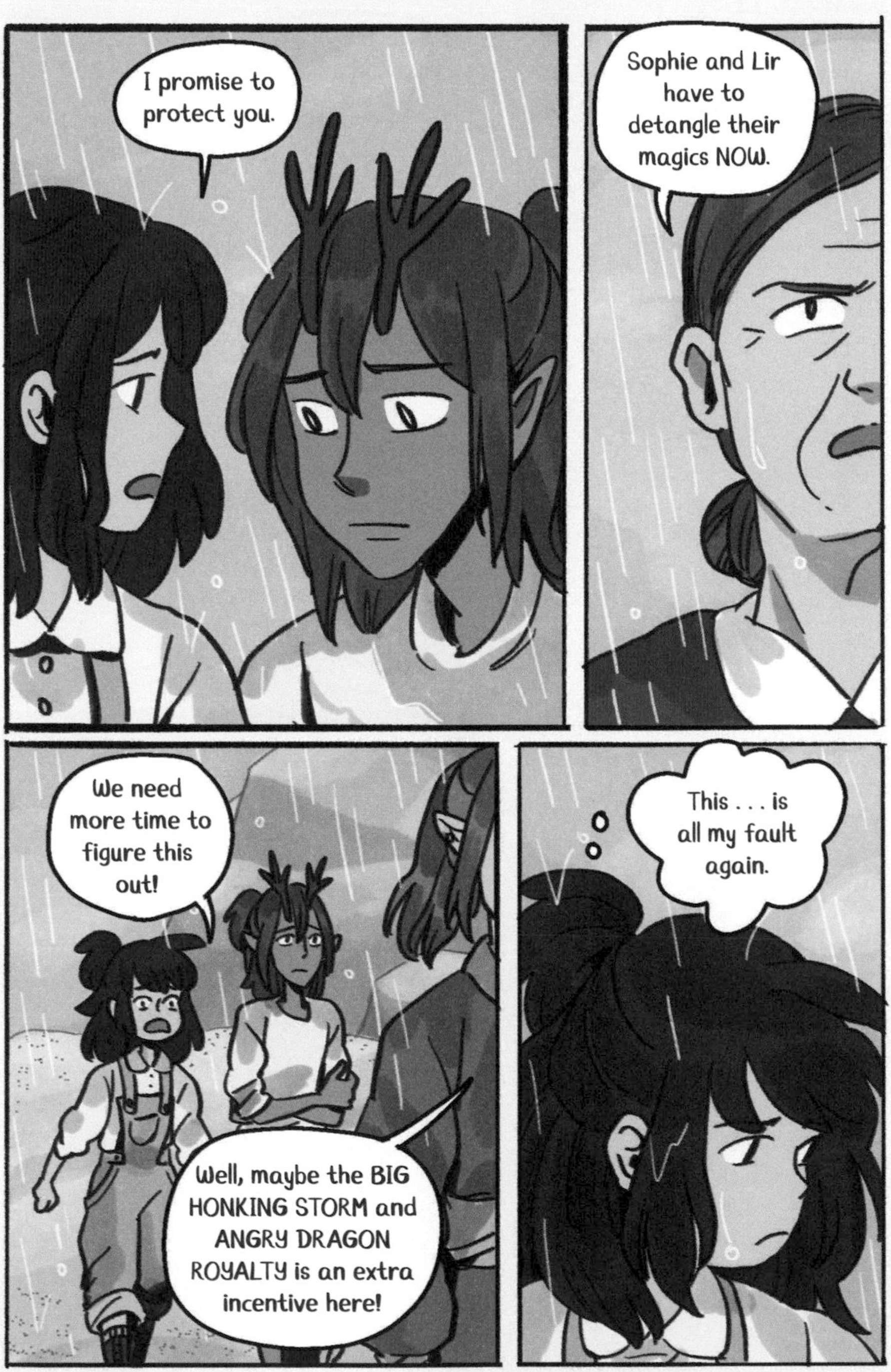
I promise to protect you.
Sophie and Lir have to detangle their magics NOW.
We need more time to figure this out!
Well, maybe the BIG HONKING STORM and ANGRY DRAGON ROYALTY is an extra incentive here!
This . . . is all my fault again.

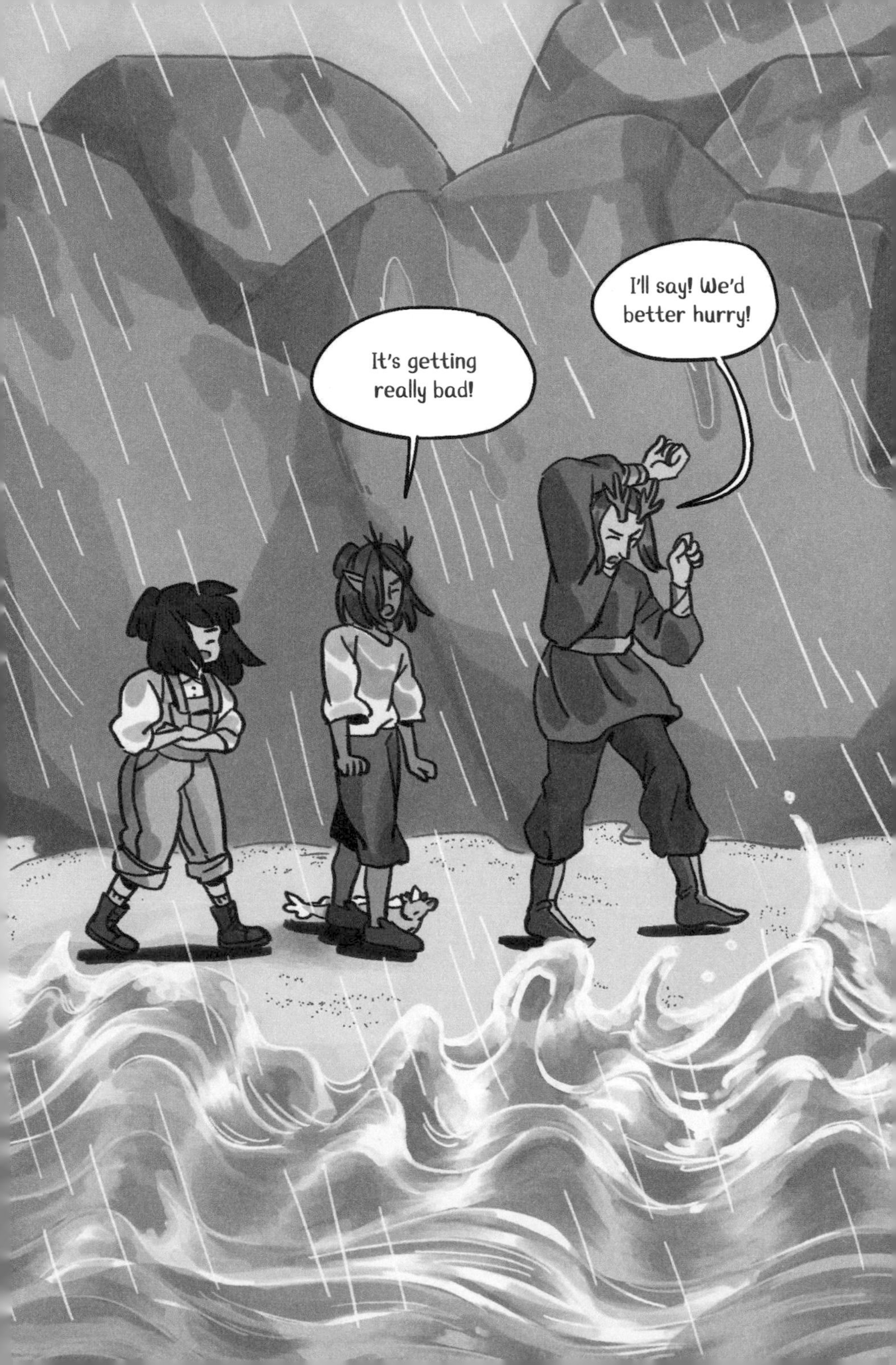
It's getting really bad!
I'll say! We'd better hurry!

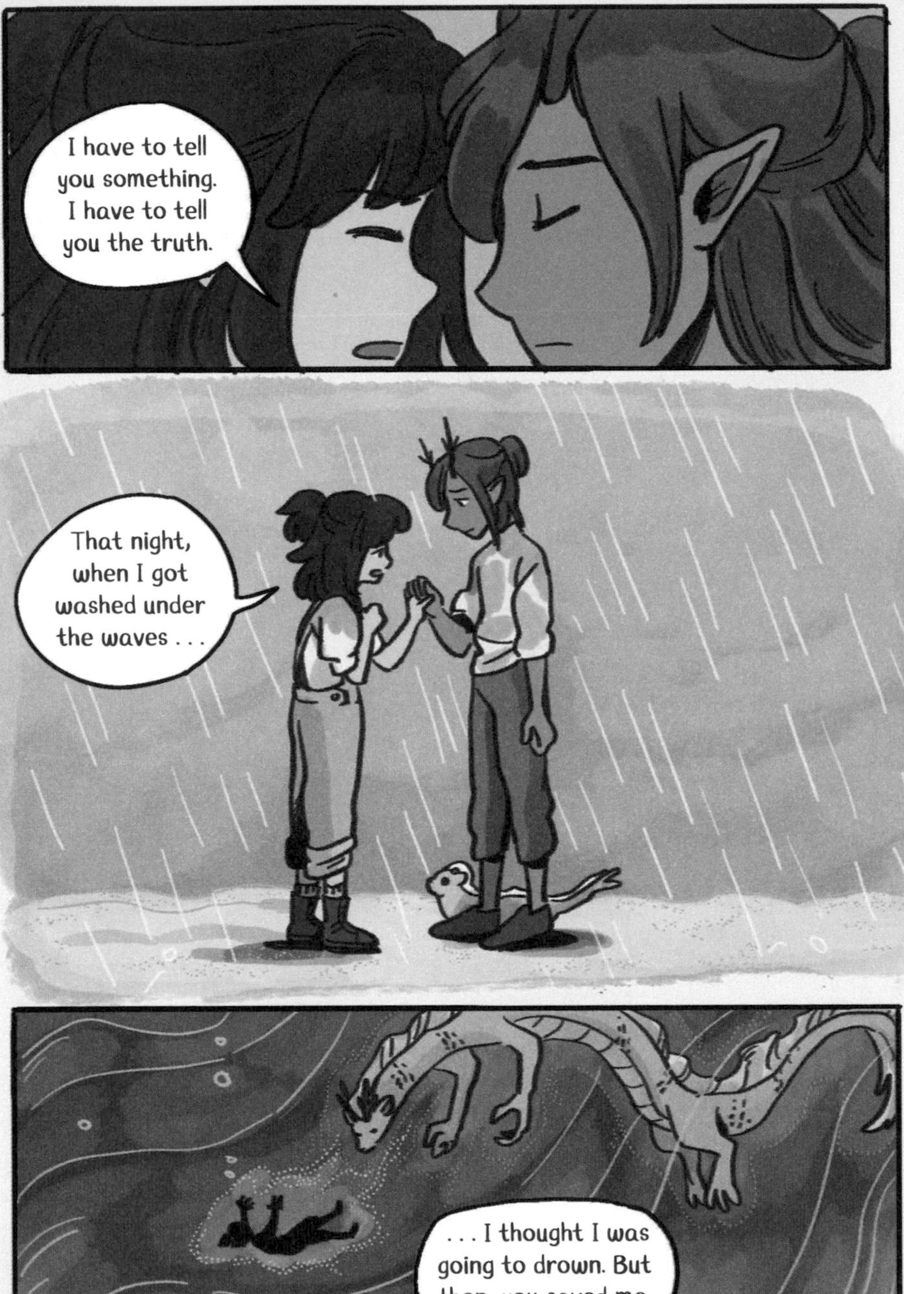
I have to tell you something. I have to tell you the truth.
That night, when I got washed under the waves . . .
. . . I thought I was going to drown. But then, you saved me.

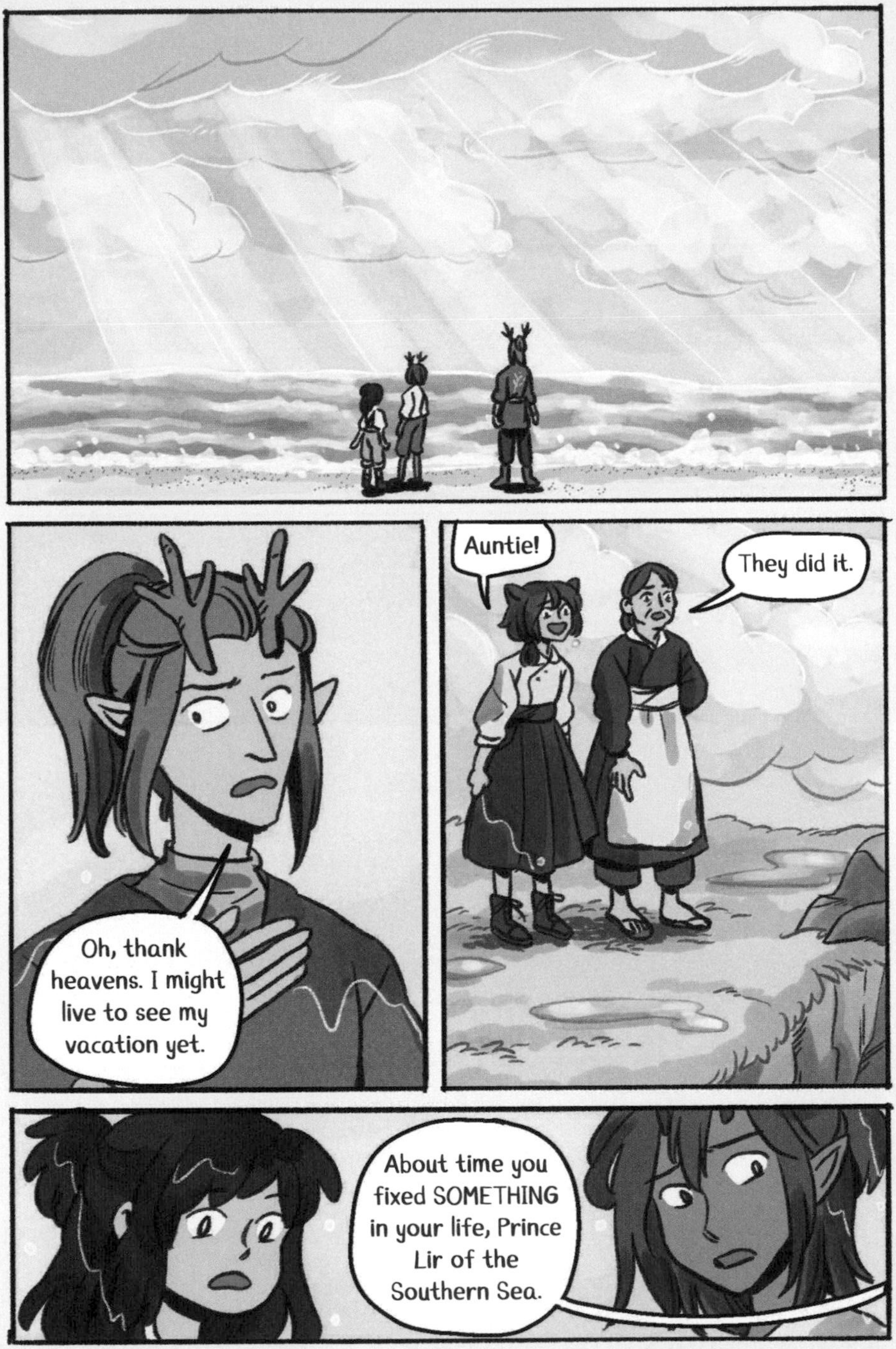

Oh, thank heavens. I might live to see my vacation yet.
Auntie!
They did it.
About time you fixed SOMETHING in your life, Prince Lir of the Southern Sea.

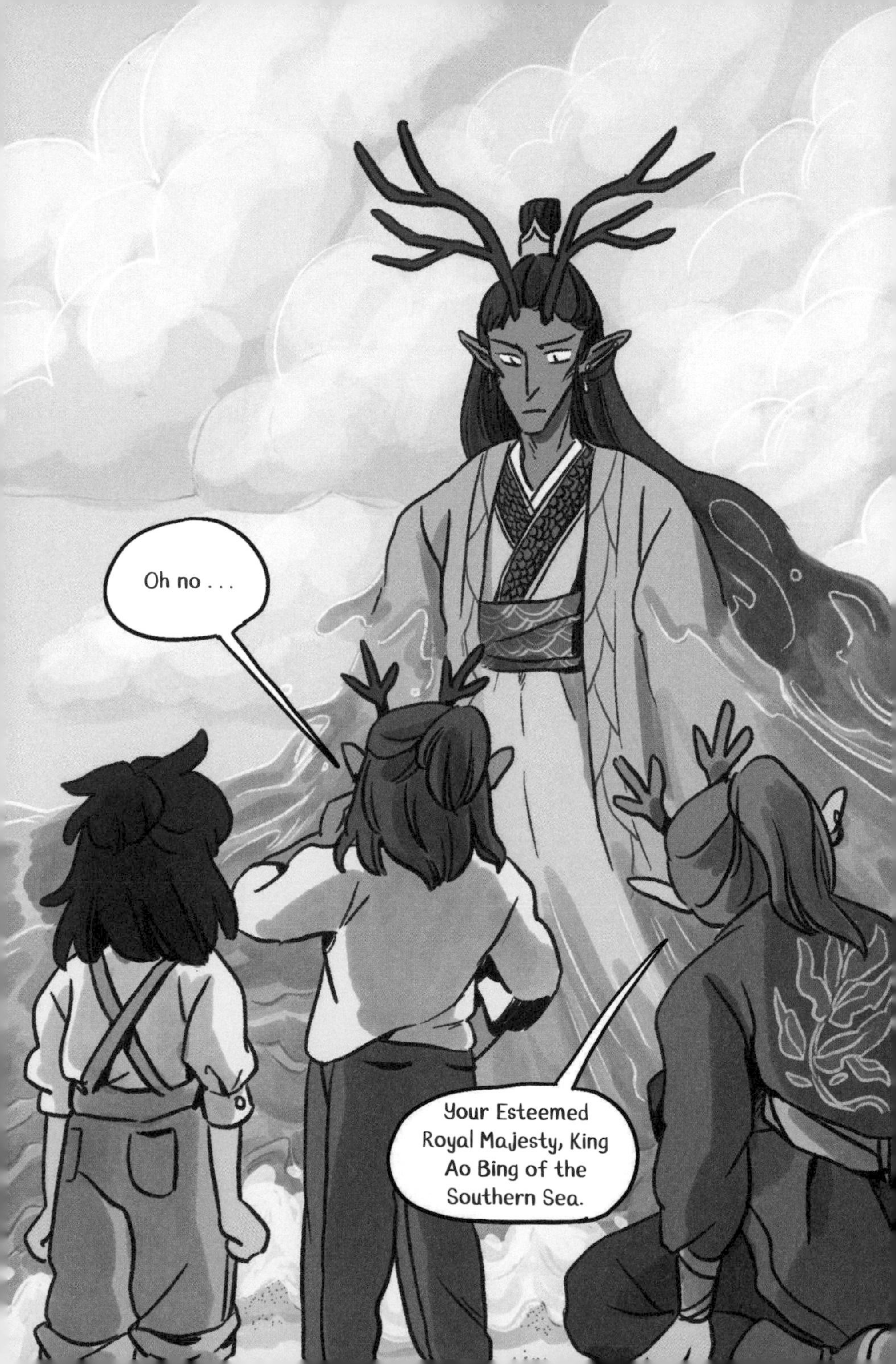
Oh no . . .
Your Esteemed Royal Majesty, King Ao Bing of the Southern Sea.

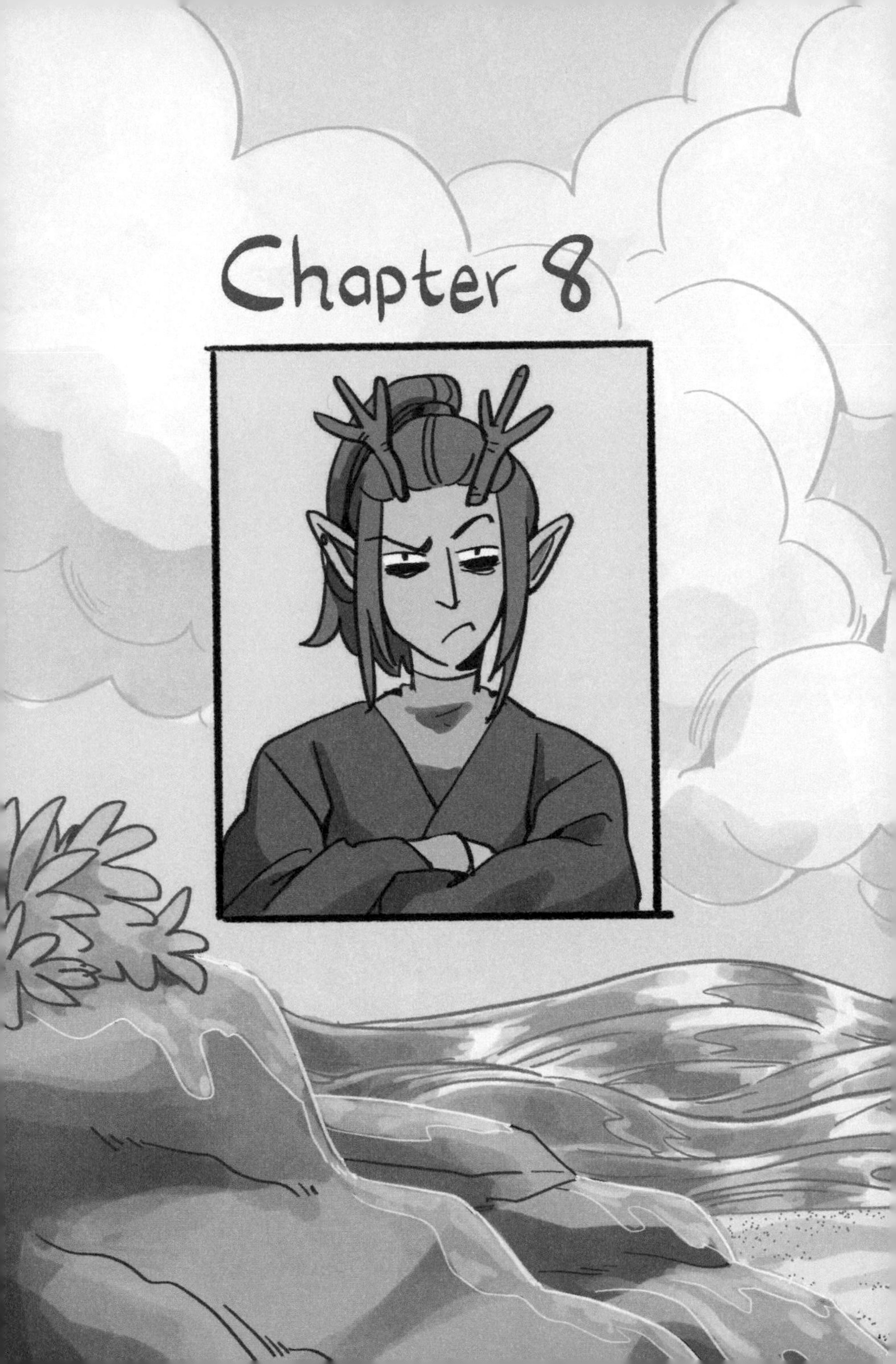
Chapter 8

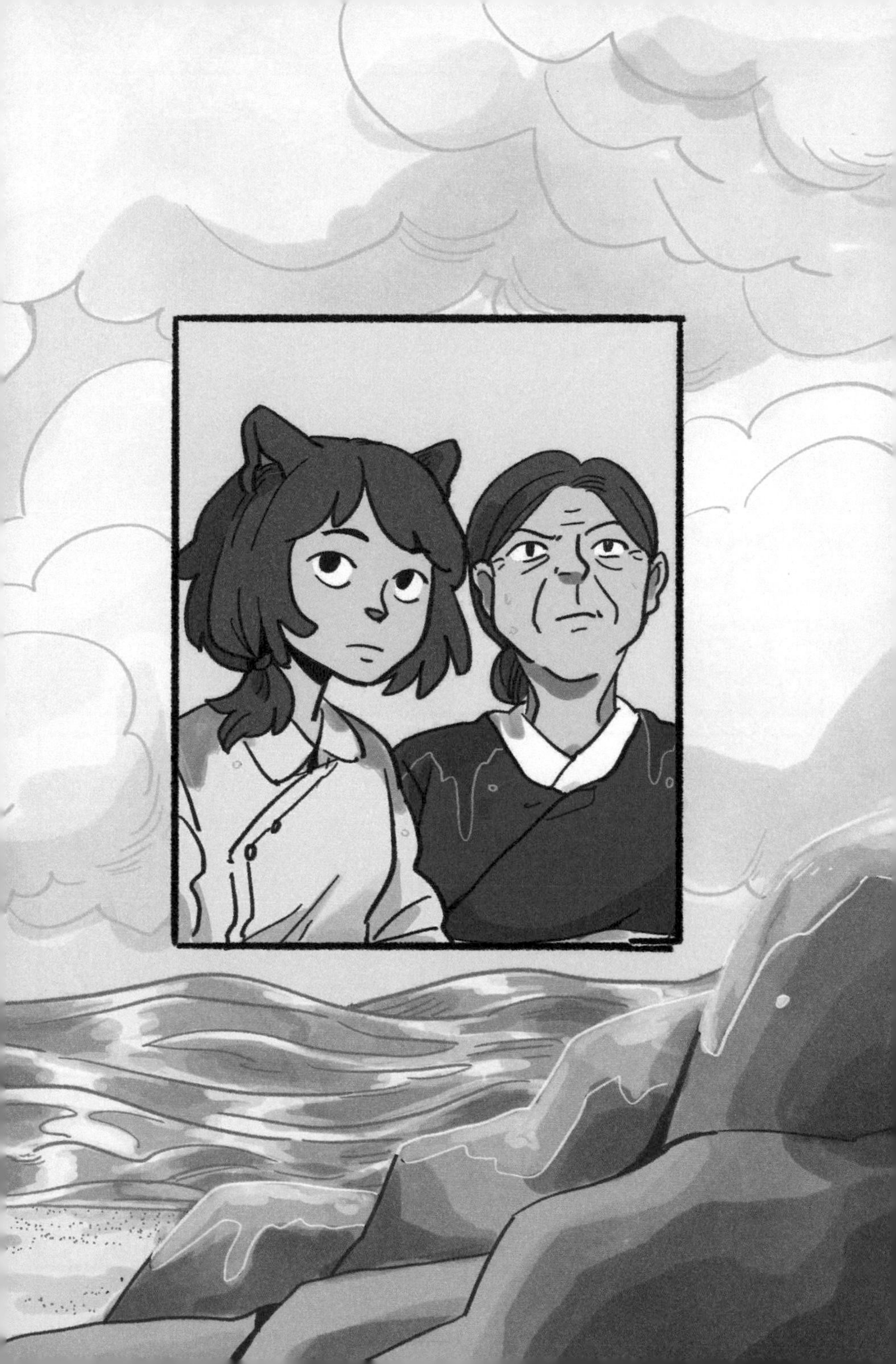

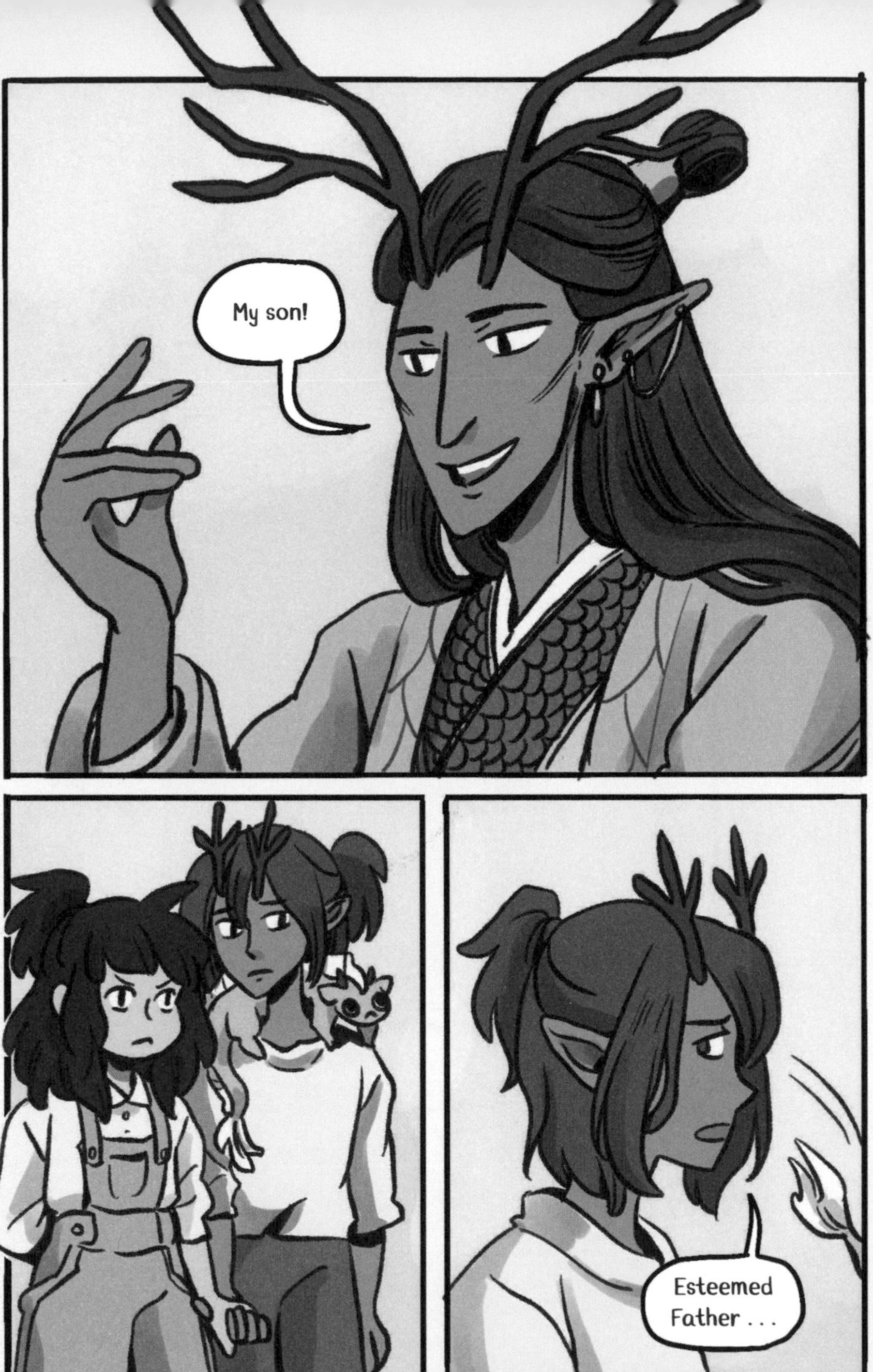
My son!
Esteemed Father . . .

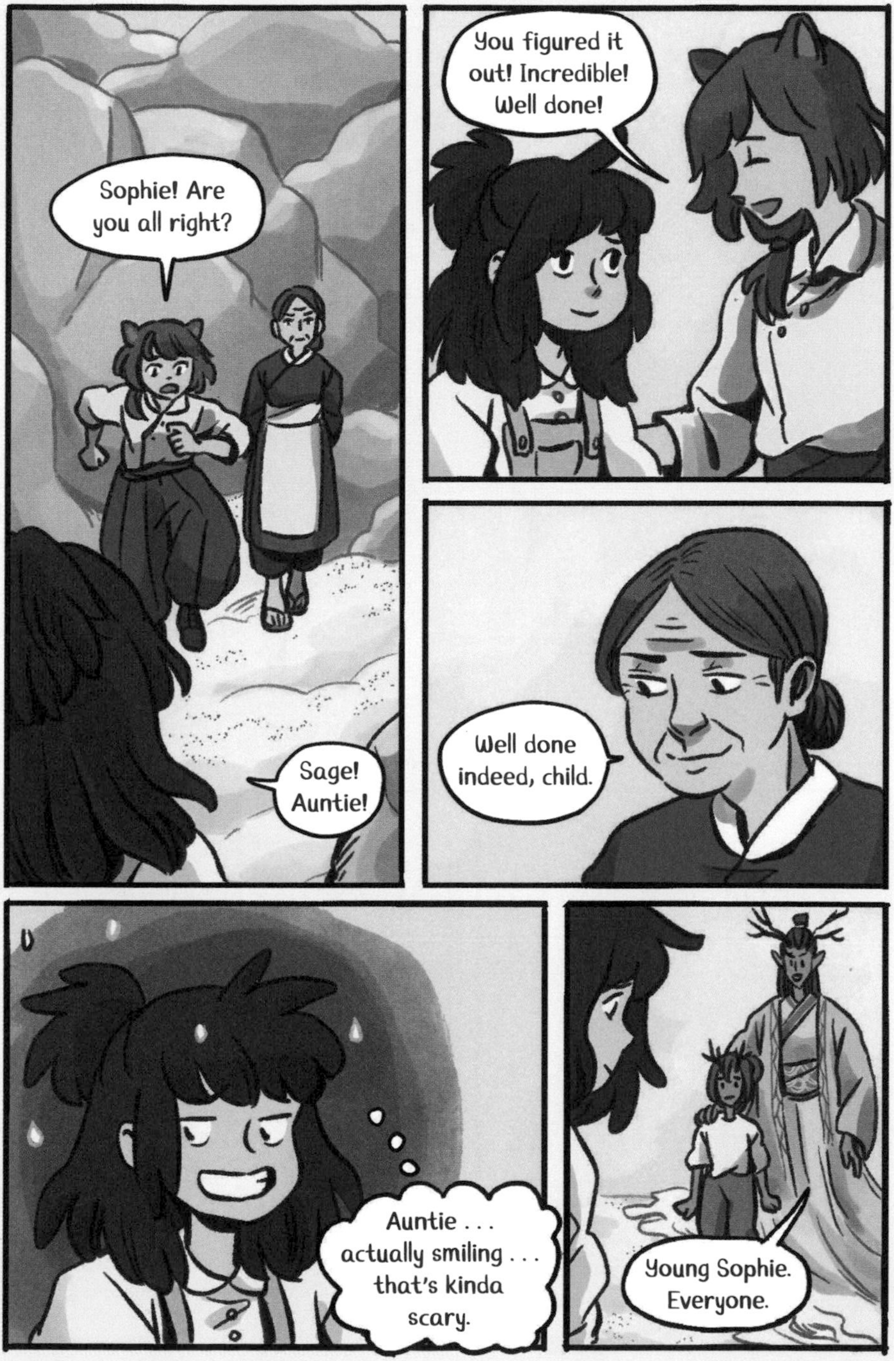
Sophie! Are you all right?
Sage! Auntie!
You figured it out! Incredible! Well done!
Well done indeed, child.
Auntie . . . actually smiling . . . that's kinda scary.
Young Sophie. Everyone.

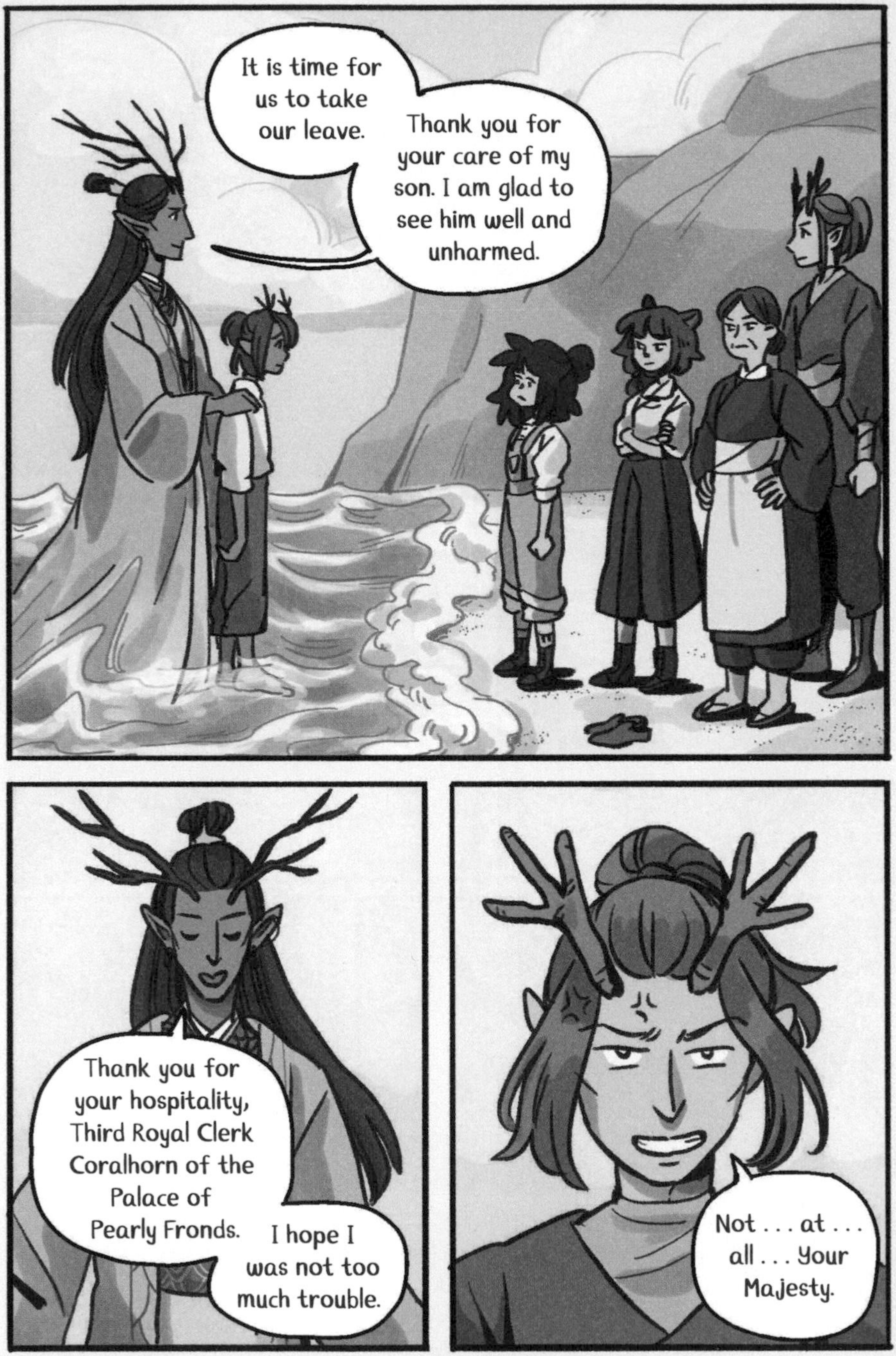

It is time for us to take our leave.
Thank you for your care of my son. I am glad to see him well and unharmed.
Thank you for your hospitality, Third Royal Clerk Coralhorn of the Palace of Pearly Fronds.
I hope I was not too much trouble.
Not . . . at . . . all . . . Your Majesty.

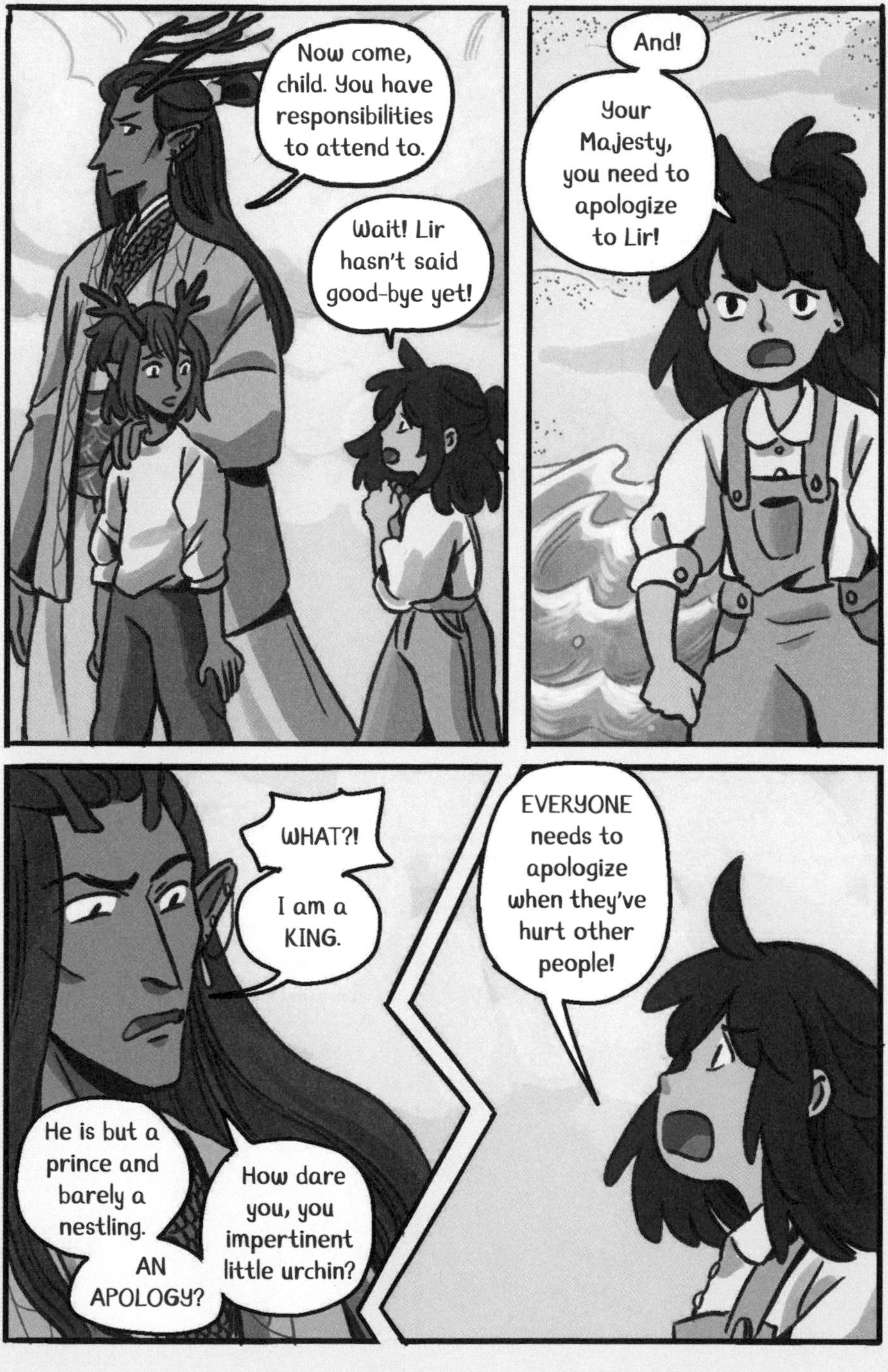
Now come, child. You have responsibilities to attend to.
Wait! Lir hasn't said good-bye yet!
And!
Your Majesty, you need to apologize to Lir!
WHAT?!
I am a KING.
He is but a prince and barely a nestling.
AN APOLOGY?
How dare you, you impertinent little urchin?
EVERYONE needs to apologize when they've hurt other people!

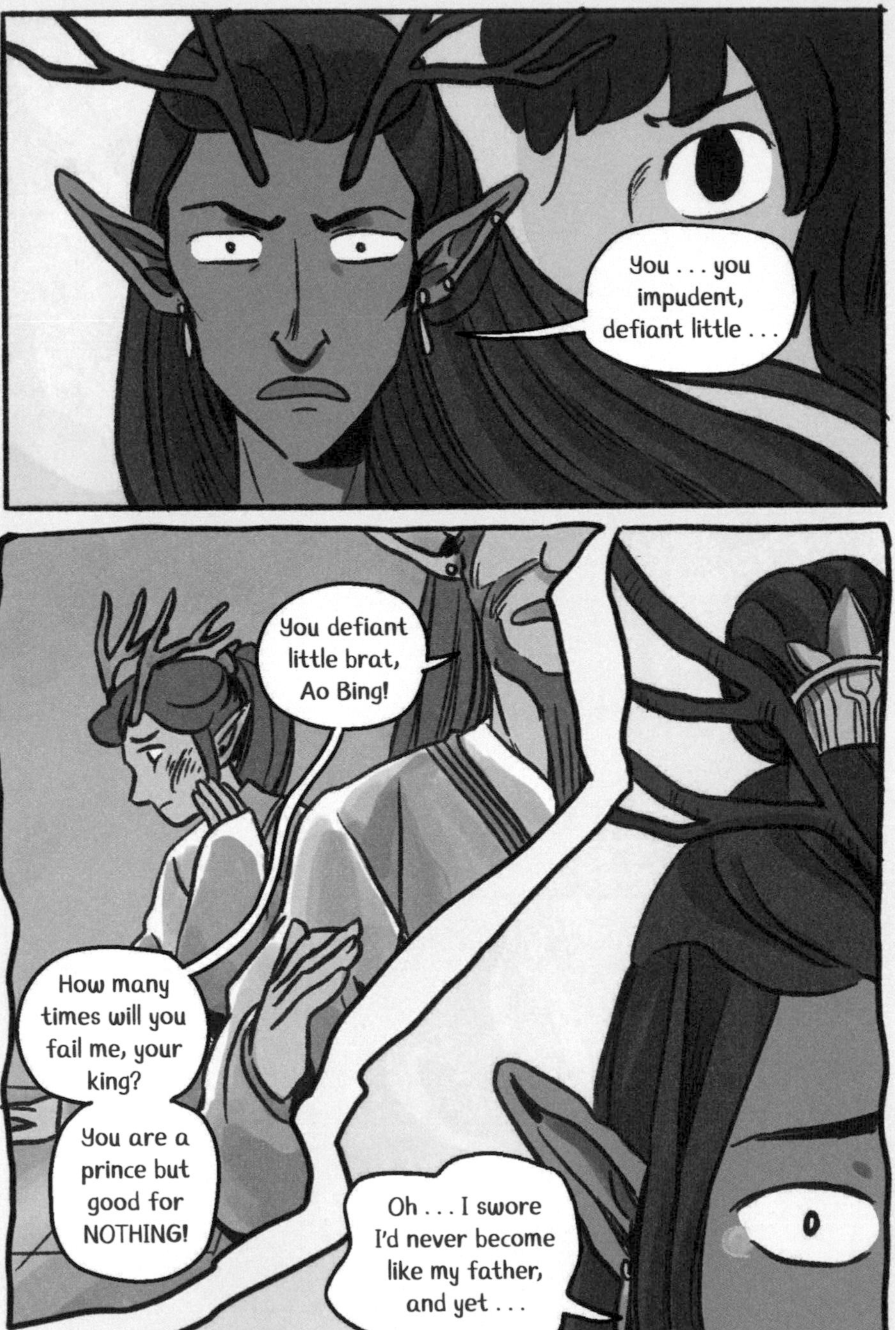
You . . . you
impudent,
defiant little . . .
You defiant
little brat,
Ao Bing!
How many
times will you
fail me, your
king?
You are a
prince but
good for
NOTHING!
Oh . . . I swore
I'd never become
like my father,
and yet . . .

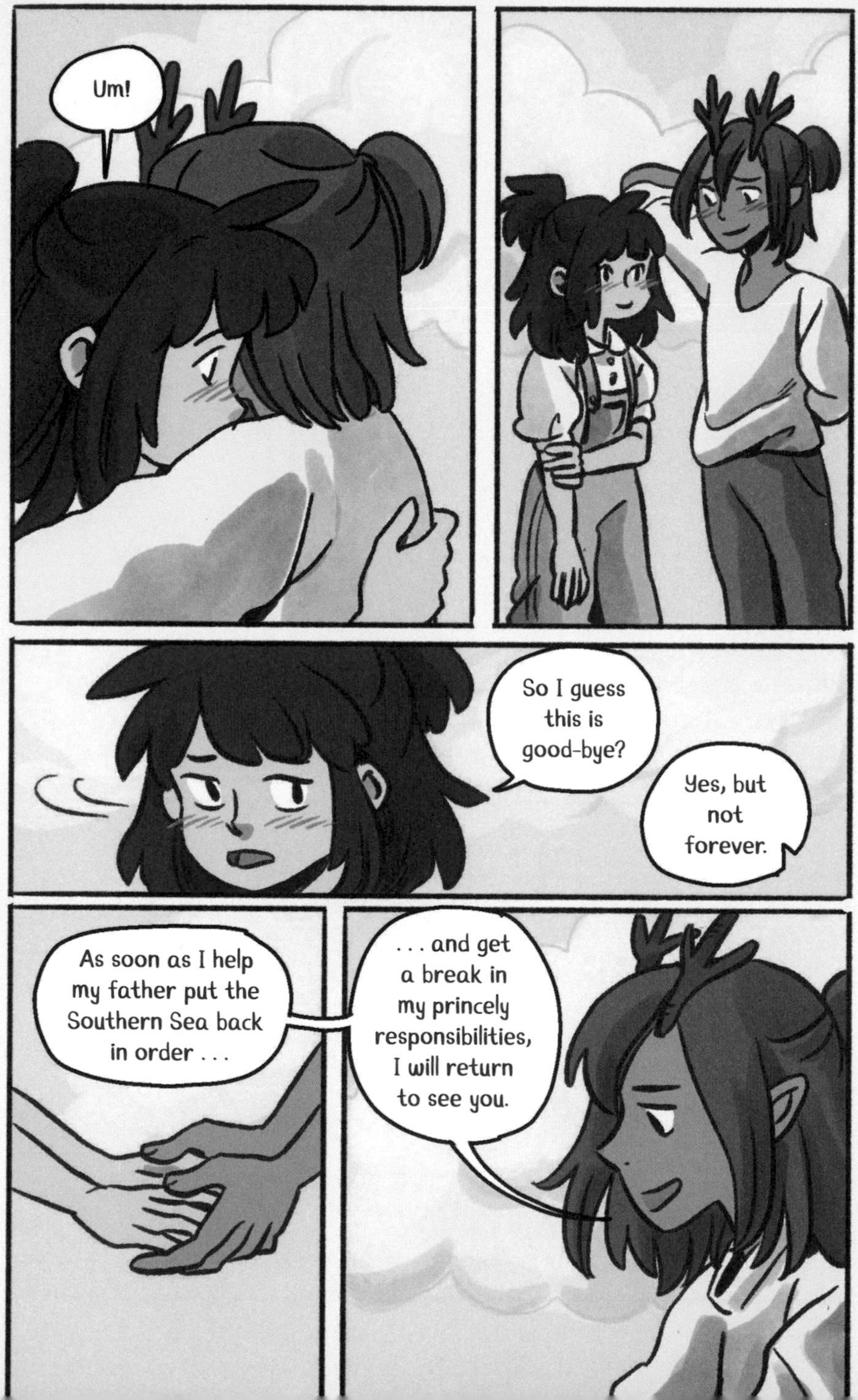
Um!
So I guess this is good-bye?
Yes, but not forever.
As soon as I help my father put the Southern Sea back in order . . .
. . . and get a break in my princely responsibilities, I will return to see you.

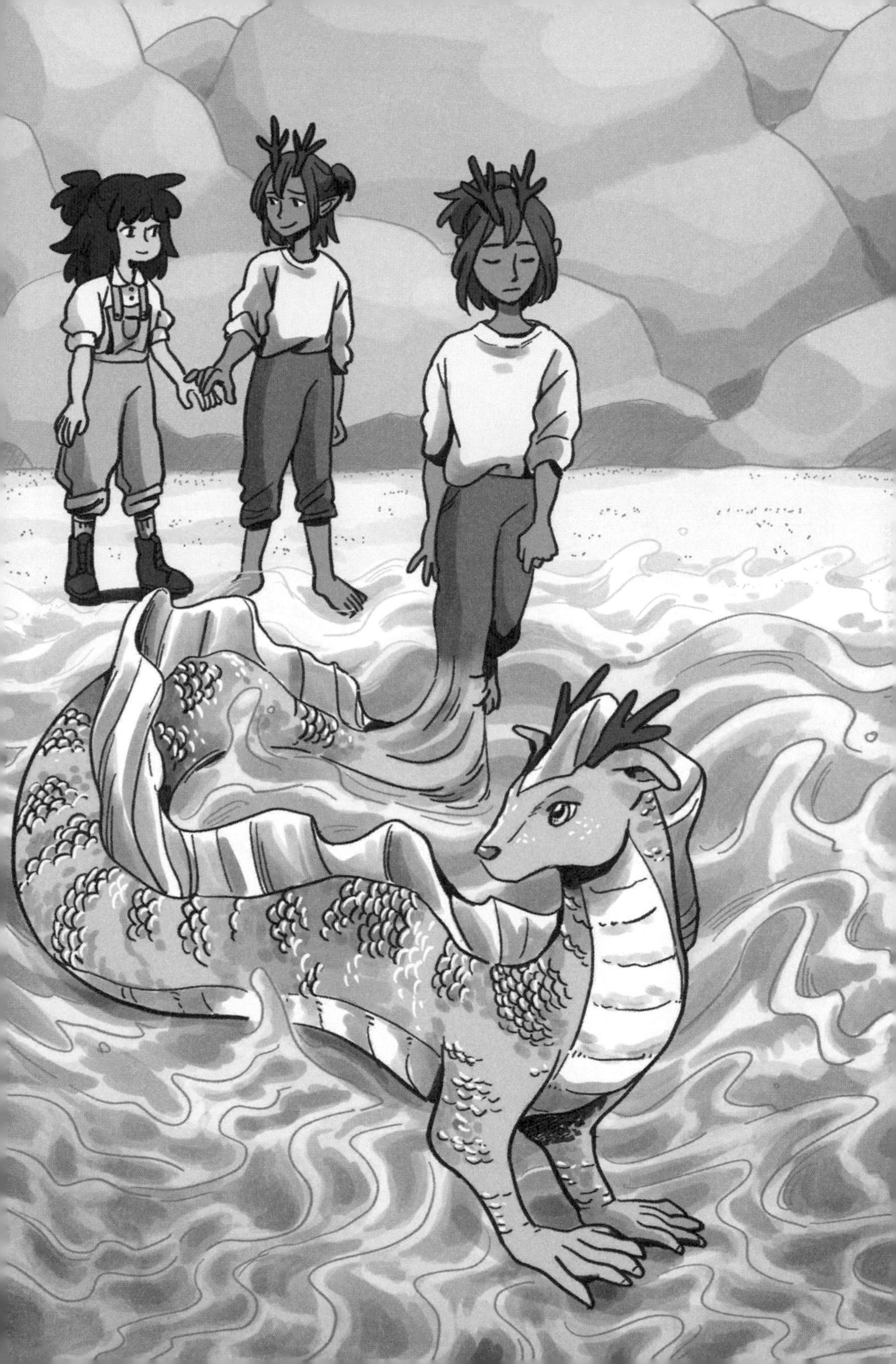

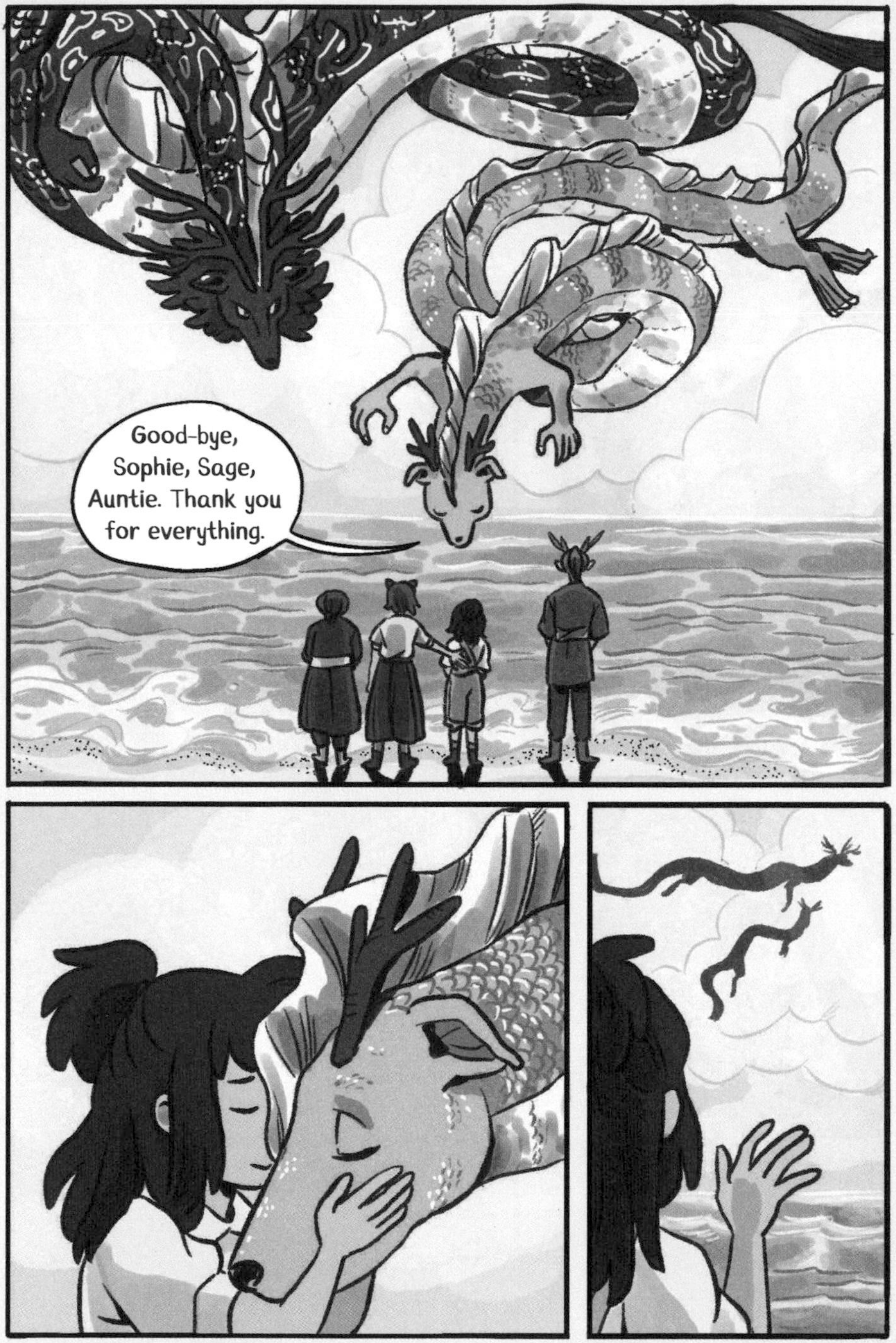
Good-bye, Sophie, Sage, Auntie. Thank you for everything.

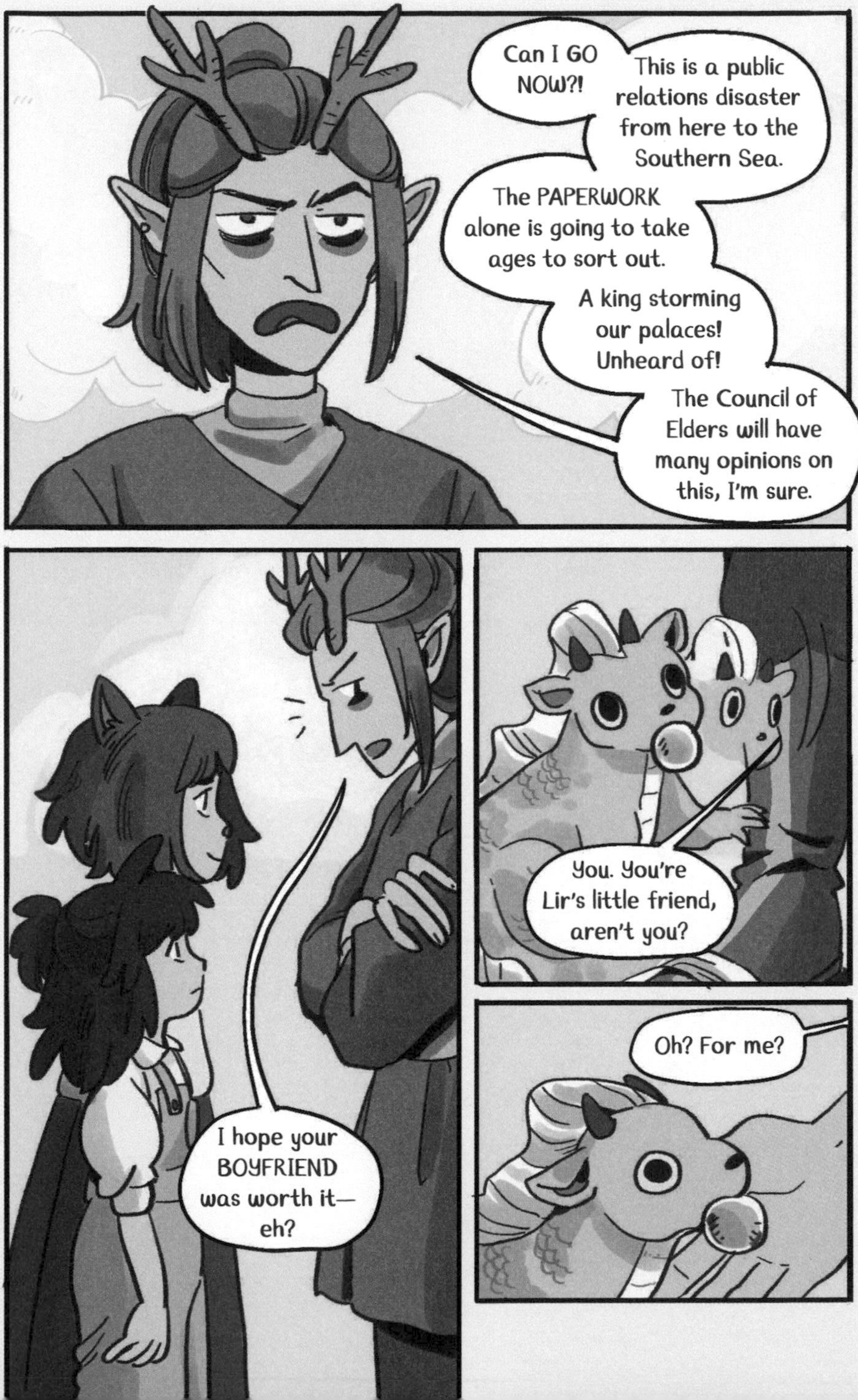
Can I GO NOW?!
This is a public relations disaster from here to the Southern Sea.
The PAPERWORK alone is going to take ages to sort out.
A king storming our palaces! Unheard of!
The Council of Elders will have many opinions on this, I'm sure.
I hope your BOYFRIEND was worth it—
eh?
You. You're Lir's little friend, aren't you?
Oh? For me?

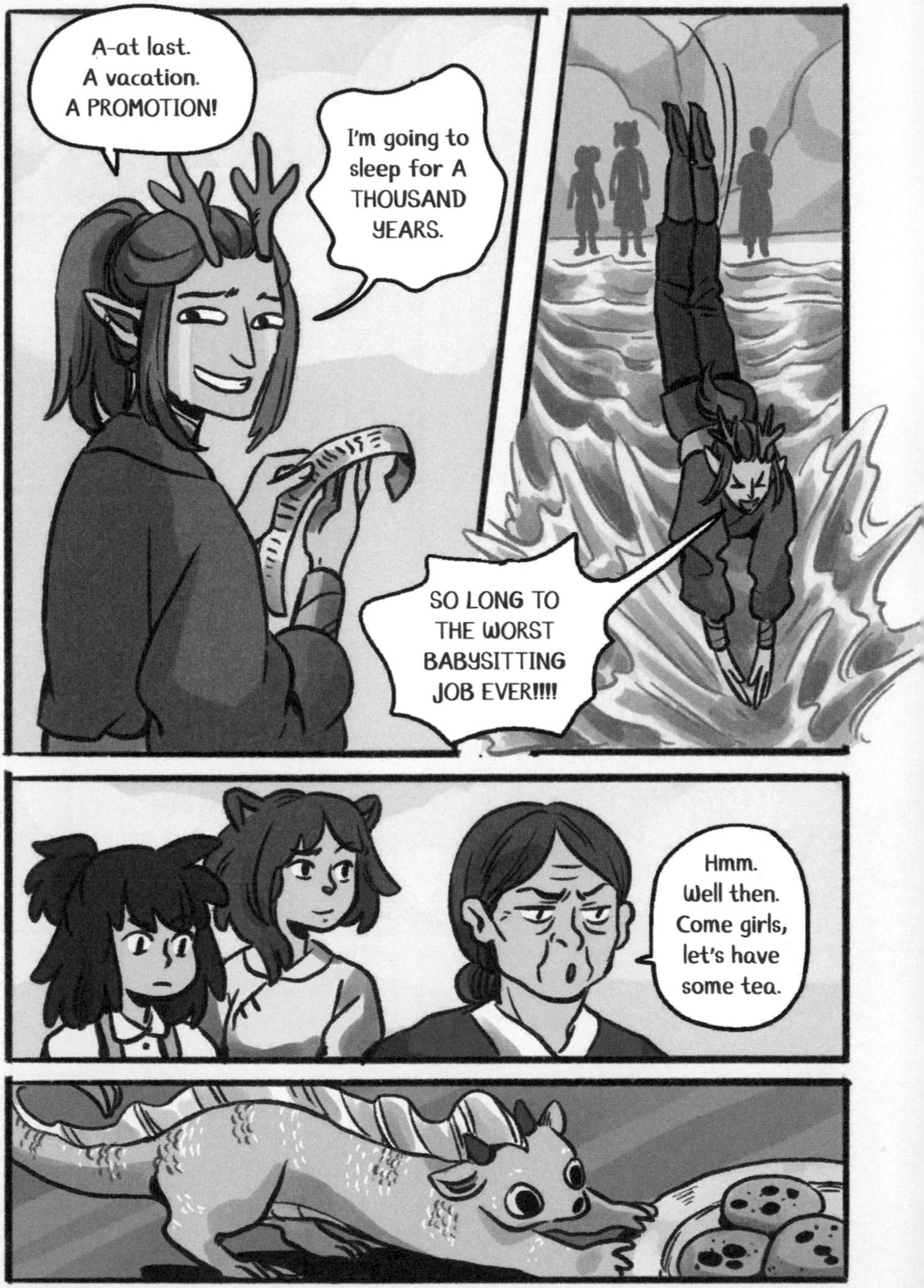
A-at last.
A vacation.
A PROMOTION!
I'm going to sleep for A THOUSAND YEARS.
SO LONG TO THE WORST BABYSITTING JOB EVER!!!!
Hmm.
Well then.
Come girls, let's have some tea.

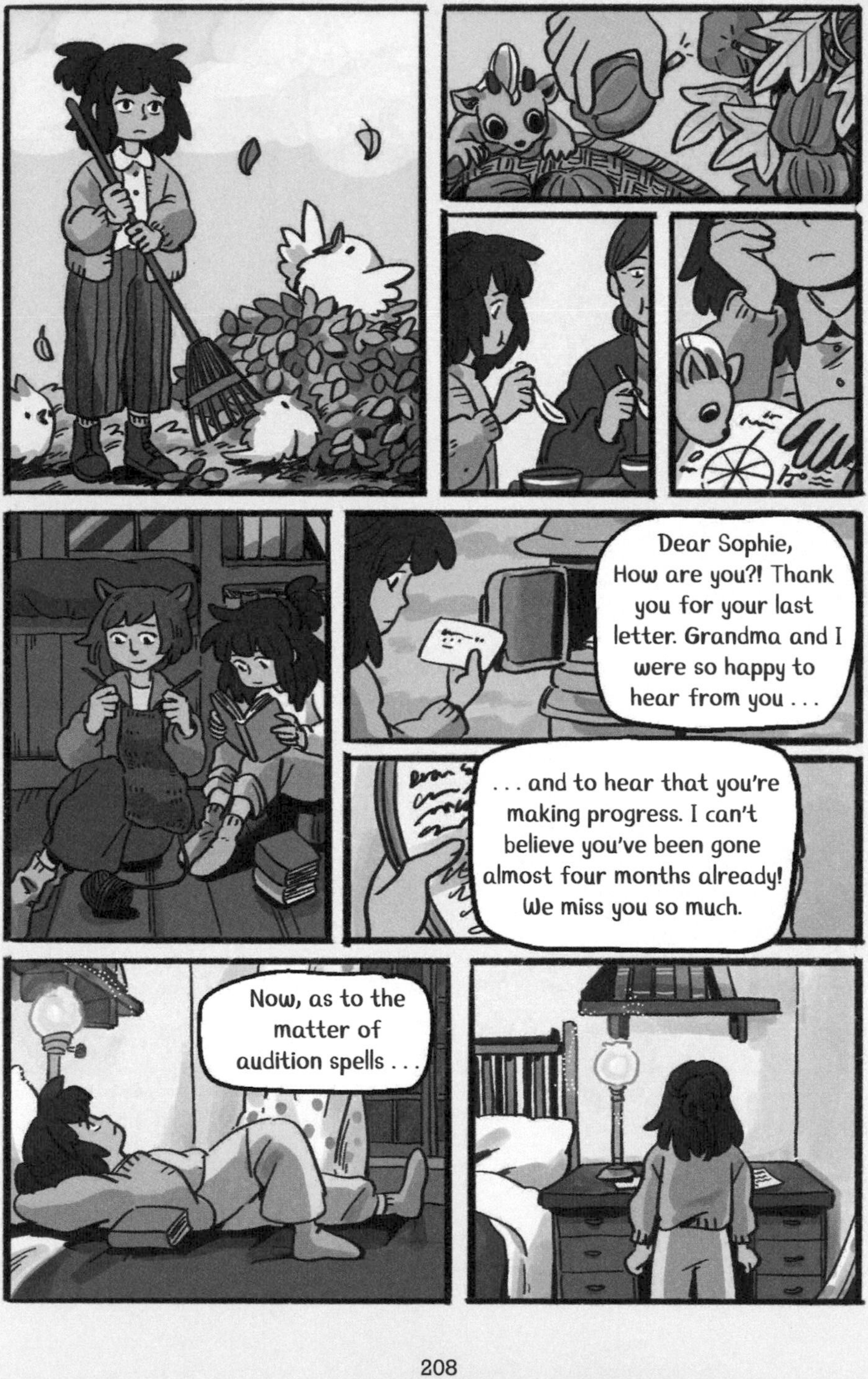
Dear Sophie,
How are you?! Thank you for your last letter. Grandma and I were so happy to hear from you . . .
. . . and to hear that you're making progress. I can't believe you've been gone almost four months already! We miss you so much.
Now, as to the matter of audition spells . . .

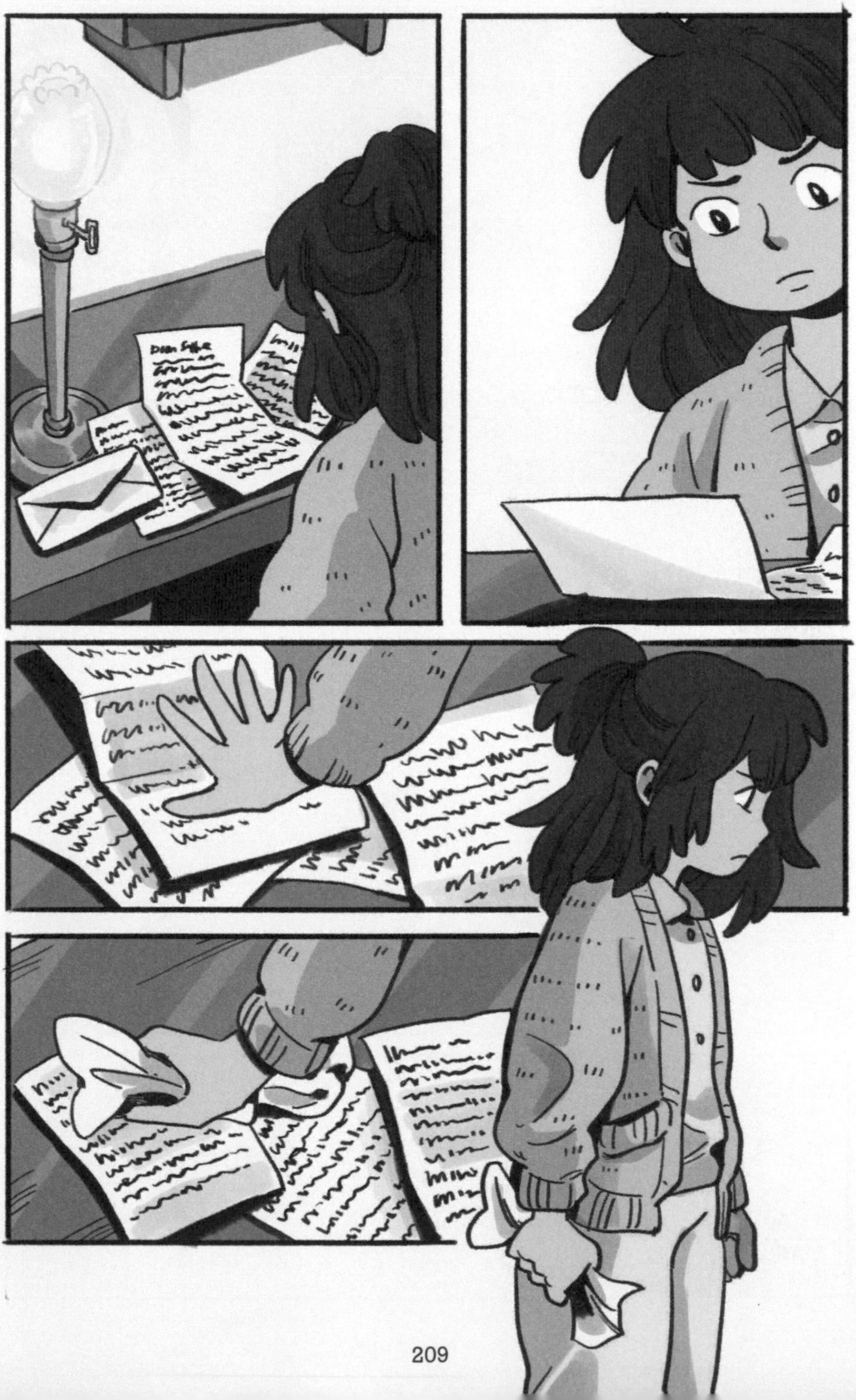

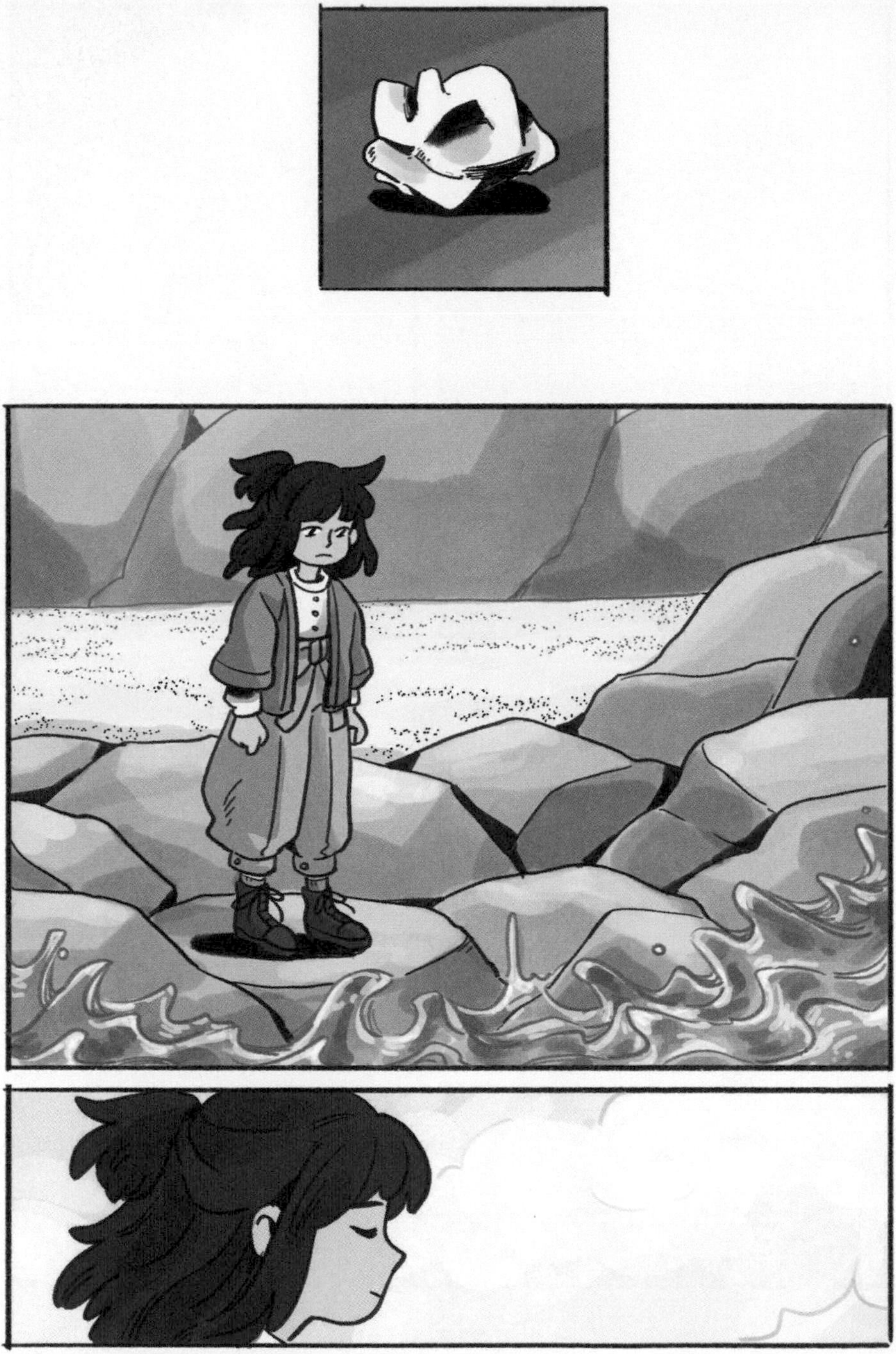

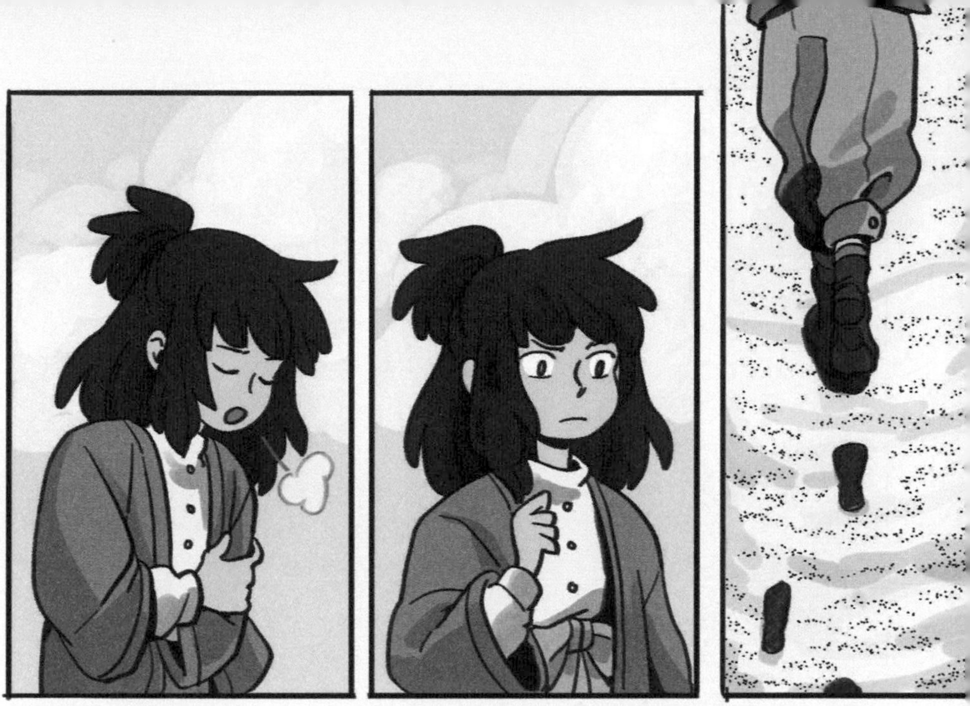

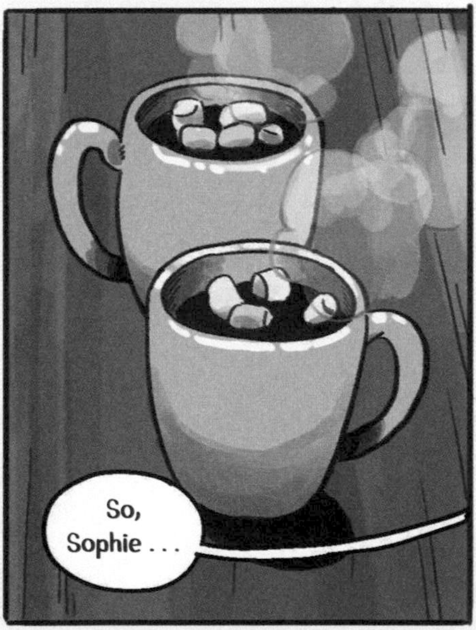
So,
Sophie . . .

Dear Mom and
Grandma . . .

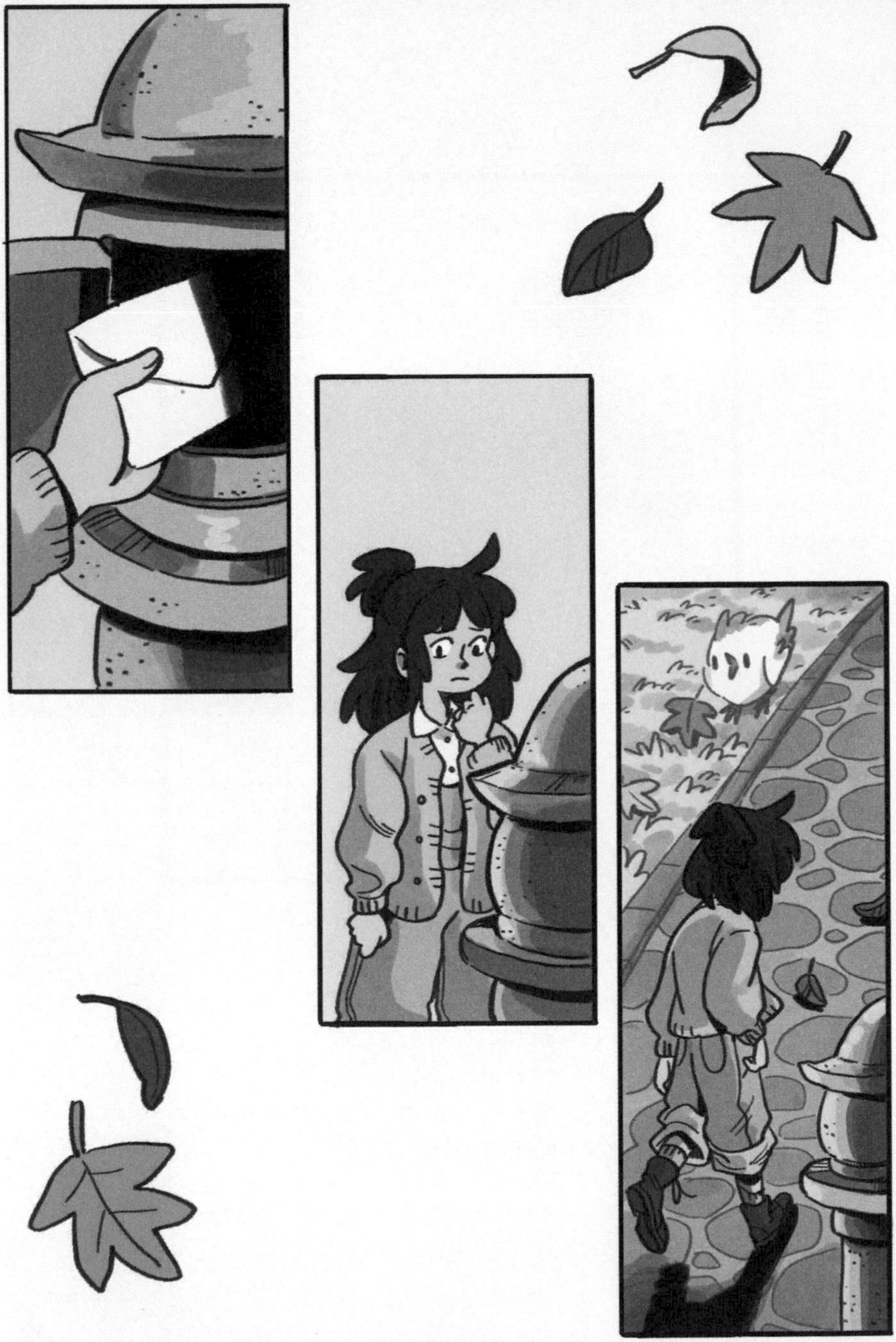

215

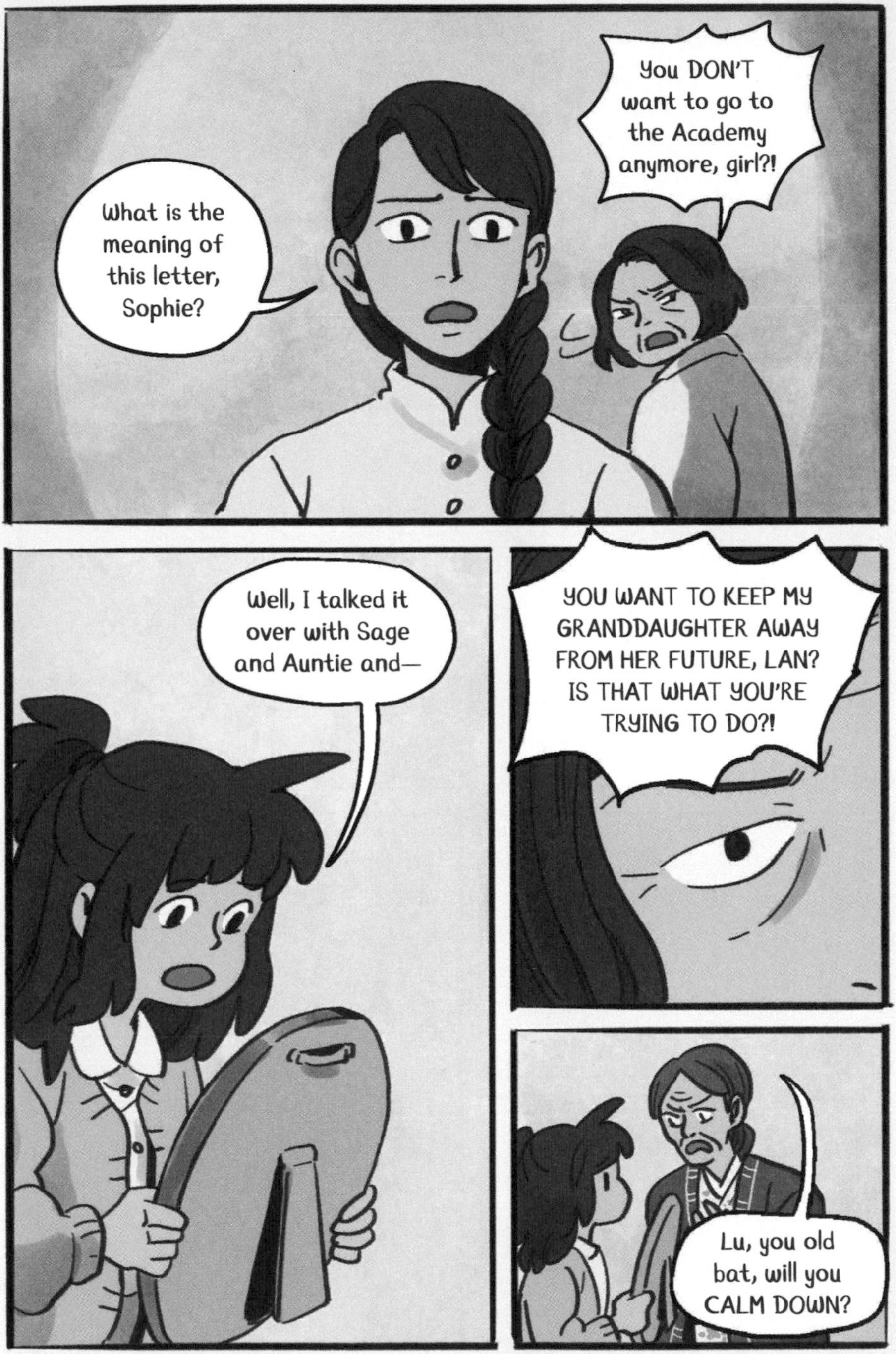
What is the meaning of this letter, Sophie?
You DON'T want to go to the Academy anymore, girl?!
Well, I talked it over with Sage and Auntie and—
YOU WANT TO KEEP MY GRANDDAUGHTER AWAY FROM HER FUTURE, LAN? IS THAT WHAT YOU'RE TRYING TO DO?!
Lu, you old bat, will you CALM DOWN?

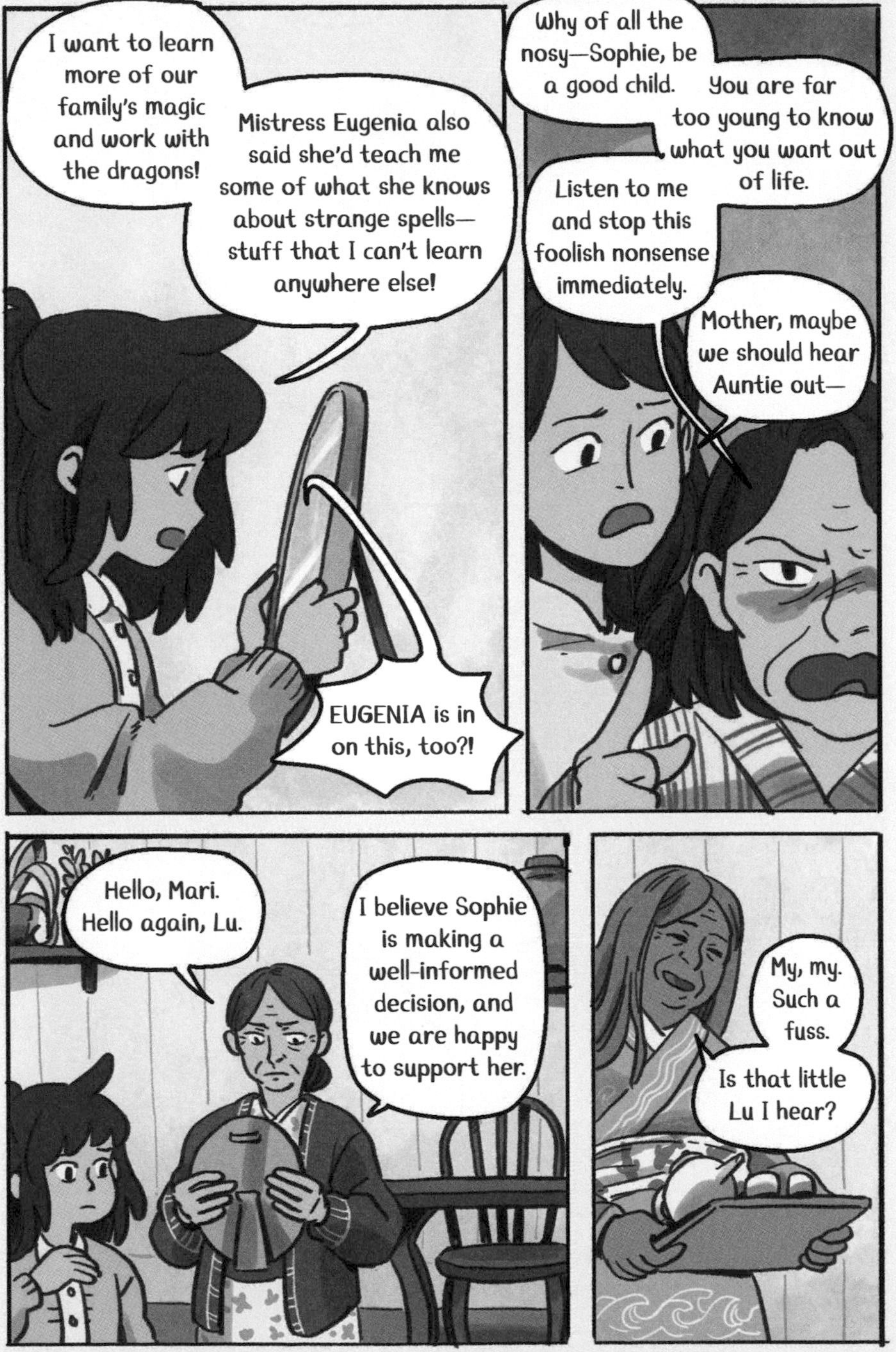
I want to learn more of our family's magic and work with the dragons!
Mistress Eugenia also said she'd teach me some of what she knows about strange spells—stuff that I can't learn anywhere else!
EUGENIA is in on this, too?!
Why of all the nosy—Sophie, be a good child.
You are far too young to know what you want out of life.
Listen to me and stop this foolish nonsense immediately.
Mother, maybe we should hear Auntie out—
Hello, Mari. Hello again, Lu.
I believe Sophie is making a well-informed decision, and we are happy to support her.
My, my. Such a fuss.
Is that little Lu I hear?

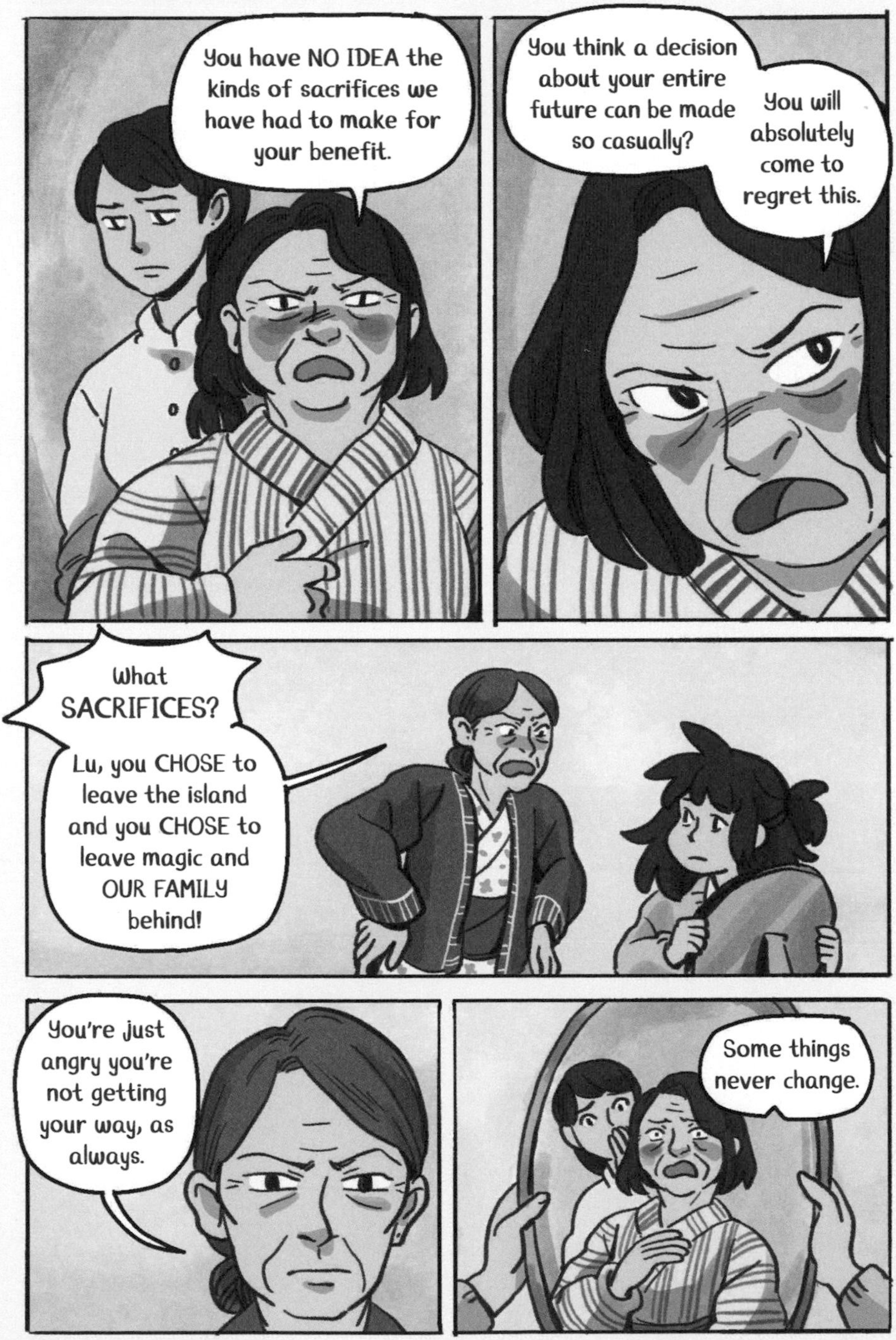
You have NO IDEA the kinds of sacrifices we have had to make for your benefit.
You think a decision about your entire future can be made so casually?
You will absolutely come to regret this.
What SACRIFICES?
Lu, you CHOSE to leave the island and you CHOSE to leave magic and OUR FAMILY behind!
You're just angry you're not getting your way, as always.
Some things never change.

Sophie, go back to the house. Lu and I are LONG overdue for a talk.

Sophie, please think—

Grandma, Auntie.

I'll be waiting for you both.

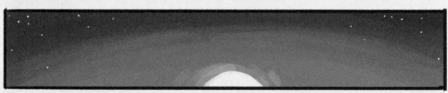

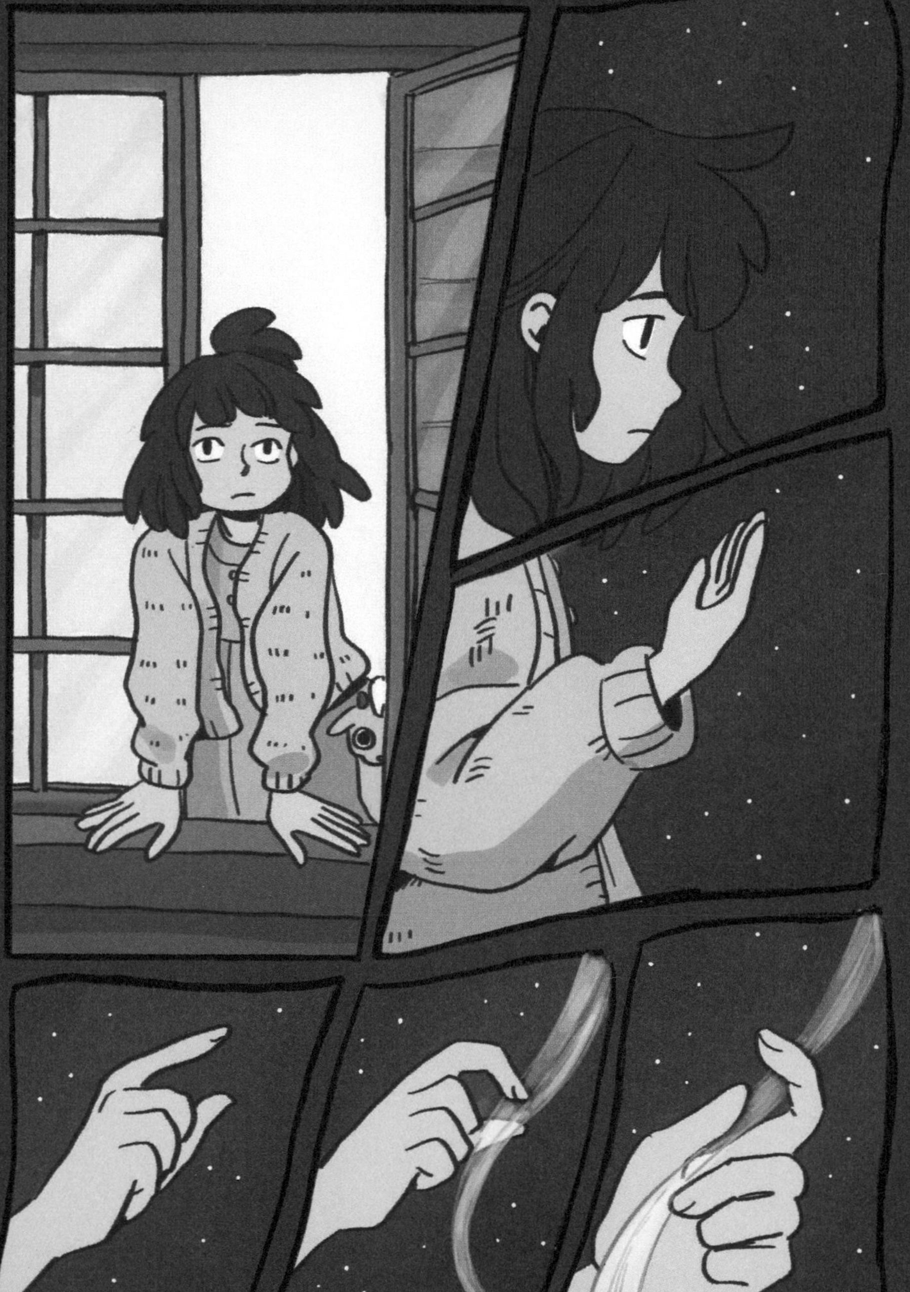

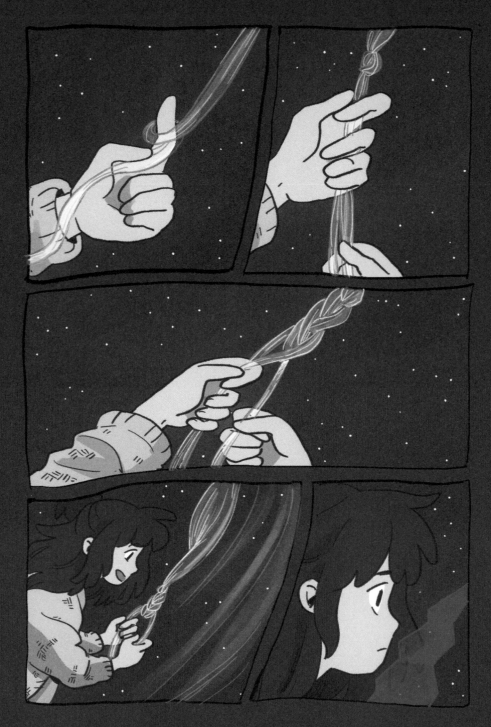

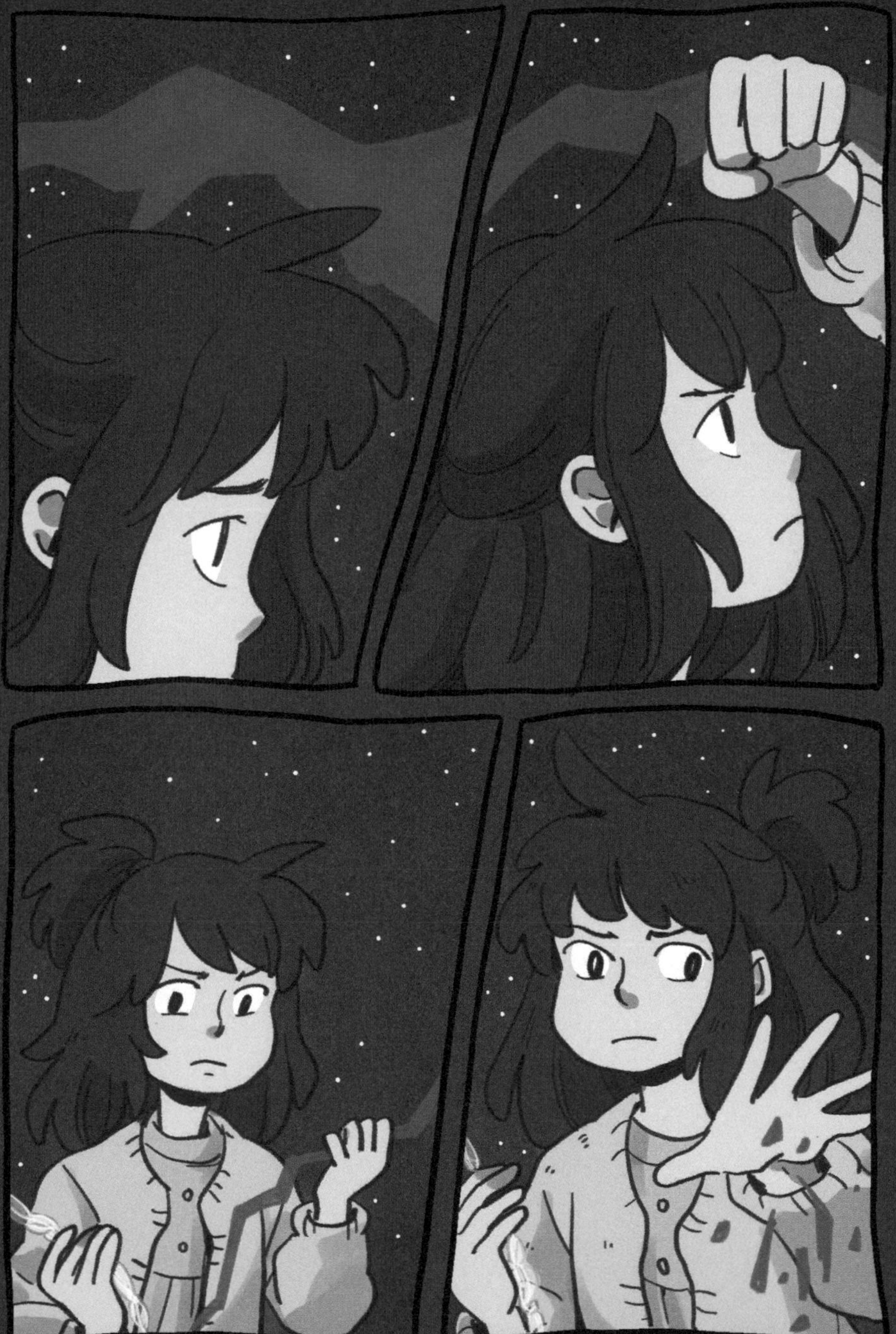

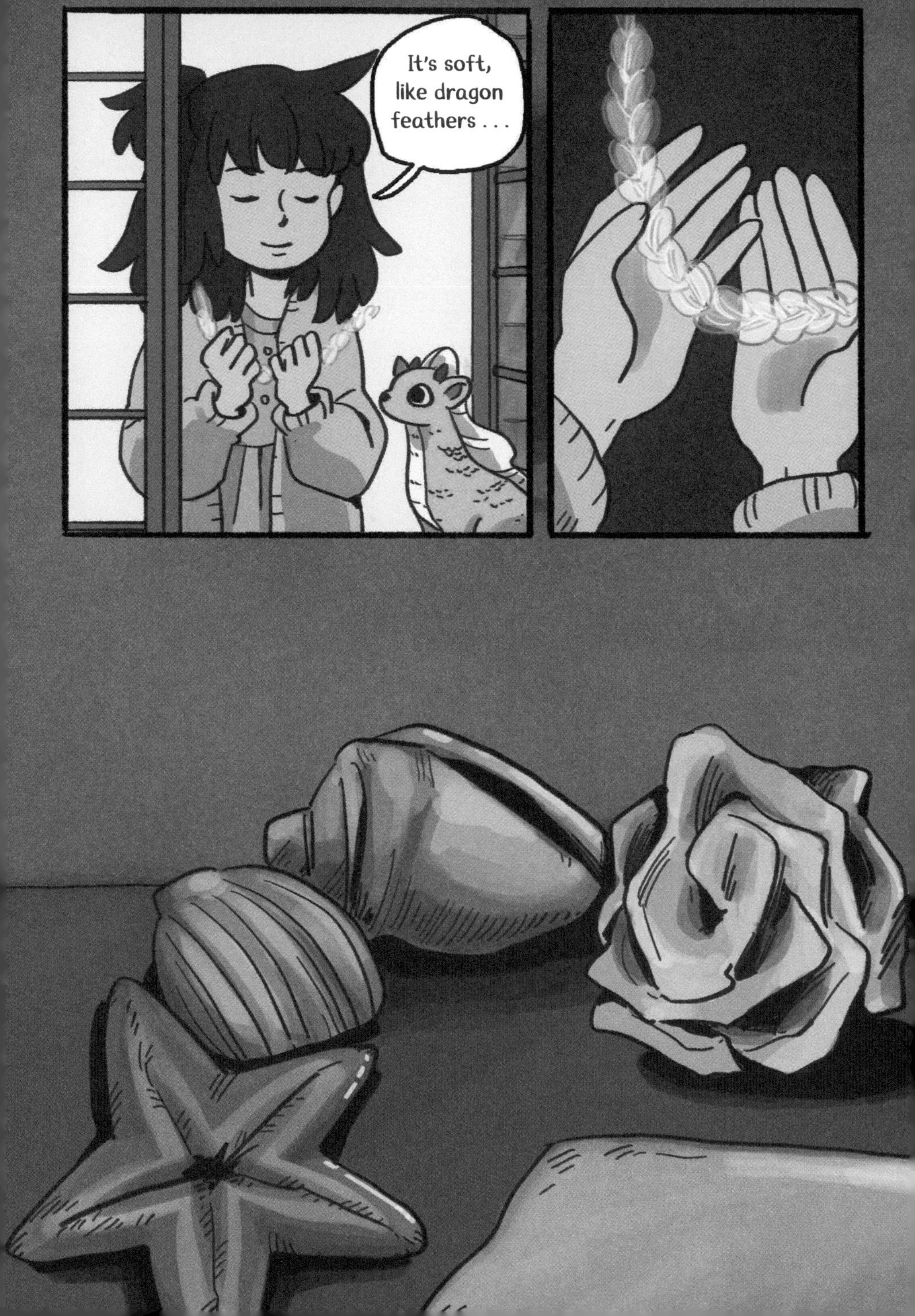
It's soft, like dragon feathers . . .

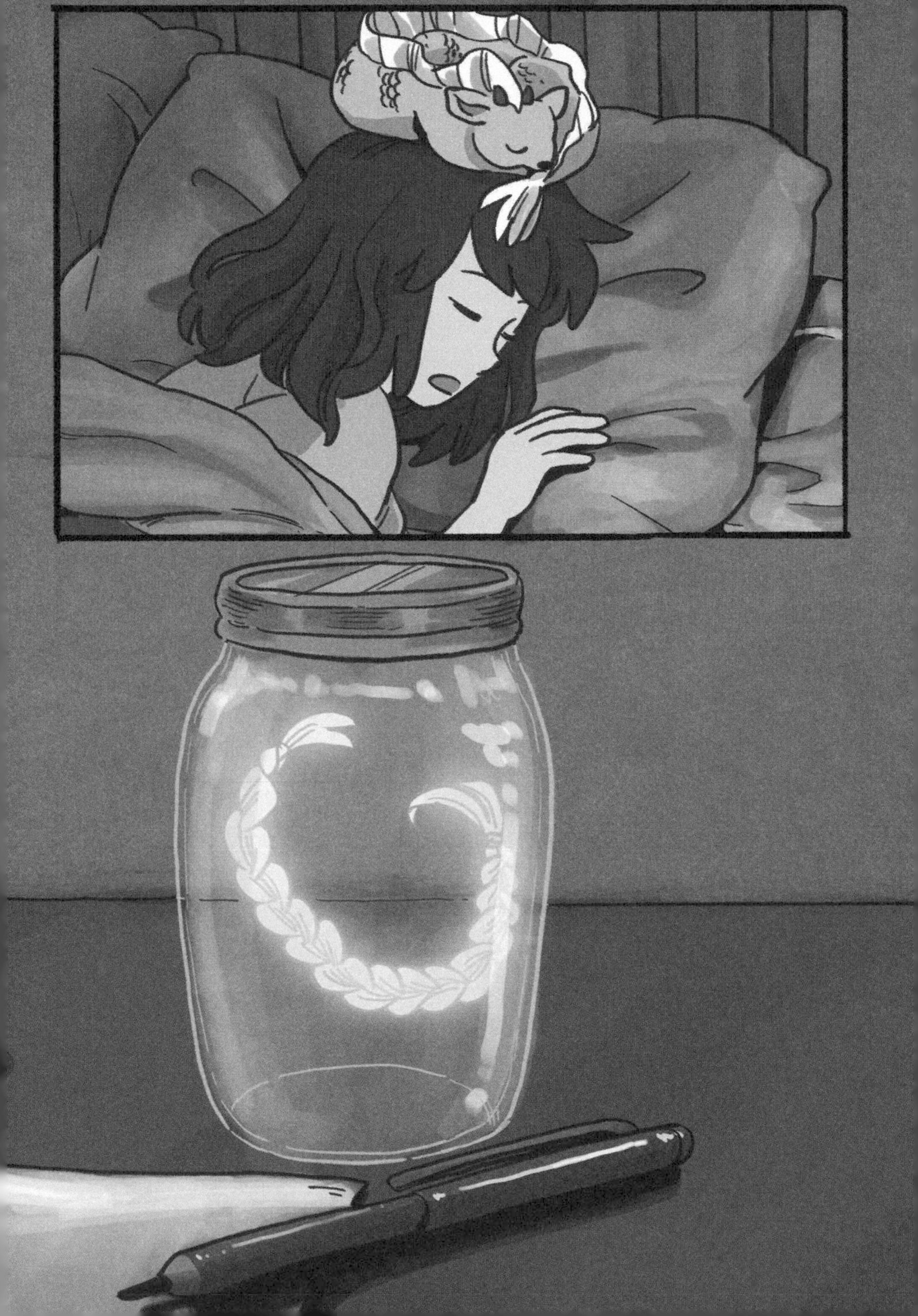

Epilogue

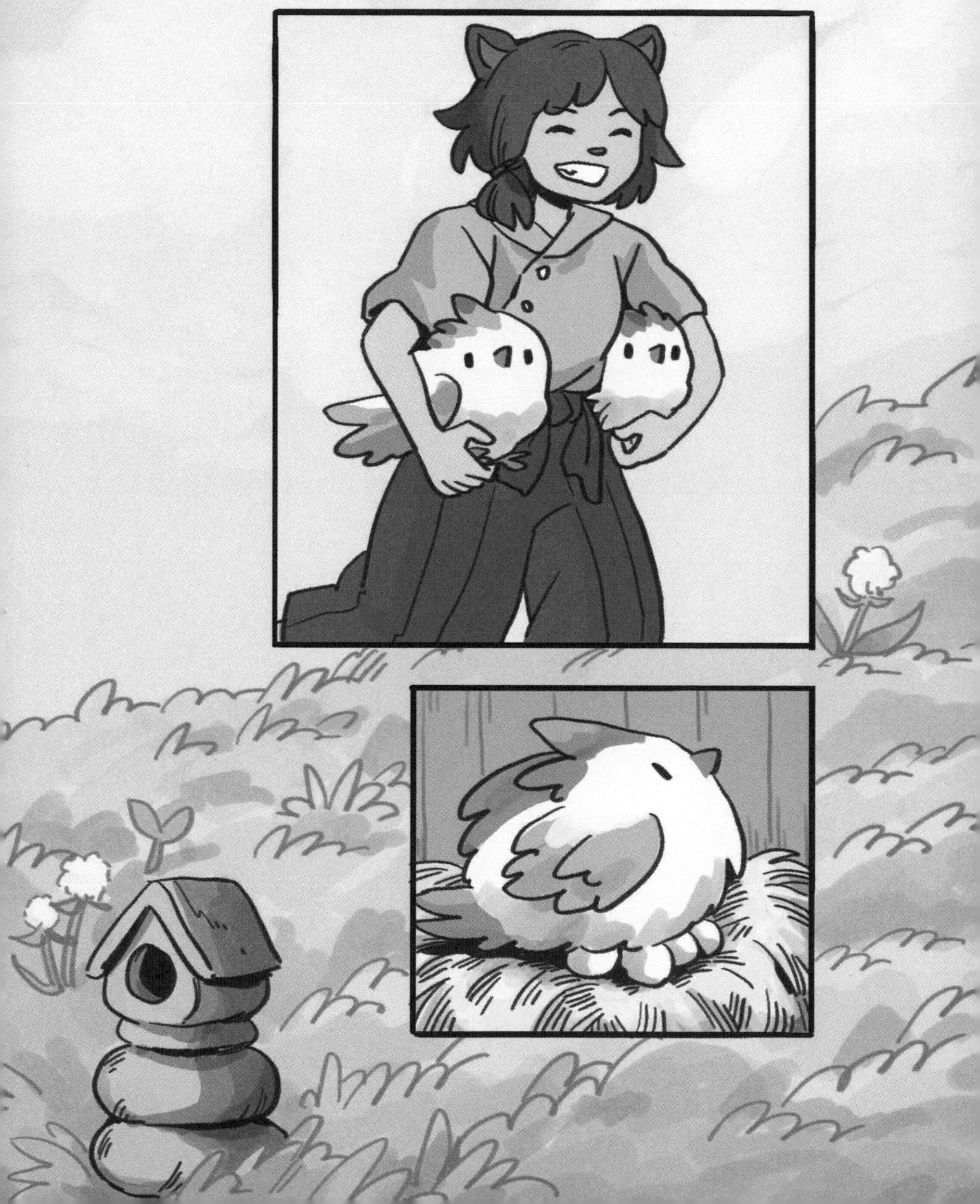

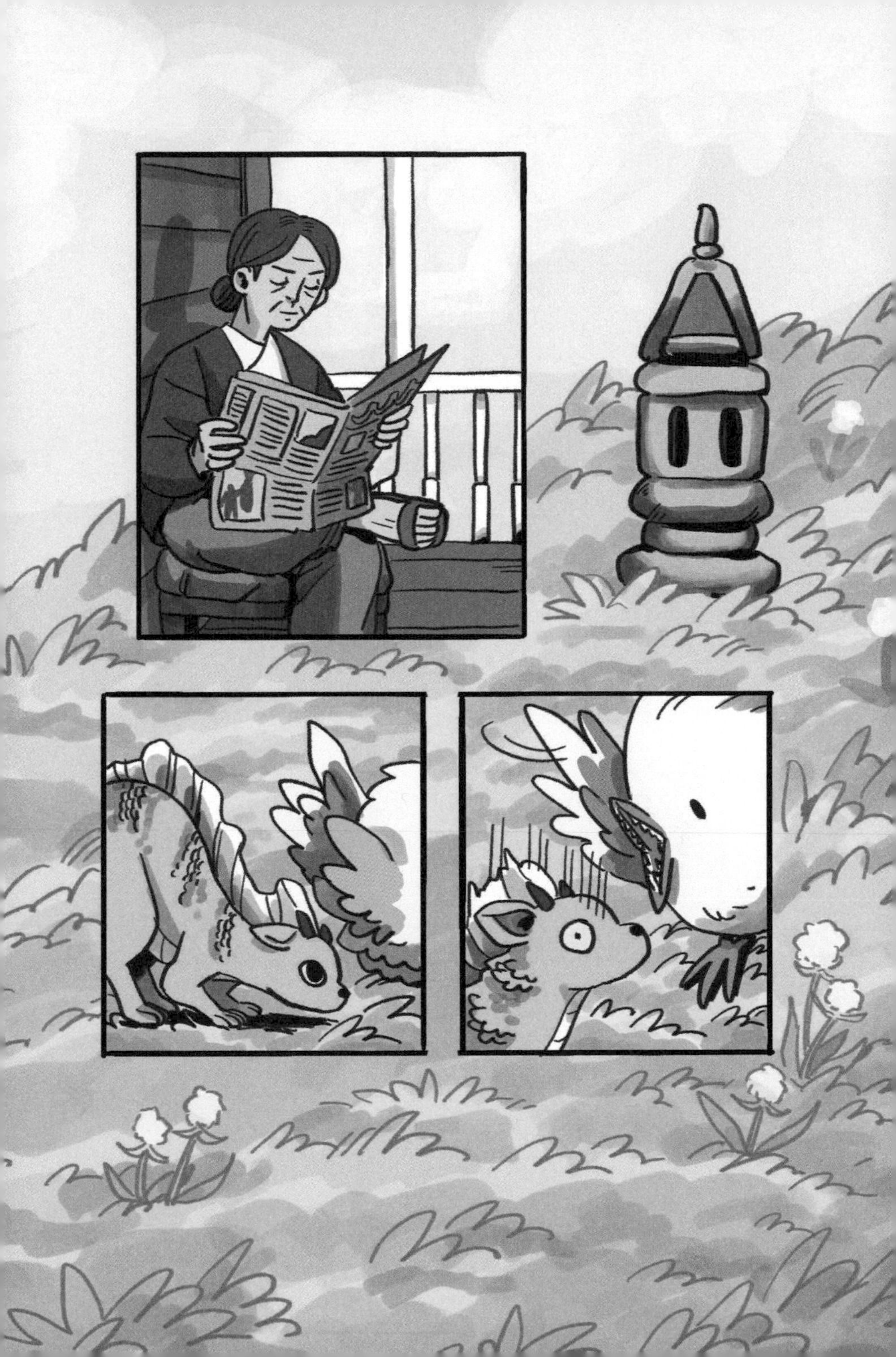

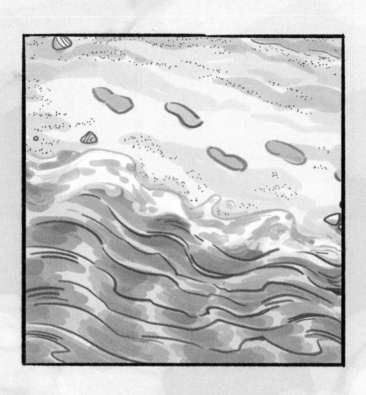

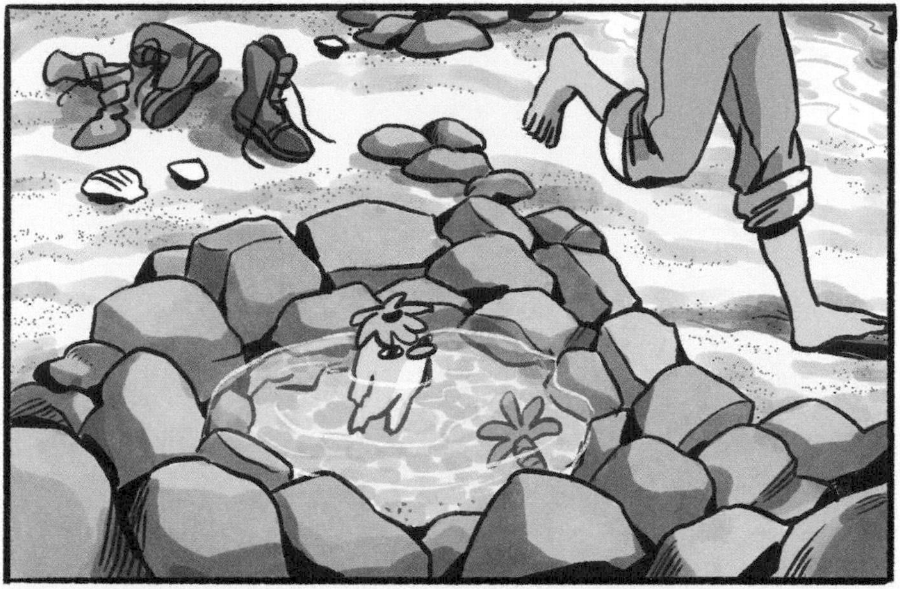

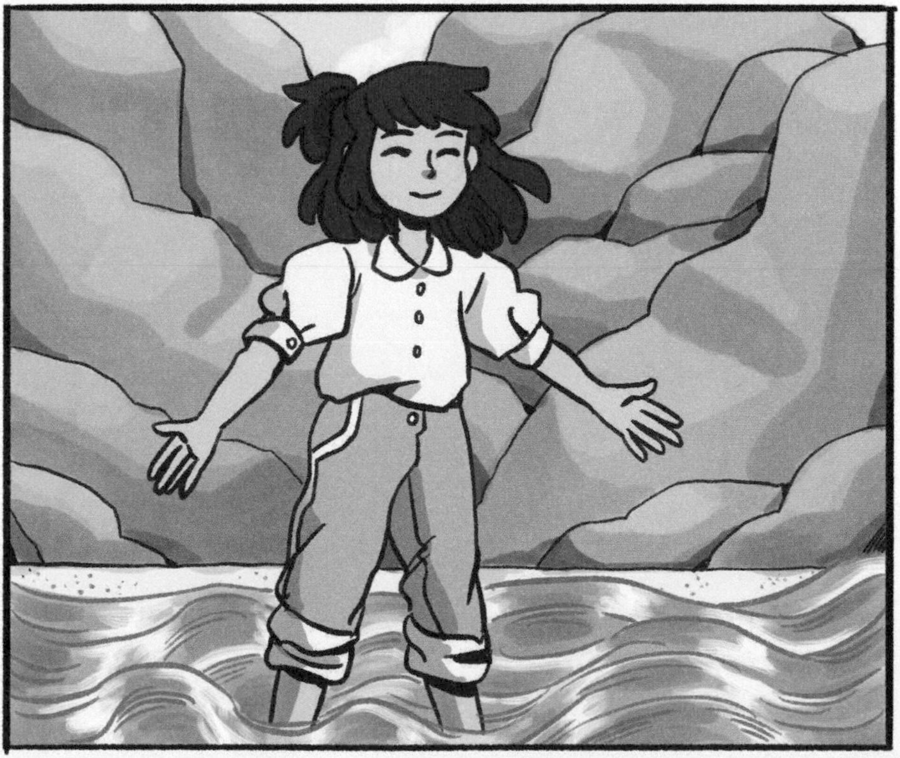

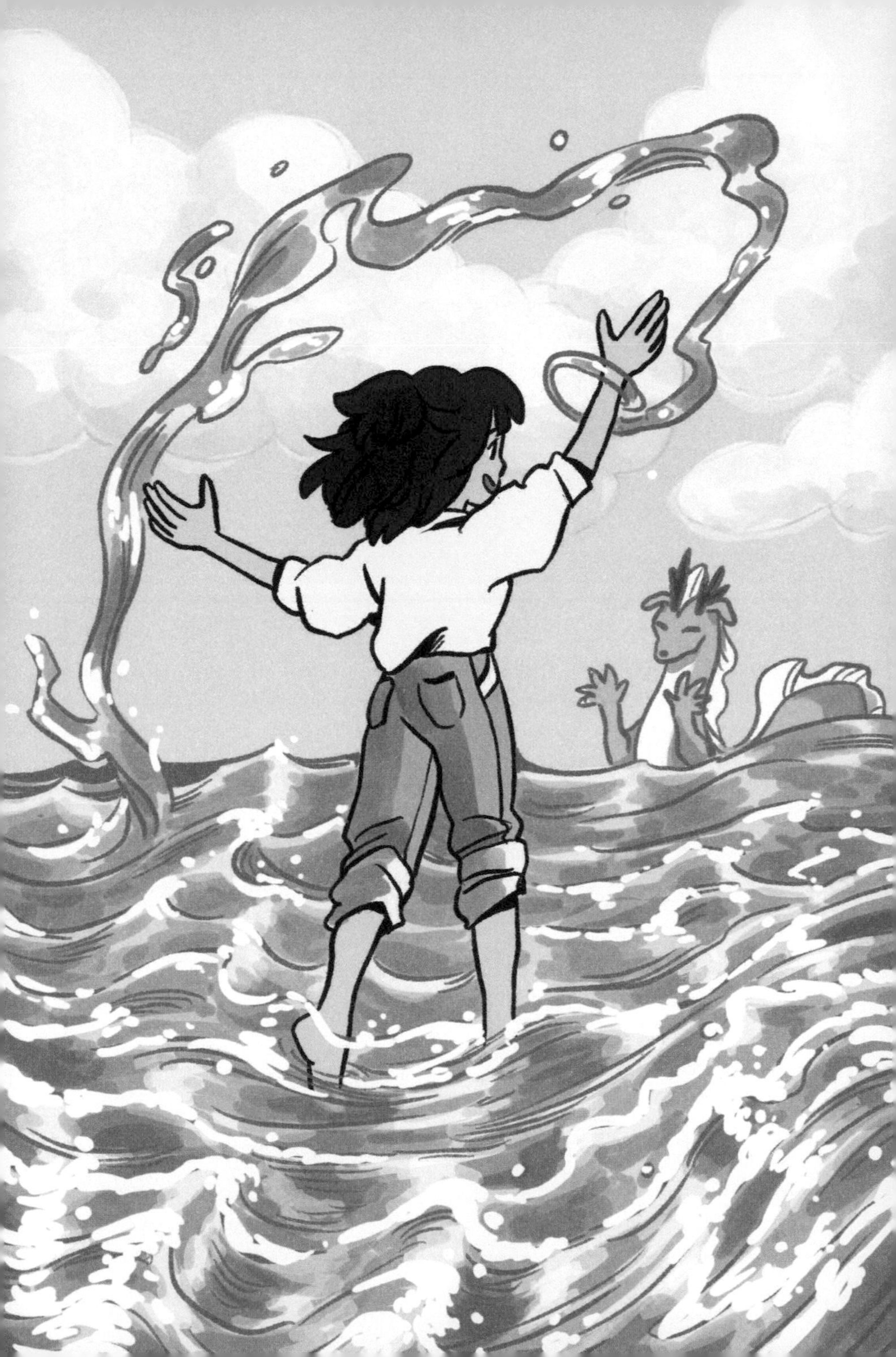

ACKNOWLEDGMENTS

Sometimes you don't know which memories you subconsciously tuck away in a drawer to pull out later for inspiration. When I was in college, my family went on a trip up the New England coast to Maine. In Acadia, I found beautiful water, lush green forests, and a charming seaside town (no water dragons to my knowledge), which, years later, would become fictional, magical Shulan. To that end, thank you to the wild New England forests and powerful Atlantic Ocean, and to my parents for bringing me there.

Thank you to Linda Camacho, my absolute superstar agent, without whom none of this would be possible. Thank you so, so much to Team *Tidesong*: Alex Cooper, who believed in the vision of this story from the beginning; Erin Fitzsimmons, for your wonderful cover treatment and art direction; Andrea Vandergrift, for putting this whole dang book together with the power of InDesign; and Cat San Juan, for turning my handwriting into an actual usable font! Thank you to Allison Weintraub for following up on all the important things I forget I also have to do as an author, such as submitting an author photo and social media stuff.

In no particular order, thank you to the friends who have encouraged me to become the best artist, and more importantly, the best person I can be: Shivana Sookdeo, Chris Kindred, Shannon Wright, Olivia Stephens, Hannah Vardit, Ethan Aldridge, Casey McQuiston, Steenz Stewart, Joamette Gil, Autumn Crossman, Kay O'Neill, Toril Orlesky, Jin Cha, Kody Keplinger, Sam Maggs, Adrienne Cho, Karuna Riazi, Aria Velasquez, Bianca Xunise, Erique Zhang, Cristy Yeung, Maya Pasini, Sabrina Chun, and Jade Feng Lee.

Thank you to my partner, Richard, for keeping the house together, the cat fed during all of my late nights, and providing endless love and support.

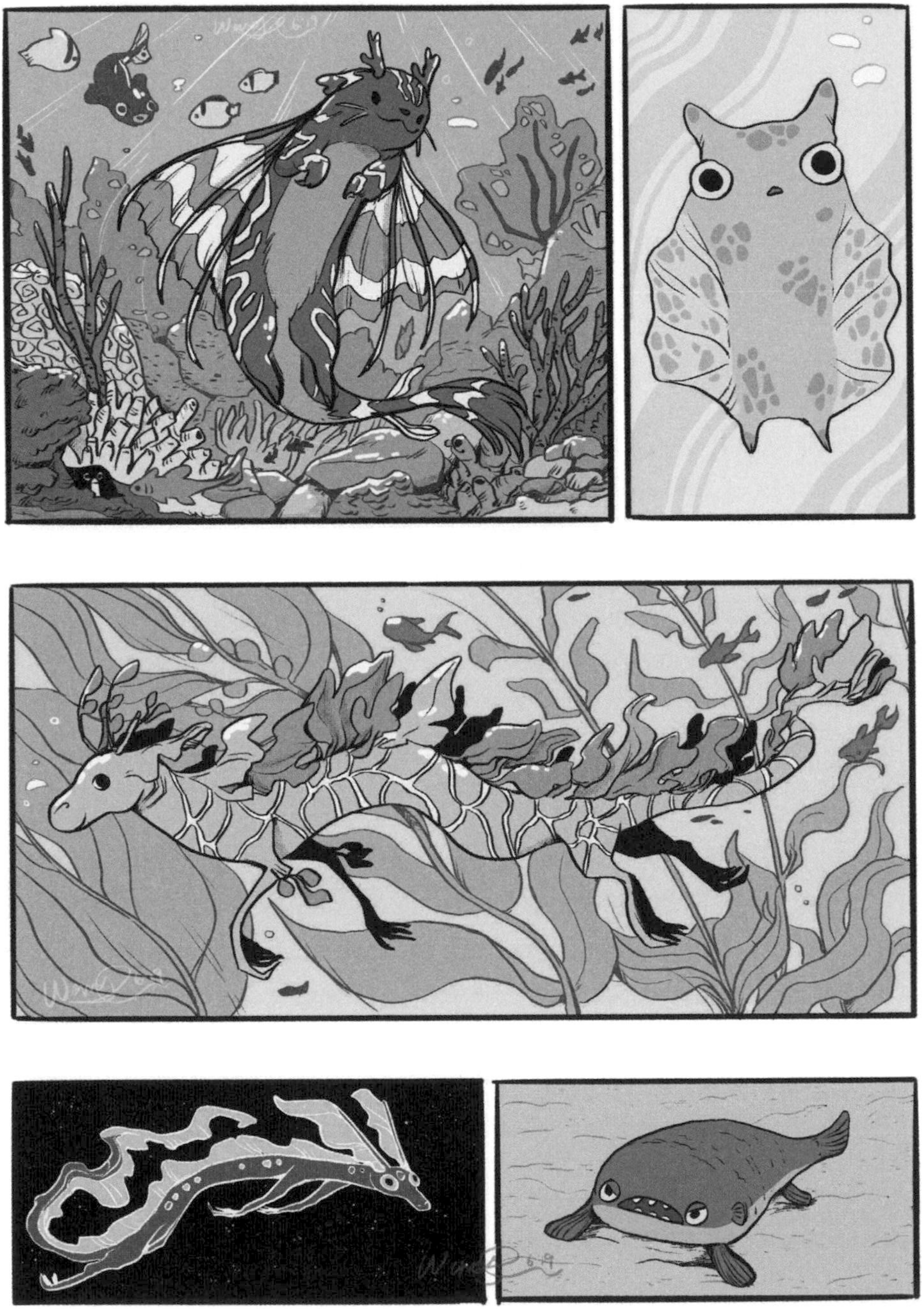

AUTHOR'S NOTE

A question a lot of people ask me is, "Where do you get your ideas from?" The dragons of Chinese mythology, which live under the sea and can shapeshift, provided a jumping-off point for the fantasy elements of this graphic novel. But I also spent a lot of time thinking about the different shapes of real-life animals and their movements to come up with the final designs for the water dragons and other creatures. Not just the bigger, charismatic ocean ones, like otters and sea lions (although I love those!), but the tiniest, almost invisible ones as well—plankton, the newborn fish, and all the little organisms that make up a coral reef. Not all of these designs made it into the final cut of the book, but they were all important when it came to building a fictional ecological backbone for the world of *Tidesong*. I am lucky to have grown up in New England, where we had all kinds of aquariums and coastal activities (tidepooling! crabbing!) for young people to learn about the incredible biodiversity of our oceans.

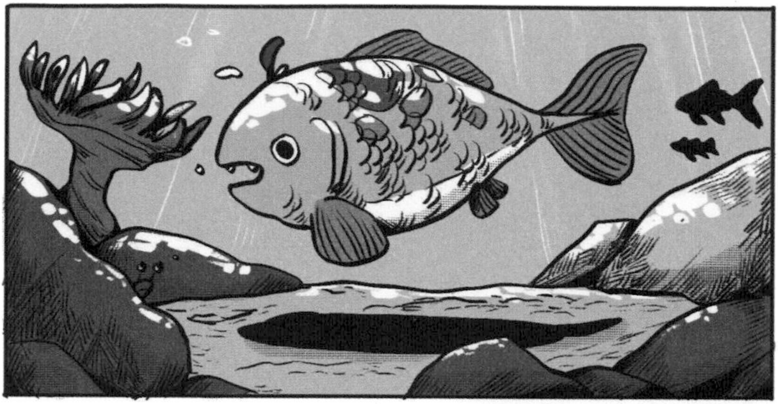

I encourage you all, if you can, to go to your school/town library or aquarium to find out more about local conservation efforts and what kinds of unique and wonderful creatures live in your area—you will be surprised, I promise.

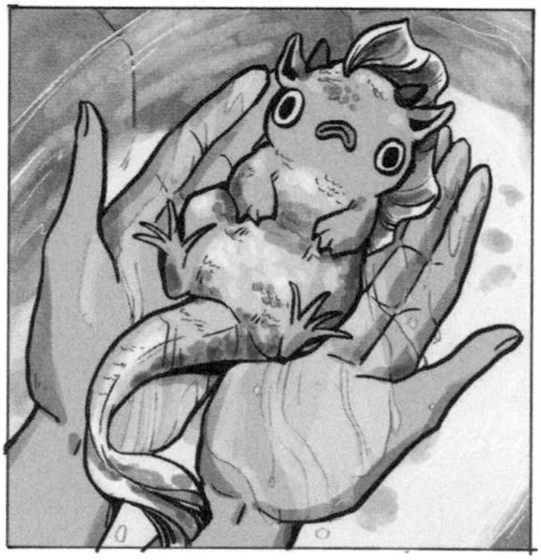

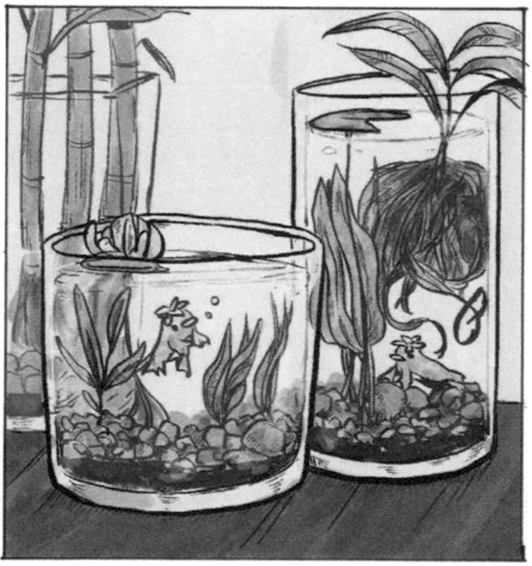

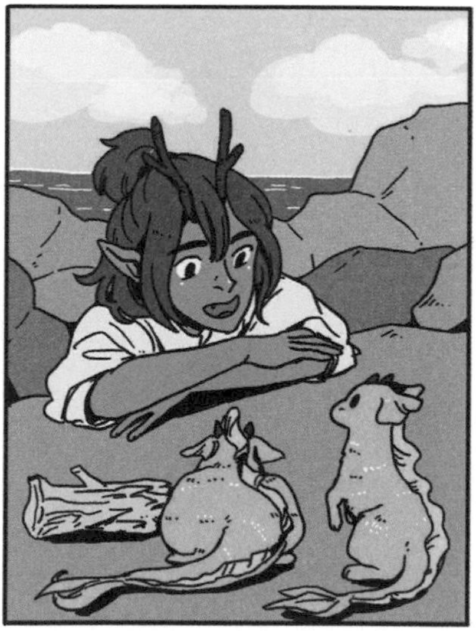